A HOMESPUN KISS

Sam reached around the back of Abby's head and pulled out the few pins that held the chignon she always wore. He wanted to see her face framed by the russet waves of her hair. When the tresses fell free, Sam filled his hands with them and fanned them over her shoulders. The ends curled over the bodice of her dress. Shorter strands wafted around her temples, casting gauze-like shadows on her eyes. She leaned toward him, and the barriers continued to fall.

"You're beautiful, Abby," he said, "and I don't think you're even aware of it."

"Oh, Sam . . ." she began skeptically as though, even now, she wouldn't believe him.

"Abby, you're not going to argue with me about this, are you?" he teased affectionately. "After all, of the two of us, I'm the only one who can see you."

"No, I'm not going to argue. I'm just going to believe for the moment that maybe I am."

Sam cupped his hand under her chin and raised her face so he could see into her eyes. In their glittering depths, he saw the beginnings of trust, not doubt . . . hope, not uncertainty. When he lowered his mouth to hers, she backed away with an imperceptible flinch, and he stopped, waiting for her to give him a sign that she wanted him to do what he very much wanted. Her lips parted slightly, just enough to invite him to taste them, and his mouth touched hers with a gentle pressure that calmed her at the same time it prompted her to ask for more. . . .

Books by Cynthia Thomason

RIVER SONG
SILVER DREAMS
HOMESPUN HEARTS

Published by Zebra Books

HOMESPUN HEARTS

Cynthia Thomason

Zebra Books
Kensington Publishing Corp.
http://www.zebrabooks.com

ZEBRA BOOKS are published by

Kensington Publishing Corp.
850 Third Avenue
New York, NY 10022

First Printing: August, 1999
10 9 8 7 6 5 4 3 2 1

Printed in the United States of America

This book is dedicated to Wilma Qualls of Kentucky. Thanks, ''Aunt Bill,'' for summers on the farm, bowls of popcorn, and all the wonderful stories. And to the memory of Joe Tom Qualls, a noble American farmer. I hope they're serving Cokes in heaven.

Chapter One

Ohio—1892

Abigail Chadwick recognized the familiar signs. Her father placed his elbows on the pulpit, threaded his fingers, and leaned slightly forward. Then he scanned the parishioners' faces with his gentle hazel eyes. He was near the end of his sermon and ready to drive his final lesson home.

The chapel hushed with expectation. Only the breezes from the ladies' fans, swaying back and forth in languid hands, stirred the warm air. Reverend Chadwick concluded his sermon in the rich, velvet baritone that had seemed as sweet as music to Abby for all her twenty-three years.

"You must love your neighbor as yourself and remember the teachings of the Samaritan who showed us that all men are our neighbors. Go now into your homes and your fields with a solemn pledge to continue your good work in the service of this community." He bowed his gray head, paused while the worshipers did the same, and intoned softly, "Let us pray."

Before bowing her own head, Abby looked to her right at the children seated beside her in the first pew. The twins, Thomas and Timothy, had stopped fidgeting, knowing the sermon was at a blessed end. Ten-year-old Susanna smoothed the worn fabric of her best cotton dress, folded her hands, and placed them on her lap. Next to her, sixteen-year-old Rebecca, her blond head raised to the rough-hewn pine planks of the crude lectern, stared in rapt attention at Reverend James Chadwick.

At the other end of the row of children, big, strong Will sidled closer to the edge of the pew, looking every bit as anxious to bolt as a rabbit waiting for its cage door to be opened. Abby smiled at the raw energy of the fifteen-year-old youth as his gaze connected furtively over his shoulder with those of the other young men of Seneca Township, each one straining to be the first outside on this summer-like day.

When the prayer ended, Reverend Chadwick raised his hand over the heads of the congregation in the sign of benediction. But before he could say the words of parting, Abby pointedly cleared her throat drawing his attention. He looked at her, and a light of recollection dawned in his eyes. He withdrew his hand.

"Oh, yes, before we leave this morning, I would ask your assistance in one more matter that my daughter has reminded me cannot wait." He inclined his head toward the five children in the front row. "The youngsters you have placed in our care are in urgent need of necessities. We appreciate all the kind donations of chickens and vegetables, and in your case, Ernest, that fine sow you sent to us last week."

The man who had been singled out for his generosity preened with pride in the pew next to Abby while Reverend Chadwick continued. "But the children need clothing and shoes, and we must ask for your help once more."

He indicated a wicker basket beside him on the simple altar. "As you leave the church today, please deposit whatever you can for the children—even a few pennies will help. The Chadwick family thanks you for your generous gifts."

After the service, when the other families had gone home, Abby herded the children to the weathered buckboard harnessed to a pair of sturdy mules waiting patiently under a centuries-old elm tree. She climbed up on the driver's bench and sat silently beside her father, afraid that if she spoke, the temper that often got her into trouble would surely show.

James snapped a practiced command, "Git up, mules," and the buckboard lurched down the rutted road toward home. He kept looking at Abby, and she figured he could tell she was near her boiling point. After all, her father knew her so well he sometimes told her what she was feeling before she had even sorted things out for herself.

He glanced up at the clear sky and rubbed his hand over his short, trim beard. "This Ohio weather can sure be a puzzling thing, can't it, Abby? Just over a week ago the wind was howling through the hills with a chilling blast, and an inch of snow covered the ground. And today the sun is out and it must be eighty degrees."

It was a tactic of her father's to try to engage her in idle conversation that would eventually lead to what was really bothering her. Abby knew that was what he was doing now.

"I've never seen an April like this one," he continued. "It's as though spring passed us by and went straight to the dog days." He steered the mules around a deep, muddy crevice in the road, a remnant of a long, harsh winter. "Yep, it's time to get the first planting of corn in."

Abby wasn't the least bit interested in the weather, but she nodded and responded with a clipped, "Yessir, Papa."

He set his elbows on his knees and turned to face her. "All right, Abigail, you might as well come out with it. Something's eating at you, and if you don't tell it, you'll be wearing that grim face for the rest of the day."

The floodgates burst. "Two dollars and thirty-three cents, Papa! That's all those nickel-nursing misers put in the basket today. I can't dress these children on two dollars and thirty-three cents!"

"Ah, so that's it. You've got to remember, Abby, it's been a hard winter and times haven't been so easy for folks . . ."

"It's been plenty easy for some, Papa—the ones who you'll notice didn't contribute anything this morning. Even after your lecture about the importance of being a good neighbor, the people of Seneca Township are as pinch-fisted as ever!"

James gave a subtle nod toward the back of the buckboard. "Abigail . . . the children."

"It's because of the children that I feel this way! Ernest Sholski puffed up like a rooster this morning, priding himself on giving us that skinny ol' pig. I'd wager he didn't even put a penny in the basket!"

"If you were a wagerin' girl, that is," James teased, trying to lighten the mood.

She managed a smile, but returned at once to her point. "Most of our neighbors can afford more than they give, I know it."

"You expect too much of folks, Abby."

"Maybe I do, but these children need so much."

"You've just got to have faith that everything will work out. We'll get by, we always have. Next week we'll just ask again, and the week after that. I'll say a special prayer tonight to thank the Lord for the blessing we received today, and I'll ask Him to shower a little measure of guilt over the heads of the ones that didn't give.'' He winked at Abby from under the wide brim of his best black hat. ''I listen to you, daughter, and the Lord listens to me. It'll all come out right in the end.''

''Papa James is right, Miss Abby,'' Rebecca said from the back of the wagon. ''The Lord will take care of us.''

''Oh, Rebec . . .'' Abby stopped short when she saw the look of hurt on the girl's face. ''I mean *Angel,*'' she amended quickly. ''Yes, of course He will.'' Then to her father, she whispered, ''Since she came to us, I never seem to remember to call her Angel. I guess I still find it strange that she made up a new name for herself.''

''Patience, Abigail,'' James admonished kindly. ''It's little enough to do for a poor lost creature who's been abandoned by her parents. It helps her get by, and after all, that's why they come to us, isn't it? To get by?''

''And because there's nowhere else to go,'' Abby added as she stuffed the coins from the wicker basket into her pocket. She looked at the children, and as always, her heart swelled with love for them. But the feeling was tainted with pity that each of the children had suffered a loss that had left a scar. ''You're right Papa. They ask little enough, but unfortunately that's what they get!''

A quarter mile from the church there was a fork in the road. The main path followed an easy curve north to Seneca Village and bigger towns further on, while the eastern path led to a narrow lane bordered by budding maple trees. It was toward the east that James Chadwick guided his mules, for it ended at Chadwick Farm. The mules plodded instinctively in the direction of the familiar path, until James suddenly tugged both reins to his chest. The animals halted and shook their large heads in obstinate displeasure.

''Look there, Abby,'' he said, pointing up the village

path to a disabled wagon on the roadside. "Someone's having trouble. We'll see if we can lend a hand. This being Sunday, there may not be anyone else along this road for hours."

As they drew near, Abby recognized the stranded traveler who was having difficulty with a large freight wagon. Everyone knew Duncan Walthrop, the hardware salesman who'd been working the rural areas of northern Ohio for years. Abby was surprised to see him crouched in mud and gravel at the rear of his wagon. He was scooping up the littered contents of a packing crate that had obviously tumbled out of the wagon and broken into splinters on the ground. Even though the brake handle at the driver's seat was pulled back and set, the wagon pitched forward and back as one of the two Morgan horses at the harness bucked and thrashed against its restraints.

James set the brake on his buckboard and jumped down to help. "Duncan Walthrop! So it's you having problems. What's happened?"

The burly drummer stopped his streak of angry epithets when he looked up at the Chadwick family, and rose to face James. He shook his hands, relieving them of clumps of mud. "Reverend Chadwick! I mighta known if anyone was to stop and help, it'd be you."

"It looks like you're having trouble with one of your horses."

Duncan frowned. "That cussed old mare just up and reared like she was full o' locoweed. I don't know what got into her, but her gyrations knocked down the gate and spilt ten pounds of nuts and bolts all over Summit County!"

James studied the unhappy mare, who didn't show any signs of cooperating. He looked puzzled, which meant he wasn't drawing the same conclusion Abby was. "Let me have a look at her, Duncan," he said. "Maybe I can figure out what's wrong."

"Don't dirty your Sunday suit, Reverend. I've got a new man helpin' me who swears he can fix anything. If he can set this problem to rights, I just might believe him."

From the other side of the horse, a tall, suntanned man in an open-necked shirt stood up to get Duncan's attention, and managed to capture Abby's as well.

"The shoe's clean," he called. "I can't find a stone or burr or anything that would have set her off." Keeping one hand firmly on the bridle, the man patted the horse's neck and spoke in a soothing tone that Abby knew should have quieted the mare . . . under normal circumstances. She also realized that these circumstances weren't normal, and the man's attempts to calm the horse only increased the animal's discomfort.

Duncan threw his hands in the air. "Well, see if there's a thorn in her harness, Sam, or check for horseflies bitin' her. There's got to be some explanation, unless that thievin' Brady at the livery rented me a mare that's missin' a few oats in her bag!"

Abby leaned back on the wagon bench and watched the man run his hands over the horse to check for biting insects. She strongly suspected he wouldn't find any, and she'd already decided not to wait much longer to come to the mare's aid.

It was during his inspection of the horse's hide that Sam glanced up and noticed the woman staring at him from the buckboard. In fact, six pairs of eyes peered over at him, but it was the woman's that held his attention. Though she sat primly on the wagon seat, he sensed that she was regarding him with more than a mild interest. She seemed to be eyeing him with a critical glare.

She called to the drummer while her gaze remained on Sam and the mare. "Mr. Walthrop, I think I might be able to help."

Duncan chuckled and shook his head. "I hardly see

how, Miss Chadwick. You just sit up there and stay clear of the trouble, you hear? You don't want to get your pretty dress all dirty.''

Duncan had hardly finished his admonition before the woman climbed down from the wagon. ''I can wash my dress, Mr. Walthrop,'' she said. ''What I can't do is sit here and watch that animal suffer!'' She removed her shoes, hiked up her skirts, and slogged through the mud toward Sam.

Though his eyes were on the determined female, Sam clearly heard Duncan's warning. ''You'd better stop your daughter, James. That mare's in a bad temper.''

''So's Abby,'' James countered. ''So I suggest we leave her be.''

Sam watched her approach with both curiosity and annoyance. What did this dainty-looking Abby Chadwick think she was going to do that he hadn't already tried? He increased the pressure of his fingers on the bridle to keep the mare from thrashing out and biting Abby's hand. He certainly didn't need any more problems. It was enough to hold the mare without having to protect this interfering female as well.

She stepped between the horse and Sam. The mare began prancing about agitatedly at the arrival of this other human.

''You're going to have to stand clear, ma'am,'' Sam ordered. ''I don't want you to get hurt.''

Abby didn't budge. ''She won't hurt me. Just let go of her headstall.''

''I can't do that. She'll come around and snap you for certain if I do.''

''No, she won't. Now please take your hand away.'' When he resisted, Abby narrowed her eyes at him and asked, ''Have you been around horses much?''

There was no point lying to her. Sam's handyman duties at the Chilton-Howe Boys' Preparatory School had never included stable chores. For that, the school hired a full-time professional groom. And Sam had only rarely been given permission to ride the thoroughbred ponies available to the young masters. "No, I can't honestly say that I have, and being around this one doesn't make me any too eager."

A trace of a smile lifted the corners of Abby's mouth as she turned back to the horse. Then her fingers worked deftly to release the buckle on the mare's bridle. "If you'd had more experience," she explained patiently, "you would have known immediately that this poor creature's bit is too loose. Her tongue's over the metal bar, and every time you pulled on the reins or tugged her bridle, she's been in considerable pain. It's no wonder this horse tried to topple your wagon."

The instant Abby removed the bit from the mare's mouth, the horse stopped prancing, and Abby was able to replace the gear properly. "There," she said, rubbing the satiny equine nose which nuzzled her shoulder, "isn't that better?"

"Well, I'll be," Sam muttered. "I guess I should thank you." The truth was he didn't know if he admired this woman or resented her. But clearly she had saved him a lot of time and guesswork.

Abby rested her arm on the horse's back and looked at Sam. "You're welcome," she said. "And don't trouble yourself because you didn't know what was wrong. It's just something you learn when you've been around animals for a long time."

The shadow from the brim of Abby's sunbonnet hid much of her face, but Sam decided that the smile he could see seemed genuine and her attitude sincere. She hadn't belittled him for his lack of expertise, and he appreciated that. He waited to see if she offered her hand to him, and when she didn't, he introduced himself anyway. "My name's Sam Kelly."

She didn't respond at first, but her gaze scanned the length of him. He was suddenly conscious of his disheveled appearance. It had been too long since he'd seen a barber, and he knew his hair covered his collar. Minutes ago he'd undone the top buttons of his shirt when the front became damp with perspiration, and he'd rolled his shirtsleeves up well past his elbows. All in all, he didn't look even remotely like the Samuel Kelly from the Chilton-Howe School, and he assumed he didn't look like anyone this woman would like to shake hands with.

"I guess I'm a sight," he said, wiping his hands on his denim pants.

A look of chagrin crossed Abby's face and brought a tint to her cheeks. "No, no, I'm sorry. You must think I'm terribly rude." She immediately thrust her hand at him. "I was thinking of . . . well, I must have been daydreaming, or something. I'm Abigail Chadwick."

As they shook hands, Sam forgot his feelings of unease and smiled at her. "Nice to meet you." He took a long, slow look at her, and surprised himself by wishing she would take her bonnet off. He couldn't even see what color her hair was, but for some reason, he imagined it was auburn. Maybe it was because he'd been able to see that her eyes were the prettiest shade of green, and green-eyed girls often had red hair. "I don't suppose you have anything cool to drink, do you, Miss Chadwick?" he finally said when it became obvious he had stared too long.

She glanced over to the buckboard. "Will one of you children see if there's any lemonade left in the basket?"

Five curious faces had been fixed on Sam and Abby, but at her request, everyone but Will scrambled to the basket to be the one to deliver the requested drink. "Here you are," the victorious Angel said, holding out a tin cup.

Abby and Sam walked over to the buckboard. Sam

took the cup and drank the contents in three big gulps. "Thanks," he said to Angel, though his smile encompassed all the children.

Duncan came up behind them, put his hand on Sam's shoulder, and gave Abby a sheepish grin. "I guess we're darn lucky the reverend and his daughter came by, ain't we, Sam? Course if I hadn't been so tied up pickin' up this litter, I'da took a look at the mare myself. I'da figured out her problem right away."

"Of course you would have, Mr. Walthrop," Abby said with a sweet smile.

Duncan cleared his throat and turned to James. "Now that all the ruckus is over, Reverend, why don't you and I talk a little business? I'll be around to your place in a few days, and I hope I can count on you for an order."

"I can't make any promises, Duncan. Money's tight, though now that I know you're here, I'll see what we're most in need of."

While the men talked, Abby placed her shoes in the buckboard and climbed back up on the seat. The twins had begun to fuss in the back, and Thomas called out, "Aren't we ever goin' home, Papa James?"

"Guess that's a sign we'd best be on our way," James said, ruffling the boy's hair.

"Thanks for stoppin', Reverend," Duncan said. "And I know Sam thanks you, Miss Chadwick."

Sam nodded once at Abby. "Hope I see you again sometime."

"That'd be nice, Mr. Kelly."

James hopped up beside her and guided the mules down the road to where he could turn the buckboard around. When they passed the freight wagon again, Sam and Duncan had finished loading the contents of the broken crate.

Realizing Abby was watching him, Sam looked up and waved at her as the buckboard passed. The last he saw of her was the wide brim of her bonnet blown back in a sudden gust of wind. Trailing over the cotton band was a lock of auburn hair glinting red-gold in the sun. "I knew it!" he gloated with a satisfied grin.

Duncan's sharp gaze passed between Sam and the buckboard. "Seems like you have an eye on the reverend's daughter, son," he mentioned casually as both men climbed aboard the wagon.

"She's not hard on the eyes, Duncan, I'll say that."

The drummer shrugged. "I guess she's got curves enough to attract a man, all right, but I've heard she can be an ornery woman at times. I never saw it person'ly, but that's how I've heard folks describe her."

"Ornery, you say?" Sam pretended to be shocked at Duncan's appraisal of the minister's daughter. "I've heard you talk about your own wife in those very same terms, Duncan."

Walthrop's good-hearted laugh rang out through the spring air. "Yeah, but that's different. My wife's got somethin' to be ornery about. She's married to *me!*"

"Poor, sainted woman!"

Sam leaned back and rested his feet on the prop in front of him. It felt good to be away from teaching in a classroom and out in the open. He liked traveling with the easygoing Duncan, and he liked working with his hands again. There hadn't been a time in his life when he'd been this free of responsibility.

The few decisions he made now were simple and immediate. His life was uncomplicated, and he no longer allowed the resentment he felt toward the man who'd fathered him and the melancholy of his past to interfere with the natural flow of his days. And until something happened to change his mind, that was the way he wanted things.

He still grieved for his mother, and it concerned him

that he'd made a promise to her that he hadn't carried out. To ease her pain and make her last hours peaceful ones, he'd told her that he would claim his inheritance. Sometimes he thought about Harland Carstairs, and the day the attorney came to Chilton-Howe with news of Sam's father's death. And the surprising conditions of Tobias Rosemont's will did pique his curiosity on occasion.

But the truth was, he didn't know when, or even *if,* he'd ever be ready to face his father's legitimate family. Right now, with the sun warm on his face, and the jostling of the wagon lulling him into serenity, he didn't give a tinker's damn about being a rich man.

James Chadwick pulled around to the back of the neat frame farmhouse and let the children and Abby off at the kitchen door. The children ran inside, but Abby hung back. She rested the cumbersome picnic basket on her hip and looked up at her father. "I was just wondering about something, Papa. You don't think you discouraged Mr. Walthrop about coming here, do you? I mean, do you think he'll still stop by to see us?"

"No, Abby, I don't think I discouraged him at all. I told him I'd see if we need anything. To Duncan Walthrop, that's as good as if I'd taken out my money pouch. He's a salesman, Abby, and salesmen live by the eleventh commandment, 'Thou shalt not miss a sale.' "

She laughed, but her eyes had a faraway dreamy look that James had never seen before. "I suppose you're right, Papa."

He drove the rig to the barn. As he unhitched the mules, James thought about his daughter's puzzling question. Looking to the clouds he said, "Daisy, you don't suppose our Abby has actually taken a fancy to that young fellow?" The possibility astounded him, and he chuckled to himself. Duncan's helper had seemed to take an interest in Abby, all right, but could he finally be the man who wouldn't turn and run from her as if the devil himself were chasing him?

Chapter Two

The following week continued unseasonably warm, the days lengthening by minutes as the temperature rose. In the village, merchants opened the doors and windows of their shops, and by afternoon found the interiors so oppressive that they retreated to their porches to wait for customers. The farmers of Seneca Township worked long hours planting their corn crops while the soil provided a warm, dry bed for the seeds. On Saturday, when five acres of Chadwick Farm lay patterned with neat corn furrows, James released the dam on the tributary of the Little White Tail River to allow nourishing water to trickle through the rows of his arid field.

On Sunday, Reverend Chadwick again asked his congregation for donations for his children, but once more the measure of sympathy from their neighbors was disappointing. Abby kept her criticisms to herself this time, but inside, her cynicism about the citizens of Seneca Township grew. It seemed there would be no end to the financial woes she and her father faced.

And on top of that, Duncan Walthrop had not stopped by the farm in the eight days since his wagon had been disabled on the road. Though Abigail hadn't mentioned the drummer's helper to her family, she certainly hadn't been able to dismiss him from her thoughts. For a whole week her mind had conjured up visions of the lean, strong Mr. Kelly with the dark hair and easy smile. All day Monday she found herself watching for the freight wagon to cross the rise that led down to the farm. But the only wagon that came to Chadwick's that day was the buckboard driven by her father.

When James returned from Seneca Village early Monday evening, he entered the kitchen he had built onto the two-story farmhouse and set his supplies on the scrub table. He was walking with a confident swagger that made Abby wonder what had brought about his lighthearted mood.

He spoke to Angel, who as usual was following him. "Why don't you scoop the flour into the bin for Miss Abby, Angel, and then start the dinner biscuits?"

"Okay, Papa James."

He walked over to the butcher block, where Abby was slicing bacon from a side of pork. She sensed he was anxious to tell her something, so she looked up at him and smiled. "You look like the cat who's found the milk pail, so why don't you tell me what's happened?"

He took a thin catalogue out of his back pocket and held it out to her. "Look what was delivered to Purcell's Mercantile today."

She wiped the grease off her hands and took the catalogue. "What is it?"

"It's put out by these two fellows in Chicago." He read the names on the front cover. "Richard Sears and Alvah Roebuck. It's chock full of useful things at prices almost anybody can afford. You just send these fellows the money, and they send you the goods."

Though Abby was skeptical, the book looked interesting. She began thumbing through the pages. "What do you mean, 'prices almost anybody can afford'?"

"Go to page twelve," James said. "Look at the prices of those shoes. You can get work boots for Will for one dollar and ten cents, and high-buttons for Angel and Susanna for only fifty cents each. And as for the twins, well, I've never known six-year-old boys to wear shoes in the summertime anyway, so they can wait."

"I've never heard of anything like this," Abby said. Her father's excitement was beginning to infect her as well. The catalogue truly held a great many marvelous things.

James hooked his thumbs under the straps of his overalls and rocked back on his heels. "You see, Abigail, I told you to have faith that everything will work out. Most folks spend their lives looking for grand and glorious miracles to believe in, but most often what we're searching for just sort of sidesteps into our lives slowly, and without a lot of fanfare, like this little book did today. It's the small miracles that happen every day that keep us going. You just have to look for them and believe."

Normally practical about most everything in her life, Abby had to agree that the catalogue was a little miracle. "Come over here, Angel," she said. "You can even pick shoes from three different styles!"

"Isn't it wonderful, Miss Abby? I knew the Lord would provide."

"I think it's more Mr. Sears and Mr. Roebuck doing the providing, Angel, but that's all right. At least there will be new shoes for the ladies of Chadwick Farm."

Angel and Abby continued poring over the assortment of useful things in the wondrous catalogue, while James, chuckling at their comments, took over the job of kneading the dough for biscuits.

"Papa James! Miss Abby!"

Will's cry of alarm carried on a sudden gust of wind that blew the eyelet curtains straight out from the kitchen window. Abby and James ran to the window and saw Will running toward the house in the midst of a whirling cloud of dust, his arm stretched to the sky. "Cyclone's comin'!"

"My God, Papa, look!" Abby's gaze froze on the twisting black cloud heading for the newly planted cornfield. The apple trees in the orchard at the edge of the field were already bending toward the approaching spiral as tender limbs and branches were hurled out of the twister and into the sky.

"Get the children into the cellar," James shouted above the rising crescendo of wind. He ran to close the windows which were not in the direct path of the cyclone.

Abby raced outside to call the children, but they had already gathered at the front porch. Grabbing arms and hands, she rushed them all across the yard to the root cellar.

Crouching in the mounting wind, she fumbled with the latch of the little-used cellar door. Swirling dust smarted her eyes, and her hair whipped around her face, stinging her cheeks as she struggled with the rusty metal until her fingers bled from the effort.

"Get outta the way, Miss Abby!" Will ordered, pushing her aside. He battered the hasp with a log until the stubborn latch slid back. When he flung open the door, the twister was bearing down on them, cutting an errant path toward the homestead. Splinters of wood and wire from the chicken coop were sucked into the outer bands of the cyclone as the squawking of terrified hens mingled with the thunderous roar of the wind.

The children scurried down the ladder that led below ground, until only Will and Abby were left on the surface. "Get down there, Will!" Abby shouted.

"I'm waitin' for you, Miss Abby. You go first."

"Don't argue with me, Will, go on!"

He hesitated a moment more, and then reluctantly swung his lanky frame onto the ladder and disappeared into the cellar. The tornado swirled around Abby's home, threatening to draw everything she loved into its demonic core. A widening spiral appeared above the roof of the farmhouse. Then the first cracks of rent tar paper and torn shingles joined the cacophony of destruction. Bit by bit, Abby's home was being sucked into the maelstrom. "Papa!" she called futilely. Her voice was carried up and away in the roaring wind. "Papa, where are you?"

She shielded her eyes against the savage attack of debris, and watched the back wall of her kitchen explode into shards of wood and glass that spun in a crazy spiral to the dark cloud above. The door of the root cellar quivered in her hands, and was nearly torn from her grasp.

Frightened cries from the children urged Abby to the cellar. For their sakes, she couldn't wait any longer. "Papa will be all right," she said, trying to convince herself it was true. "He'll find shelter." She climbed down the ladder and pulled the door over her head, sliding the interior bolt across.

When she landed on the packed dirt floor, she felt an ominous rumbling beneath the soles of her shoes. She watched the cellar door billow in and out, its flimsy bolt straining against the awesome power of the wind.

The little group in the dark root cellar crouched together, some with hands over their ears to block out the howling wind. The twins buried themselves in Abby's skirt and cried. Susanna whimpered, and Angel mumbled an incoherent prayer. Will stalked about clenching his fists and muttering his frustration at not being able to defend their home. Abby stroked the twins' heads and prayed for her father's safety. He had to be all right. Anything else was unthinkable. Moments later, it was all over.

*   *   *

When Abby emerged from the root cellar, she scanned the littered farmyard for James, oblivious to the tattered remains of her life. A deep, devastating loss permeated the air around her, and it seemed even more destructive than the damage done to Chadwick Farm. She sensed the storm had changed forever the life her family had built together in the lazy swells of Ohio's rich Appalachian plateau.

She called her father's name repeatedly, only dimly aware that the youngest children wandered around the yard picking up bits and pieces of furniture and clothing and turning them over in their hands. When she felt a fluttering at her ankle, Abby looked down and covered her mouth to stifle a sound that was part sob and part hysterical laughter. She picked up the single page from the Sears and Roebuck Catalogue that was pressed against her leg, and let the breeze carry it out of her hands to the sky. Had it only been minutes since James had brought the book to her and she and Angel had admired the items in the pictures?

Now she didn't even know where her father was, and the catalogue and mementos of her life were ripped to shreds. Her throat constricted painfully, and for a moment she didn't think she could take another breath. She had to find James. None of the rest of it mattered.

"Are you all right, Miss Abby?" Will asked, coming up behind her.

She grasped his shoulders and shook him. "We've got to find Papa. He could be hurt."

"We'll find him, Miss Abby. Don't worry."

They went to the house and stepped through the gaping hole that had once been the southern wall. Sunlight filtered through the fast-moving clouds overhead, spearing shafts of amber light onto the maple floor. There was no longer a roof to block the sun's rays, and there was no sign of James.

Will searched the other rooms and returned to the kitchen.

"Did you find him?" Abby asked.

He shook his head as Susanna came around the back of the house, her normally composed little face pale with fright. "Miss Abby, Will! There's nothing left of the barn. It's all blown apart, and the mules are just walking around like they're lost!"

Abby's heart hammered with fear. "God, no," she cried. "Papa!" The terror she saw in Will's eyes told her he was having the same thought.

They ran outside, heedless of the meandering animals that had lost their shelter. The barn that James Chadwick had built ten years before had been reduced to rubble. Pitchforks and hoes and other farm tools were scattered in an area a hundred yards around the barn's perimeter, their metal parts bent and handles broken in half. Hay bales had been rent apart, and their dusty contents littered the yard and blew into Abby's mouth and hair. She picked among the splintered lumber and called her father. When she lifted one ragged section of wood and saw a wrist and hand, she screamed for Will.

He reached her in seconds, and together they clawed at the beams and twisted lumber while a frantic prayer to spare her father's life raced through Abby's mind. When they uncovered James's face, she stared in horror at the blood dripping down his neck. His lifeless, vacant eyes told her he was dead.

She knelt in the devastation and scratched through the broken lumber, flinging the pieces away from her father's body. "No, Papa, no, don't leave us," she cried, until Will took her arms and lifted her to her feet.

He held her while she strained against his grip, needing to shelter James, wanting to pour her own life back into his still form. "Let me go, Will," she beseeched him. "Papa needs me."

"You stay back now, Miss Abby," the boy said. "I've got to close his eyes and dig him out the rest of the way. You go on back to the house and let me do this." He slowly released her and began clearing the rubble.

Abby's shoulders sagged and her body shook with violent tremors. "Is this what your faith brought you, Papa?" she cried. "Where are your small miracles now?" She raised a fist to her mouth, but could not stop the flow of bitter words. "Is this an act of your merciful God?"

Will knelt in the dirt and dust and stared up at her, halting his grisly chore. Her gaze was drawn to his. She looked into wounded brown eyes clouded with pain almost as great as hers. He was coping with his own grief and trying to make sense of what was senseless, and her words hurt and confused him.

She closed her eyes, freeing the stinging tears which coursed down her cheeks. "I'm sorry, Will," she whispered, reaching out a trembling hand to him. "Forgive me." She turned away and walked back toward the house where the little ones and Angel huddled together in the gathering dusk watching her, still unaware that something even more terrible than the storm had happened.

When Abby swiped at her tears, they mingled with the grit and grime of destruction and scratched like sandpaper against her skin. She drew a deep, shuddering breath and set her back in a rigid posture. There was much that needed to be done.

"I'm not goin' back to school, Miss Abby," Will announced two days later as he put on James's old suit jacket. The coat fit snugly over Will's broad shoulders, and Abby studied his stern expression as she threaded a string tie under his collar. "I've only got two months to go anyway, and then I'll be done for good, so what's the difference?''

Abby took the large hand that extended a full two inches beyond the jacket sleeve. "Will, I know why you're doing this, but I don't want you to miss out on any schooling. You're so young ... you shouldn't take on a man's responsibility yet.''

Will smoothed a shock of sandy blond hair off his forehead and grinned. "Now, you and I both know that I was never much of a student anyway. And as for responsibility, you and the kids need me here much more than I need to be cipherin' numbers in the village schoolhouse.''

She couldn't argue with him. Getting Will to do his lessons had always been a struggle. Even when he tried, he was never very successful. And she did need him at the farm. She desperately needed every spare hand she could find. Thankfully, some of their neighbors had shown up the day after the storm to hammer wood planks over the eaves as a makeshift roof, but that was only the beginning of what needed to be done to rebuild Chadwick Farm—not to mention the crop that had to be put in during the spring months. The work to be done was staggering, and Abby knew she couldn't do it all herself. She placed her hand under Will's chin and nodded her agreement. "What would I do without you?''

"You won't have to find out, Miss Abby," he said. "I'll always take care of you.''

"And I will too," Angel said. She turned around for Abby to fasten the top button of her best dress. Even in their primitive conditions, the family had managed to dress respectfully for James Chadwick's funeral. "Remember, we have to have faith. Any minute now, Papa James is going to come in that door and remind us of that. I hate to say it, Miss Abby, but you have been lacking in faith lately, and you're going to disappoint Papa James.''

Abby pressed her lips together to control her mounting impatience with the girl. "Angel," she said after a moment, "do you know where we're going today?"

Angel avoided Abby's eyes and looked out a window at some indefinite point on the horizon. "The twins say we're going to put Papa James in the ground today . . . that he's dead—but I don't believe it. Even if I see it with my own eyes I won't believe it. God wouldn't just take him away from us—not when we need him so badly."

"Sometimes things just happen, Angel, bad things, and we have to accept them," Abby said.

Angel's bright blue eyes glistened with tears. "But I still see Papa James, Miss Abby. Truly I do, and I'm not touched like Will says."

After giving Will a stern look of reproach, Abby ran her hand over the girl's platinum hair. She remembered her father telling her that Angel imagined a special place that helped her to cope in a difficult world, and Abby now understood the blessedness of being able to do that. Lately she found herself wishing she could retreat to Angel's beautiful existence of halos and gossamer wings. "It's all right, Angel," she said. "Sometimes I still see him too."

Abby, Will, and Angel loaded James's coffin on the buckboard, and the family began the short trip to the church where he had preached. Mr. Purcell, who owned the mercantile, also served as undertaker for the few deaths that occurred in Seneca Township each year. He had come out to the house and prepared the body; now all that was left was to commit the remains of James Chadwick to rest for eternity in the small cemetery in back of the chapel.

They were halfway to the church when a smart two-wheeled buggy belonging to a neighbor approached from the opposite direction. The driver hailed the buckboard, and Will stopped.

"Good morning, Martha," Abby said to the middle-aged woman in the buggy who was holding a toddler on her lap.

"Abigail. I know this is a bad time, but misfortune has a way of building on itself." She refused to look Abby squarely in her eyes as she held the light-haired little girl away from her lap. It was as if she feared the child would wrinkle her dress.

"Isn't that Lizzie O'Donnell?" Abby asked.

"It is. Her parents were killed in the storm, and she was just discovered today. One of Ernest Sholski's boys found her wandering around her parents' place and brought her to me, though heaven knows why. I can't raise a child at my age. I fed her and cut up some old tablecloths for diapers, but that's all I can do. Being as you're equipped to handle orphans, it seemed only logical . . ."

"I've got more than I can handle, Martha. Surely you must know that. We're just burying Papa today."

"I know, and I'm sorry, Abigail, but this child's got nowhere else to go. She seems like a good baby." When Abby still hesitated, Martha added, "I know you need help, Abigail, and I'll send Arne around to help you one day soon. I promise I will, but you've got to take this child."

The little girl kicked her legs furiously as she was held suspended away from Martha Swenson's ample body and the security of the buggy. Instinctively Abby reached her hands out and took the wiggling bundle. "Hello, Lizzie," she said. "I guess you're coming home with us."

"Thank you, Abigail," Mrs. Swenson said. "We'll be seeing you soon." She elbowed her silent husband, and he nodded, turned the buggy around, and headed back toward the village.

Abby settled the child between her and Will on the driver's seat, and the frightened toddler began to cry. "It's all right, Lizzie," Abby said, smoothing her hand over the girl's soft, springy curls. She looked over her shoulder at the wide-eyed children in the back of the buckboard. "Someone get me a biscuit from the basket, please."

"I will!" Angel said, coming forward with the requested goody. "You did the right thing, Miss Abby," she said. "Papa James will be proud of you."

Abby only sighed and put the biscuit into Lizzie's plump little hands.

Three days later, Duncan Walthrop's freight wagon emerged from the canopy of leafy maple trees and crested the rise that led down to Chadwick Farm. This was one of Duncan's last stops, and he was counting on the reverend to spend five or ten dollars as he usually did. As the Morgan horses drew closer to the farmhouse, Duncan screwed his face up in alarm. "Looks like that twister we heard about tore this place up plenty, Sam."

He halted the team a few yards from where Abby was bent over an oak tub, scrubbing clothes against a tin washboard. She had glanced up several times as the wagon approached, but had returned immediately to her labor as if the arrival of the drummer held no importance for her.

When Duncan set the brake, Abby finally dropped the garment she was washing into the tub and looked up at him from under the brim of a wide straw hat. "Morning, Mr. Walthrop," she said, and nodded at Sam.

"Lordy, Miss Chadwick, that cyclone sure made a mess of things around here."

"Yes, it did," she answered wearily. She passed a damp arm across her forehead.

"You remember Kelly here, my helper?"

"Of course." She acknowledged him again with a glance.

"Hot day, isn't it?" Duncan noted. "Sure could use a drink of water, Miss Chadwick."

She stood and pointed to a well several feet away. A wooden bucket hung from the crank rod. "Help yourself. The water's cool and fresh. The well's about the only thing I can still count on working around here these days."

After Duncan jumped down and headed for the well, Abby removed her hat and shielded her eyes with her free hand. She watched Sam climb off the wagon, but her eyes were void of any reaction to him. If was as if she were looking but not really seeing that his white shirt gleamed in the sun and his thick crop of dark hair was now groomed and clean.

He'd never have admitted it to Duncan, but when Sam learned they were going to the Chadwick Farm, he'd taken extra care with his appearance. He hoped to make a better impression on Abby Chadwick than he had the last time, but now that he was standing face-to-face with her, his preparations seemed lost on a vacant stare.

Sam felt the need to say something to cover an awkward silence between them. "I'm sorry about what happened to your place, Miss Chadwick."

The tentative smile she gave him was touched with sadness, as were her jade-colored eyes. In defiance of despair, however, sun-gilded tresses of red hair blew around her face and neck. One long strand settled on the front of her beige cotton blouse, curling above her breast. Sam remembered Duncan telling him that Miss Chadwick didn't do much to pretty herself up like other ladies did, but Sam saw a flawless simplicity in her that outshone artificial beauty.

Duncan returned, wiping the excess water from his mouth with the back of his hand. "I see Will comin' this way from the cornfield," he said, "but where's the reverend? No doubt with your barn tore up and the house damaged, you're gonna need a lot of tools. I promise to give James a good price.''

Abby lowered her gaze to the ground. ''Papa died in the storm, Mr. Walthrop.''

Sam looked from Abby to Duncan. The casual expression on his employer's face had been replaced with shock, and his mustache couldn't hide the frown that pulled at his mouth. ''I'm awful sorry to hear that, Miss Chadwick,'' Duncan said. ''I was mighty fond of your daddy. You must be havin' a rough go of it now.''

''We're managing,'' she said. ''Everyone is pitching in.''

As if on cue, Will came around the back of the house and stood beside Abby, towering a head above her. ''That's right, Mr. Walthrop. We're gettin' along fine here.''

''I'm sure you are, Will. Is there anything you need? I'll help you as much as I can to replace your tools and equipment.''

''We won't be buying anything just now, Mr. Walthrop,'' Abby answered. ''Maybe next time you're through.''

Sam noticed the hoe in Will's hand, and saw that Duncan was looking at it too. It was held together with a flimsy metal band, and the blade was bent at the end. The two men seemed to share the same thought as Duncan sniffed the air around him. ''Is that soup I smell comin' from your kitchen, Miss Chadwick?'' She nodded, and he turned to Sam. ''Are you hungry, Sam?''

''Yessir, I sure am.''

''If you were to offer us a bowl of that soup, Miss Chadwick,'' Duncan said, ''I'd see my way to replacin' that hoe Will's holdin'. And I might throw in a pound of nails for a cup of coffee.''

Will stepped forward. ''We don't need charity . . .''

Abby raised her hand. "I think Mr. Walthrop's offering us a fair deal, Will, and I'm going to take it," she said. "Come into the kitchen, or what's left of it anyway."

Duncan motioned for Sam to follow Abby inside. "You two go on ahead. I'll just find that hoe in the wagon and weigh out those nails."

Sam followed Abby into a cool parlor and through a short hallway to a sun-warmed kitchen that had sections of plywood serving as its roof. Pinpoints of light filtered through the canvas weave of the tarp stretched over the wood. He studied the workmanship, or lack of it, evidenced by the hasty repairs and said, "This isn't going to keep you dry, Miss Chadwick."

"So far it hasn't had to. It hasn't rained a drop since the twister. We're having to irrigate every day, and the river's getting low. I think I'd trade a leaky roof for a good downpour right now."

Abby poured water from a pitcher into a bowl and washed her hands while Sam looked around the kitchen. Wood slats from a corn crib covered the shattered windows. Several portions of scrap lumber had been nailed together to serve as a table. The legs of the few chairs showed the shiny tips of new nail heads, indicating they had recently been repaired. The door of the oak icebox hung on its hinges with wire, and the ventilator pipe on the wood-burning stove was bent in two places before it exited the west wall of the house. There was no southern wall at all. The interior was protected by more sheets of canvas.

Abby pulled an apron off a hook near the stove and tied the ends around her waist. When she noticed Sam surveying the damage, she said, "It used to be a pleasant enough kitchen."

"It's not so bad," he said kindly. "Your repairs show a lot of ingenuity."

"Someone taught you good manners, Mr. Kelly. You found something nice to say in spite of what you see."

She stirred the soup in a cast-iron pot and glanced toward an area a few feet away. Sam followed her gaze. On the scarred maple floor, a child slept on a quilt, her thumb plugged securely into her perfectly round little mouth. A mop of strawberry curls, just slightly lighter than Abby's hair, covered her head.

When he saw an unmistakable fondness for the baby in Abby's eyes, Sam wondered if there were a special relationship between the two of them. Did the child have the same jade-green eyes? Before he considered the propriety of his question, Sam blurted out, "Is she yours?"

Abby's eyes widened slightly. "I didn't give birth to her, but yes, I guess you could say she's mine, for as long as she wants to stay. The soup's ready. Why don't you sit down, Mr. Kelly?"

She put a dented tin bowl on the table in front of him, and the tempting aroma of its contents drifted up to his nose. Then she removed a checkered cloth from the top of a reed basket in the center of the table to reveal a crusty loaf of bread. She carved a slice and handed it to him.

"Sure looks good," he said appreciatively.

She poured two cups of coffee and sat down across from him, wrapping her fingers around her steaming mug. Sam noticed her reddened knuckles and short, jagged nails. These were hands that had seen hard work, and he admired the fact that she didn't try to hide it. There was no pretense that he could see about Abby Chadwick, making her very different from the girls he remembered coming to Chilton-Howe.

Young ladies often strolled the manicured campus on weekends with their brothers or suitors, but they never wasted their conversations on Moira Kelly's illegitimate son. Once in a while, despite the glowers of her escort, a lady would stare overlong at young Sam as he trimmed the tall holly hedges or raked leaves in the fall, but there was almost always a cool disdain in her eyes.

There were times, however, when Sam imagined he'd seen something else broiling beneath a girl's safe, haughty appraisal of him from under her parasol, a craving, almost, that tempted even as it scorned him. As he grew older, Sam recognized the secretive glances for what they were . . . forbidden, well-disguised desire for what the girl could not, or should not, want. But Abby was different. She seemed somehow untouched by prejudice or convention. Or maybe Sam was different, his past buried in Cooper's Glen, Pennsylvania, far from this simple country farm.

Abby's voice cut through his reverie. "Watch for chips of pottery when you drink. Sometimes the hot coffee makes these old mugs crumble."

"You mean if I break a tooth, it wasn't the coffee?"

"Well, it could be that too," she said, laughing softly. "My coffee has a reputation for being too strong." Her gaze shifted from him to the canvas wall beside them. "We used to have a fine set of Blue Willow china that my mother got as a wedding gift," she said. "We kept it in a hutch that stood right there, and it had a border of little bluebirds flying around an Oriental garden with a pagoda in the center. After Mama died, we didn't use it much, but whenever we did, like at Thanksgiving or Christmas, I used to dream of faraway places. After the twister, the china was broken into so many pieces that we couldn't repair any of it. Neighbors three miles away found bits of it in their yard. And the hutch—Will used the wood to make a bed for Lizzie." She smiled. "Maybe you're right, Mr. Kelly. I guess we are ingenious at that."

"I know for certain that you are, Miss Chadwick. I remember your talents with the mare that day."

She shrugged off the compliment. "So where are you from, that you've avoided an association with horses?"

He told her a little about Cooper's Glen and about meeting Duncan.

"So you haven't known Mr. Walthrop long?" she asked.

"Just long enough to know he's a good man."

"That's true. Papa always liked him. He's been coming around here for years."

"Duncan spoke highly of your father, Miss Chadwick. I'm sorry about what happened to him."

He realized that she'd probably heard such shallow expressions of sympathy from a hundred people, but he hoped she believed that he meant it, because he, of all the others, could understand her sorrow. He thought of his mother, and as a fresh jolt of grieving coursed through him, he knew that if she had been snatched from him without warning, her death would have been even harder to bear. "Truly I am," he repeated.

"Thank you, Mr. Kelly."

"How will you manage here, Miss Chadwick?" he asked suddenly. "How will you get by?"

For a long moment their eyes locked, his searching for an answer, and hers a fathomless swirl of green that spoke of her hopelessness even as they swallowed his next heartbeat. "Not on faith, Mr. Kelly," she said, "not anymore."

Chapter Three

Sam noticed Duncan in the doorway before Abby did. The drummer stood hesitantly on the threshold to the kitchen and watched them with keen observation.

"Come on in, Duncan," Sam said. "You're going to like Miss Chadwick's soup."

Heavy footsteps echoed through the house toward the kitchen. Will came up behind Duncan and peered into the room, looking first at Abby and then Sam. "What's going on here?" he asked.

"Nothin', Will," Duncan answered quickly for all of them. He put his arm around the boy's shoulder. "I was just tellin' Miss Chadwick that the hoe has passed your inspection, and you prob'ly can't wait to get back to work."

"I can wait," Will grumbled. "I just came in to get my lunch."

Abby jumped up and set places for Will and Duncan. Will picked up his soup, but made no move to sit. Instead he stood across the table from Sam and stared at him over the rim of his mug.

Sensing the boy's animosity, Sam finished his lunch, letting Duncan cover the tension in the air with chatter. "I've got some things to check on in the wagon," Sam said after a moment. He got up from the table and headed for the exit. "Thanks for the meal, Miss Chadwick."

"You're welcome, Mr. Kelly. Anytime." As Sam was leaving, he noticed Will sit at the table and reach for a large slice of bread. It seemed the boy's appetite had suddenly returned.

Minutes later Duncan joined Sam behind the house at a makeshift lean-to that had been built against a large willow tree. It scarcely protected the few tools that Abby and Will had been able to salvage from the wreckage, and Sam was sifting through them, a scowl on his face and a tablet and pencil in his hand.

"What're you doin', Sam?" Duncan asked.

"Look at this mess, Duncan. Everything's in need of repair. I've just now put the handle back on this seeder, but the wheel won't even turn. And this plow blade needs replacing. How can these people plant a crop when their plow isn't even functional! I've made an inventory of just the barest necessities that they're going to need." He handed the paper to Duncan. "Most of what they already have can be fixed, if that boy Will knows what he's doing, but he'll need these new parts to do it."

Duncan scratched his head. "I don't imagine Will's too handy at fixin' things. And anyway, how are you proposin' to fill this list? I feel sorry for Miss Chadwick too, but I can't let her have these things for nothin'. Otherwise this whole trip would amount to naught."

"I know that, Duncan. I'll pay for them."

"Miss Chadwick won't take your charity, Sam."

"Then we'll tell her we're letting her have everything on credit."

Duncan shook his head. "This is farm country. These folks know that they can't depend on their crops to pay their bills. They pay cash, and Miss Chadwick prob'ly knows that more than most after what happened here."

"Then we'll just leave everything here in the lean-to without saying anything to her. After we're gone, what can she do?"

Duncan pointed at the tablet. "I don't mean to stick my nose into your business, son, but where're you gonna get the money to pay for all this?"

"You owe me two weeks' wages, Duncan, and besides, when you picked me up in Cooper's Glen, I never said I was a pauper . . . I said I was looking for a job, that's all. You assumed the rest."

Duncan snorted his surprise. "Oh? So now I s'pose you want me to believe you weren't some drifter with but one carpetbag to his name? You're really some highfalutin blue blood, and you flagged me down just so you could have an adventure sellin' farm tools!"

Sam looked away from Duncan's probing gaze. He didn't feel much like a blue blood, but the drummer wasn't far from the truth. "Of course not. I needed the job. But I had a few dollars saved up."

"And now you're gonna spend 'em on this run-down place?" Sam set his lips in a firm line, and Duncan gave in. "All right, then, if you're bound and determined, let's get the goods unloaded and be on our way. I want to be back in Cuyahoga Falls by dark. There's no place to stay in that one-horse Seneca Village."

Sam and Duncan worked quickly to unload the hardware from the wagon. Thankfully, the willow tree kept their activity hidden from the house. When they finished, they rode the wagon around to the front porch, and Abby came out, balancing Lizzie on her hip. Abby handed the child a package wrapped in brown paper. "These are the friends we made the sandwiches for, Lizzie," she said, "and you may give them to the nice gentlemen."

Duncan took the bundle from Lizzie's outstretched hand. "Thank you, pretty miss," he said, and nodded at Abby.

"It's just some bread and cheese, but it might ward off the hunger before you get back to town."

"I'm sure it will, and I thank you kindly, Miss Chadwick."

Sam was sitting on the wagon bench with his elbows on his knees. A well-worn leather hat dangled from his hands, and he twisted it around by its brim. When Abby's gaze rested on him, his hands stopped moving and the hat hung motionless. It was as if those green eyes could reach across the patch of dirt that separated them and see into his soul. At the very least they stirred a reaction in him that he couldn't deny. He returned the smile she gave him with his own.

"It was nice seeing you, Mr. Kelly," she said. "Maybe you'll come back sometime."

Sam figured she was just being polite, but it bothered him more than he wanted to admit that he would probably never see her again. He didn't know where he'd be or what he'd be doing when Duncan came back this way the next time. He put his hat on and touched the brim with two fingers. "Maybe so, Miss Chadwick, and good luck to you."

She held up Lizzie's hand. "Say good-bye, Lizzie. Tell the nice man bye-bye."

"Get along, horses!" Duncan coaxed gruffly, and the Morgans headed away from the house. When Sam looked back, Lizzie was running around the yard chasing after a clucking hen, but Abby hadn't moved. She remained on her front porch until the wagon had crossed the ridge and moved into the lane of maple trees.

When the roof of the farmhouse disappeared on the

other side of the rise, Sam attempted to concentrate on Duncan's explanation of their itinerary. But his mind kept going back to Chadwick Farm and the almost insurmountable problems faced by its mistress. How could one woman and six ragtag orphans hope to mend the broken buildings and rebuild their lives? What would they do when winter came?

Sam looked at Duncan, saw his mouth moving, but his words had become as insignificant as the buzzing of insects in the tall grass by the side of the road. Suddenly Sam was asking himself a lot of questions. Was this where he wanted to be . . . on a wagon heading east? He had no home, no family to go back to. Or could he see himself at the end of the lane where a proud woman with more than her share of misfortune seemed to be calling him back?

He gave up pretending to listen, took a tablet and pencil from under the wagon bench, and began sketching lines and angles. Within minutes, a clear likeness of the Chadwick farmhouse appeared on the page. Triangular rafters met in a pitched angle over the extension where the kitchen roof had been, and Sam's numbers and notations were scribbled all around the diagram. He was aware that Duncan had been watching his drawing, alternating his gaze between the road and the tablet. So he wasn't surprised when Duncan asked, ''What the heck are you sketchin' tie beams and trusses for, son?''

Sam looked over at his boss and announced confidently, ''I can do this, Duncan.''

Duncan grabbed the tablet from Sam and stared at it in disbelief. ''You're not considerin' what I think you're considerin', are you?'' He clearly disapproved of the plan before he even heard it.

''I can put the roof and back wall on that kitchen. I know I can.''

Duncan handed the tablet back and leveled his eyes on

the road. "Drawin' a fancy picture is a lot different from buildin' a roof, son."

"I know that, but where I worked before I fixed lots of things. Like I told you once, most anything can be repaired using a few simple rules of carpentry and geometry."

"Look here, Sam, the only calluses on your hands are the ones you got since you hooked up with me. When I picked you up in Cooper's Glen, I knew you were a strong lad, but your hands were too pretty. I figured you hadn't done a lick a' work in your life. Now you're tellin' me you can raise a roof?"

"That's exactly what I'm telling you. It's been a while since I had to use those skills, but it's coming back to me."

Duncan frowned and gave the reins an extra slap, as if he were trying to hurry the team further away from Chadwick Farm. "You'd best forget this notion, son. I can't wait for you to finish the roof, and I ain't got time to help build it."

Sam tapped the pencil against the tablet and stared at the diagram. Then, paying no heed to what Duncan had said, he declared, "Stop the wagon, Duncan. I'm going back."

Duncan hauled back on the reins, and the horses stopped. He did a quarter turn on the bench and stared at Sam. "What's got into you, Kelly? You can't walk out on me now. You promised to stay on till we were back in Pittsburgh." Sam started to speak, but Duncan didn't let him. "What is it about Abigail Chadwick that got you to come up with such a crazy plan? After all, she's just a woman—good-lookin' enough, I guess, but I've told you she's a contrary female. It's one thing to try and be a decent man, Sam, but you're prob'ly too decent for your own good."

Sam didn't deny that Abigail Chadwick had caught his

eye, but the fact was, until he'd envisioned her seeing the results of his labors, he hadn't decided for certain that he was going back. Now he knew he couldn't be content with his life on the road any longer because Abby and her plight had touched his heart and, for now, had given new purpose to his life.

There were few certainties for Sam, but one was that he wasn't going back to Chilton-Howe. And another was that he had no desire at the moment to face the Rosemonts and claim his inheritance. That could come later . . . if ever. But for the time being, while he sorted things out, Chadwick Farm was a good place to be. He didn't explain all this to Duncan, knowing it wouldn't make any sense to the drummer anyway. He countered Duncan's argument with a simple rationale that expressed the basic truth of his decision. "You said this morning that the Chadwick place was near the end of your territory. Most of your merchandise has been sold. You really don't need me any longer, and these people do. I can do some good here."

"Oh, you think so?" Duncan shot back irritably. "I'll tell you somethin' you seem to have forgot, Sam. In a few hours those orphan kids are gonna come over that rise from the township school and plop themselves down right in the middle of that mess. Think about that for a darned minute. And I heard that the one girl isn't right in the head." Duncan's index finger made a circle at the side of his face. "Folks say she's always havin' visions. Are you ready to be a daddy to some other bullfrog's tadpoles?"

Sam considered Duncan's question, then answered, "I think it's all the more reason I should stay."

"And what if Miss Chadwick don't want you there? She's been runnin' things her way for a good long while now."

"And probably doing a good job of it too. But if she doesn't want me, then I'll go."

"And what about Will? He eyed you like you was bringin' smallpox down on 'em."

"Once I show him I'm just there to help out, he'll be glad to relinquish a little responsibility."

"And that's the only reason you're goin' back . . . just to help Miss Chadwick out?" Duncan's voice held an accusation, and Sam knew what it was. "I saw the way you two were lookin' at each other when I came in the kitchen. For Pete's sake, Sam, she's the minister's daughter, and you'd do well to remember that! Her daddy may be gone, but I guarantee that James Chadwick's presence hangs over that place day and night!"

"I've never been afraid of ghosts," Sam said as he jumped down from the wagon and ran around to get his clothes. He opened his satchel and dropped in the tablet and pencil. Then he came back to the front of the wagon and leaned on the footrest. "I figure we've only come a mile or so from the house. I'll head back on foot."

Duncan fixed his gaze straight ahead and picked up the reins once more. "Don't count on me to wait here for your sorry backside if she throws you out."

"I won't. If she doesn't want me to stay, a good long walk will be just what I need to think things through. Maybe I'll see you in town after all!"

Duncan looked down at Sam and shook his head, but he managed a bewildered half grin as he drew some bills out of his pocket and thrust them at his helper. "Here's what's left of your pay. Like I said, Kelly, you're a good man; I hope it don't prove to be your undoin'. I'd bet more than these wages that those stars in your eyes are snuffed out pretty quick by that woman and her brood."

Sam only shrugged. "Maybe, maybe not. Good-bye, Duncan, and thanks for everything. I'll see you next time you're by." The wagon lumbered forward, and Sam turned around and headed back to Chadwick Farm.

Abby was aware of movement on the rise before she actually turned from her clothesline to see a man coming down the path. She recognized his leather hat and lean frame, and knew at once it was Mr. Kelly. When her heart beat a little crazily against her rib cage, she attributed it to concern over the circumstances that had brought him back.

She had just finished hanging up the last of the laundry. Drying her hands on her apron, she walked toward Sam, meeting him halfway. "Mr. Kelly, has something happened? Did you have trouble on the road?"

"Nothing like that," he said. "I came back on my own. I've decided to stay and help you."

At first she didn't think she'd heard him correctly. After all, why would anyone, especially a stranger, suggest such a thing? "Did you say you want to stay here and help out?" she repeated.

"That's right."

An unexpected, unfamiliar, but not unpleasant quiver began deep inside her, but Abby's innate skepticism won out over all other emotions. From behind the stern mask she'd fixed on her face, she said, "I don't recall asking you to do that."

"You didn't, but you seem to possess considerable common sense, and I doubt you'd be foolish enough to turn down willing help."

A few moments passed while Abby contemplated the many implications of Sam's decision, and she finally said, "And just why *are* you so willing, Mr. Kelly? Why would you want to offer your services in this tarnished Eden?"

"You act as though you suspect an ulterior motive, Miss Chadwick, and there isn't one. All I want is to help your family out in exchange for a place to stay. I need to think some things through for myself, and your farm looks like a good place to do that.''

She planted her fists on her hips. ''What is it exactly that you need to think about?''

''Nothing in particular,'' he said a little too quickly. ''Just things in general. Duncan doesn't really need me any longer, and I don't have anywhere I have to be for a while.''

Deciding he was deliberately avoiding her question, Abby said, ''Did Mr. Walthrop fire you?''

''No.''

She narrowed her eyes suspiciously. ''Are you wanted by the law, Mr. Kelly?''

''No.''

''But you are in some kind of trouble?''

''If you mean am I hiding from somebody who's going to show up here one day and blow my head off, no to that too.''

Abby took a step closer to Sam and openly appraised the clear charcoal eyes set in his strong, handsome face. He seemed to mean every word he said, and yet he was proposing a situation that most people would consider absolute folly. ''Don't you have family somewhere who will be wondering about your whereabouts?''

A dubious glimmer flashed for just a second in Sam's eyes, and Abby suspected that a secret lay buried inside him, but he shook his head without giving her a clue as to what it could be. ''Nobody's wondering about me at all,'' he said simply.

Abby finally reminded him of the situation that she knew would make him turn tail and run as fast as he could. ''You do realize, Mr. Kelly, that I'm raising six orphans on this farm?'' She pointed to a blanket hanging on the laundry line. ''And every one of them is as different from the other as the patches in that quilt.''

Sam stood his ground and didn't even blink. "If you're trying to scare me, Miss Chadwick, you'll have to pick something more terrifying than children."

She sighed in frustration, but inside, a small flicker of hope flared where only desperation had been before. Still, she couldn't quite accept that this man, who barely knew her, was willing to help scratch an existence out of what was left of her farm. "So I'm supposed to believe that you're offering yourself to Chadwick Farm for a bed and some solitude?" She knew her voice sounded harsh and her tone unappreciative, but she wanted him to know she was not yet convinced of his sincerity.

Sam dropped his satchel on the ground, pushed his hat back on his head, and stared at Abby from beneath the strands of thick black hair that fell across his forehead. He rubbed his hand across the back of his neck, easing tense muscles.

"Miss Chadwick," he began in a deceptively calm voice that soon gave way to exasperation, "you are without a doubt the most hardheaded woman I've ever met when it comes to accepting the simple truth that someone is just trying to lend you a helping hand. Hasn't anyone ever done you a good turn? Or have you pushed every person with good intentions out of your life with the same narrow-minded suspicions?"

She gasped her indignation as Sam wisely backed away from her. The raw nerve he'd struck was tingling on the surface of her skin and threatening to erupt in a show of temper. She turned her back to him, and tapped her toe in the dirt until she had calmed her nerves. She had to admit he wasn't entirely wrong. She didn't accept shows of kindness very well, but then, she'd never really had many offered.

She looked back at Sam and saw that he was watching her warily, though the suggestion of a smile she let curl her lips seemed to relax him. "Maybe you are just a kind man, Mr. Kelly, and God knows I can use your help, but there are a lot of problems with what you're suggesting that you may not even be aware of.''

He widened his stance comfortably and folded his arms across his chest. "Okay, name one."

"Well, for instance, where are you going to sleep? We barely have enough room as it is."

"I guess it's customary for strangers like me to bunk in the barn, isn't it? But I know you're lacking in barn hospitality right now. Where do the other fellas sleep?"

"In a loft above the parlor."

"That'll suit me just fine. I'm used to much worse being on the road with Duncan." He stuck his hand out toward her. "Now do we have a deal or have you come up with another problem?"

"I can't pay you."

"I know that." He kept his arm outstretched.

Abby looked at the strong, capable hand with its light dusting of dark hair on the knuckles. Sam held it confidently in front of her, and when she glanced up at his eyes, she saw the same confidence reflected there. "We might have a deal . . ." she said hesitantly.

"What now?"

"I don't even know your first name, Mr. Kelly, and yet you're proposing that we live and work together almost like family."

"You just forgot my name. I told you what it is on the road the other day." A teasing grin lifted the corners of his mouth. "Where *are* your manners today, Miss *Abigail* Chadwick?"

She smiled openly at the joking criticism, and decided that since she was so close to accepting his offer, what harm could it do to suggest that there might be some humor after all beneath the hard shell of the minister's daughter. "My manners, or lack of them, seem to be the only thing we have in common, Mr. Kelly. After all, you're the one inviting yourself to stay."

His soft gray eyes hinted of subtle admiration. "My name's Sam, Abigail . . . Abby, just plain Sam."

He pushed his hand closer to her, and she took it, tentatively at first, but he grasped hers firmly, and they shook decidedly one time. He kept the pressure of his fingers on her wrist a little longer than was necessary, and their eyes locked. When she turned away, Abby saw that Will had stopped working and was leaning on the brand-new hoe watching the scene at the farmhouse with great interest.

"Why? Why'd you do it?" Will asked later that night after the littlest children had gone to bed and Sam had taken a lantern into the yard to repair some tools. "Why'd you hire *him?*"

"I didn't *hire* anyone," Abby answered curtly. "Hiring implies paying a salary. You know that I can't pay Mr. Kelly to do what he's offered."

"That's another thing. If he's not being paid, then why's he doing this? What's he after anyway?"

Abby threw down the towel she'd been using to wipe the supper dishes and glared at Will. He was being every bit as distrustful as she had been and forcing her to justify a decision that she knew in her heart was irrational. "Maybe he's not after anything," she said angrily. "Maybe he's just doing a kindness where one is sorely needed. Did you ever think of that?"

"That's what I think."

Abby and Will turned toward the kitchen entrance as Angel came in. "Miss Abby's right, Will," Angel said, "and I think you'd do well to remember the story of the Good Samaritan. He stopped on the road to help the beaten man and asked nothing in return. Maybe Sam is just like the Samaritan, sent here by Papa James to help see us through our troubles.''

Will answered Angel with a disgruntled scowl. ''That's just plain stupid . . .'' A sharp look from Abby silenced him.

''I don't think it's a bit stupid, do you, Miss Abby?'' Angel asked, casting wide, hopeful eyes on Abby.

''I think it's a wonderful thing to believe, Angel,'' Abby said evasively, but Angel seemed to accept it as agreement. Giving Will a triumphant glare, she sauntered from the kitchen.

When she'd gone, Abby raised a finger to Will and opened her mouth to reprimand him.

''I know what you're gonna say, and I'm sorry,'' he said. ''I should never have called her stupid, even if nearly everything she says is. I just don't see why you didn't lean on me instead of some stranger. Don't you trust me?''

Will Buckman might be the size of a full-grown man, despite his fifteen years, but Abby knew that inside he was still a boy coming to terms with emotions he couldn't even identify. She suspected that he had ideas about being more to her than just a valued friend and member of her family. She straightened her back and raised herself to her full five feet four inches, though it still left her considerably shorter than Will. ''Don't you trust *me,* Will?'' she said. ''According to the people of Seneca Township you're going to have to for at least a couple more years.''

She hated having to remind him of his place in the family, but she couldn't let him dream of assuming a role he wasn't ready for or a relationship that would never happen. She kept her eyes on his until he looked away, pretending to worry over an imagined speck of dust on the floor.

''If it makes you feel any better,'' she finally said, ''I don't intend to lean on anyone, Mr. Kelly included, but

I'd be a darn fool if I didn't accept a willing hand when it was offered, for all of our sakes.''

Will's heavy booted foot continued to swipe at the floor until Abby leaned her face down to his and looked up into his eyes. She picked up the towel from the table and smiled at him. ''And speaking of willing hands . . . since you ran Angel off, I could use a pair to dry these dishes.''

He took the towel, stepped beside her, and reached for a plate. In a few minutes, they got the job done.

Chapter Four

Abby's kitchen had a new door, and she was quite certain it was the finest one in all of Summit County. It was a double Dutch door made of sturdy ash, and Sam told her that when the wall surrounding it was finished, she could leave the bottom part closed to keep out the chickens, and open the top to let in the sun and the breeze. Abby couldn't wait to use it, so one night, when she finished sweeping the floor, she turned the shiny brass knob that opened her door and swept the litter into the yard. She could just as easily have swept it under the canvas sheets that still hung on either side of the frame, but that wouldn't have been at all memorable—and certainly not as much fun.

She visualized the way her kitchen would look when Sam was finished with it. In the short time he had been at Chadwick Farm, he had framed in the wall with two-by-fours, installed the door, and fashioned a wide window over the sink. Now, when she looked out through the pink-hued dusk, she could see the neat rows of budding corn plants, their slender shoots stretching through the loose soil.

With painstaking effort, life was returning to Chadwick Farm. Even the wounded apple trees showed signs of recovery, as fragrant pink blossoms appeared on the twigs, promising the spring season that Papa James had said had passed them by.

Sometimes Abby didn't see Sam for hours at a time, for while he was working on the house, she and Will, with little Lizzie nearby, worked in the field to put in their crop with the newly repaired tools. But Abby could always hear the tapping of Sam's hammer as he mended her house, with much the same rhythm as a seamstress's needle mends a rend in fabric. And after dinner, when Abby and the older children tended to chores, Will and Sam went to the field and worked until dark.

But tonight Sam had stopped his labor earlier than usual because Susanna had asked for his help. It was with an unsettling sense of familiarity that Abby listened to Sam's voice in the background as the bristles of her broom kept a steady accompaniment.

"So let's see," he said to Susanna. The girl leaned forward, cupped her chin in her hand, and listened intently. "It says here that Mary has three dresses, a plaid one, a checkered one, and a flowered one. She has four pinafores in different colors, red, green, blue and yellow." Susanna followed Sam's finger as he traced the words in her math book. "How many different outfits can Mary put together by arranging her clothes in all their possible ways?"

He looked at Susanna and patiently waited for an answer. Finally she sat up straight, and with a puzzled look on her face, said, "The colors have to match, don't they?"

"I don't know," he said. "I think we should assume that they do match."

"Well, then, does Mary have any hair ribbons?"

"The book doesn't mention ribbons."

Susanna twisted her finger around the blue satin ribbon that held the chestnut hair at her crown. "Miss Abby gets my ribbons from the ruffles on Urline Ralston's old dresses. I have five different colors, and if Mary did too, then she would have to match those with her dresses and pinafores. Think how hard it would be to choose all the right outfits then!"

Sam stifled a grin, but he managed to convince Susanna that he took her concerns seriously. "I don't think the person who made up this problem had any idea that it would become so complicated or that he would be dealing with the fashion sense of such a mature . . . How old are you anyway, Susanna?"

A coy grin tugged at the girl's mouth. "How old do you think I am?"

"Well, from the way your eyes are twinkling with mischief, I'd say you're about twenty-one."

"Twenty-one? Heavens, no. Then I'd be almost as old as Miss Abby, and all the girls at school would call me an old spinster like they do her. I don't think I'd like to be one of those."

The broom slipped out of Abby's hand and rattled to the floor. She retrieved it quickly and resumed sweeping without looking at Sam, though she was certain he had heard the noise. Only a deaf person would not have heard it, and only a blind one would be ignorant of the flush on her cheeks.

"And just what is a spinster, Susanna?" he asked, gallantly pretending not to notice the disturbance behind him.

"I don't know, but when the other girls say it, it doesn't sound very nice. Do you know what it is, Sam?"

He nodded. "A spinster is a lady of fine quality who, although she has undoubtedly had many suitors, has not yet selected the one who would be just right for her. She is a woman of uncompromised taste, and she will not be satisfied with the first beau to come courting.''

The wonder in Susanna's eyes suggested a new respect for Abby's position. "Then I think I would like to be one after all,'' she said. "Can I be a spinster now, Sam, when I'm ten?''

"Oh, no. You have some living to do yet. It is only by having experiences that you grow into such a worthy position.'' He tapped the end of her nose and added, "And one of those experienccs is dealing with difficult math problems, so you should turn your attention to this one, and I suggest we stick to just what's written in the book.''

Susanna finished the problem easily, and asked for permission to play with the twins until bedtime. When she'd gone, Sam settled back in his chair. Abby was aware of his watchful gaze as she leaned the broom against a cupboard and removed her apron. She tucked errant strands of hair into the bun at her nape and smoothed her skirt.

"You look awfully pretty for a spinster,'' he said after a moment.

The flush returned immediately to Abby's face. "I've known for quite some time that you're a fine tutor for the children, Sam, but I've never before realized that you have such a silver tongue.''

His eyes grew round as his smile broadened. "What? You didn't like my explanation to Susanna?''

"It's not truthful. If the girls at school are being mean and spiteful, then Susanna should know it for what it is. The fact is, and you know this, most women my age are married, and some people around here do think I'm rather strange . . .''

"Haven't you had any suitors, Abby? I can't imagine that you haven't.''

"Not that it's any of your business, but yes, some. I've

just been too busy here on the farm for much courting. You might expect too that not many men are interested in a woman with a built-in family. And truly, I haven't had the desire to pursue a relationship with the gentlemen who came around—''

''Aha!'' Sam interrupted jubilantly. ''Then it *is* a matter of selectivity, just as I said to Susanna. You haven't found the right one yet. You needn't be so defensive, Abby. Whether or not a lady has attached herself to a man does not make her more, or less, of a woman. In fact, I've seen enough clinging vines to know that independent women are more interesting.''

''Then why must everyone else use the word *spinster* as if it meant haggard old crone?''

Sam's dark eyes lost their teasing, and the angles of his face took on hard lines of gravity. ''I'll tell you something, Abby. It's about my mother and how a circumstance of her life made a hell of her existence in a small community much like this one. Moira Kelly was a good woman, but she was never married, and I'm quite certain that through the years, she would have been much happier to be called merely a spinster than some of the other labels the good people of Cooper's Glen attached to her because she had a son out of wedlock.'' He closed the math book, and stood up from the table. ''A word is just a word, Abby, and out of some people's mouths it often lacks forethought and substance. I learned long ago to pay no attention to what some folks say.''

He left the kitchen, and as Abby watched him go, she felt both stunned and privileged that Sam had allowed her to see a crack in the rigid isolation he imposed around his feelings. She finally had a glimpse of his well-guarded past. Even though she still knew very little about Sam Kelly, she laid her hand against her emotion-warmed cheek and remembered with absolute clarity that he'd said she looked pretty.

* * *

Most nights, after chores were done, when the children were in bed, Abby sat on the porch to enjoy the cool air, and Sam took a lantern and went to the lean-to by the willow tree to work by himself. He always returned after the house was quiet for the night. Though Abby was in bed, she knew when he came in because the screen door squeaked one last time, and the old ladder creaked as he climbed to the loft.

She listened to him settle down on the cotton-ticking mattress, and afterwards fell asleep too. She didn't know what he did during his time alone, but she respected his need for solitude. After all, he'd told her that was one of his reasons for choosing to stay at Chadwick Farm.

This night, after Sam left the house and Abby said good night to the children, she stood on the porch and looked across the yard to where the light from his lantern sent amber beams between the wood planks of the lean-to. The yard was awash with pale moonlight, and seemed to draw Abby down the porch steps and in the direction of the lantern's glow. She reached the entrance to the lean-to, and saw thin shavings of wood float to the ground even before she could see the skillful hands whittling the limb.

She stepped inside and leaned her shoulder against the willow tree that supported the shelter. She knew Sam was aware of her presence, and he didn't seem to mind the intrusion. Her gaze shifted from the concentration in his eyes to the whimsical figure he was carving. "What is it?" she asked softly, feeling that she was somehow inter-rupting an artist.

He looked up at her and smiled. "If you can't tell, then I must not be very good."

"Well, it's not finished, is it?"

"No, but here, this one is." He reached down·beside

the stool he was sitting on and handed her a wooden statue. Dowels passed through the figure at its joints, allowing the arms and legs to swing freely. A carved wood pistol was glued onto one round hand, and leather strips were tied to the legs, dressing the figure in chaps. On top of the oval face with its triangular eyes and hollowed-out grin, a flat leather hat covered corn-silk hair.

Abby held the statue so that it danced in her palm. "It's wonderful."

"Thanks. It's called a hickory cowboy. I learned to make them when I was a kid. We had lots of hickory trees in Cooper's Glen. The other day when I was down at the river I saw one, and it put me in a mood to make a couple of these again."

"What are you going to do with them?"

"I've heard Thomas and Timothy talk about cowboys a lot. I thought they might like to play with them."

"Oh, they will. Both boys say they want to be cowboys when they grow up, though I don't think either one of them has ever sat on a horse. Papa used to walk them around on one of our old mules once in a while and they'd holler 'giddy-up,' but the mule never paid any mind." She handed the stick man back. "This was real nice of you, Sam. The boys will be surprised."

He shrugged. "They're good lads, and I've always liked making things. It's a way to occupy my hands while my mind is free to wander."

Abby wished she knew where Sam's thoughts traveled during his hours alone in the lean-to. Mostly she wondered if he had decided to move on soon. And if he had, how would she feel about that? He certainly hadn't made her any promises beyond helping out for a time, but his leaving was a possibility she didn't want to think about now. "Did you make things for a living before you met Mr. Walthrop?" she asked, avoiding what was really on her mind.

He nodded. "I built a few things, repaired things, did some general handyman work—nothing too fancy, but I learned a lot, I guess." He studied the newly whittled spot on the figure, and ran his thumb over the natural patina shining in the lantern light. "I've always had a fondness for good wood, and hickory's some of the best." He scooped up a handful of the shavings and handed them to Abby. "Here, smell these."

She did. They smelled tangy and slightly smoke-cured.

"Kind of makes you want to curl up and make a bed of a whole lot of them, doesn't it?" he said.

"It does indeed." Abby watched the tendons flex in Sam's arm as he resumed shaving the twig. Each stroke of his knife removed practically the same amount of bark, so practiced and measured were the fluid movements of his hands. There was contentment in creativity, and Sam had found it. And, she admitted, there was contentment for her in having him around. Watching him work, she realized that the true reason she didn't want to think about Sam leaving didn't have anything to do with the help he'd provided on the farm. The truth was, she didn't want him to go. He had repaired a lot more than a house and some tools since he'd arrived. He had quietly been repairing broken lives too.

As her gaze rested on the shadows playing around the handsome features of his face, Abby wanted to tell him how grateful she was, how much she would miss him when he left . . . how much she wanted him to stay. Instead she only sighed and pushed away from the willow tree. "I'll leave you be," she said. "I'll see you in the morning."

"Abby, wait a minute." He put the figure down and motioned her back into the lean-to. "I want to talk to you about something, and now seems as good a time as any."

She straightened her back to brace herself for bad news.

She couldn't ignore the ribbon of dread that snaked down her spine. This was it. Sam was going away. "All right," she said calmly, keeping her emotions hidden.

"It's more a favor really." He pulled up an empty crate and indicated she could sit on it. When she did, he said, "It's about Angel."

Relief, more powerful than she would ever have thought possible, washed over her. "Angel?"

"She wants to go to church again, and she says you won't go. I want to know if it's all right with you if I take her and any of the others who want to go too."

Abby drew a deep breath to fight an automatic tensing of muscles in her neck. She avoided Sam's searching gaze. "There's not even a minister there. No one has replaced my father, so what's the point of going?"

"But they're still having services on Sundays. I checked. There must be prayer and singing at least. Angel needs to go, Abby. There's a big hole in her life, and religion is the only way she can fill it."

"Why didn't she tell me this?"

He regarded her with a knowing, sympathetic gaze. "She didn't think it would change your mind."

"She's right, it wouldn't. I won't go to church, Sam. I can't. I just don't think it makes a difference anymore." She stood up and turned away from him. "But you take her if you want. I won't stop you."

"And if you decide to go . . ."

"That's not likely." She stepped out of the lean-to, but stopped before going to the house. With her back to Sam, she said, "Thank you for your kindnesses to the children. Right now they need someone like you." Without waiting for a response, she left him alone again.

Sam didn't have any trouble getting Thomas and Timothy to follow him out to the water pump behind the house on Saturday night for a bath. But he did have a hard time convincing them that while a dousing under a sprinkling can would be good for them, it wouldn't be for their hickory cowboys. Once he stripped down to his flannel drawers and helped the boys out of their clothes, he persuaded the twins to leave the cowboys on a log bench away from splashing water. Then the boys let him wash their hair and scrub them down thoroughly with Abby's castile soap.

When they were finished, Sam plopped both towel-dried youngsters down on the small back porch with a stern warning for them to wait outside until Miss Abby called them in. "Remember now," he said, "the girls are having their baths in the kitchen. They're not quite as adventurous as we men, and they like their privacy. So you must not go in until they're done." Even though the six-year-olds nodded seriously, Sam added, "And no peeking." When he came back after his own shower, the boys were still facing forward, their cowboys engaged in a rousing shoot-'em-up.

After breakfast the next morning, the children of Chadwick Farm donned their best clothes, combed their hair, and waited for Sam to take them to church. Angel and Susanna helped the boys button their shirts and hook their suspenders before they primped a few extra minutes in front of the parlor mirror.

Sam hitched the mules to the buckboard, and came into the kitchen to inspect the children. "Will you look at the handsome lads and pretty lasses," he said. His appreciative whistle made Susanna giggle and Angel blush.

He then spoke more loudly than was necessary for the small group gathered around him. "It's time to go." He looked over their heads and down the hallway to the front of the house, and seeing no one, asked, "Has any of you seen Miss Abby since breakfast?"

"I did," Thomas offered, his curving smile chasing

the freckles up his cheeks. "She was outside feedin' the chickens. She said I didn't have to do it this mornin' since I was goin' to church."

So she wasn't even going to tell them good-bye. Sam tried to shrug off his disappointment. "Well, then, Angel, you bring the basket and let's go." He lifted the canvas sheet and let the children pass through.

A voice brimming with teasing caught him off guard as he followed Angel outside.

"You'd better hurry Mr. Kelly, or you'll make us all late." It was Abby, calling from the buckboard seat where Lizzie was perched in her lap.

Angel gave Abby her most beatific smile. "You're doing the right thing, Miss Abby, and . . ."

"I know what you're going to say, Angel. Papa James will be proud of me."

"Well, that's true," Angel said after thinking a moment. "But I was going to say that *I'm* proud of you."

"And so am I," Sam added, climbing up beside her and taking the reins. He rested his elbow on his knee and smiled appreciatively at the pretty picture she made from the ruffled trim of her bonnet to the tip of her shoes peeking out from the hem of her skirt. Her dress was the color of the underblade of sweet meadow grass, so light it made the irises of her eyes seem a brighter green than usual. If the dress was faded from wear and washing, it didn't matter, because the skirt was covered all over with little daisies that looked as hopeful as a new yellow dawn.

"What are you looking at, Sam?" she asked. "Can't a lady change her mind?"

"Sure she can. I'm just surprised that the lady who did is you."

"There's nothing wrong with that, is there?"

"Oh, no, ma'am," he said, pulling his gaze away from her and snapping the reins. "Nothing whatsoever. You just amaze me sometimes, Miss Chadwick, that's all."

"It's not so amazing. The last thing I want to do is give you a swelled head, Sam, but you might have had something to do with my decision to come today." She lowered her voice. "I did think a little about what you said in the shed ... about Angel. Maybe I have been somewhat blind to her needs lately."

He gave her a slow, easy grin. "Don't give it a second thought, Abby. Your vision's obviously improved since then."

All the way to the canopy of maple trees, Sam stole glances at Abby's profile, noting the smile that stayed on her lips. He thought of Duncan Walthrop, and mentally chastised the drummer. *You see, Duncan, she's not so ornery after all. In fact, even after all her troubles, Abby Chadwick seems possessed of a sweet disposition and a willingness to compromise. And the most appealing auburn hair. And a soft, full mouth. And a fine figure ...*

Sam let go of a pent-up breath and shook his head to clear his mind. What was he doing, listing Abby's attributes like that? He smiled to himself, realizing how that fair skin of hers would turn scarlet if she only knew what he'd been thinking about.

"I guess Will didn't want to come this morning," he said after a few minutes.

"No. He can be sullen at times, like today. But he'll snap out of it."

"He's having a hard time with me here. I noticed his bad temper started when I decided to stay." There was a slight nod of Abby's head. "I think he'd like nothing more than to see the backside of Sam Kelly crossing over that rise for good."

"I'm sorry he's made you feel that way, Sam. Did he tell you he wanted you to leave?"

"Not in so many words, though yesterday he asked me how long I planned on staying."

Abby's head snapped around, and her eyes fixed on

Sam with a curiosity so intense, it bordered on a much stronger emotion—one he couldn't identify. Then, just as quickly, she leveled her eyes on the road again. "Oh? And what did you tell him?"

Sam had only recently begun to think seriously about this matter himself. He knew he couldn't stay at the farm much longer, especially since he was running out of what little money he'd had when he arrived. But he could always come back. Abby's unreadable profile gave him no clue as to what answer she expected . . . or wanted from him. Finally he said, "I told him I needed to finish the repairs on the house, and help get the rest of your sale crop in. Then I said I'd have to go. Probably by the middle of June."

"I see." Her voice sounded distant and hollow.

"Will seemed to ease up a bit when I told him that."

"Well, of course Will's feelings are important."

Sam tried to see her face, but she pulled at the wide brim of her bonnet and hid her features. After a moment she said, "There is the matter of money we need to settle."

"What do you mean?"

"You've already spent much more on the farm than I've given you from our savings. It's obvious you've been dipping into your own pockets." The bonnet brim rippled in the breeze, but still revealed nothing of Abby's face. Her words, though, were flat and her tone methodical, as if she were closing a business deal. "I appreciate what you've done," she continued, "but provisions must be made to pay you back. I've been getting a little from the sale of the eggs, and so far the fall harvest looks promising . . ."

"I never expected you to pay me back, Abby," he said. "I've only contributed a small amount, and only because I wanted to. I just wish I could stay long enough to build you a barn. But that takes more money than I have right now. I want you to forget this notion of owing me any-thing.''

"I can't do that. You'll leave your address and an accounting of what you've spent, and I'll send what I can till it's all paid.''

Her voice left no room for argument, and they rode on in silence. Sam couldn't follow her instructions anyway, since he had no idea what his address would be. Rosemont Manor? There was money enough there, all right, but Sam had pushed the matter of his father's will to the back of his mind, and wasn't anxious to think of it again.

There was always Chilton-Howe. He could return to his little room in the dormitory. He'd taught enough classes to pay back the administrators for their funding of his university studies, and they'd promised him a modest salary if he continued to teach there.

But the truth was, even after all the hours of thinking at Chadwick Farm, Sam still had not decided on a direction for his life. All he knew for sure was that at this moment he was sorry he'd brought up the subject of Will. What had started out as a beautiful morning had taken an ugly turn.

He risked a look at his silent companion. She sat rigidly straight, staring at the road while she perfunctorily smoothed the downy curls on Lizzie's head. If she knew he was watching her, she didn't even give him the satisfaction of a sideways glance.

"What will you do this winter about a barn?" he asked after the quiet was beginning to rankle his nerves. "Where will you keep the mules and the cow when it gets cold?"

"I'll board them out, I guess," she answered mechanically. "Don't concern yourself. I won't let the animals freeze, Sam."

Freeze is right! He resisted a very real shiver that crept around his neck in the frosty atmosphere of the buckboard. Relieved when he came to the church, he pulled alongside the other wagons and buggies and set his brake. The children jumped out, and he came around to help Abby down.

"If you'll just take Lizzie," she said, handing the child to him, "I can manage on my own."

He set Lizzie on the ground, and watched Abby turn around and hook the toe of her shoe between the spokes of the wheel to step down. "I've never doubted that for a minute," he said.

Despite the absence of a minister, there were almost as many people in the church as attended when James Chadwick preached, and nearly every head turned when Abby and her family entered the double doors and proceeded down the center aisle to a pew in the middle. The front pew, which had always been reserved for the minister's family, was now occupied by Ernest Sholski and his gangly boys. When she felt Mr. Sholski staring at her, Abby sent him a scathing look that made him shrink slightly into his starched collar. "Old coot," she muttered. "Didn't take him a month to wipe us off the roles and take our seats!"

"What did you say?" Sam asked as the children filed into the pew.

"Nothing. Never mind."

Abby smiled at Melissa Mitchum, who sat in the pew behind her. Melissa was the one woman Abby considered her true friend. After Abby sat down, Melissa shifted the baby in her lap so she could lean forward, close to Abby's ear. "Why haven't you come by to see me?" she whispered. "Tongues are waggin' about you as fast as a jack-rabbit's heartbeat." She rolled her eyes toward Sam. "I heard you had a gentleman staying on the farm. He's a fine-looking specimen, Abigail. You must tell me what's going on."

Abby cast a quick glance at Sam. Thankfully, he was busy settling the children into their seats, and seemed unaware of Melissa's secretive comments. Facing forward, Abby let her answer hiss out of clenched teeth. "Nothing is going on, Melissa. Now hush or he'll hear you!"

"Well, if nothing is going on, then you're daft, Abby Chadwick! Good-looking men like him don't come around every day. You can't let him get away!"

Abby kept her face pointed away from Sam. "I don't *own* him, Melissa! He's just helping out, then moving on. There's nothing more to say."

Abby was grateful when the mellow chords of the organ halted all further conversation. At the front of the church, Martha Swenson poked her stoic husband in the ribs, and he rose to his feet, clutching a hymnal in his hand. Abby bit her lip to keep from chuckling at the somber, black-clad figure of Arne Swenson. She hadn't heard the man put two sentences together in all the time she'd known him, yet apparently Martha had prodded him into leading the singing.

In his drawling Swedish accent, Arne said stiffly, "If you all vill turn to page twenty-seven in yer books, ve vill sing *Abide vis Me*." He paused while everyone turned pages in response to his suggestion, but before he signaled the organist, he surprised Abby by saying, "I'm sure I speak fer all of us, ven I say velcome back to Miss Abby and the children."

Once again her family was the object of attention as heads nodded in their direction. While she knew that everyone in Seneca Township had respected and liked her father, she knew just as certainly that those sentiments did not always include her. Nevertheless she politely acknowledged the curious stares of her neighbors and smiled at Mr. Swenson. "Thank you, Arne," she said, remembering how he'd been one of the men who'd come around after the storm to construct a makeshift roof over her kitchen.

It was no surprise to Abby minutes later when Ernest Sholski read an Old Testament scripture about how God had showered Abraham's family with riches. He followed the lengthy reading with a parable about his own success, which he attributed to being in God's special favor. It gave her some satisfaction to see that most of the hardworking farmers around her yawned behind cupped hands during Ernest's boastful recitation. Everyone knew that he lived on his wife's inherited wealth while he dabbled at raising livestock.

The congregation stood as Arne raised his hand, and the first strains of the closing hymn filled the small room. Abby was listening to the clear, sweet tones of Angel's voice when the double doors at the rear of the church suddenly burst open and banged against the walls.

The singing stopped abruptly, and all heads turned toward the disruptive noise. Gasps of surprise and alarm rose in a muffled crescendo from the pews.

As shocked as everyone else, Abby stared at a hulking silhouette blocking the sunlight at the entrance. A monster of a man strode down the center aisle, his wild stare darting among the pews as his heavy boots thumped along the thin carpet. When he reached the retreating Arne Swenson, the man spun around and faced the people of Seneca Township.

His worn overalls were imbedded with a charcoal grime that emitted a foul stench, alien to the rich, earthy smells of farm country. Beefy arms thrust from ragged shirt-sleeves and ended in tightly clenched fists. His large head moved from side to side, causing greasy strands of gray hair to brush his shoulders. The man's lips quivered with undisguised rage as he faced the congregation.

Ernest Sholski cleared his throat and stammered, "What's the meaning of this? Who are you?"

"My name's Tucker Brandywine," the loud voice boomed. "From West Virginia."

So that's it, Abby concluded. She had just identified the grimy soil that seemed a part of the man's skin and clothing. Coal dust.

"What do you want, Mr. Brandywine?" Ernest Sholski ventured in a timid voice.

"I want what one of you stole from me. You done took what was mine and I want it back!"

Ernest's cheeks puffed out in fear and indignation. "I don't know what you're talking about. This is a God-fearing community. Not a man here would steal from his neighbor. What is it that you think has been taken, Mr. Brandywine?"

"My daughter, that's what! And someone in this *God-fearin'* town of yours has her!"

Chapter Five

It took several minutes for Tucker Brandywine to calm down enough to tell his story to the people of Seneca Township. Panting with pent-up anger, he sat on the edge of a pew and croaked out the explanation of how he'd come to their village this Sunday morning. For just over a week, he had been living on a twenty-acre plot of dry, tired land covered with weeds and boulders. On this spot stood a ramshackle one-room cabin that had fallen into pitiful disrepair even while its previous owner still lived there.

Tucker explained that one day this same man, Clive Fitzsimmons, whose solitary existence had long been the subject of speculation and gossip by the people of Seneca Township, came looking for work at the Blue Bottom Mining Camp in West Virginia, where Tucker had lived. Since a man's background and even his qualifications were not very important to the employers at the Blue Bottom, Fitzsimmons was hired on the spot. In less than a week, he had resumed his habit of looking at life through the bottom of a whiskey bottle and starting arguments with anyone unlucky enough to be in his vicinity. One of his chief adversaries at the camp was Tucker Brandywine.

"Of course Fitzsimmons was no match for me," Tucker boasted to the attentive crowd in the church. "I'd bested him many times in fistfights before the damn fool made the wager which cost him his farm. He was snookered up plenty when he challenged me to a wrestlin' match he had no hope of winnin'. 'Let's make things interestin',' he says to me, struttin' round the camp like a banty rooster. 'I'll put up my place in Ohio, a fine spread,' he tells me, lyin' like the sidewinder he was. So I says, 'Sure,' and I wagered a poke with my . . ."

Tucker clamped his lips shut, and glanced furtively at the listeners nearest him. "Well, never mind what I wagered. It don't matter anyhow, since I didn't have a ghost of a chance of losin'."

"And then what happened?" someone from the back of the crowd asked.

"What d'ya think? I beat his sorry arse till he warn't much more than a bloodied corpse."

Susanna gasped and turned to Abby, who tried too late to cover the girl's ears. She caught Sam's eye and nodded toward the twins, who did not seem the least distressed by the colorful tale, but were listening with wide eyes and open mouths. And, Abby realized, Sam was almost as enthralled.

Andrew Purcell of the mercantile laughed out loud. "So you just up and left West Virginia, with nothing more to go on than Clive Fitzsimmons's description of his place?"

Tucker turned fiery eyes on the shopkeeper, and Mr. Purcell grew red-faced from choking back his amusement. "How was I to know the bastard was a cheatin' river rat?" Tucker declared. "He crawls to my cabin the next day and hands me a deed, and says, 'Here you are, Tucker

Brandywine, and you're as lucky a man as I've ever come across.' Now I'm the fool 'cause I took him at his word. I come here to find out there's more varmints holed up in that shack of his than lives in the whole of the Blue Bottom! I was a sight better off facin' the devils in the mine shafts than I am tryin' to scrape a livin' out of Fitzsimmons's worthless hellhole!''

Abby was becoming impatient. She sensed that Mr. Brandywine was enjoying his questionable celebrity and wandering too far off track. "But sir," she said, "what about your daughter? How does she fit in this story?"

He turned beady eyes on her that suggested he didn't like being interrupted. "Well, a' course I brung her up here with me. She stays around for a day or two, then vanishes, gone like a puff o' smoke, and I ain't seen her for a week."

"And you're just now looking for her?" Abby exclaimed. It was unbelievable! Tucker blanched, but didn't answer her. "Do you think she missed her home and friends in West Virginia? Maybe she's trying to get back there."

Tucker shot Abby a demeaning look that told her what he thought of her theory. Rubbing a grimy finger over a pool of spittle in the corner of his mouth, he mocked, "Now that's a bucket that won't hold water, missy. First of all, Emma ain't got no friends, and second, she ain't smart enough to light out on her own. 'Sides, she ain't never cared where she called home, long as she had a mat to sleep on and somethin' to stop the growlin' in her belly."

His eyes turned fierce and threatening again, and drew a steely line on the people closest to him, including Abby. "No, missy, she's been stole for certain, and I aim to get her back."

"Mr. Brandywine," Ernest Sholski intervened, "there's not a man here that doesn't sympathize with your plight." He swept his arm in a circle to encompass his neighbors. "We're all parents, and we consider our children to be our God-given gifts. Why, we wouldn't think of . . ."

Tucker stood abruptly, leveled furious eyes on Ernest, and balled his fist into a weapon. "I'd lay money right now that it was you who done it, the way your jaw's flappin' with all that self-righteous dung . . ."

Abby's mouth flew open, and she was just about to hurl an indignant rebuttal at Tucker when Sam stepped in front of her and pushed her back a step. "What does your daughter look like, Mr. Brandywine?" he asked calmly. "How old is she? We'll need something to go on when we search for her."

Tucker squinted one eye tightly shut, and peered at Sam with a malevolent glare that softened after a moment to dubious interest. He rubbed his jaw with thick, curled fingernails, and his gray stubble of beard rasped like sandpaper. "You believe she's been took?"

Sam shook his head, "No, sir, I don't, but if she's still in Seneca Township, we'll find her." He looked around at the congregation, and a few of the other men were nodding in agreement. Probably to avoid getting on Tucker's bad side, Abby decided.

"All right, then." Tucker drew a hand across the middle of his chest. "She's about this tall." His finger poked the end of his spine. "Her hair's about yay long, and it's light-colored, I guess. She claims to be fifteen. I don't recollect for sure."

"Okay," Sam said, "that will help. Do you remember what she was wearing the last time you saw her?"

"She ain't got but two dresses, but I can't tell you which one was on her." He cocked his head to the side as if trying to recall more details, and when one occurred to him, his wide mouth parted to reveal a smattering of stained teeth. "I can tell you this, though. She's as lazy as a West Virginia dog in the summertime."

Abby couldn't keep quiet any longer. "How can you talk about your daughter that way? You don't know where she is or even if she's . . ." Sam gave her a warning look that made her bite back her words in spite of her anger, but she glared at the menacing eyes of Tucker Brandywine without blinking.

"You git her back, boy," Tucker said to Sam, though his stare never wavered from Abby's face. "I got to have that girl, you understand?"

The search for Emma Brandywine was organized by noon, and by one o'clock, eight teams of two men each had set off to scour the countryside in their assigned sections. On the way back to Chadwick Farm, Abby let loose with her opinion of Emma's father. "I've never seen such a vile, selfish creature!"

From the back of the buckboard, Timothy grabbed the wagon seat, sat up on his knees, and declared, "Yeah, Sam, you shoulda punched that ugly ol' man for talkin' so mean!"

Sam looked over his shoulder at the boy and smiled. "Tim, Mr. Brandywine might have deserved that, all right, but a man's got to learn that there's a time to fight and a time to give way. This was a time to give way."

"How does a man know which one it is?"

"He just does, I guess. It comes with getting older and hopefully wise enough to think about what's really important. Right now, that's finding the girl."

Sam told Will about Emma when they got home, and the two of them searched the acreage of Chadwick Farm, the apple orchard and woods bordering their fields, and the nearby banks of the Little White Tail River. For all the men involved, the search continued Monday and Tuesday, but by dusk Tuesday evening, when no trace of the girl had been found, the realities of the farmers' lives dictated that their livestock and crops could no longer be ignored. The investigation into Emma Brandywine's disappearance was reluctantly abandoned.

"That poor girl," Abby said late Tuesday night after Sam and Will came in from the latest meeting at the church. "I hate to just give up. I feel like one more day might bring about the results we're hoping for."

Sam stirred the smoked pork stew Abby had put in front of him. "I know, I feel the same as you do, but Arne Swenson is right. The girl could be anywhere. And if she has met with a fatal accident or become the victim of an animal, then her body could be hidden so well that we're not likely to find it even after days of searching."

"Don't talk that way, Sam. I don't want to think about it." Abby was grateful the younger children were in bed and couldn't hear Sam's very plausible account of Emma Brandywine's fate.

"Well, I'm glad we're done foolin' with the whole thing," Will said, swinging his long leg over the back of a kitchen chair and sitting down. "Nobody even knows this Tucker Brandywine, and yet we all drop our chores and do his biddin'. I'm tired of it. We don't even know if there ever was an Emma! Nobody ever saw her."

"Why would a man lie about a thing like that?" Abby asked.

"You saw him, Miss Abby, so you should know why. He smelled like a warthog and probably has the morals of a mangy tomcat too."

"Will!"

"I'm sorry, but I think this fella's been leadin' us all down a path just to stir things up. All I know is that I've got three acres of string beans to get in before the week is over, and I say we forget about him."

Abby looked at Sam, and he shrugged his shoulders.

"Who knows? Maybe Will's right. I agree that we can't go on looking indefinitely."

"How does Tucker feel about us giving up the search?" Abby asked.

Sam set his spoon against his bowl and leaned forward. "That's the strangest part. Every time anyone's gone by his place to report, he's been sitting on his porch like he's just waiting for us. I don't think he's ever gone out to look for his daughter himself. He still maintains that one of us took her and says he's not about to let the matter drop, but that seems to be the extent of his worrying."

Abby sat down and folded her hands on the table. "Still, it's a sad thing when a child's been hurt, and it breaks my heart to think of her."

The following evening Will skipped supper, and while there were still three hours of daylight, he walked over the rise and away from the farm. He needed some time to himself, and lately he'd gotten precious little of it. Halfway down the road to the fork, a narrow trail cut east through thick stands of willow and oak trees and snaked through the woods to the bank of the Little White Tail where the river was its widest and fastest-flowing.

Will trekked through ground cover of wild ferns and sumac. Acorns fallen from overhanging pin oak trees crunched under his feet, and winged seeds of sugar maples spun around and around in the golden haze of the setting sun, the more hardy ones embedding themselves in the underbrush eventually to spread tiny roots. As far as Will knew, there being no evidence of other footprints, no one but him had traversed the dense thicket in a long time, but he pushed through it with ease.

He approached the river by following what remained of an old Iroquois trail that the Indians had used when carrying their canoes from the great Cuyahoga River to the smaller White Tail. Portage Path, it was still called by some of the older residents of the Ohio plateau, who remembered when the Iroquois still lived there close to the white settlers. Pieces of Indian artifacts could still be found along the footpath if one were curious enough to look and knowledgeable enough to recognize them.

Will stopped at the edge of the river when he saw a wild grapevine hanging from a low branch and coiling over the roots of its mother tree. Taking his knife from his boot, he cut off a section of the vine about six inches long and a half inch in diameter. He took a kitchen match out of his pocket and struck it against a rock, then held it against the vine, puffing at one end until the other glowed red. Sweet-smelling smoke curled upward. The burning end crackled as Will pulled smoke into his mouth and swirled it into his cheeks before letting it out again. It felt good to be smoking on his way to his place again.

As the early evening shadows grew long, Will walked beside the riverbank and breathed in the rich, musty scent of dark, moist soil mixed with the sweet smell of sumac blossoms. He passed a stand of shagbark hickory trees, and thought of Sam and those silly little cowboys he had made for the twins. Sam was so pleased to have found one lone hickory tree at the edge of Chadwick Farm. What if he knew about the dozens of trees that grew along the Little White Tail River at this point? Will decided he wouldn't tell him.

Soon the hickories gave way to gray paper birches and balsam poplars that thrived in the dampness at the river's edge. When the river narrowed at an old portage point, Will saw a familiar landmark that told him that he was nearing the most anticipated part of his journey. Half a canoe, its ridged underbelly facing upward, lay partially in the water. It was made of birch bark, the only material the Indians trusted because it grew stronger with age, the bark fibers tightening each time the canoe dried in the sun. When this canoe was new, and had not weathered the seasoning of many crossings, Will guessed that it had split in two in a raging current and had been left by its maker, who'd either intended to repair it later, or had drowned in the churning water of the Little White Tail. Will had passed the canoe many times, but he never removed it from the water, knowing that it would remain where it lay long after he was gone. It didn't need man's help to persevere.

He heard the Big Deer Falls before he saw it. It sounded like a hot summer rainstorm and thundered its anger because its power and energy were confined to a prison of giant, worn boulders. It plummeted from where he stood to a clear pool forty feet below. Streams of foaming water fell over jagged rocks, splitting into torrents that cut a boiling trail to the spring.

Will climbed down damp rocks bordering the falls, each step taking him closer to the blue-gray shadows of the gorge, nature's icebox, continuously freshened by a cool, clean mist rolling off the pool to the shore. The gorge had been carved by a glacier centuries ago and was still forming, renewing itself each spring when the water flowed heavily again. Will felt exhilarated and privileged that he, and only a handful of white men before him, had found this path to the camp of the Iroquois.

A short way from the spring, before the gorge became dense forest again, there was a cave, a great wide curving wall of granite and shale topped with white pines and oaks and chestnut trees. The entrance to the cave was bordered by berry bushes, wild plum, and sweet crab apple trees. The cave was known as Lucy Cameron's Kitchen.

All his life Will had heard the tales of white men, the stories of Johnny Appleseed, and Paul Bunyan, but it was the legend of Lucy Cameron that he believed in. Captured by the Iroquois in the early days of the settling of Ohio,

Lucy lived in the cave and worked for her captors. Their drawings and strange symbols remained yet on the cavern walls, and Will studied them each time he came. He didn't know what had finally happened to Lucy, but her kitchen had become his private world, where he lived with the myths of the Indians just as she had lived with the reality of them.

He entered the enchantment of the cave, and stopped dead, his gaze fixed on an eerie red glow in the center. His nerve endings tingled with alarm. He wasn't alone. A fire burned inside a ring of rocks on the floor of the cave. He hadn't smelled it from a distance because he was still smoking the grapevine.

A quick, nervous glance around the burning circle produced other evidence of intrusion. A squirrel, skinned and skewered on a green limb, sat on the rocks near the fire. Chestnuts, hickory nuts, and buckeyes were drying on a rack made of twigs, while berries, glistening with moisture, lay on a giant sycamore leaf.

His bewilderment gave way to a seething anger at the unseen trespasser. Perhaps he was being watched. He should be frightened, he knew, but he was too furious to be cautious. Besides, he didn't have time to think about what he should do, because he sensed movement behind him just before he heard a primal howl. He spun around, and a creature wielding a firebrand over its head charged directly at him.

Will's mind immediately registered several important details about his attacker. The creature was small and human and probably female and came at him with flailing arms, churning feet, and wild, tangled hair. And to a victim caught off guard, she was unquestionably dangerous. She swung her torch at Will's midsection, and he sidestepped the thrust. She raised her arms and aimed her weapon at his head, but he ducked, feeling the sting of flying sparks on his face.

"What the devil!" he swore. "What are you tryin' to do?"

"Knock your head off, that's what!" the creature howled back.

When she lowered the heavy torch to regain her balance and launch a new attack, Will saw his chance. He charged at her, knocking his shoulder into her stomach and slicing at the fist holding the firebrand with the side of his hand. The club fell to the ground and rolled over in the dirt, extinguishing the blaze. Will heard the girl's breath swoosh from her lungs as she hit the floor of the cave, clutching her abdomen.

She lay perfectly still, moaning in pain, and Will approached her cautiously. When she didn't move, he bent over her, trying to see her face, but her long hair covered her from forehead to waist. "Are you gonna be okay?" he asked.

With the speed and ferocity of a caged animal, she targeted her bare foot at Will's groin. Only his quick thinking and agility enabled him to avoid the well-placed kick. That was enough. He grabbed both her wrists and yanked her to her feet.

"Git your hands off me!" she bellowed, while her bared teeth bit at the fingers that gripped her like a vise.

"I'd like nothin' better, if I thought for a minute you wouldn't keep tryin' to kill me!"

She stopped fighting, tossed her head back, and glared at him. He pulled her to the fire and forced her down in the dirt. "Don't you move," he ordered, and miraculously she remained still.

Will paced back and forth in front of her, his eyes vigilant and his breathing labored as his mind reeled with shock. Finally he said simply, "You've got some explainin' to do!"

With a dirty hand, she flipped a mat of filthy hair off

her face. "Me? What about you? This here's my place, and you can jus' turn your arse around and git out of it!"

"This is *my* place," Will countered, protecting what had always been his.

"Oh, yeah? And who made you king o' the cave, you big, stupid jackass?"

In all his fifteen years, Will had never heard a female, even the meanest of them, talk like this one did. He could only stare at her, not knowing what to say, or how to deal with her. She defied any of his notions of what a female should be like. All at once he realized where he had heard similar language from an equally unkempt human being, and everything fell into place. "You're her, aren't you?" he said, almost mystically.

"Who her? What are you talkin' about?"

"You're Emma Brandywine."

"Don't talk crazy. I ain't never heard the name and don't know any such person. You're a cotton brain if there ever was one."

"Oh, no, I'm not. Look at you. You're just like your daddy said. Little and skinny with ugly ol' hair and a raggedy ol' dress." He wrinkled his nose at her. "And you smell like your stinkin' father too. You're Emma Brandywine, all right, and you're the reason this town's all put out."

She crossed her arms over her chest and peered at Will through slitted eyes. "You're one for the madhouse, you are."

"How did you get here?"

"Well, how did *you* get here? I 'spect I came the same way." She spread her arms out beside her. "You don't see no wings sproutin' so's I could fly down to this hole, do you?"

"No, I mean, how did you know about this place?"

Just like her father did, Emma had a way of cutting a person down to size with a steely glance. "I was fixin' to take me a holiday, and I read about this paradise in a picture book.''

''You've got a right smart tongue for someone who's in a peck of trouble,'' Will warned. ''I want the truth from you, now!''

She bit her lower lip and stared at him. He could tell she was sizing up her chances against his height and weight. She picked up a large stone and clenched her fist around it as far as her tiny fingers would let her. Will prepared to duck, but she turned and flung the rock across the cave, admitting defeat.

''All right,'' she grumbled. ''I jus' stumbled on this cave, that's all. I was runnin' and not payin' much mind to where I was goin' and ended up here. Are you happy now you know?''

''What were you runnin' from?''

''None a' your business.''

''Him? Were you runnin' from Tucker?'' Her gaze darted away from him just long enough for Will to know that he was right. ''Why? What'd he do to you?''

''Nothin'. He didn't do nothin'. I thought I told you to mind your own business.''

Will threw his hands up in frustration. ''This *is* my business, and you're in it! I've been comin' here all my life, and you can't just wander in like a sod squatter and claim rights to it.''

''Well, that's exactly what I done, and I ain't goin' nowhere.'' Emma crossed her legs Indian-style, thrust out her chin, and appeared as immovable as a granite statue.

What was he to do? Will was running out of patience with Emma Brandywine. She wouldn't tell him what was wrong. Yet she wouldn't leave. ''Get your stuff together. You're goin' back up top with me. I'm turnin' you over to your daddy so he can take care of you and the folks of Seneca Township can forget all the trouble you've caused.''

She scrambled to her feet and squared off with him. "I don't need nobody to take care of me!" she protested. "Least of all my pappy. And I couldn't give two warts off a frog about the people in this stupid town."

"All right then, have it your way. Stay here if you want. I'll just go over to Fitzsimmons's place and tell your daddy where you are. He can come get you!"

Satisfied that he'd had the final word, Will stomped toward the cave entrance, determined to do just as he said. He would get rid of this bothersome girl one way or the other. He was almost to the spring when he felt a tug on his arm and heard her voice, now small and scared. "Don't do that. Don't tell my pappy."

He looked over his shoulder at her, and through all the dirt and grime he saw fear in her eyes.

"Please," she said.

He squinted his eyes to shut out her face while he thought. "You can't stay here forever," he said. "It'll get cold and you'll run out of food."

"I know. By fall I'll be gone. I promise. You can have your place back. Just please don't tell my pappy you saw me. I can't go back to him. I just can't."

Her pleading was the most pitiful thing he'd ever heard. After uttering a mild oath under his breath, he gave in. "Okay, I won't tell him for now, if you promise to get out." He saw her narrow shoulders sag in relief. "But you're gonna get sick."

"What d'ya mean? I'm fit."

He pointed to her assortment of nuts. "You won't be if you eat those buckeyes. They're poison. Nice to look at, but . . ."

"I won't eat 'em. Thanks, and for not tellin' too."

He nodded, and started to go again, but something drew him back. When he looked at her this time, she seemed so tiny and helpless, stepping back into the shadows of the cave, even though he'd just had enough proof that she wasn't exactly helpless at all. "Maybe I'll come back now and then to see how you're doin'," he said. "Is there anything you need? I don't have any money, but I maybe could get some little thing for you."

Her eyes lit up and she smiled at him, and for just an instant all the dirt and grime seemed to disappear. "I sure would fancy a mug of milk, even if it's not cold by the time you get here. And some bread . . . a biscuit maybe. Would that be too much trouble?"

"No. I can bring you those things."

"What's your name anyway?"

"Will."

"That's a good name. Strong like. Fits you real fine, Will."

He lifted his hand in an offhand wave. "I'll see you again, Emma."

"There's just one more thing, Will." He raised his eyebrows in question. "I saw how you was lookin' at me before and heard what you said about me not smellin' so good. Do you think you could bring me some soap? And some turpentine?"

"Turpentine?"

She fingered a stringy mass of dull hair. "I got me a passel a' them itchin' bugs on my head. They're 'bout to drive me to distraction. Turpentine'll kill 'em."

"I'll be back as soon as I can, Emma."

As he climbed back up the rocks by the waterfall, Will thought that being orphaned maybe wasn't the worst thing that could happen to a person.

Chapter Six

The image of Emma Brandywine, tattered and hungry, stayed with Will for two nights, and since he had once been without a home or place to go like Emma, he was determined to make things better for her. Therefore, he only waited two days before telling Abby that he wouldn't be home for supper again.

She stopped washing dishes and looked over her shoulder at him. "Why not, Will? Where are you going? Are you meeting friends?"

He hated lying to her. "I might be. I'm goin' down to the Little White Tail and do some fishin'. I imagine somebody'll show up to keep me company. If you're worried about the work I'll be missin', I promise . . ."

"I'm not concerned about that at all," she said. "I want you to go off and have some fun. You haven't had much this summer, and the fishing weather won't last forever."

"And Sam?" Will knew that his absence in the evening

would mean more work for Sam, and for the first time he was grateful that Sam was around to pick up the slack.

"I don't think he'll care. Besides, you'll make it up by starting extra early tomorrow, won't you?" There was a glimmer of teasing in Abby's eyes that told Will she didn't really mean it.

"Yeah, I will."

"You go on then. When I'm done here, I'll get Lizzie and meet you out by the cabbage field. We might be able to finish planting before you go off this afternoon."

Will took his hat from the porcelain hook nailed to a panel of white pine that made up the newly completed interior wall of the kitchen. He placed it snugly on his head and started out the door. "Wait a minute," Abby called. He turned slowly, afraid she'd changed her mind. "I'll save some bacon and butter beans for you tonight in case the fishing's not too good."

He slowly let out his breath. "Thanks, I might need it."

He crossed the farmyard, glancing over his shoulder at the house a few times before he reached the apple orchard. Then, without going on to the cabbage field, he ducked behind a wide tree and knelt down next to a large rock. Rolling it over, he uncovered a canvas bag that held the supplies he'd been getting together a little at a time when no one was watching him.

He checked them over to make sure everything was still there. Soap, a pint tin of turpentine, an old crockery cooler for milk, a wood bowl and fork, a mug—the worst one from Abby's kitchen so she'd be less likely to miss it, a one pound bag of flour, a sugar square, some leavening, and an old cast-iron muffin tray. He pictured Emma's delight when he showed her how he could make an oven from the rocks in the cave so she could make drop-biscuits every day till the milk ran out.

"Just a few more things," he muttered to himself as

he closed the bag tight again. "And I can't get those until I know Miss Abby's gonna be outta her room for a while."

He returned the bag to the hole and pushed the rock into place. Then he shoved his hands in his pockets and headed with a light step toward the field of newly planted cabbage.

Lunchtime provided Will with the opportunity to gather the other items he intended to take to Emma. Sam had stopped putting the siding on the exterior wall of the kitchen, and had come in to talk with Abby while she prepared the noon meal. From Abby's bedroom, Will could hear their voices coming from the rear of the house, so he knew they wouldn't discover what he was doing.

A large camelback trunk sat at the foot of the bed that had been Papa James's until Abby took over his room. Will lifted the lid, hoping that the scent of camphor pellets wouldn't drift into the kitchen. He waited a moment until he was satisfied that no one was coming to investigate, and then rummaged through the contents of the trunk. He pulled out two of Papa James's old linsey-woolsey shirts that had been laundered and put away. He knew that Abby intended to give him the shirts this fall when it got cool, but in the meantime, Emma could use them at night in the chilly cave.

Next he removed a faded quilt. The picket-fence border was ragged in places from years of washing, but it was clean, and Emma would be glad to have it. He considered taking other items, but was afraid that anything else, like the feminine clothing and nicer linens, would be missed. Tucking the things under his arm, he ran out the front of the house and doubled back to the tree that marked his hiding place.

He had just finished concealing the goods in the canvas bag when he saw a four-passenger buggy come down the lane to the farmhouse. From a distance, Will recognized

Ernest Sholski riding as passenger. He didn't know the
tall man sitting beside him holding the reins.

Will came back to the house just as Abby and Sam
came out to meet the buggy. A look of concern was on
Abby's face, and Will knew why when he saw the five-
pointed star on the pocket of the driver's shirt.

"Afternoon, Ernest," Abby said coolly, then shifted
her gaze to the sheriff. She knew who he was, but she
couldn't remember any other time he'd been to the farm.

"Abigail, you know August Hawthorne, Summit
County Sheriff," Ernest said.

The sheriff touched his hand to the brim of his wide
tan hat. "Miss Chadwick." He then turned his attention
to Sam. "I've come to see Mr. Sam Kelly. Are you him?"

Sam stepped up beside Abby. "I am."

"What's this about, Sheriff?" Abby asked. Her mouth
felt dry and her throat scratchy.

"It's about the disappearance of Emma Brandywine,
ma'am. It seems the girl's father, Tucker Brandywine,
thinks that Mr. Kelly here might know more than he's
telling."

"What? Sheriff, that can't be," Abby declared. She'd
feared from the beginning that Tucker Brandywine was
going to cause trouble in Seneca, but to accuse Sam—
the idea was ludicrous. "It was Sam who suggested that
we search for Emma."

"I know. Mr. Brandywine told me that. But he also
said that Mr. Kelly didn't put up much of a fuss when
the search was called off. Is that true, Mr. Kelly?"

"True enough, I guess, but I wasn't the one that called
it off."

"Maybe so, but Mr. Brandywine thinks you might have
planned the search to throw suspicion away from yourself."

Abby recalled how Sam had searched for Emma for hours at a time, and how bad he felt when she wasn't found. "Sheriff, you can't possibly put any stock in this farfetched notion," she protested.

"It's not just that, Abigail," Ernest Sholski said. "It's also the fact that Sam is new to the community. Nobody really knows anything about you, Kelly."

Ernest gave Sam what was no doubt meant to be a pitying glance, but Abby knew darn well that there wasn't an ounce of true compassion in him.

"I'm sorry," Ernest continued, "but you could be guilty of any number of crimes from before you came here, and none of us would know about them."

Abby was growing angrier by the second. She narrowed her eyes at Ernest Sholski, and was pleased to see him squirm on the buggy seat.

Sam, on the other hand, looked very much in control, and his voice was calm when he said, "Sheriff, I wanted that girl found as much as everyone else did. I swear to you that I didn't have anything to do with her disappearance."

"That *sounds* good, Mr. Kelly, but it's no *proof* that you didn't have something to do with it. I'm going to ask you to come back with me to Akron. We need to ask you some questions and run a check on you."

"You're taking him to jail?" Abby demanded in disbelief.

"Just for a couple of nights, ma'am, for questioning. With any luck we can have this matter cleared up soon, and I'll bring him back."

Sam's face was expressionless, and Abby had no idea what he was thinking. If he wasn't going to fight this injustice, then she would have to do it for him. She glared at Ernest Sholski, who avoided her eyes as his cheeks flushed scarlet. "You've had something to do with this, Ernest, I know it! You probably put this crazy idea into

Brandywine's head in the first place. That's why you're here butting into someone else's business as usual!''

"That's not fair, Abigail," he squawked in defense. "I just came along to show Sheriff Hawthorne the way. In fact, I even suggested that he send a telegraph to that drummer, Duncan Walthrop, to see what he had to say about your . . . er, houseguest.''

"I'm afraid Duncan doesn't know much more about me than you do, Mr. Sholski," Sam said.

"That's what we found out," the sheriff concurred. "While he claimed you were a good worker, he admitted he didn't even know where you came from." Hawthorne climbed down from the buggy and approached Sam. "You might want to bring a change of clothes, Mr. Kelly."

Abby wrapped her hand around Sam's arm. She tried to keep her voice steady, but a slight tremor betrayed her emotions. "Can they do this, Sam?"

"Apparently they can." He patted her hand and smiled at her. "Don't worry. I didn't do anything. I never have. And remember, you had the same suspicions about me as these fellows do, when I first came to stay with you. Everything's going to be all right."

She managed to smile back at him, but that was only until he went into the house. When he was safely out of earshot, she turned back to the sheriff. "I've been with this man day and night for weeks, Sheriff, and I know he's innocent of anything that disgusting Tucker Brandywine accused him of!"

Suddenly Ernest Sholski's eyes opened wide and his lips curled up in a smug grin. Abby realized what impression she'd just given him about Sam and her, and felt the heat of embarrassment. Being all too familiar with the gossip trail in Seneca Township, she knew she might regret her words. "Stop looking at me like that, Ernest!" she bit out.

The sheriff chuckled and inclined his head toward her.

"We'll find out if Kelly's innocent as soon as we can, ma'am. I hope you're right."

Sam came out a few minutes later with his valise. He leaned down to Abby, whispered a few sentiments of encouragement, and gently squeezed her arm. Then he followed the sheriff to the buggy.

After the three men rode down the lane and over the rise, Abby sat heavily on the front porch steps. She saw Will come over to her, and realized he must have witnessed what had just happened. "Do you believe this, Will? The sheriff thinks Sam knows where the Brandywine girl is."

"That's just not possible, Miss Abby," Will said. "Don't worry. Hawthorne'll find out Sam doesn't know anything and let him go."

"Do you really think so?"

"I'm sure of it."

Will nodded his head with such firm conviction that Abby started to feel better.

"I don't think anybody knows where that girl is," he said. "Sam's just got to be innocent ... of kidnapping Emma Brandywine anyway."

The hesitation in Will's answer made Abby wonder. What if the sheriff discovered something else about Sam? What if her first instincts had been right after all, and he'd been hiding out at her farm all this time? "No, no," she muttered to herself, shaking off a shiver of apprehension. "I know this man too well."

"Oooh, this stuff stinks somethin' awful!"

Emma's protestations nearly drowned out the rumbling of the waterfall. Will raised his head from the rock oven he was building in the cave and called out, "Do you want me to help you?"

A squeal answered him. "Don't you come anywheres

near me, Will! I've got nothin' on but my drawers, and I don't need you over here gawkin'.''

Will grinned as he added another carefully selected rock to the igloo he was shaping. He poked a stick among the glowing wood coals in the fire pit, deciding that they were just about ready to transfer to the oven. ''Just hold your nose then, Emma, till you're finished,'' he shouted. ''And don't forget to follow that dousin' with the soap. I can't imagine sittin' in the same cave with you smellin' like turpentine!''

A few minutes later Will was spooning a doughy mixture onto the cast-iron tray when Emma came in the cave. She had put on one of Papa James's shirts, and it hung down past her knees. The sleeves had been rolled up several times and gaped open halfway between her wrists and elbows, revealing skinny arms. It was hard to believe that she was even fifteen, she was so tiny inside the big shirt.

She twisted her hair, and drops of water ran down the shirtfront and onto the floor of the cave. Raking her fingers through the wet mass, she said almost shyly, ''I guess I could use a comb.'' He made a note in his mind to bring her one. She looked down at the solid round structure he had completed. ''So that's your oven, huh?''

''That's it. I was just gettin' ready to move the coals over, and then we can bake the biscuits.'' He shoveled red coals onto a log paddle he had shaved down to work like a spatula, and slid the embers into the bottom of the oven. A pair of large rocks made a rack for the tray of biscuit dough. ''Just a few minutes, and they ought to be done.''

Will and Emma sat down together by the oven to wait for the biscuits. After a little while she said, ''Will, I got to tell you somethin'.''

''What's that?''

"You're not a cotton brain at all, like I said before. Fact is, I think you're about the cleverest boy I ever met."

He sat a little straighter, and felt a warmth that had nothing to do with his nearness to the oven. "And you don't stink anymore either," he said. "And your hair's really kinda pretty." He studied the color of it in the yellow glow from the embers in the fire pit. It was not as white as Angel's, but Tucker had been right. Emma's hair was light-colored, almost like wheat, and it was nice. "You think you killed all of those bugs?"

She wrinkled her small nose at him. "I know I did. There ain't a bug in Ohio that could survive what I just done to them itchers! And once I bury that ol' blanket I been sleepin' on, their kin'll be just as dead." She leaned close to the oven and sniffed appreciatively. "I hope you'll see fit to come back again sometime, Will."

He knew that he would.

From the cabbage field, Abby saw the sheriff's buggy come over the rise. Her hand flew to her chest, and she could feel her heart pulse against her palm. It was definitely Sam sitting next to August Hawthorne. In the two days that he had been gone, many of the same wild notions she'd thought of when he left had been running through her mind. What if Sam was guilty of some terrible crime? What if he decided that since he was already away from her and the children, he would leave Seneca for good without even saying good-bye? She didn't know which set of circumstances would have been worse.

As the buggy drew nearer, Abby pressed her lips together to keep a bubble of laughter from bursting forth in hysterical relief. All her worrying was for nothing. Sam had come back. She scooped Lizzie up from her blanket between the neat rows of cabbages and ran to the farmhouse, arriving just when the buggy did.

Sam jumped down and reached around the seat to retrieve his valise. Then he went to Abby and grinned down at her. "Looks like that extra mouth you've been feeding has come home hungry again," he said. "And not with a price on his head."

"Thank God," she whispered. "Are you all right?"

"None the worse for the wear." He responded to Lizzie's plea for him to take her, and lifted the laughing child onto his shoulders. "And how's the saucy Miss Elizabeth?"

It seemed so natural for him to be there, standing in front of her house, with her. "We've missed you," Abby said softly.

"*We* have, have we? It's always nice to be missed." She could tell from the glint in his eyes that he knew she was speaking for herself. But God help her, why should she pretend she hadn't missed him when she had, more than she'd ever believed possible, and she had lain awake both nights thinking of him.

She turned away from him, afraid that her eyes would reveal more of her emotions than she wanted him to see, and faced the sheriff. "So, you see, Mr. Hawthorne, Sam Kelly's not the despicable man that Tucker Brandywine painted him to be. You could have saved yourself a lot of time and trouble by taking my word for that."

The sheriff propped his boot on the footrest and shook his head. "You're right about that, Miss Chadwick, but if either one of you had told me some of the details of this man's life, I might not have taken him in at all, so some of the blame is yours."

Apparently August Hawthorne knew more about Sam than she did, but Abby wasn't about to let on that she was in the dark. "Well, Sheriff, the obvious virtues of a simple, hardworking man like Sam Kelly should be evident to even the most novice investigator."

A hearty guffaw from the sheriff made Abby step back

in bewilderment. "That's a good one, Miss Chadwick," he said. "Simple and hardworking . . . as hard as a man works with his eyes glued to a book and his hands on a quill! I'd have never thought for a second that your hired man here had been educated at a fancy boys' prep school in Pennsylvania. Why, the dean himself sent me a telegram thanking me for giving him information on the mysterious disappearance of Mr. Kelly. Seems they want him back at his teaching job awful bad."

Boys' preparatory school! Teaching job! The words resounded in Abby's ears, and it took all her willpower not to let her surprise show to the sheriff.

More revelations about Sam quickly followed as the sheriff kept talking. "And if that's not enough, the university Sam went to praised him as a scholar. Said they'd never had the first black mark against him. 'A serious student with a strong sense of ethics and moral values,' I believe were their exact words."

Hawthorne gave Abby a look that combined admiration with disbelief. "I don't know how you've managed to keep this fella away from his books and blackboards, ma'am, plowing your fields and hammering your nails, but you've earned my respect!" With a chuckle, August Hawthorne turned his horse around and called back over his shoulder, "Good luck to you, Sam, and sorry about the trouble."

Abby didn't hear Sam's farewell to the sheriff. A tremor, which had begun as a slow, steady thrumming of dread deep in her stomach, reached her ears with a thunderous roar, blocking out Sam's words. For days she'd been living with the fear that he might actually be guilty of some crime in the past, and she had nearly convinced herself to graciously forgive him and let him stay. But she never once imagined that Sam would have come from an aristocratic background, and this new information made him seem as far removed from her as a boys' academy was from the Seneca Village schoolhouse.

She closed her eyes tightly shut, trying to erase the image of the sheriff's grin as he praised Sam. All she could see against her eyelids were visions of Sam wearing fine clothes, carrying books across a neat, landscaped campus . . . Sam in an ivy-covered classroom, teaching rich people's sons like himself how to succeed in a gentleman's world . . . Sam escorting well-dressed ladies to dinners and concerts. And to think she'd praised him for making wooden cowboys!

Her eyes snapped open again at the sound of Sam's good-natured chatter. "It's good to be back, though I guess there's a pile of work I've got to catch up on." Carrying Lizzie, he started up the two steps to the porch and glanced back to see if Abby was following him. She refused to look at him, and he asked, "Abby, is something wrong? You can see I'm perfectly fine. They treated me quite well, actually."

She raised her face and leveled her eyes at him. "I'm sure they did, Sam. After all, you must have been the guest of honor at our little backwoods jail!" She brushed past him, hearing her skirt rustle against his pants leg. Once inside the house, she jumped at the crack of the screen door she had just let slam behind her.

Chapter Seven

Sam followed Abby into the kitchen and set Lizzie down on the floor. He handed her a toy, and when he was confident she would stay occupied for a while, he confronted Abby. "Why do I get the feeling that we're having an argument, but I'm the only one who doesn't know the reason?"

She kept her back to him and began pounding a mound of dough on the scrub table, punching her fist into it as if it were a living thing—one she wasn't at all fond of. "How would I know why you get any feeling, Sam? It's not like you've ever told me anything about yourself." The fabric of her dress stretched taut across her shoulders as she worked. White puffs of flour rose from the table when she picked up the dough and slapped it down again.

"There's not much to tell you . . ." he ventured cautiously.

"Just plenty to tell the local sheriff, and you only lived in his house for two nights!"

So that's it, he thought. Sam smiled, only because he

knew she couldn't see it. "Jealous of the sheriff, are you, Abby? Well, don't be. You're much prettier than he is."

Her hands stopped moving, and Sam watched her back straighten as she drew in a long breath. It occurred to him then that maybe he shouldn't be making light of this situation. After a threatening silence, he found himself thankful that she wasn't slicing bread with a sharp knife instead of kneading dough.

"What's the name of it?" she asked. The lump banged against the tabletop again.

"What?"

"The boys' school you went to."

"It's called Chilton-Howe. It's rather small, only two hundred students . . ."

"Exclusive, you mean?"

"Yeah, I guess you could call it that."

"I've heard of it." She gave him a smug look. "Yes, Sam, every so often we country folk actually hear of a place that exists all the way across the state line." She returned her attention to the table. "As a matter of fact, Ernest Sholski tried to get his oldest boy admitted there, but they wouldn't take him. Herbert probably didn't fit the mold as well as you."

"I didn't fit any mold, Abby." He walked to the side of the table and looked at her profile. "Is that what's bothering you? That I didn't tell you where I went to school?"

She pressed her hands against the table, and leaned forward. "You never told me anything, Sam, and now I'm finding out you're not who I thought you were."

"I answered every question you asked me."

"Yes, I guess you did. Maybe I just didn't ask the right ones. Maybe I was afraid of the answers."

"And now you're disappointed?" She looked up and he saw the hurt in her eyes, though he still didn't feel he should be held responsible for putting it there.

"You're not like us, Sam, and for a while, I hoped . . . thought maybe you were." She covered her mouth with her hand as if she were trying to stop the flow of her words. His eyes fixed on the slender fingers dusted with flour.

"Abby, I'm not like anybody at Chilton-Howe, anymore than you're like anybody in Seneca Township. I told you about my mother, who she was and the shame she lived with."

She looked at the raw timbers of the new ceiling and stifled a bitter sound, half sob and half laughter. "Oh, yes, your mother . . . Miss Kelly, who had a son out of wedlock; yet she still managed to scrimp together the money and reputation to send him to private schools and university. Yes, I remember you mentioning her, Sam."

"It wasn't like that."

"Oh, how you must look at us here in Seneca Township, with our simple ways. We must seem comical to you, Sam. You must find a great deal of amusement in the staid, sheltered boredom of our lives while you sit by yourself night after night. This must seem like a funny little place you've picked to hide in, whatever your reasons."

He reached her in one long stride and turned her to face him. Grasping her shoulders firmly, he shook her, and despite the surprise on her face, he didn't let go. He was a hard man to anger, but she had done it by judging him unfairly and without provocation. "You know I don't believe that, not for a minute. True, you don't know my background, but you do know *me,* Abby, and after all these weeks, to pretend you don't is to make a sham of the time we've been together. It's dishonest, Abby, and you're as honest a person as I've ever known, so don't play games that are beneath you."

She closed her eyes. Moisture gathered on her lashes, vanquishing his attempt to stay angry at her. His grip on her shoulders relaxed, and before he knew what he was doing, he began stroking her arms. His hands moved up and down the coarse fabric of her blouse. He spoke softly but urgently. "In my quiet evening hours I do think of this place, the children ... you, but I never scorn the simplicity of what you have. I cherish it. It's noble and uncomplicated, and it's life at its most genuine level. And Abby, trust me. What you have perceived me to be, that's what I am, no more, no less."

When she raised her gaze to his, her eyes glistened with tears. "You still don't understand, do you, Sam? You're educated, scholarly. You've grown accustomed to things I'll never have, never even see probably. You're *somebody,* Sam, and I'm ..."

Her voice trailed off, and the full impact of what she was trying to tell him hit him with the force of a punch. Could this really be Abigail Chadwick—the confident, opinionated woman whom Duncan Walthrop called "ornery"? The spinster of Seneca Township who held her head high despite the opinions of her neighbors? The same woman who would have stood against the thundering Tucker Brandywine in church? The one who looked so vulnerable and wounded now?

Pulling her into his arms seemed like the most natural thing to do. The scent of flour and sweet-cream butter rose up to his nostrils, and he breathed in the fresh, pure smells that he had unknowingly come to associate with her. She rested her cheek against his chest, and he toyed with a loose strand of hair that trailed down her back. She was trembling. Her tears dampened his shirt. Abigail Chadwick was actually weeping in his arms.

"Abby, listen to me," he whispered against her hair. "How can you possibly believe that you're not somebody too? In fact, you are quite possibly the most accomplished somebody I've ever known. Look what you do every day—care for six children who love you, manage a farm and most of the people surrounding it, drive a team of mules pulling a buckboard or a plow . . . attract a genius like me with your determination and pride and make me feel like I'm the lucky one to be in your midst.''

He heard her sniffle and felt her trembling increase. He was alarmed until he sensed her lips curling against his chest. Her voice rose up to him with a smug cockiness. ''Don't forget my knowledge of horses, Sam.''

''How could I?'' he said, releasing her and looking down into her eyes. He brushed the last remaining tear from under one and smiled. ''I'll never forget that, since I'm very sure you won't let me.''

Lizzie had tired of her play and had crawled over to them. She tugged on Abby's skirt, demanding attention. Abby ran a finger under her nose and bent to pick the child up. When she stood again, her eyes were clear and dry. ''I really don't know what brought that on, Sam. It's certainly not like me to behave so . . .''

''Confused? Uncertain at times like nearly everyone is?''

She nodded. ''Anyway I'm sorry, and I want you to know that you don't owe me any explanations. Fact is, inside I was proud of you when I heard the sheriff sing your virtues, and now I can admit it.''

''That's just because you were relieved to learn I might actually have some.''

''Not true, Sam. Like you said, I know you, and I never really doubted that, not ever.''

He ruffled Lizzie's hair, but his smile was for Abby. ''Well, then, girls, since we've cleared this up, I'll get to work. I don't want anything else to jeopardize my job today.''

When Sam left the kitchen, Abby returned to her chores, but for the rest of the day, questions tumbled around in her head. By evening she was no closer to having answers. Sam Kelly was an even bigger mystery to her now that she knew more of his past. Why had he been traveling with Duncan in the first place? And why hadn't he returned to a place where he was obviously needed and respected? What was he running from if it wasn't the law?

The one thing she did know was that he'd said he was leaving in June. She had to accept that because why, oh, why, would a man like Sam Kelly ever want to stay with the spinster of Seneca Township and her brood of needy children . . . no matter how much she wanted him to.

When Sam went to bed that night, the incident with Abby was still on his mind, and his conscience battled with his common sense. Did he have an obligation to tell her any more about his life in Cooper's Glen or about his father's family at Rosemont Manor? He didn't think so. After all, he would be leaving Chadwick Farm soon, and while the idea of going filled him with a nagging despondency, what other choice did he have? He had no money left to finish rebuilding the farm. And even if he found a way to stay, how would Abby react when she heard the details of his unfinished business with the family of Tobias Rosemont?

It bothered Sam that the knowledge Abby had gotten from August Hawthorne didn't tell the whole truth about Sam's time at Chilton-Howe. The sheriff didn't know that Sam's mother was a maid and her illegitimate son earned his education by doing odd jobs and tutoring. At the very least, Sam knew he was guilty of the sin of omission by not clearing up the facts as August viewed them.

The sheriff had said that Sam's record revealed an almost unearthly perfection in his exemplary journey through Chilton-Howe and later the university. Hawthorne hadn't found any black marks against Sam in all his years as a youth, but Sam knew that there were some.

Besides being the outcast son of the Irish woman who cleaned the offices of professors, he had managed to anger campus administrators on more than one occasion.

He remembered one such incident with astounding explicitness. For years after it happened, Sam could close his eyes and still picture what she looked like, almost smell the scent of bleach and soap and spicy sausage that always lingered on her hands and clothing.

Greta Belcher, "Fraulein" as the students called her, worked in the laundry at Chilton-Howe. Sam didn't know much about her . . . only that she had emigrated to America when she was sixteen years old, but he remembered when she first came to work at the school. He was barely seventeen, and she was twenty-eight, and when he first saw her, his eyes and mind were incapable of encompassing every inch of her imposing frame. To Sam, she was the female equivalent of a Norse god, with her uncommon height and big bones, a crown of thick hair like yellow sisal, and the figure of a buxom Viking maid.

She had greeted him with a smile so wide it practically disappeared around the sides of her broad face, and she batted eyelashes that seemed too heavy to be lifted by ordinary lids. Heavy braids pinned on the sides of her head were like coils of mooring rope. He didn't know what jobs she had had before, but she was so pleased to be working at Chilton-Howe that she actually caused Sam to wonder at his own disparagement of the school and his position there.

She fancied Sam right away, and told him so in her thick German accent that made him both alien and enchanting, like a mythical creature from the Black Forest. The privileged boys at the school noticed her too, from far away, and commented about her from behind cupped hands in the shaded alleyways between venerable Chilton-Howe buildings. Through their muffled laughter, Sam heard them talk about the Fraulein's "pair of tankards

that come round a corner a full thirty seconds before the
rest of her.'' Mewling with boyish lust, they vowed they'd
grab any chance to ''suck of her special brew.''

But it had been Sam Kelly whom she singled out.
''You're not like the others,'' she'd told him. ''There's
a darkness in you, Sam, like the pitch in my own soul.''

She persuaded him to meet her in the laundry room
after dark one night, and he had gone, anxious, excited,
and still innocent. He remembered the first time Greta
closed the door to the laundry and without hesitation
unbuttoned his shirt and rubbed her bleach-whitened
hands over his chest. She'd unfastened his trousers and
dropped them to the floor while he stood spellbound,
watching her fingers dance over his flesh with skill and
impatience. When he was naked and she was disrobing,
she'd said only, ''You're a right handsome lad, Sam
Kelly. You'll pleasure me fine as I will you.''

Every part of her was round and full, overflowing with
the essence of who she was and what she wanted. She
pulled him down onto a mound of soiled sheets and covered him with her body. He remembered thinking it was
surprisingly firm, her white skin taut over well-muscled
arms and legs. She buried his face between her large
breasts, the only soft part of her, and moved over him,
exciting him in ways he'd been too fearful to imagine.

He came to her whenever he could escape the gentle,
trusting scrutiny of Moira Kelly, though it was not as
often as Greta asked him to. And each time he learned
more, discovering what pleased a woman. He was the
student she had always yearned for, and she was the
master of her classroom.

Eventually, however, young Sam tired of Greta's dominance over him. He grew irritated when she constantly
hushed him with a stern word whenever he tried to talk
to her about the weightier subjects that were sometimes on
a young man's mind. She guided his awkward movements

with her hands, praising him when he did well, but not permitting him to experiment too much. He wanted more from Greta Belcher, but she wanted no more from him. Sam would have broken away from her on his own, but before he could, they were caught on the laundry room floor by a night watchman who had heard strange sounds.

Sam was certain it would be the end of his stay at Chilton-Howe, and he agonized over what that would do to his mother, who would likewise be without a position. The guilt lay upon him like a leaden weight, sometimes threatening to smother him with its intensity as he waited for disciplinary action to be handed down by school authorities.

He pleaded forgiveness from his mother, and vowed that such indiscretions would never happen again. Moira Kelly begged her employers to be lenient with her son, citing his excellent work record and commendable reputation in the classroom. In the end, it was Greta Belcher who was sent away from Chilton-Howe while Moira and Sam were permitted to stay. The incident was never mentioned again, and Sam went on to achieve distinction in his duties at the school and his classroom studies.

In all the years since, while he practiced the fine art of discretion, none of the women he'd known and the relationships he'd shared with them had stayed in his mind with the purity of remembrance like the first time with Greta Belcher. Yet as he lay on his mattress in the loft of the Chadwick farmhouse, he tried to recall the details of Greta's face, as he had many times in the past, and was astonished to find that he no longer could. Nor could he remember the others. Each face that began to form in his mind was suddenly fringed with auburn hair; each pair of eyes were tinted a haunting green, and each pair of lips was full and rosy and could laugh at a child's antics as easily as they could frown at an injustice. He shook his head, but the face of Abby Chadwick would not go away, and he took it with him into his dreams.

For the next few days, Sam worked extra hard, Abby noticed, either to make up for time lost in the city jail or to get as much done as possible before he left in the middle of June. His frenzied efforts meant that the spring crop was planted ahead of time, the exterior wall of the kitchen was finished and stained to match the rest of the house, and the roof was nearing completion. The tools that could be repaired were all in good working order, and generally the farm was in a far better state than it would have been had Sam not impulsively come to stay. Despite all Sam's claims to the contrary, Abby did indeed owe him more than she could ever repay.

The first week of June brought idyllic days of summer with warm, dry afternoons and cool, fresh evenings. It would have been among the happiest times of Abby's life had the thought of Sam's departure not been on her mind almost constantly. She didn't bring up the subject of his leaving again, knowing he would tell her when he was ready to go, but she never doubted that the day would come.

One afternoon when the older children were at school, and Lizzie was taking her nap, Abby took advantage of some free time to plant flowers in the little bed by the front porch of the farmhouse. Sam had brought her the seeds from Mr. Purcell's store, and the thought of seeing colorful marigolds and zinnias in bright yellows and oranges helped to cheer her. As she pushed the tiny seeds into the damp soil, she listened to the tapping of Sam's hammer on the roof, as steady as a heartbeat and, though she tried to deny it, almost as vital to her existence.

She looked up when she heard a buggy approach the house. Two women, both dressed in somber attire, were on the driver's seat. Their colorless dress, and the rich appointments of the carriage, prompted Abby to correctly identify them. ''Now what could those two be doing here?'' she muttered as Martha Swenson and Harriet Sholski stopped a few yards from her.

''Good afternoon, Abigail,'' Harriet said, her stiff lips moving just enough to get the words out.

''Harriet, Martha,'' Abby acknowledged. ''What brings you ladies out this afternoon?''

''We've come on county business, Abigail,'' Harriet said. ''I have some news for you regarding the children in your care.''

Abby's heart skipped a beat. Good news at last, she thought. Perhaps her neighbors had finally come through with a sizable donation to help them out. ''I'll certainly be grateful to hear it,'' she said.

Harriet nodded. ''I'm sure you will . . . under the circumstances. We've found permanent homes for the children, Abigail—all but the youngest, that is—and we're still pursuing possibilities for Lizzie O'Donnell.''

It was as if Abby had been made of straw, and all at once the stuffing were being ripped out of her. Her legs felt too weak to support her. She leaned back against the porch railing and concentrated on drawing a deep breath so she would be able to speak. ''You what? Harriet, you can't be serious!''

''We're absolutely serious, aren't we, Martha?'' A ridiculously long feather on Martha Swenson's bonnet bobbed up and down as she nodded her head. ''We realize how much a burden the children have become, and we set about trying to relieve you of it . . . with a great deal of success.''

''But the children live *here*. They can't go anywhere else. I won't hear of it!''

''It's out of your hands, Abigail,'' Harriet stated with authority. She took a document out of her reticule and held it up for Abby to see. "It's official. We waited until the circuit judge came to the village and he signed the appropriate papers for the youngsters to go to their new homes. They're being adopted, Abigail. I should think you'd be happy for them."

Abby looked from one to the other of the women, her disbelief growing as a cold fear overtook her. "But Will has lived here for three years, and Susanna and Ang . . . Rebecca almost two years. And the twins—they're just getting used to being here. You can't uproot them, Harriet. You can't!"

When Abby didn't bother to take the document, Harriet shoved it back in her bag. She pursed her lips in impatience for a second, then said, "It should make you feel good, Abigail, to know that we've found all respectable homes. Mr. Vanovitch and his wife in Akron are adopting Will."

"The knacker?" Abby didn't try to hide her disgust.

"Don't be unkind, Abigail. The collection of dead animals is an important job. After all, the poorer townsfolk can't afford the best cuts of meat, and they rely on Mr. Vanovitch's market. And besides, his business has increased since he's set up the tanning shop."

"But he'll have Will doing man's labor, and he's still just a schoolboy."

"Is he in school now, Abigail?" Harriet asked haughtily. Receiving no answer, she said, "I thought not. Be assured that he will attend regularly with the Vanovitches."

"And Susanna and Rebecca?"

"That worked out especially well. They will go together to the inn in Cuyahoga Falls. They've added ten new rooms, and the girls can earn their keep housecleaning. It's a respectable position for them both, and considering their humble beginnings and Rebecca's . . . well, shall I say *odd* propensity for fantasy, as much as either of them will probably ever hope to achieve. The innkeeper and his wife will see that they're well cared for. Now as for the twins . . . there's a childless older couple in Mansfield who have agreed to take them . . . very stable people.''

"Stop it!" Abby cried. "You haven't found them loving homes. You've signed them on as apprentices! You can't do this. The children are happy here."

"Abby, you said yourself—many times, I might point out—that the children are constantly lacking the barest essentials, and now with Reverend Chadwick gone, it's not likely to get any easier. We really feel . . .''

Little by little Harriet's words faded into the background, and as Abby watched the older woman's mouth move with more of her self-righteous babble, her anger slowly gave way to a growing suspicion. Something wasn't making any sense. Why would these two women suddenly take it upon themselves to improve the lot of orphaned children they had previously given no thought to at all? Just a few weeks ago, Martha Swenson had dropped Lizzie O'Donnell in Abby's hands, and now she was claiming to want to find her another home, one more appropriate. Abby knew instinctively that there was more to this than these two women were telling her, and she was determined to find out what it was.

She stood up straight and faced the women squarely. "What's really going on here, Harriet? Martha? Everyone in the township knows the children have a good home here. How did you get the judge to sign those papers?"

Abby waited several moments until Martha Swenson finally nudged her companion. "I'm going to tell her, Harriet. I'm not afraid to."

"I'm certainly not afraid to either, Martha," came the clipped response, "but if it makes you feel better, then go ahead. I was just hoping to avoid a scene, that's all."

"One of you better tell me, ladies," Abby said, "or a scene is just what you're going to get!"

Martha stuck her head out of the buggy and gave a

cursory search of the farmyard. Then she leaned forward and whispered, "It's that *man*."

At first Martha's statement didn't make any sense. Abby stared at her trying to read meaning into her tight little face. Finally full comprehension came to Abby, and a throaty chuckle sputtered from her lips, because the notion was ridiculous even considering the seriousness of the situation. "Sam? You mean Sam Kelly?"

Martha gasped at Abby's flippant reaction. "Of course. You're living without benefit of marriage with that man, Abigail, and the whole community knows it."

"The people in this community know absolutely *nothing* except what their narrow little minds conceive to be true. Where were these so-called *good people* when Chadwick Farm was blown half to bits? Where were they when Papa was killed? Nowhere! It was Sam Kelly, a stranger, who put us back together, not the upright citizens of Seneca Township!"

"But Abigail, you told Harriet's husband that you have been living with this man . . ." She drew a long uncomfortable breath and pressed her palm against the bodice of her dress. "Day and *night*. What kind of example is that for impressionable children? And you know practically nothing about him. I swear, Abigail, your father would turn over in his grave if he only knew . . ."

"My father would *rise* from his grave and haunt both of you if he could hear one word of this absurd conversation!"

"There is no call for rudeness, Abigail," Harriet admonished. "We are only doing what is best for the children. Besides, it's not just Sam Kelly we're concerned about. You can live in your home any way you choose as long as your behavior does not affect innocent children. Judge Wilcox agreed with us wholeheartedly that a single woman is not capable of providing good care for the county's needy children, and that is the basis for this decision.''

"Oh, poppycock, Harriet. That's just an excuse and you know it. That opinion belongs right out there in the field with the rest of the cow chips!''

"Abigail! How dare you speak to me . . . ?'' Harriet's scolding was abruptly cut short when she stared in shock at the figure coming around the corner of the farmhouse.

When she saw him, Abby became aware for the first time that the hammering had stopped. But she clearly heard Sam's cheerful whistling as he walked toward them, hurriedly buttoning his shirt over his bare chest.

"Oh, sorry, ladies,'' he said, managing a boyish blush of embarrassment. "I didn't know Abby had company. How are you this beautiful afternoon?''

His smile was so engaging and his mood so lighthearted that Abby didn't know whether to laugh or scream at him. His sudden appearance right now, though, was like a minstrel's at a funeral—completely out of place. Both women in the buggy muttered a hasty greeting as they kept their eyes glued on the brazen young object of their scorn.

Sam strode up to Abby and passed his arm around her back, settling his hand possessively on her shoulder. "I hope you ladies will come calling often now that you've heard the news,'' he said.

Abby glanced at the look of pure enchantment on Sam's face as she heard Martha Swenson ask, "What news is that, Mr. Kelly?''

"Abby didn't tell you?'' he said, beaming at her. "I've asked her to marry me, and she said yes. I'm the luckiest man alive!''

Chapter Eight

Harriet Sholski's gasp competed with the string of tremulous *oh, my*'s uttered in Martha Swenson's shrill soprano.

"I can see you ladies are surprised," Sam acknowledged with a wide grin. "No more than I was when Abby agreed to be my wife."

"And no more than I am at this moment," Abby said through clenched teeth. She felt Sam's hand tighten on her shoulder, and didn't know if the gesture was meant to prompt her to go along with him or to keep her from crumpling to the ground with shock. Probably both.

Sam looked at the women in the carriage and back to Abby before raising his eyebrows in innocent confusion. "Did I interrupt something, Abby? I guess my manners could use some polishing if I did."

"No, no, Sam," Abby answered. "Your manners are the last thing I'm worried about now."

Harriet cleared her throat and adjusted her position on the driver's seat until her back was straight as a pole. "Well, Abigail, it seems that congratulations are in order.

You might have told me about this impending marriage during our little conversation.''

''Yes, indeed, you should have, Abby,'' Martha echoed. ''This announcement may very well affect the judge's decision.'' She glanced at her more formidable companion for confirmation. ''Mightn't it, dear?''

Harriet leveled a look of extreme annoyance at her friend before turning stern eyes on Abby. ''I suppose so, Martha. It appears that the insignificant details of her upcoming nuptials momentarily slipped Abigail's mind.''

Sam's fingers poked the soft flesh of Abby's upper arm. ''You don't consider our marriage 'insignificant' at all, do you, sweetheart?''

''Of course not,'' she answered in a voice that was much stronger than she would have thought possible under the circumstances. She even risked hurling a barb at the bristling Harriet Sholski. ''How could any girl forget about the most joyous day of her life? Surely you remember the pleasurable anticipation of your own wedding to Ernest, Harriet.''

The older woman's lips formed a tight pucker, which prompted Abby to hide a fleeting, satisfied smile behind her cupped hand. ''I didn't say anything because Sam and I haven't announced our plans to anyone yet,'' she continued. ''You know how I feel about my privacy. Like most of the people in Seneca Township, I mind my own business.''

Harriet Sholski's eyes narrowed to slits as if she suspected she were the target of Abby's sarcasm, but the amiable smile Abby plastered on her face kept the busybody from squawking her offense. ''I guess it will be all right if you mention my upcoming marriage to the circuit judge now, though,'' Abby said sweetly.

''You intend to file for permanent guardianship of the children then?''

''Naturally.''

"Very well, Abigail. Since you have decided to alter your living arrangements to those befitting a good Christian woman, I'll inform Judge Wilcox of your plans." Harriet drew the reins through her gloved hands, preparing to leave. "There's just one more thing. This wedding . . . it will take place soon, I presume?"

Abby faltered for a moment, and Sam jumped in. "Very soon, Mrs. Sholski. We've already begun the arrangements."

"I'll be waiting to hear what those arrangements are, Mr. Kelly. Good day to you."

Sam lifted his free hand in a casual wave. "So long."

As Abby watched the carriage pull away from the house, Martha Swenson's voice drifted back to her. "It is rather romantic, isn't it, Harriet? He really is a nice-looking young man, don't you think?"

Abby couldn't hear Harriet's response, but an extra snap of the reins on the horse's back and a hastening clip of horseshoes on the hard-packed dirt told her that a scowl had no doubt settled on the woman's dour face.

When the carriage disappeared over the rise, Abby whirled around to face Sam. "Do you realize what you've done?"

"Just proposed marriage," he answered with understated and aggravating blandness. "Though not very gallantly, I'm afraid."

"Not very *gallantly?* You're worried about being gallant, and I'm wondering how I'm going to hold this family together once this story leaks out!" She flung her arms wide in frustration. "I know you were just trying to help, Sam, but really, that was the most irrational, impetuous act . . ."

"Now, Abby, hold on a minute. I happen to believe that was the most rational thing I've ever done in my life. At least it seemed the most direct means to an end."

"Meaning what?"

"Those two fire-breathing dragons are gone, aren't they? They're dropping the campaign to take the children away, right?"

"Oh, sure, for the next few days maybe," Abby conceded. "But they'll be back. As soon as they realize that we didn't march down the aisle, they'll just resume their little witch-hunt against me, and this time with more ammunition."

Though she believed her situation was becoming more hopeless by the minute, Abby couldn't stay angry with Sam for long. After all, he had only tried to come to her rescue. "Oh, Sam," she groaned, "I know your heart's in the right place, but you've only made things worse! Now they can add that I'm a liar as well as the village tart."

He answered her with a self-assured shrug. "But you don't *have* to be a liar, Abby. And neither do I. Do you think I didn't mean the proposal?"

She turned away from him, her mind already churning with schemes designed to appease Harriet and Martha. "Of course you didn't mean it, I know that."

"But I did. I'll marry you, if that's what it takes."

His words penetrated her frantic search for a solution, and she struggled to grasp the confusing implications of his misguided chivalry. She stared at him in disbelief, not trusting herself to speak. What had come over Sam Kelly, scholarly, ethical man he was supposed to be, to suggest such a thing? Did he really believe this was the best way to handle the problem? Did he believe that she would accept his desperate expression of charity?

Even if he did care for her the way a husband should, which she knew very well he didn't, then it was obvious his nose had been buried in a book for too long, because he knew even less about romance than she did—which was pitifully little. His offer kept repeating in her mind. *"I'll marry you, if that's what it takes."* Well, I definitely *have an answer to your gracious proposal, Sam Kelly,* she thought. *Thanks, but no, thanks! I'll find another way.*

Intending to deliver her answer with firm conviction, Abby faced Sam and saw that he was looking at her with a sheepish grin and rubbing the back of his neck. "That didn't come out exactly the way I meant it to," he said as if reading her mind. "What I meant to say is that I *want* to marry you."

She gave him her most humbling stare, the one that always made everyone sit up and take notice. "Don't do me any more favors, Sam. The new kitchen is more than enough and has quite certainly turned my head."

"Come on, Abby. This is no time to hide behind hurt feelings. Just listen to me for a minute. There's a lot more at stake here than you and me. The future of these kids is the real issue, and as crazy as it sounds, I've come to think of them as my kids too. I can't let those self-righteous biddies take them away from you . . . from us."

She looked out toward the apple orchard, but continued to listen. "For God's sake, Abby," he argued, "people have married for a lot worse reasons than we have. Look at all the arranged marriages they have in Europe, and there are still mail-order brides who travel to the Northwest. Some women actually go across the country to wed strangers!"

"Why don't you advertise for one of them then?"

"This isn't about them! It's about us and how we can keep these kids!" There was a tremor in his voice that said he was losing patience. "I'm just trying to tell you that people marry for position, or money, or . . ."

"Love?" she said more bitterly than she'd intended.

He expelled a long breath. "The lucky ones, I suppose, but frankly I haven't known many of those." He walked around her and forced her to look at him. "We get along, don't we?" She kept her face expressionless and he relented with a tone of restrained amusement. "Okay, maybe not at this moment, but at least most of the time. You think I'm good with the kids, don't you?'' She managed a slight nod of agreement. "I think you're a wonderful mother. I told you that the other day, and it would be a serious mistake if those children were taken away. Face it, Abby, getting married is the best, possibly the *only* way to insure that they can stay right here where they belong.''

She didn't want to admit that his outlandish idea probably had merit, but she could think of no other way for them all to stay together.

He must have sensed a softening in her attitude, because a smile pulled at his lips. "Once you admit that I'm right, and that you really have to marry *someone,* you'd just as soon pick me as anyone else, wouldn't you?'' He paused a moment before adding with exaggerated schoolboy enthusiasm, "I know I'd pick you.''

Abby couldn't hold back the fickle chuckle that surely betrayed her. "Gee, Sam, maybe I've been all wrong about you. You *do* have this endearing romantic side.''

He laughed. "Maybe I do at that. Maybe you're just the woman who can find it.''

"Aren't you forgetting one thing?''

"What's that?''

"You're going away in a few days. Remember, you already bought your ticket. It's only a one-way fare, isn't it?''

A worried frown erased the smile from his face. "It is for now,'' he admitted, "but I'll come back. I've got some business to attend to, Abby, that's all, and I don't know for sure how long it will take me.''

"What kind of business?''

"It's just a job back in Pennsylvania,'' he evaded. "It's a way to earn some of the money we're going to need. An old friend got it for me, and I've got to go.''

She wondered why he was so hesitant to give her any

details about his trip. What kind of a job could he be going to that he couldn't tell her about? "Is it teaching?" she asked.

"No. Teachers are as poor as church mice, even those at Chilton-Howe were. I've got to make a good living now more than ever. But just as soon as I can, I'll tell you where I'll be and when I'll be back. And I *will be back,* Abby. In fact, I'll return in time to get that barn done before the first snow falls, and I should have plenty of money to do it."

Abby cocked her head to the side and regarded him warily. "Are you teaming up with a bank robber, Sam?"

"My friend's as saintly as a judge, I promise you. Now, are you going to marry me or let those old crones win?"

Jubilant voices in the distance drew Abby's attention to the rise. The children were coming toward them, bookbags swinging empty at their sides since it was the last day of school. Sam placed his hands on the sides of Abby's face. "Here they come. You've got to decide soon. Do we tell them they're staying right here with us or that they have to pack their bags?"

She studied his handsome face, deciding it was also a kind, strong face grounded firmly with intelligent, caring eyes. Could this possibly work? She knew he was serious about marrying her and protecting the children, though why he would make the commitment was still baffling. There were vital questions that had to be answered. "Why are you doing this, Sam? You could have so much, and we'll only hold you back."

His dark gaze captured hers with such intensity that she knew what he was about to say came from his heart. "If you say yes, then I'll feel like I already have what most men search their whole lives for. I've learned a lot about values since I came here, about what's really important. I want a home, Abby, and this family. It sounds crazy, I know, but I think I sensed that when I first came here with Duncan. It's just that simple.''

"Oh, no, Sam Kelly," she whispered fiercely. "I suspect it's far more complicated than that. There are parts of you that I haven't begun to know yet, and reasons you're searching for an anchor in your life. I just don't know what they are.''

He didn't deny it. "Trust me, Abby. I won't let you down. I'll take care of you.''

One more question remained to be asked, and it was the one whose answer Abby feared the most. "How will you feel if I fall in love with you, Sam? Are you prepared for that?''

If he was stunned by her direct question, he didn't show it. In fact, he answered with unflinching confidence. "I have considered that possibility, and I intend to try my hardest to see that you do. In fact, if we end up loving each other, I'll consider that a pretty fair bonus for saving these children, and I won't be a bit surprised by the outcome. I'm a patient man, Abby. I won't pressure you to do anything you're not ready for. I'll wait for you.''

It was a good answer, and she realized that she'd been holding her breath the whole time he delivered it. She released most of her misgivings in a long, slow sigh. Dear God, she wondered, was it possible that she loved him already? Could she love a man she knew so little about, or was she the biggest fool ever born? She couldn't turn away from his gentle, searching eyes. She couldn't turn away from the chance he was offering. Maybe it was time for Abigail Chadwick to accept someone on faith. Maybe it was time to believe again.

He inclined his head toward the approaching children and circled her waist with his hands. "Are you ready?'' he asked.

"Oh, Sam, this is the right thing to do, isn't it?''

"Why don't you ask them?" he said as the children gathered around.

Angel clasped her hands behind her back and watched Sam and Abby with puzzled interest. The twins, who normally would have been tugging at Sam's shirtsleeves, stood a few feet away gawking at the strange look on his face. And Susanna, who as usual went right to the heart of a matter, exclaimed to her adopted siblings, "They're touching each other!" Then, speaking for all of them, she bluntly asked, "What's going on between you two?"

At Sam's nod of encouragement, Abby said, "Sam and I have something important to tell you."

One evening a week later, Abby sat on the mahogany settee her mother had brought all the way from Hartford, Connecticut, when she married James Chadwick. Sam had asked Abby to wait for him in the parlor because he had something to discuss with her before they were married the next day. He came into the room holding a pen and piece of paper. After turning up the wick inside the amber chimney of a kerosene lamp, he sat down next to her. "Everyone's asleep," he said.

"All except for Will. He's out again, but it's quiet, and we can talk."

He took the hand that rested on her lap, placed it on his knee, and covered it with his own hand. The pads of his fingers pressed lightly into her palm, and she felt the current from his touch flow through her veins.

"You're not going to change your mind, are you?" he asked with a tender smile.

She let out a shaky breath. "No, but I'm surprised I feel this nervous. Almost like a real bride."

He lifted an eyebrow and sat back to scrutinize her features. "But you *are* a real bride, Abby. This is for keeps, you know. True, we don't have the Reverend James

Chadwick to lead the ceremony, but when the circuit judge pronounces us man and wife, it's just as binding.''

"I know.''

"It's not going to be a very memorable day for you, though. Not like most girls have. I'm sorry. Maybe someday I can make it up to you.''

"I think there will be plenty to remember about tomorrow,'' she said. "How many brides are attended by the six children they're raising, and how many see their husbands off for weeks right after the ceremony?'' Though she tried to keep their conversation light, she dreaded having to say good-bye to Sam, even if it was for a short time. She hid the depth of her feelings by understating her desire. "It'd be nice if you didn't have to leave after we sign all the guardianship papers.''

"Do you really mean that? I figured you were looking forward to a long honeymoon without me.''

He was matching her casual attitude with one of his own, and Abby wondered if they were both doing the same thing—hiding the uncertainty of their future and their chaotic emotions by making them seem trivial. She knew that was what she was doing.

He shrugged. "Maybe it's best this way. I think you need some time to get used to the idea of having a husband. And some time to miss me.''

"And if I don't miss you at all?'' Listening to the sound of her words, Abby realized she could never play the part of a flirt. Coyness was not in her nature, and it was all she could do to refrain from shouting, "Oh, but I will! I will miss you every day you are gone!''

He squeezed her hand once before releasing it and picking up the paper on his lap. Then he winked at her as though he knew what she was really thinking. "Call me an optimist,'' he said. "I'm just absolutely certain you will. Now, about this paper.'' His voice changed to a business-like tone. "I've written down some things you'll need to know.'' The pen tip followed the lines on the paper. ''You can contact me through this man, Harland Carstairs. This is his address in Fox Hill. It's a little town just north of Pittsburgh. He'll know where I am and how to reach me.''

''Will you be staying with him?''

''No, but not far away. I'll probably be staying where the job is.''

''Is Mr. Carstairs the old friend who got you the job?'' Abby asked. Sam nodded. ''What sort of work is it?''

''Just labor, but it should pay well.''

''Will you be working hard?''

''After working here, anything else seems like a holiday!'' he exaggerated. He followed the teasing statement with one of telling sincerity. ''But at Chadwick Farm, the rewards have been worth it.''

She looked down at her hands folded on her lap, and he chided her gently. ''Why, Abby, are you blushing at a little honest flattery?''

''I'm not a blusher, Sam. I should think you'd know that.'' She answered with quiet indignation, though she didn't look up at him for fear he'd see telltale color on her cheeks. And she was afraid that if she looked at him, she'd blurt out that what she was feeling went far beyond a schoolgirl blush.

For the first day or two after Sam's proposal, Abby had stubbornly refused to even think about what she'd done. She wouldn't allow herself to admit that she was actually marrying a man she had only known a short time and one who hadn't said he loved her. If she didn't give credence to the idea, then she didn't have to consider the niggling doubt that she was indeed a hopeless fool who was destined never to realize true romance. So what if she never experienced burning passion? She could live without passion. After all, she told herself, romance had existed for a very long time only in her dreams.

Despite her best efforts, though, the reality of her decision began to sink in. As she became more accustomed to the idea of marrying Sam, a comforting warmth settled deep inside her that made her chores easier and her days sunnier.

Then for the past two days, she'd been positively giddy with the thought of becoming a wife. She tried to keep her feelings locked inside, but she wondered that the whole world couldn't see that Abigail Chadwick had changed. And if the changes weren't evident on the outside, it was enough to know that a light burned steadily on the inside, and she could feel its heat every time she thought of Sam. It especially happened when he was near, and his affectionate pats came more often and his warm gaze washed over her from across the table or across the room. She felt the light inside glow brighter, and she wondered that he didn't feel its heat.

Sam leaned down to better see her face, and when she lifted her eyes, he said, "Why the serious look, Abby? Is something bothering you?" He touched her face with the gentlest caress.

If you only knew, Sam Kelly. "It's . . . it's nothing," she stammered. "Just silly notions have come to me, that's all."

"You want to tell me about them?"

How could she tell him all the things she was feeling, when she doubted whether he was feeling any of them at all? She hoped the little smile she gave him would mask her embarrassment. "I guess I'm just happy to be marrying you," she admitted simply. "I think maybe you should know that."

Her eyes beckoned him like a shimmering magnet, drawing him into the mirror to her heart, and he realized that whatever he said now would hold a great significance for both of them. He sensed that Abby was on the verge of a great discovery, and she was asking him to explore it with her. His face inched closer to hers. "It pleases me to hear that, Abby."

Up to that moment, Sam had always thought of Abigail Chadwick as attractive and fair. He was certainly tantalized by her womanly, lean figure and her clear, expressive eyes. She was an admirable lady in all respects. He'd known that from the first time he saw her. But suddenly, he found her astoundingly beautiful. In the golden light from the lantern, her face was the flawless porcelain of a child's, her green eyes soft and shimmering. All at once, without warning, Abigail Chadwick took his breath away, and his feelings for her broke through some of the barriers that stubbornly remained between them.

Sam reached around the back of her head and pulled out the few pins that held the chignon she always wore. He wanted to see her face framed by the russet waves of her hair. When the tresses fell free, Sam filled his hands with them and fanned them over her shoulders. The ends curled over the bodice of her dress. Shorter strands wafted around her temples, casting gauze-like shadows on her eyes. She leaned toward him, and the barriers continued to fall.

"You're beautiful, Abby," he said, "and I don't think you're even aware of it." His hands rested on her shoulders, and she trembled.

"Oh, Sam . . ." she began skeptically as though, even now, she wouldn't believe him.

"Abby, you're not going to argue with me about this, are you?" he teased affectionately. "After all, of the two of us, I'm the only one who can see you."

A pleasant tingling crept up her neck to the roots of her hair. "No, I'm not going to argue. I'm just going to believe for the moment that maybe I am."

Sam cupped his hand under her chin and raised her face so he could see into her eyes. In their glittering depths, he saw the beginnings of trust, not doubt . . . hope, not uncertainty. When he lowered his mouth to hers, she backed away with an imperceptible flinch, and he stopped, waiting for her to give him a sign that she wanted him to do what he very much wanted. Her lips parted slightly, just enough to invite him to taste them, and his mouth touched hers with a gentle pressure that calmed her at the same time it prompted her to ask for more.

She offered no resistance when he drew her close, and the kiss deepened. He slanted his head to find better access to her mouth and put his arms around her back. His mouth moved over hers, and he felt the tension in her lips melt away as she yielded to his embrace with increasing eagerness.

She moaned softly, and he slid his tongue against the line of her mouth. Moving his hand up and down her spine, he urged her nearer until her breasts brushed against his shirt. In that instant, when Abby's body felt warm and inviting against his, the little hard-back settee suddenly became uncomfortable, confining, and completely inadequate for caressing the soft curves of his bride's supple form. Sam longed to take her hand and lead her to the big featherbed in James Chadwick's old bedroom.

A startled cry caught in Abby's throat, but she didn't draw away. Instead, she arched her back and reached around his neck, letting Sam know that she wanted the kiss to continue as much as he did. He pulled her more tightly into the beckoning circle of his arms, and she came willingly. With what little reason Sam still held on to, he marveled that once again Abby had amazed him. He had discovered that buried beneath her cool, efficient exterior, she was a passionate, exciting woman. The pressure of her hand pushing against his chest brought him back from the swirling haze of desire. "Sam, Sam . . . the back door." Her voice, muted and sweet, warned him. "It must be Will."

A reluctant smile crept onto his face. "Will who?"

A husky young male voice called out, "Miss Abby, I'm home!"

"That Will," she said, hurriedly smoothing the placket of her blouse and tucking the ends into the waistband of her skirt.

"Of course. I remember him now."

As Will's footsteps sounded along the short hallway from the kitchen to the parlor, Abby searched the rug in front of the settee for the piece of paper that contained Harland Carstairs's address. It had fallen from Sam's lap moments before. She picked it up, cleared her throat, and pretended to be reading the paper when Will came through the doorway. "So this is his name, right, Sam?" she said with an effort to keep her voice steady.

Stifling a chuckle, Sam answered, "Absolutely, first and last, in that order."

"Good. I'll keep this handy in case I need it." She looked up, catching Will's puzzled stare. "Oh, Will, I didn't hear you come in. Did you have a nice evening?"

Will looked suspiciously from Abby to Sam, and he nodded. "You two ready for the big day tomorrow?" he asked after several moments of silent appraisal.

"Ready and willing," Sam answered, standing up. "And to that end, I think I'll go on to bed." He bent down and placed a chaste kiss on Abby's cheek. "Good night, Abby."

"Good night, Sam," she said briskly. She watched him leave the room and heard his footsteps on the ladder to the loft, only slightly aware that Will had taken his place on the settee.

"So is this wedding really okay with you, Miss Abby?" Will asked.

She switched her gaze to Will's worried face. "Whatever do you mean?"

"There's been considerable talk in the village that you're doin' this just so you can keep the young ones.

It's awful nice of you, but it seems like a powerfully hard thing to do if you don't have feelin's for Sam.''

His big brown eyes were full of concern for her, and Abby touched his arm. "It's sweet of you to fuss about me, Will, but everything's going to be fine.'' She ran her hand over her shoulder where Sam's hand had been, and she couldn't suppress a contented sigh. "As a matter of fact, I do have feelings for him,'' she said. Then in case Will found her too bold, she added, "He's a good man, Will. Don't you think so too now?''

"Yeah, he's come around all right. And he's playful with the little ones. They like him fine.'' He nodded wisely. "I guess he'll do for you, Miss Abby. I just wonder if you feel for him what a woman's supposed to feel for her man.''

"Why, Will Buckman . . . what do you know about those kinds of feelings?''

He shifted his feet on the hook rug and looked down. "I'm not sayin' I know anything,'' he said. "I'm just imaginin', that's all.''

"Well, someday you will,'' she assured him, and when she saw him smile, she wondered if perhaps he already did.

Sam Kelly and Abigail Chadwick were married the next morning after a three-and-one-half-hour drive in the buckboard to the county seat. Abby wore her green dress with the yellow flowers. She carried a bouquet of daisies Angel had made for her that morning, and had allowed Angel to wind a few extra flowers through the spirals she'd fashioned on Abby's crown with the curling iron.

Will, straight-backed and staid, stood as best man for Sam, and Angel, dreamy-eyed and ethereal, was maid of honor for Abby. This left Susanna in charge of the younger children, who had been told to sit quietly in back of Judge

Wilcox's office. It was a position that she readily assumed and managed with success.

When the short ceremony was over and the marriage license had been signed, Judge Wilcox immediately granted guardianship of the six Seneca Village orphans to the Kellys. He wished them all well, and went on to other pressing matters of the day.

With the two hours that remained before his train left for Pittsburgh, Sam took his family to lunch. For most of the children it was their first time in a restaurant, and it was an exciting experience despite the heavy eyelids of the youngest ones, who had risen that morning well before their accustomed times.

At the train depot, Will moved into Sam's seat in the buckboard and took the reins while Sam and Abby walked to the waiting train. Sam set his valise down in the loading area, and tried to think of something to say to his wife that would make his parting easier for both of them. "I want to stay, you know that, don't you? If there were any other way to get the money . . . "

"I know."

He smiled down at her, and his soft gray eyes held a promise. "Someday we'll have a proper honeymoon and stay in a fine hotel with waiters to bring us our food."

"And seven beds?"

"Sure. Seven beds." He took her hands. "You should be all right for a while. There's enough money to see you through until I get my first paycheck, and when I come back we'll start over, the right way." He pulled her into a tight embrace. "Good God, Abby, I didn't think it would be this hard to leave."

She felt his heart beat against hers, and squeezed her eyes shut to stop the flow of tears that threatened to spill down her cheeks. "Take care of yourself, Sam," she whispered. *And please, please, come back.*

The conductor announced final boarding, and Sam

leaned over and kissed her. "I'll miss you," he said in a husky voice. Then he picked up his bag and backed toward the slowly moving train.

"I'll miss you too," she called, but he had already turned and was sprinting toward the platform of a passenger car, and she didn't know for sure if he'd heard her.

She waited until the train pulled out of the station and she could no longer see him waving. Then she headed back to the buckboard and the children, who she hoped would sustain her in the weeks to come. Before she reached them, she looked at the sky. *Papa, help me,* she mouthed in a silent plea. *Help me to have faith in this man who has made more promises than perhaps he can ever hope to keep. You once told me I've got to have faith in my fellow man, and my heart believes in Sam, but my mind, Papa, is traitorous. It is telling me now that I am a fool to trust in promises. Sam Kelly, my husband, may never return.*

Chapter Nine

What was left of a hazy afternoon sun seeped through the trees that lined the Erie rail tracks and cast rippling olive-hued reflections on the window next to Sam's head. Ashen clouds streaked across a blue-gray sky that threatened rain at any moment. Sam thought it only fitting that a dreary dusk was descending over the monotonous countryside, adding impetus to his increasing gloom.

He knew it was guilt he was feeling. He'd had enough experience with it to know when he was caught in the web of self-recrimination. He thought of Abby standing beside the depot in Akron, watching the train take him away from her and toward a destination she knew so little about. *Why don't you tell her the truth?* he had asked himself over and over again during the long afternoon, but the answer was obvious. Facing his father's family wasn't going to be easy. Sam truly believed that a relationship between the Rosemonts and him would never develop satisfactorily, and in fact, was likely to produce bitter animosity.

Why involve Abby in a situation whose outcome was questionable at best, and in reality, was probably doomed from the start? Besides, Abby had made it clear to him that money and position, even when she had only *assumed* they existed, only increased the differences between them. Sam had no desire to test his union with his new bride, and her tentative faith in him, with speculative riches.

It was definitely true that the Kellys needed money, even Rosemont money, desperately, and it was this realization that drove Sam to the journey he was taking today. But he was well aware that the Rosemonts would not welcome him into their family circle. He fully expected to be scorned by his half brothers, just as he had been scorned through all his youth by their peers at the Chilton-Howe School. And if that were so, Sam had made up his mind to take what he could from his father's legitimate family and return to Abby as soon as possible.

At least there was one man who championed Sam's right to his inheritance. Harland Carstairs almost made it seem as if it was Sam's *duty* to claim what was bequeathed to him. A vision of Carstairs's face formed before Sam's eyes, obliterating the bleak scenery outside the train window. It was an honorable, trustworthy face with serious gray eyes and strong, confident planes. A fashionable handlebar mustache, perfectly groomed, swept down from the lawyer's upper lip. Sam could picture the curled and waxed ends twitching slightly as Carstairs told him about the will. In fact, Sam remembered everything about that March afternoon as if it were yesterday . . .

"Sam, you've got a visitor." The secretary from the dean's office interrupted the tutoring session Sam was having with three students. Sam looked up from the blackboard and questioned the messenger. "Who is it?"

"It's an attorney from somewhere near Pittsburgh. He's

with your mother right now. Dean Hendricks says it's okay for you to stop what you're doing and see what it's about.''

When Sam entered his mother's small bedchamber, he noticed two things immediately. One was that the imposingly large frame of the soberly clad attorney nearly filled the tiny space not occupied by Moira Kelly's bed and medical equipment. The other was that his mother looked unusually well, considering the advanced state of her consumption. She was wearing her best dressing gown, and she had covered her lank hair with a frilly nightcap. The pink ruffles framing her face and an uncharacteristic glint in her eyes made the ravages of the recent winter months practically disappear from her visage. Moira almost looked like a girl again . . . until she spoke.

''Samuel, come to me,'' she rasped, fighting to keep from coughing. Her thin fingers reached out to him, and he crossed the narrow room to grasp her hand. ''Samuel, a miracle has happened, one that I have prayed for since the day you were born.''

He looked from his mother's expectant face to the staid, controlled countenance of her visitor. Moira's fingers pressed urgently into the palm of Sam's hand. ''This is Mr. Harland Carstairs, from Fox Hill, Samuel. He's your father's representative, and he's come to tell you that your father has recognized you at last. You will finally get what has been your due.''

Sam had lived with his mother's fantasies since he'd been a toddler on her lap, listening to her tales of a great house and a life befitting a young prince, but he'd never made her dreams his own. He'd learned through the years to nod courteously at her and then push the illusions to the back of his mind, knowing they had no place in the life he led every day. So he looked at Harland Carstairs and gave him an indulgent smile meant to explain away the meanderings of his mother's imagination.

"How do you do, Mr. Kelly," Carstairs said, shaking Sam's hand. He held a legal document up for Sam's inspection. "I've brought a copy of your late father's will, and I think you'll find it of great interest."

Hearing in this offhand way that his father was dead meant nothing to Sam. When he wasn't forced to listen to his mother's ungrounded fantasies about Tobias Rosemont, Sam gave the man no thought at all except to loath him for exiling his mother to a life of drudgery and condemnation. Sam had never wanted anything to do with his father, and he certainly had no use for whatever pittance the man might have left his illegitimate son to salve his conscience.

If Harland saw the indifference in Sam's eyes, he was not put off. "I'll briefly explain what it says, Mr. Kelly, though I'm certain you will want to peruse its contents more carefully in your own time." Squeezing his considerable bulk between the wooden arms of the one narrow chair in the room, Harland drew his spectacles from his vest pocket and rested them on his nose. Then he laid the document on his knee and scanned through preliminary pages before stopping at the important provisions of the will.

He looked up at Sam and cleared his throat. "Basically, Mr. Kelly, your father left you one third of the House of Rosemont, a highly successful furniture manufacturing empire which he inherited from his own father and which he guided to new heights of profitability in the last thirty years." Removing his glasses, Carstairs tapped the will with the earpiece. "It's a considerable fortune, young man."

"Samuel, my prayers have been answered," Moira Kelly whispered from her bed. "Now you can assume your rightful place in society. You have been invited into your father's world at last—the world you belong in."

A fit of coughing seized her, and Sam raised the flame

under the kettle on the paraffin stove. Pungent herbal vapors filled the room. "You see what you've done with your nonsense, Mr. Carstairs," he chastised. "It's important for my mother to remain calm. You should have discussed this with me privately."

The attorney smiled at Moira Kelly. "I'm sorry for your mother, Mr. Kelly, but this is not nonsense. It's fact. There are provisions, of course, conditions which must be met."

Sam responded with a derisive snort. "That doesn't surprise me. I'm quite sure that I won't be any more favorable to my father's *conditions* than I am to the acceptance of his entire bequest!"

"Listen, Samuel!" his mother said sharply. "You must hear what this man has to say. Go on, Mr. Carstairs. My son will pay heed."

"The only conditions are that you learn the workings of the House of Rosemont. Your father has provided a good salary for you while you apprentice in various departments of the company. You will be expected to alternate between the sawmill and the manufacturing plant. After a brief tenure of three months, which I think you will agree is reasonable, you will automatically be granted interest in your father's company as provided by the will."

"One third of the company, you said?"

"That's right."

"And the other two thirds?"

"They are bequeathed to your half brothers, Frederick and Simon. They will oversee your progress and guide you in assuming your place with them at the head of the company."

Already surmising the answer, Sam inquired, "And how do my brothers feel about this?"

For the first time since their meeting, Harland Carstairs appeared less than self-assured. So, Sam had found the wrinkle in Tobias Rosemont's well-thought-out last request.

"I will be honest with you, Mr. Kelly," Harland said. "Frederick and Simon have contested the will in court. They hired their own attorney right after Mr. Rosemont died and sought to have the document overturned. Obviously they weren't successful or I wouldn't be here today."

"And do they know you're here today, Mr. Carstairs?"

The attorney peered at Sam over the rim of his spectacles. "They know this visit is inevitable, just as they know that I am honor-bound to uphold your interests in this matter. I'm on your side, young man, make no mistake about it."

Moira Kelly's faint voice carried weakly over the hissing of the kettle. "You see, Samuel. It's meant to be. All you have to do is claim what is rightfully yours."

"Yes, Mama, yes," Sam said, placating her. He could see that this unexpected turn of events had sapped his mother of needed strength, and she was growing weaker by the moment. "You just rest now. I'm going to walk Mr. Carstairs outside now. Then I'll come back and speak with you."

"Tell him you'll go to Fox Hill, Samuel, tell him."

He nodded and patted her hand before indicating that Harland should leave the room. Once in the hallway, Sam decided to dismiss the attorney as quickly as possible. "You can see what my situation is here, Mr. Carstairs. My mother is ill, and I wouldn't consider a change in my life at this time. I can't leave her."

"Of course, Mr. Kelly, I understand. But if and when you decide to act upon your father's last wishes, you need only contact me, and I'll arrange a meeting involving you, Frederick, and Simon. And seeing your mother today, I can't help believing that my news will prove to be a godsend for you in the future."

Sam followed Harland's gaze, and he knew the meticulous man was scrutinizing the dreary details of the Chilton-Howe employees' dormitory—the drab, windowless walls of the narrow hallway, the peeling paint on the wood plank floor. The attorney even discreetly wrinkled his nose at the musty odor coming from mildewed plaster moldings at the ceiling before he said, "Perhaps when you are able to consider a change in location, your father's bequest will hold a certain appeal to you."

In the outdoor courtyard, Harland walked to a fine buggy waiting at the end of the walk. He turned to Sam and raised his eyebrows in question. "I can expect to hear from you, Mr. Kelly?"

Sam knew the time for polite discussion had ended. "I'm afraid you've misjudged me, Mr. Carstairs, and consequently wasted your afternoon by coming here. You see, the truth is, my father's bequest will *never* hold any appeal to me."

Carstairs frowned. "What are you saying?"

"Just this. I'm not interested in whether or not Tobias Rosemont assuaged his guilty conscience on his deathbed. In fact, I hope that by turning down his belated gesture of magnanimity, I can have the pleasure of imagining his soul burning in Hell."

An odd smile, just visible beneath the attorney's handlebar mustache, suggested admiration. He stepped up into his carriage and picked up the reins. "Don't let pride limit your possibilities, son," he said. "Your father, self-serving bastard that he may have been at times, did attempt to make amends for his mistake—albeit late."

"You're wrong, Mr. Carstairs. He never made amends to the one person who deserved them. He used my mother when she was his maid and then banished her from his home. It's too late for him to make it up to her now."

Harland waved an index finger at Sam from beneath the leather canopy of the buggy. "Ah, Mr. Kelly, you forget. I saw the light in your mother's eyes when she heard the provisions of the will. When she looked at you and imagined what you could become, I knew Tobias Rosemont's debt to her was paid.''

He released the brake and stared straight ahead at the tree-lined drive that led to the exit of the Chilton-Howe campus. Without looking at Sam he said, ''I left the will on your mother's bureau. Read it, Mr. Kelly. You don't have to decide today. But remember this . . . one should never throw away the keys to the kingdom without knowing which doors they open.'' Then he flicked the reins on the horse's back and his carriage pulled away.

One week later, Moira Kilbourne Kelly died in the same little room where she had given birth to her illegitimate son twenty-six years earlier. The few mourners who gathered around her grave site were servants at the school like Moira had been and one full professor who had always appreciated the gleaming pen tips she aligned in a neat row on his desk.

When the service ended, Sam disposed of his mother's few belongings, packed his clothing, and walked away from Chilton-Howe. He had no destination in mind, but within hours a jovial drummer passed him on the road. Duncan Walthrop offered Sam a job and an escape from Cooper's Glen, with its bitter past. Pushing his father's will to the back of his mind, Sam climbed on board with the drummer, happy to be heading away from western Pennsylvania, and toward Ohio.

That was over three months ago, and now Sam was back. It was nearly dawn when the train arrived at the depot in Pittsburgh. Sam couldn't see a reason to waste money for a few hours' rest in a local inn, so he walked to a nearby meat and produce market and waited for the distributors to open. The first businessman to raise his

loading dock door wore an apron embroidered with the
name "Stavinsky's Pickle Company." Seeing the same
name on a freight wagon in back of the market, Sam
asked if the man's delivery route included Fox Hill. He
was told it did. The proprietor agreed to let Sam ride
along with his driver for a small fee. That settled, Sam
climbed aboard the wagon, which smelled faintly of brine
and garlic, and rode beside the reticent driver as he headed
out of Pittsburgh through the increasing morning traffic.

When they reached the village of Fox Hill, the sun was
high in the sky. The first indication Sam had that he
was in the Rosemonts' hometown was a wooden placard
tucked into a stand of shady oak trees by the road. The
artistically chiseled letters on the sign identified the village
to visitors, and proclaimed that Fox Hill was established
in 1802, and nearly one fourth of the current residents
were direct descendants of Mayflower Pilgrims.

"They say the people are as pedigreed as their dogs,"
the previously silent wagon driver said, pointing to the
sign. "And prob'ly as thick with fleas, if you ask me! Over
yonder's the village square," he said, pointing toward a
plush green carpet of mowed grass and several well-
tended gardens surrounding an ivy-covered gazebo.
"Course wagons ain't allowed down the main street. We
got to stick to the back lane."

Before the wagon veered toward a narrow road used
for commercial traffic, Sam scanned the buildings that
made up Fox Hill's picturesque business district. The
venerable old edifices were architecturally pleasing with
their Georgian symmetry and red brick facades. He
noticed that the park, which the driver had called a
"square," was actually an oblong. The village hall stood
at one end, while a large Presbyterian church occupied
the other. Two-story shops and offices ran along each side,
and Sam realized that inside one of the sunlit windows,

Harland Carstairs was probably sitting at his desk conducting the day's business.

The wagon bypassed the square and proceeded along a path that took them around the backs of the buildings. They stopped at the rear entrance of a cafe, and the driver unloaded a pickle barrel. "I'll just get off here," Sam said.

The driver nodded a silent farewell, climbed back onto the wagon bench, and drove off. Sam cut through an open arcade between two buildings, and searched the numbers on storefronts to locate the attorney. He found the name of Carstairs on a brass plaque with a hand engraved under the address. The index finger on the sign pointed up a narrow set of stairs to the second floor.

Sam gave his name to a matronly secretary, the only employee in the reception area. She had no sooner announced his presence through the interoffice transmitter than the door to the attorney's office opened and Harland came out with a wide grin on his face. "Well, Sam Kelly, are my eyes deceiving me?"

"No, sir, they're not." Sam took Harland's proffered hand.

"Where have you been? I contacted Chilton-Howe, and they knew nothing of your whereabouts after your mother died. I was sorry to hear about that, by the way."

"Thanks. I've been traveling for a while, here and there."

Carstairs put his arm around Sam's shoulder and ushered him into his office. "You're here now, and that's all that matters. I'm pleased that you've come to your senses. Now let's get busy."

Two hours later, when Sam was certain he knew all the important details about the will, he stood up and bade Harland Carstairs good day.

"You're not considering going to Rosemont Manor alone, are you?" the attorney asked. "I think I should go with you just so Frederick and Simon are absolutely clear on your position."

"Thanks just the same, Mr. Carstairs, but I'm sure they're clear enough without you telling them again. Besides, I'd just as soon do this on my own. I'll let you know if I need you."

The attorney patted Sam on the back. "I like your style, young man. I think you'll do okay. You will let me drive you?"

"If it's not far, I'll walk. All I need from you is directions."

"That's easy enough. If it makes you feel any better, I think you're equal to the challenge, Sam. Just head east out of the village and then cut north on Sawbuck Road. Rosemont Manor is only a half mile from the junction."

Sam picked up his suitcase and left the office. Before he had reached the outer office door, Carstairs's secretary responded to her employer's buzz. She neglected to close the door when she went in to see Harland, and Sam heard the attorney's muttered remark. "Miss Merriweather, I feel like I've just led an innocent lamb to slaughter."

Chapter Ten

It was late afternoon when Sam stood at the gate to Rosemont Manor. The house was huge, and so architecturally impressive that it *almost* lived up to the impossibly lavish descriptions Sam had heard from his mother for so many years. Situated on top of an expansive rise, the mansion sprawled across the tree-covered summit. Three stories of multipaned windows built to a central turret that dominated the structure likened it to an English castle. Magnificent broad-leaved trees on the hilltop flanked the house on each side. Perfectly manicured shrubs and evergreens cut in geometrical shapes dressed the drive and front lawn.

Sam opened the wrought-iron gate and entered the property. He estimated that the house was at least three hundred yards from the gate, all of it uphill, and he trudged up the drive, hearing the white gravel crunch under his heavy boots. When he reached the double entrance door, he drew a deep breath and raised a lion's-head knocker.

A middle-aged butler in a spotless black suit and

starched white shirt answered after only one knock. "May I help you?" he asked stiffly, but not unkindly.

"Yes. My name is Samuel Kelly. I've come to see Mr. Rosemont."

"Mr. Frederick or Mr. Simon?"

"I'm not sure," Sam answered. "Both, I would expect."

"Unfortunately neither is home at the moment. Have you tried the factory?"

"No, I haven't. I was hoping that I could wait until they return."

The butler lowered his gaze from Sam's face and fixed it on the suitcase he held. "Is this a business matter, Mr. Kelly? Are you seeking employment?"

Sam smiled. "No, nothing like that. May I come in?"

After several seconds of silent debate, the butler opened the door wide enough for Sam to enter the foyer. Then the man crossed to a set of pocket doors at the side of the hall and motioned for Sam to follow him. After sliding one of the portals along its well-oiled runner, he said, "You'll be more comfortable in here, Mr. Kelly." He pointed to the worn satchel, which had once belonged to Reverend James Chadwick and now dangled from Sam's hand. "Allow me, sir."

Sam relinquished his suitcase and the butler exited, pulling the door closed behind him. Sam examined his surroundings. Never in all his life had he seen furnishings like those in the Rosemont drawing room. Even the richly appointed administrative offices at Chilton-Howe paled in comparison with the showy trappings of Victorian opulence that fed Sam's gaze.

Though he'd seen photos of proper Victorian rooms, Sam knew very little about furniture, a fact that had both amused and perplexed him since he'd made his decision to investigate the opportunities at the House of Rosemont. But he knew at once that he didn't care for the furnishings of his father's parlor. The huge room provided seating for two dozen people, yet there didn't appear to be any chair that invited a guest to actually sit.

Sam viewed each piece of furniture with an eye to which part of the body it was most likely to offend. A pair of low open-ended sofas with carved fretwork backs looked punishing to the spine. Four straight-backed throne chairs had wide wooden arms that ended in open-mouthed lions' heads with ivory teeth protruding exactly where one's fingertips would most likely rest. An ornate chaise next to one of the three fireplaces might have been tempting, but the mahogany neck of a ridiculous-looking swan arched at a sharp angle right where a sitter would hope to put his own neck. And scattered about the room were fragile-looking wicker chairs and ottomans that Sam couldn't imagine supported more than ten pounds. He decided to stand.

The other pieces in the room were far more decorative than utilitarian. Massive cabinets, sideboards, and étagères, with more ornamentation than storage capabilities, filled nearly every available wall space not relegated to heavy damask draperies and dark, foreboding European art. Sam raised his brows in skeptical amusement as he realized he might very well be standing in the middle of a life-sized House of Rosemont catalogue!

The drawing room door opened with a quiet hiss, and the butler joined Sam once more, his fastidious dress and demeanor making him an appropriate addition to the grandiose setting. He carried a silver tea set, which he put on a serving table. Sam watched the butler's practiced hands moving over the teapot and cups until he became aware that someone else had entered the room. A female clad entirely in black moved across the floor with a subtle swish of satin until she stood just a few feet away from him.

She was tall and thin and stood still as a fence post.

Her gray hair was pulled severely away from a hollow, angular face. Dark shadows under pale gray eyes stood out against the sharp plane of prominent chalk-white cheekbones. Her colorless lips were pinched into a tight circle. Tiny lines radiated from the edges, making her mouth resemble a child's drawing of a sunburst.

She never relaxed the white-knuckled ball her hands made at her waistline as she peered at Sam through eyes that condemned him with a piercing glare. "So you're Moira Kelly's son." It was more an accusation than a statement.

"Yes, ma'am, I am."

"We thought you'd come, though with the passage of time we rather hoped you wouldn't."

"Sorry to disappoint you, whoever you are," Sam responded with a purposely impertinent grin.

The woman pursed her lips even tighter while she narrowed her eyes like a hunter scoping his prey through his rifle sight. Her white neck stretched up from her stiff black satin collar. "I am Delilah Rosemont," she announced as if it were a title and not just a name. "Tobias Rosemont's widow, and the mother of his sons."

Sam felt his temperature begin to rise, and he balled his fists at his sides. The slow simmer must have been evident in the color of his face, because the butler discreetly stepped between him and Mrs. Rosemont. "Shall I serve the tea now, madam?" he asked, his voice the essence of cool rationality.

Delilah fluttered her hand in the air and nodded. Then she leveled her stern gaze on Sam once more. "I want to make something absolutely clear to you. Though it is true that you were the only . . . *mistake* my husband produced, you should know that Moira Kelly was certainly not the only dalliance he pursued during his lifetime. You don't believe for a moment that Tobias Rosemont felt anything other than the most primal instincts for your mother, do you?''

Without realizing he was doing so, Sam accepted a serving of tea from the butler. The delicate teacup rattled on its saucer in Sam's trembling hand. It was the only sound in the cavernous room until he spoke moments later. ''Not that it's any of your business what I believe, but the truth is that I don't give a damn what Tobias Rosemont felt about anything. I'm here today, as you know, because of a bequest revealed to me by Harland Carstairs. And unless it directly relates to the execution of the will, I would prefer it if I never heard your husband's name.''

''Tea, madam?'' Again the soothing voice of propriety from the vigilant butler.

Delilah took the cup. ''Aren't you just a little concerned that I might fling the contents in Mr. Kelly's face, Kitridge?''

''Yes, indeed, madam. The thought crossed my mind.''

Delilah looked at the butler. A slight slackening of her rigid lips cracked the granite lines of her face, but it was not enough for Sam to believe that blood flowed through her veins instead of ice water. ''You needn't worry, Kitridge. By suggesting that we avoid mentioning my late husband's name, Mr. Kelly and I have discovered one bit of unstable though common ground.''

She turned her gray eyes on Sam again. ''I have already telephoned my sons, Mr. Kelly, and they are on their way home now. I'll leave you alone to gather all your wits about you while you await their arrival. You will find yourself a combatant in a battle of wills, and I should warn you to prepare all your weapons. As the principal spectator, I assure you that I hope you are soundly defeated. Good day to you, Mr. Kelly.''

With a static crackle of her satin skirt, and a clipped order to Kitridge to bring her tea to her sitting room,

Delilah Rosemont flounced from the drawing room followed by the butler carrying his silver tray.

Despite his earlier appraisal of the furnishings in Rosemont Manor, Sam suddenly felt the need to sit. He chose the closest chair, and sank into it, regardless of the wood-carved grapevines that poked into his shoulder blades. *No wonder they don't mind this furniture,* Sam thought. *You have to have some soft edges to notice the hard ones!*

For a half hour, the only sound that kept Sam company was the ticking of a mammoth grandfather clock, which stood between a pair of elaborate French doors leading to the back garden. The tranquillity was abruptly broken just after the Westminster chimes heralded four o'clock. A commotion in the drive drew Sam to the front window, where he saw a carriage approaching at a fast pace. When it reached the main entrance, the coachman pulled hard on the reins to halt the straining horses. The door of the coach was emblazoned with a gilded rose, the same insignia Sam had noticed on much of the parlor furniture.

Rosemont Manor crackled with energy when the brothers arrived home. Sam watched with mounting curiosity as a groom appeared at once to hold the reins while the coachman stepped down and opened the carriage door. Kitridge waited at the entrance, and took the black bowlers and attache cases surrendered by the fashionably dressed gentlemen who stepped down from the phaeton.

Listening through the sliding doors, Sam heard the brothers come inside the house to be greeted by a woman who questioned with obsequious formality whether or not they desired refreshments. And then he heard Kitridge's voice again. This time the butler acted as valet, offering to relieve the Rosemonts of their jackets. The servants were dismissed with curt authority by one of the brothers, and finally Sam's anticipation ended. The drawing room doors were opened, and Tobias Rosemont's other two sons stepped over the threshold.

Sam stood to face his brothers. Nothing was said by either of the Rosemonts, but the austere demeanor of the older man led Sam to believe that he was in command of his slightly built sibling. His eyes, cold and unblinking with determination, spoke volumes about his opinion of Sam and his apparent intentions to finally avail himself of the benefits of the will.

"I am Frederick Rosemont," the older man declared, hooking his thumbs in the slits of his vest. "This is my brother, Simon. It is not necessary to introduce yourself, sir, for we most certainly know who you are."

Sam decided from the start that Frederick Rosemont ruled his empire by intimidation. His large stature and imposing stance no doubt helped him to do this. Bushy sideburns, like thick peach-colored moss, extended half-way down his cheeks from his abundant red hair. An impeccably trimmed carrot-hued chin beard created an air of undeniable authority on his stern face. Like his mother's, Frederick's eyes glinted like molten steel.

Young Simon, whose fair, thin face was unexpectedly etched with lines of anxiety, looked as though he'd spent his entire life trying to catch up with the authoritarian Frederick . . . unsuccessfully. Though nearly six feet tall, the frail-looking Simon stood slightly behind his older brother and was practically lost in Frederick's broad shadow. His wavy blond hair was parted in the middle, as was the style for young gentlemen, and framed his light blue eyes. Unlike his brother, Simon's pale visage was beardless. Sam couldn't help wondering if that was from choice or a lack of material to work with. He felt a slow grin lift the corners of his mouth.

"Do you find something amusing about the situation we find ourselves in, Mr. Kelly?" Frederick asked.

Sam shrugged. "Only slightly so at this point, but I have a feeling that our situation will prove more humorous as the afternoon wears on."

"You have an impudent tongue, don't you?"

"Actually, no," Sam said. "I'm quite respectful unless the occasion demands otherwise."

"I think you'll find that I demand the respect of everyone around me, and I get it—even from the lowliest apprentices trying to work their way up in the House of Rosemont. That is why you're here, isn't it? To proceed with the rather stringent working conditions of my father's will?"

"That's exactly why I'm here, and I'm as aware of the conditions in the will as I'm sure you are."

Without taking his eyes off Sam, Frederick spoke to his brother. "Simon, pour us all a brandy. You do drink brandy, don't you, Kelly?"

"Brandy will be fine."

"I remember your mother, Kelly. After all, I was eight years old when she left. She was an excellent maid as I recall. Rather timid but then, that's just the sort of deportment one desires in a servant. How is Moira, by the way?"

The muscles in Sam's jaw clenched, and he suppressed the inclination to throttle Frederick. Instead he responded in a well-gauged threatening tone. "My mother is no concern of yours, and I would appreciate it if you would not defile her name again by bringing it up in this house."

Frederick raised his eyebrows in mock innocence. "I see I've angered you, Kelly. So sorry." He stepped forward and handed Sam a glass of brandy. "I won't mention her again. Why don't you sit down so you can enjoy your drink. Simon, join us, won't you?"

Sam sat on one side of a large marble coffee table, and the Rosemont brothers sat on the other, the lines of offense clearly drawn. Frederick crossed his legs and sat back in his chair. "Let's get down to business, shall we? It seems that the three of us are locked in by that damnable will, but we should get a few things straight from the start." He leveled a challenging glare at Sam. "Exactly what do you know about Gothic and Renaissance Revival furniture, Kelly?"

"Only that I'm probably sitting on it."

An indulgent smile tilted Frederick's mouth. "Right you are. The House of Rosemont employs five highly skilled European craftsmen to design its furniture, which is highly sought after by the finest families in Pennsylvania and beyond. We then hire twenty loggers to cut down the trees to make it, fifteen men to cut the logs, and forty to build the furniture. The days are long and the work is hard. The most grueling part is probably the sawmill. You realize that's where you'll start, don't you, Kelly?"

"That's what I was told, and it's fine with me." He tried to find a more comfortable position in the throne-like chair he was sitting in. "Since I really don't care much for the finished product, I'd just as soon work with the lumber."

Frederick's bushy red eyebrows climbed up his forehead. "Shame on you, Kelly. I hope Father didn't hear that. He was a big man, and we'd certainly feel the ground rumble if he rolled over in his grave. But since we're agreed on the essentials of this plan, I'll have Kitridge arrange transportation for you to the mill each morning."

Apparently finished with their conversation, Frederick rose from his chair and walked to a sideboard to set his glass down. He turned back to Sam before leaving the room and asked, "Do you have a place to stay, Kelly?"

"Not yet."

"We'll put you up here while you're working for us. You'll have to find other facilities, however, if you decide to remain in Fox Hill. Rosemont Manor was left to my mother. It would be her decision to invite you for an extended stay." He raised an eyebrow at Sam. "I don't expect that to happen."

"Nor do I, but I'm sure your temporary hospitality will be acceptable," Sam said, rising to stay at eye level with Frederick.

"Fine. Simon, take Kelly to the pantry and find Kitridge. He can accompany our guest to the carriage house. There's a cozy little room in the attic, Kelly. You'll be comfortable there. You can take your meals in the kitchen. Good afternoon."

Simon stood up and waited for his brother to leave the room. Then he walked over to Sam.

As far as Sam could remember, the younger Rosemont hadn't said a word since arriving home. Sam looked at him and grinned with sarcasm. "A big-hearted man, your brother. Nice of him to offer the attic room, unless of course he has an ulterior motive—like to keep an eye on me."

"I wouldn't know," Simon said dryly.

"Oh, I'll bet you do, and you're just not telling me. I've got a hunch that genuine cordiality doesn't run in this family."

"Frederick can be downright charming when he wants to be," Simon stated. "Well, come with me. I'll take you to Kitridge."

Sam trailed behind Simon until they reached the hall-way. Then he maneuvered to walk abreast of him. "Tell me something, Simon," he said. "You haven't said much. I suppose you're about as happy to have me here as the disagreeable Frederick is."

"My brother speaks for me most of the time."

"I see. I don't imagine anyone has considered that there could be some advantages to having me on board. Lessening of the work for everyone? Introduction of fresh ideas? More free time for you two fellas to pursue leisure activities? You do have lives outside of the House of

Rosemont, don't you? You both seem like such happy, congenial sorts.''

They entered the kitchen, and Simon faced Sam. His bland expression gave Sam no clue as to what he was thinking.

''I don't guess I believe that there are *any* advantages having you here,'' Simon said. ''Especially since Frederick doesn't seem to find any. As for me, I just don't think it's fair.''

Now we're getting somewhere, Sam thought. ''What's not fair?''

''You never even knew him. I lived under his roof all my life, did his bidding, listened to his complaints, tried endlessly to please him, never knowing till after he died that it couldn't be done.'' A darkness clouded Simon's eyes, and his voice was tinged with bitterness. ''I've earned my share of the House of Rosemont. You got one third handed to you, and you never did any penance at all.''

Sam could have laughed out loud, but he didn't. Simon truly believed that he alone had a monopoly on misery. ''There are different kinds of penance, Simon,'' Sam explained. ''If you knew anything about me, you'd know that I paid for being his son . . . maybe more than you did.''

Simon's gaze remained on Sam's face, but his focus seemed to be far away, in the darkest recesses of his mind, on a memory perhaps. ''I don't see how. Like I said, I've earned my share. I might even say I've earned yours too.''

The butler came in from the pantry and observed both men. ''Can I be of some assistance, gentlemen?''

''Yes, Kitridge,'' Simon answered. ''Frederick has determined that Kelly can stay in the carriage house. You're to take him there and see that he takes his meals with you.''

"Yes, sir, right away." Simon strode out of the kitchen without another word, and Kitridge smiled faintly . . . the first smile that Sam had seen alter the staid demeanor of the Rosemont's butler. "I'll get your bag, Mr. Kelly. And might I say, welcome to sunny Rosemont Manor, sir."

Sam put his hand on the butler's arm. "Have they always been such a brooding lot, Kitridge—even before the old man died?"

"Quite, sir. To my knowledge, brooding is inherited genetically from Rosemont family ancestors. If I may be so bold as to admit hearing gossip, Mr. Samuel . . . now that I know who you are, I understand you might be in line to inherit some of it yourself."

"Not me, Kitridge. My mother was Irish. Even one lucky shamrock in a man's family tree banishes all the grim foreboding of a dozen dark English castles!"

Chapter Eleven

The first week of July brought near-perfect conditions for the crop that had been planted on Chadwick Farm in the last few months. The days were sunny and dry, while many evenings the sky opened up and gifted the earth with cool, nurturing rain. One warm afternoon when Sam had been gone ten days, Melissa Mitchum's small one-horse buckboard appeared over the rise. Abby saw her friend wave and came from the field to meet her.

"Abby!" Melissa called. "I've brought a letter for you."

They met in front of the house. Abby took the envelope Melissa held out to her. "I picked this up at Purcell's. It's from Sam," Melissa said. "Why you ever let that fine-lookin' man get far enough away to have to write a letter I'll never know. A woman's got to keep a firm grip on her man if she wants to keep him in line."

The envelope shook in Abby's hand. "Thanks for bringing this by, Melissa."

"First one you've got?" Melissa asked. Abby nodded.

''Well, then, I'll just be on my way since I know you're anxious to start reading.''

Abby tore her gaze from the bold clear handwriting on the envelope. Melissa was absolutely right. All she wanted to do was read the letter. ''You don't have to go, Melissa,'' she said halfheartedly. ''Let me get you some lemonade.''

''Thanks anyway, but I've got Jacob asleep in the back, and I want to take advantage of the solitude driving home. Besides, you've got a 'Please don't stay, Melissa' look in your eyes. I'll leave you alone, and someday you can let me know what was in that letter.''

''I will. We'll have a good long talk soon.''

Melissa turned her wagon around and headed away. Abby sat on the front steps and leaned against the porch rail. She fanned her face with Sam's letter, letting her anticipation grow while she imagined what it contained. A letter from Sam . . . proof that he hadn't gone away and forgotten about them. She looked at her name, Mrs. Abigail Kelly, written in Sam's educated script, and eagerly opened the envelope flap.

Dear Abby,

I'm sorry for the time it has taken for you to hear from me. As you'll be able to tell, I've written bits and pieces each day I've been here, and now I'm sending them all at once.

First of all, I'm fine and I hope the same is true for all of you at Chadwick Farm. I miss you all—Timothy and Thomas's endless questions and games, Susanna's good-natured attempt to control her brothers and sisters, Angel's quiet gentleness, and Will's bold footsteps into manhood. And, of course, Miss Elizabeth's infectious giggle, which I think I hear at least twenty times a day carried on a breeze from the west.

I think of the children through the long afternoons,

*and visions of them keep the loneliness away. I
believe more than ever that we did the right thing.
I hope you still feel the same.*

*Did I mention that I miss you, Abby, most of all?
Images of you come not just in the daytime, but at
night as well. I see your face in the oddest places—
in the sunflowers by the road, in the glow of the full
moon, and in the sun on my windowpane. I chuckle
as I read this because it appears I think of you with
the soul of a poet.*

*The time is passing so slowly; yet I stubbornly
count the hours and days until I can come home.*

"What is it, Miss Abby? Is it a letter from Sam?"

Abby looked up when she realized Susanna was talking
to her. She wondered that she could even hear the girl's
chatter over the thrumming of her own heartbeat. "Yes,
it's from Sam," she said, making room for Susanna on
the step. "Sit down and I'll read it to you. He says he
misses you . . . all of us terribly."

*My job is going very well. I'm working in a saw-
mill, and the men I've met are helpful and fair. I'm
here about ten hours a day, and when I go back to
my room I'm often too tired to do much more than
have supper and go to bed. The money is good, as
you can see from the banknote enclosed.*

Abby felt in the envelope and pulled out a crisp document from a bank in Fox Hill, Pennsylvania. Sixty dollars!
She stared at the figure for a full minute before she allowed
herself to believe that it was actually such a large amount.

"You look happy, Miss Abby," Susanna said. "It must
be an awful lot of money."

"It's not a king's ransom, Susanna, but it'll do to get
that barn started when Sam comes home."

"And buy some rock candy at Purcell's?"

Abby shrugged, giving in easily. "That too, I suppose."

"What else does Sam say?"

There is one thing about working in the sawmill that I think would break your heart, Abby. There are boys barely older than Susanna laboring as long as the men. They work as millmen's assistants, dust blowers, and sawyers, and their chances of losing a finger or a hand are almost as great as for the cutters.

They're a good bunch of boys. They hoot along with the screech of the circular saws when they hit a knot, and when the dust piles grow big enough, they climb on top and flap their arms like wild crows, squawking at the tops of their lungs. It's comforting to know that they're still little boys inside, though it grieves me to see them work so hard and receive so little pay for their families.

Susanna had giggled at Sam's description of the boys, but her face grew indignant when she heard of their unjust treatment. "Sam must do something to help those boys, Miss Abby. He would never let something like that happen to us."

"No, he wouldn't, but those boys are not his children. I'm sure he would like to help them if he could. But listen, the next part of Sam's note is much better."

I live in a small room above the carriage house belonging to some very rich people. I say the room is small. Actually it makes me wish for the expanse of the necessary room at Chadwick Farm! I can lie in my bed, which is very comfortable by the way, and nearly touch the wall on both sides of me. But

I have two large windows that I open at night, and the breeze is fresh and cool.

I also have a wood desk which must be about the size of those at the Seneca School. When I sit in the chair, my knees chase my chin, but you can see that the desk works properly because I'm writing this letter at it right now.

You needn't worry about what I'm eating. Though my meals are not nearly so good as yours, Abby, I make do with the bland, simple fare of my wealthy landlords. Actually, their larder makes Ernest Sholski's evening meal look like the vittles of a pauper! Thankfully the cook here is generous about letting me use her kitchen and partake of the leftovers.

My thoughts are always on coming back to all of you. Please tell the children they are all in my prayers, and tell Angel that I'm grateful to her for helping me to open communications with God. I think, now, that He listens to me sometimes.

My fondest dreams are of you, dearest Abby. I long to be with you and start our life together.

Sam

Without reading the last lines of Sam's letter aloud, Abby folded it carefully and slipped it back into the envelope. "Well, I guess we needn't worry so much about Sam anymore," she said. "It seems he's doing quite well."

"I'm going to tell the others about Sam's letter, Miss Abby, and I'm going to tell them you read it to me first!"

Susanna bounded down the stairs, but Abby stopped her before she could brag to her siblings. "You know what, Susanna? I don't feel like working anymore today, how about you?"

The joy of adventure shone in Susanna's eyes, and

Abby knew her triumph over hearing the letter first was forgotten in favor of a possible escapade. "What do you feel like doing, Miss Abby?" she asked.

"I'm suddenly in a very lighthearted mood, and I'd like to do something fun. I know what! Let's ask Will to watch the boys so we girls can go down to the Little White Tail and swim. Would you like that?"

"Oh, I would! I'll get Lizzie and tell Angel."

Ten minutes later, the girls of Chadwick Farm ran through the apple orchard to the banks of the river. They stripped to their camisoles and bloomers and jumped into the cool, refreshing water. They swam and splashed each other and squealed with delight until they all climbed out, laughing, onto the grassy bank.

Tucker Brandywine crouched behind the bushes that grew thick in the moist soil along the Little White Tail. He parted the branches that obscured his view and peered at the women who had just come out of the water. They were smiling and teasing each other, and their mellow womanly voices crept through his veins like warm syrup. He squinted to better see the delectable curves of the two older women. Their bodies were outlined by the clinging fabric of their wet undergarments. He was close enough to see droplets of water on their chests and firm breasts pressed against soaked cotton.

"Gall dang that half-witted Emma!" he muttered under his breath. "I could tan her hide for running off like she done without a thought for my well-bein'. I'm beginnin' to miss that child somethin' awful."

The girl with the pale hair picked up the baby and held her over her head so the child could pluck a maple leaf. The simple gesture emphasized the budding peaks of the girl's supple young body. She twirled the laughing baby around and around in a teasing dance that fed Tucker's hungry stare. *That 'un's about Emma's age,* he thought. He tugged at the material between his legs where his trousers had suddenly grown tight and uncomfortable.

The repositioning did not provide the relief he craved, and he began fumbling with the buttons on the front of his pants. All the while he kept watching, letting his imagination feed his lust while he abandoned all caution. He emitted a low animal-like growl that had been building inside him. Startled by his own voice, he leveled his gaze on the face of the woman, the one they had called Abby in church. She had dared to challenge him that Sunday, and for that reason, and others, he had not forgotten her.

A look of horror suddenly appeared on her face, and her startled gaze scanned the brush where he hid. She snapped orders to the girls, and they grabbed their dresses and bonnets. She picked up the baby and ran behind the others toward the apple orchard.

Staying low to the ground, Tucker bolted from the river as fast as his awkward posture allowed, but he was a good distance away before he was convinced that the woman hadn't set the hounds after him.

For as long as Abby could remember, Leland Madison's family had operated the gristmill on the Cuyahoga River, and Wednesday was always the day the huge millstone was set to grind corn. Therefore, as she did once a month, Abby loaded bushel baskets with shucked corn and drove the buckboard beyond Seneca Village to where the mill was situated in a grove of oak trees on the riverbank. The swift current of the river provided just the right power for the paddle wheel to turn the three thousand pound stone when the miller opened the water gate.

Milling day was a social event for the farmers. Though the wagons began lining up at dawn, no one seemed to mind the wait for his turn at the stone. The women caught up on local gossip, the men smoked cigars and played betting games on the tails of wagons, and during the summertime, the children laughed and played by the side of the road and swam in the river.

Since becoming one of the wedded majority, Abby had found that her standing in the close-knit community had taken a turn for the better. Even Claudia Madison had come out of her office, where she weighed the corn and calculated charges, and congratulated Abby on her nuptials. Word of Abby's marriage had spread quickly, for she answered questions about Sam numerous times.

"I think you'd better bring that husband of yours home soon, Abby," Melissa Mitchum urged. "Otherwise the ol' hens around here will start to think you're a terrible shrew and you ran him off before your marriage even got started!"

Abby laughed. "Let them think what they will. I've had three letters from Sam, and he's determined to stay until we've saved enough money for the barn." With girlish enthusiasm she told Melissa a little about Sam's life in Fox Hill. "He's working in a big furniture factory, and he says that rich people buy what he makes. When he describes the furniture in his letters, it sounds so extraordinary that I can barely imagine it."

"Enough about his letters," Melissa said. "I want to know if you miss your husband."

If you only knew! "Of course I do. In fact, much more than I ever thought I would. Sometimes I find it hard to remember exactly what his voice sounds like or the true color of his eyes. I know it was a nice voice and they were kind, beautiful eyes, and his face, which I remember clearly, was the most handsome . . . but the details, they get kind of lost somehow."

Melissa put her hand on her hip, stepped back and gave Abby a teasing appraisal. "Who would ever have thought—Abigail Chadwick as smitten as a lovesick calf.''

Abby thought about her friend's declaration and nodded. ''You know, I think you're right. And Melissa, I do want him to come home. I know when winter sets in I'll be glad he's built that barn, but right now when the weather's mild and the flowers he bought me are blooming, it's hard to believe that a stupid barn's all that important.''

A baby began to fuss several wagons down the row, and Melissa strained to see where the noise was coming from. ''There's Jake waving me to come back. Little Jacob must need me.'' She gave Abby's hand a gentle squeeze. ''It'll all turn out right in the end, my friend,'' she said. ''You just have faith.''

After Melissa had gone, Abby looked up at the sky and remembered when her father had said those same words. ''Are you putting words in people's mouths now, Papa?'' She was smiling when she picked Lizzie up from the back of the buckboard where she had been playing in a mound of spilled corn. ''Look at you, messy child,'' she said, wiping Lizzie's hands.

''Nice mornin', ain't it, ma'am?''

Abby whirled around and stared into the dirt-streaked face of Tucker Brandywine. Her breath caught in her throat. ''What are you doing here?''

A grin slashed across his face revealing several brown teeth. ''It's a free road, and I was just havin' me a walk on it. That's okay with you, ain't it?''

''I can't stop you, so why don't you just go on walking, Mr. Brandywine?''

He leaned his elbow on the footrest of Abby's buckboard. ''In due time, Miz, Miz . . . Kelly, ain't it? I heerd you got married to that fella that I suspicion knows somethin' about my sweet Emma.''

''You know very well that Sam knows nothing about

your daughter. I have my own suspicions that you might know a lot more about what happened to her than you're telling. Either that, or Emma just ran off on her own to get away from you!''

The grin on Tucker's face spread, and pushed the dirt deeper into the creases around his lips and nose. ''You've got a right sassy way about you, Miz Kelly. If that husband of yours is any kind of a man, I'll wager that he'll beat that orneriness out of you one day.''

''Then once again you've shown that you don't know anything about my husband. Now go on your way. I'm sure you've got important business down the road.''

He rubbed his chin and appeared thoughtful. ''Naw, can't say that I have. Right now my bizness is tryin' to be neighborly to you. I ain't found this town too friendly since I moved here, and I'm lonely what with Emma off somewheres. It come to my mind that you might be feelin' kinda lonely yourself. I understand Mr. Kelly is over in Pennsylvania.''

''I am not in the least lonely, Mr. Brandywine. I have a houseful of children to keep me company for the brief time that my husband is away.''

''I recall seein' your fine family, ma'am.'' Tucker stood up straight and searched the area around them. When he saw what he was looking for, he pointed his thumb toward a tree some distance away. ''That 'un there's one of yours, ain't she?''

Abby followed his bold stare to where Angel sat against the tree. A long chain of clover rested in her lap and she was twining more slender stems into her handiwork. Just knowing that Tucker Brandywine was watching Angel made Abby sick to her stomach, and she couldn't hide her disgust.

Tucker seemed to enjoy seeing the revulsion on her face. ''She's a purty thing, kinda feather-headed from what I hear, but then a gentle nature's what's important, don't you think, Miz Kelly?'' He reached out to touch Lizzie's curls. ''Just like this little one . . . sweet as can be.''

Abby jerked Lizzie out of his reach, and Tucker laughed, bringing Abby's anger to its boiling point. ''Don't you touch her! And stay away from my family! I saw you the other day at the river, Mr. Brandywine. Don't bother to deny it. You were watching us.'' Abby clutched Lizzie fiercely to her chest. ''Don't you ever set foot on my property again, I'm warning you!''

Her threat only heightened his amusement, and he raised his eyebrows in mock horror. ''You're scarin' me, Miz Kelly, and that's not a bit neighborly. I was just about to ask if I could come to supper sometime. With Emma gone I ain't been eatin' too regular . . . not that she was ever much of a cook.'' He leaned close to Abby, and she turned her face away from his leering grin. ''What d'ya say, Miz Kelly? Could I come to Sunday supper?''

Abby was trembling so violently that she had to lean against the wagon to steady herself.

''We've got to move up, Miss Abby,'' Will said, coming around the back of the wagon. ''We're about to lose our place . . .'' Will's gaze froze on Tucker, and he took a menacing step toward him and demanded, ''What do you want?''

Although slighter in frame than Tucker, Will was almost as tall, and Tucker backed away from him. ''Just talkin', boy, that's all. Nothin' more.''

Will stared at Tucker's face and asked, ''Are you all right, Miss Abby?''

''Yes, Will, but I think Mr. Brandywine should move on now.'' If there was ever a time for Will's hotheadedness to take over, this was it, and short of allowing a downright brawl, Abby decided to let him take charge.

Will planted his feet far apart and leaned into Tucker.

"You heard her. Go on and get outta here! And don't you ever come near any of my family again!"

"I'm goin'. I didn't cause no harm, boy." Tucker touched the brim of his worn hat and bowed clumsily. "Good day to you, ma'am." Then he ambled down the road, passing the other wagons without stopping.

When he'd gone, Abby expelled the breath that she didn't even realize she'd been holding. She fought off a strange dizziness. "That man gives me the creeps, Will."

She wasn't prepared for the vindictiveness she saw in Will's dark eyes. He screwed his face into a mask of loathing and clenched his fists at his sides. "I hate him, Miss Abby. I hate him so bad I could kill him."

She could only stare at him as he climbed into the wagon, picked up the reins, and moved the mules forward in the line.

Two evenings later, Will paced around the interior of the cave known as Lucy Cameron's Kitchen, though he'd come to think of the cave now as, simply, Emma's. He was feeling anxious, and he knew Emma could tell.

"What's tormentin' you, Will? You're actin' as nervous as a cat on a lily pad." She was munching on a fried chicken leg he had brought her, and she licked her fingers with a wet, sucking sound.

He stopped pacing and looked at her. "I don't know how long you can go on livin' here, Emma."

The drumstick halted halfway to her mouth, and Emma stared at him. "Are you throwin' me out, Will?"

"No, of course I'm not. But it just isn't right you stayin' here all the time. What if you got sick or somethin' and I didn't get to come for a few days? What if an animal crawled in here some night and scared you? Or some person? What would you do then?"

She gave him a playful grin and pulled a chunk of dark

meat off the chicken leg. "If that's all that's eatin' you, Will, you can just stop your bellyachin'. Look at me. Since I met you I musta put on a good five pounds. I'm as fit as I've been in my whole life. And there ain't a critter on earth that I'm scared of, leastways not a four-legged one. And as for the two-legged kind, there's only one o' them that frights me, and he ain't likely to stumble on this place."

Will stooped down to be at eye level with her. "That's where you could be wrong. It's time to stop pretendin', Emma. I know you're scared of your daddy. I think I figured out why, and if you don't want to tell me, that's okay. But how do you know he won't find you here? You forget, I've seen him, and he's as mean and shifty-eyed as any man I've ever come across."

She shrugged her shoulders. "He's mean, all right, but I'll tell you one thing. He ain't never took a step he didn't have to, and that surely means he won't go traipsin' down this gully." She nodded once with determination. "No, sir, I ain't never gonna see Tucker Brandywine here, Will."

He snorted with exasperation. "I'm just talkin' possibilities, Emma! Anything's possible. It tears me up to think about that plug-ugly snake layin' his hands on you. I'm tryin' to do what's right for you ... protect you, and I can't do it by leavin' you here on your own day and night."

Emma put the chicken bone on the dirt beside her and wiped her fingers on her shirt tail. Then she put her tiny hands on Will's. "Don't you know nothin', Will Buckman? You've protected me better 'n anybody in my life has done. I never felt safe for one whole day till I found this place and met you. Look what I got now ... a clean place to sleep, three changes of clothes, a full belly, a little oven that makes drop-biscuits, and every so often a glass a' cold milk. If I wasn't lookin' into your face right now, Will, I'd swear you was Father Christmas.''

He wanted to stay stern and act like an adult, but he couldn't help himself. Emma always made him smile. ''You make it darned hard to argue with you,'' he said.

''Then don't.''

She stood up and walked around the cave, which had changed considerably from the first time Will had found her there. It was almost as if she took pride in her granite house. Her clothes were always clean and neatly folded, her crude utensils washed and stacked by the oven.

And Emma herself—that was the biggest change of all. She'd already used up two bars of soap, and her hair was always neatly plaited and tied with one of Susanna's discarded ribbons. Her face and hands were clean and she smelled as good as Abby or Angel. What had once been hard and rough and spiteful was now soft and kind and trusting, and every time he saw Emma, Will was more proud of her and happier to be with her. She was just about all he thought of, and when two or three days went by and he didn't see her, he missed her sorely.

He went to her and held her arms. ''Someday you've got to come back on top,'' he told her. ''You know you do.''

''Someday I will . . . as long as you go with me. I know that in the end I'll prob'ly do what you tell me, but for now I think I'll just stay here and have you come see me when you can. You're the best friend I ever had, Will . . . or even fancied havin'. God strike me dead if I don't mean that.''

Her blue eyes sparkled in her delicate little face, and when Will put his big hands on her cheeks, she gave him a smile so broad that it touched both his palms. He thought she was beautiful. ''Emma, can I kiss you?''

She didn't back away, but her smile faded. ''No, Will, you can't.''

He dropped his hands. "Why not?"

" 'Cause it's my rule, never to be broke. Ain't nobody ever gonna kiss me 'cause it's just too personal a thing. I swore long ago that if any man tried to kiss me, I'd bite his tongue off."

"Emma! Why don't you like kissin'?"

"Don't know if I like it or not. I ain't never tried it. Folks have tried it on me, but I always turn my head before their lips land. I can't see why I should let a body put his lips on my mouth and drop spit down my throat. That's why you can't kiss me, Will."

He shook his head sagely. "I think you're missin' out on somethin' good. I kissed a girl once, a couple of times even. She wasn't nearly as pretty as you, but it made me know that kissin' was pure enjoyment."

"You're a big liar, Will!"

"I am not! Kissin' is fun."

"Not about that, you big dope. About the part that she wasn't as pretty as me."

It took him a moment, but Will finally laughed out loud. "I got to bring you a lookin' glass, girl. You got to see for yourself. You're darn pretty, Emma, and if you ever came out of this cave, there'd be a whole lot of people who'd tell you so, me most of all."

She regarded him through narrowed eyes. "You really mean that?"

"Well, of course I do."

"Then, maybe, just *maybe,* but only 'cause it's you, we might try kissin' sometime. I ain't makin' no promises, though."

He grinned at her. "No promises, that's okay. I'm goin' now, but I'll see you in a day or so."

He had already started climbing the rocks to the surface of the gorge when she called him back. "I changed my mind. I want to try it now."

With one giant leap he hit the ground again and went

to her. Placing his hands on her waist, he raised her to her toes. Her eyes were wide and luminous, but she didn't look afraid. When he lowered his head, he saw her lids slip down over her eyes just before he closed his own and his mouth touched hers.

Her lips were rigid at first, but as he pressed down, they became more pliant and yielding. After a few seconds, Will raised his head. He knew the kiss could have been better, but, oh, what promise it held!

An impish grin met his eyes when he looked down at her. "You really make me mad, Will Buckman," she said.

"Why?"

" 'Cause you're most often right about everything! Now get outta here and leave me be."

He was still smiling when he crested the top of the gorge and walked along the bank of the river toward home.

There was a feeling of optimism on Chadwick Farm during the first week of August. Abby's bank account had been increasing steadily, and Sam had indicated in his letters that he would be home in plenty of time to build their barn. "Just a few more weeks," he'd promised, and Abby anticipated his homecoming with an excitement that was unlike any feeling she'd ever had before.

It began as a gentle stirring, a pleasing quiver, deep inside her, and flowed through her bloodstream to tingle every responsive nerve. Sam wrote over and over that he couldn't wait to come home, and Abby realized with a sense of pure joy that she felt the same way.

No one had seen Tucker Brandywine since the incident at the gristmill, and Abby believed that he had heeded her warning. Even if he were still in Seneca Township, he had obviously decided to leave her family alone.

It was with renewed hope that everyone's attention turned to school again. All the children needed clothes, and Abby decided to go into Cuyahoga Falls and buy yards of flannel and linsey-woolsey for the boys and colorful cotton ginghams and prints for the girls. Each child would have at least one new hand-sewn outfit when school started.

It took several hours to make the journey beyond Seneca Village to the larger town, and Abby planned to make an outing of it. The four younger children were eager to go with her and enjoy the store-bought sweets she promised them. Since such luxuries had never appealed to Angel, she elected to stay home and tend to chores around the farm. Still cautious about leaving any of her brood home alone, Abby extracted a pledge from Will that he would stay with Angel until the rest of the family returned.

Abby loaded a picnic basket on the back of the buckboard, and Susanna climbed on the driver's seat next to her. The twins and Lizzie settled into the back and they left the farmhouse, waving good-bye to Angel and Will.

Will began his chores, but with no one to watch over him, he found it hard to keep his interest on his work. He hadn't seen Emma in three days, and he was anxious to know she was all right. With the sun warming his back and a cool breeze floating through the apple orchard from the Little White Tail, his thoughts kept returning to the cave in the gorge. He finally gave up the futile attempt to weed the family's vegetable garden and went in search of Angel. He found her inside mending a pair of Timothy's pants.

She looked up at him and smiled. "Do you want something, Will?"

"Yeah, I do. I was wonderin' if you'd be okay here by yourself for a little while, just a couple of hours. I've got an errand to run."

"Of course I will. You go on. I'm going to see to Miss

Abby's flowers in a little while. I thought I'd cut some of the earliest bloomers while they still have such lovely color and bring them inside to add a little cheer to the kitchen. I think God meant for us to bring the beauty of nature into our lives whenever we can, don't you?"

"I don't know, Angel," he said impatiently. He wondered for the thousandth time why she never answered a question with a simple yes or no. With Angel, everything she said had to come packaged in a sermon. "I'll be back soon," he told her, and darted from the house before she could trap him into listening to any more of her chatter. He had an important goal on his mind. *This could be the day I finally convince Emma to come back here with me,* he thought.

From behind the largest tree in the apple orchard, Tucker Brandywine watched Will exit the house and lope over the rise away from the farm. He waited a while longer to see if anyone else came out of the house. Seeing no one, and noting the absence of the buckboard, he decided with a satisfied snicker that he had indeed picked a lucky day to pay a visit on Chadwick Farm.

Life hadn't been treating Tucker kindly. The coins he'd made from the few odd jobs he'd picked up had run out, and he was plagued daily with a discouraging rumble in his belly. "Since you won't be neighborly to ol' Tucker like you ought, Miz Kelly, I'll just take what I need to survive."

He lumbered across the yard to the back corner of the house. From that vantage point he could see plump tomatoes bending on vines, and pepper, onion, and carrot plants tempting him from the vegetable garden. He flattened his back against the outside wall of the house and slid to an open kitchen window. Looking in, he saw a loaf of freshly baked bread on the table. The door to the pantry was open, and he imagined what tempting goodies were there for the taking. And it certainly looked like there was no one to stand in his way of grabbing all he could get.

He was just about to go around the corner of the house and enter through the rear when he heard the front door open. *Damn! I don't want to tangle with that contrary Miz Kelly again. Or worse, suppose her husband picked now to show up!*

Tucker scooted along the wall to the front corner of the house, and stopped when he heard someone come down the porch steps. When he peeked around to size up the obstacle to his success, his lips curled up in pure delight.

"Why, this day's gettin' better all the time," he muttered. "It looks like they done left the addle-brained one here by herself. I have a hunch I can get my belly full and an aggravatin' itch scratched at the same time."

Chapter Twelve

The one they called Angel knelt by the flowers in front of the house and touched several of the blooms. A strange little smile was on her face, a smile that Tucker believed was a sure sign of her slow-wittedness. She went to a lean-to with a wood-slat roof that was nailed to a large willow tree in the side yard. Tucker waited until she was inside before he followed her.

He looked into the opening of the shed where crates and assorted farm tools leaned against the tree. A plywood wall closed the structure in from the rear, which meant there was only one way out, and he was blocking it.

Angel's back was to him, and she was looking through an assortment of hand tools. She selected the ones she wanted and put them in a basket. Though little light came through the spaces between the wood slats, Tucker watched her for a while with his arm propped against the shed entrance. He didn't need light to remember what the girl looked like when she came out of the river that day nearly a month ago. He could still see the sun on her pale, damp hair and her wet clothes pressed against her slender young body. And he didn't need light to appreciate the girl today. Her long hair streamed down her back, and she tempted him with her youth, feeding an immediate and intense arousal.

"Good day to you, purty miss," he said, grinning in anticipation of her surprise.

She gasped and spun around, but the shock on her face lasted only a moment, and was replaced with the same puzzling smile that seemed to be a mark of her character. "Oh, hello," she said. "I didn't know anyone was here."

"Didn't mean to scare you none," Tucker said.

"It's all right. I just had my mind on my chores and wasn't paying much attention, I guess." She cocked her head to the side and peered closely at him in the dim light as if she were trying to clear away the cobwebs in her brain and find a place for Tucker's face. "Do I know you?"

"I seen ya a time or two," he said. "Your name's 'Angel,' ain't it?" She nodded. "That's a right purty name for a bee-ootiful gal."

Her smile broadened. "Do you really think so? Will thinks it's stupid. Truth is, it's just a made-up name, and the only one who ever liked it much was Papa James." Her eyes glowed when she said his name. "He's a real angel, you know."

"I heerd he passed on. Terrible shame."

"Are you a friend of Papa James?"

Tucker thought about answering truthfully, but he figured a lie was likely to get him a lot farther with this girl. "Oh, James and I go way back. We was friends when we was no more 'n tykes runnin' around in britches. Fact is he told me to come round here and check on things."

Angel's face brightened with delight. "Then you see him too?"

"How's that?"

"Since he died . . . You see him in visions like I do?"

Tucker's grin spread all the way across his face. This was going to be so easy. "All the time," he said. "Why, he just come to me the other day and told me to look in on you . . . you 'specially, more than the others. He must a' had a powerful love for you, gal."

"He loved all of us, not me more than the others. But I think he knows how much I love him."

Tucker ducked his head and came all the way into the shed. The girl watched his movements and accepted his presence as though he ought to be there. She didn't back away or show any of the disgust that so many people did when he got too close. *If this don't beat all,* Tucker thought. *This girl is as trustin' as a moth flittin' around a flame . . . and just about as smart. Well, come on over here, little moth, and feel my fire!*

"Tell me somethin', purty angel," he said, looking down at her. "Did my ol' friend James ever kiss you?"

"In February he did."

"What d'ya mean?"

"It was my birthday, and we had a party. Miss Abby baked a cake and gave me a sweater she knitted herself, and Papa James gave me a Bible with a saying in it that he wrote himself. Then he kissed me right here." She touched her index finger on her forehead, and Tucker nearly laughed out loud.

"Why, that ain't no kind of a kiss," he chortled. "Didn't he ever kiss you straight on the mouth where a girl purty as you ought to be kissed?"

Angel's brows drew together in thought, and a wrinkle appeared on her forehead. For the first time, Tucker saw a flicker of confusion in her eyes. He'd started her thinkin', all right.

"You mean like Sam kissed Miss Abby at the train station?" she finally asked. "Like married people do?"

"That's right. Didn't James ever do you that way?"

"Papa James would never do that. We weren't like Sam and Miss Abby. That's another kind of love."

Tucker got down on his haunches to better see into her eyes. "Girl, I think the time has come for ol' Tucker to show you what kissin's all about. I think Papa James is lookin' down from the hereafter and wantin' you to learn. You're fully growed and ripe as a peach, gal."

He grabbed for her arm, but she shrugged away from him. "What's the matter, Angel? Are you shy?" he asked, giving her his biggest grin.

A strange look came over her face. It wasn't fear, exactly. But the poor, muddleheaded creature was perplexed plenty, as if she'd just decided that maybe he shouldn't be trusted. She stood up and reached for her basket of garden tools. "I don't think I want you to do that," she said. "And I don't think Papa James would want you to either."

She tried to walk around Tucker, but he thrust his arm out to stop her. He noticed the first sign of fright when she spoke. Her voice was soft and weak and quivered like a fiddle string. "Please excuse me. I have my chores to do."

He stood up so his large frame filled the narrow opening to the shed. He certainly didn't want her running out into the yard. His legs weren't so good anymore, and chances were he wouldn't be able to catch her if she took off. "Your chores are to make me feel welcome, ain't they, gal? Ain't I a guest here?"

He kept his arm at the level of her chest, and she pushed against it. When he wouldn't give way, the strangest little whimper came from her throat, like the mewling of a wounded cat. Tucker moved his head from side to side, smacking his lips and chasing her mouth with his. She kept turning away from him. "Come on, little angel," he pretended to beg, "just one kiss for ol' Tucker."

There was raw fear in her eyes now, and in the trembling of her lips as she tried to bite down on them. She was shivering so much that even the pale, springy hair around her face danced to a tune of panic. "Let me go outside," she pleaded, gasping for air. "Please let me out of here."

"I'll let you go, just as soon as you're nice to me."

Her choking cries filled the shed, and Tucker groaned in disgust. "Quit your bawlin'. You sound like a boot-kicked puppy. I ain't gonna hurt ya. I just want to have a little fun with ya. I wager you'll like it if you give me half a chance."

He put his hands on her shoulders and pushed down until her knees buckled under her. "Wh . . . what are you doing?" she sobbed.

"We can't have no fun standin' here like a couple a' scarecrows. I'm just layin' you down so's we can have a go at this."

"You're . . . you're going to hurt me, I know you are."

Pushing her the rest of the way to the ground, Tucker placed his hands in the dirt on either side of her face and leaned over her. "No, I ain't. I told you that. You are the most simpleminded gal I ever seen. If you just be still, you won't find nothin' hurtful a'tall."

She pushed against his chest, but Tucker wasn't about to let her get away. He put his weight on his knees and lowered his head, pressing his mouth on hers. Her lips were misshapen because he'd caught them in a scream, but Tucker didn't care. He kept kissing her. It felt so damn good to taste a woman again.

She wriggled underneath him, and he sat back on his heels, stilling her with his bulk. Then he moved his hands over her clothing remembering what shapes lay beneath. A moan tore from his throat as he kneaded one small breast.

Then the scream that he had silenced with his mouth rent the air. She followed it with wails of terror and such pitiful pleadings that Tucker couldn't ignore them. She was going to ruin this for him if he didn't stop her. Even though he knew there was no one on the farm, he couldn't let her go on screaming. There might be someone on the road who'd hear her and come running. "You got to stop that caterwaulin', gal," he said, his voice husky and strained. Instead of obeying him, she only hollered louder, thrashing her head from side to side.

"I told you to stop that," he ground out between clenched teeth. "As worthless as she was, my Emma never once . . ." He bit off his own sentence and stared at the writhing girl beneath him. "But you ain't my Emma, now are ya? I got to learn you a whole new set a' rules." He closed his big hand around her throat and squeezed, just enough to close off her air passage and stop that awful wailing.

Her cries stilled to shuddering, silent sobs. She gasped for the little air he allowed into her lungs, and he sighed with relief that the horrible noise had stopped.

Then suddenly, the strangest thing happened. All the fear disappeared from her eyes as a gray veil settled over them, leaving only dull, colorless orbs to stare at his face. She stopped moving and just looked at him with a blank pair of holes where her frightened eyes had been. But she was quiet . . . almost too quiet. Tucker raised his hand from her throat. "That's the way to be, little angel," he said warily, his eyes fixed on the lifeless stare.

Still straddling her, he managed to unfasten his buttons and pull his trousers down his thighs. He next fumbled with the tiny buttons on her dress, his big fingers awkward and clumsy. He gave up after a moment and rent the fabric, sending the buttons scattering to the ground. All the while she kept looking up at him, dry-eyed, not blinking, not crying, just looking.

He shrugged off an eerie dread that had come over him, threatening to spoil his plans. "Oh, no, you don't,

gal. You ain't gonna spook me with your crazy eyes."
He continued his work until a strange muttering, low and
even, came from her barely moving lips.

"The devil walks among us. Save me, Papa James.
The devil walks among us. Smite him down, Papa James.
The devil walks among us . . ."

Tucker jumped up from the rigid form, whose only
sign of life was the monotonous mumbling of the lips.
"Don't you put no spells on me, little witch."

"The devil walks among us. Smite him down . . ."

Tucker's palms grew sweaty and the muscles between
his shoulder blades shivered. Grabbing at his loose pants,
he went to the entrance of the shed and looked out. He
scanned the sky, half expecting a bolt of lightning or a
clap of thunder . . . some sign that he was about to be
felled for his sins. Seeing none, he turned around and
narrowed his eyes on Angel. Her neck was showing the
welts he'd left there, her clothes were rumpled and her
hair was spread in the dirt, but still the only part of her
that moved was her lips. "The devil walks among us
. . ."

"Don't be an ol' fool, Tucker Brandywine," he scolded
himself. "This here's about the easiest poke you've ever
had. This half-witted gal can't hurt you." He rubbed a
hand along his chin and chuckled nervously. "Truth is,
this cotton noggin won't even remember what happened
today. You're free as a bird on this 'un." He dropped
his trousers to his ankles and waddled back over to Angel,
determined to get the job done.

Will couldn't believe his good luck. When he first saw
Emma in the cave, he told her his family, all but his sister,
were gone for the day, and asked if she would come back
with him just to see what Chadwick Farm was like. He
promised her that they'd stay off the lane and make their

way through the thickest cover of trees and brush. No one would see her, and she could get a look at where he lived. Then, as soon as she wanted, he'd take her back to the cave. "It's a good place, Emma," he told her. "The people there are real nice, and someday maybe you'll decide you want to live there. Say you'll come with me."

He didn't think she would, but Emma surprised him by saying yes. When they came over the rise to the farm, Will realized that he'd only been gone a little over an hour. Abby wouldn't be back for a long time, and Emma could stay at least through dinner.

As they approached the farmhouse, Emma said, "Won't your sister tell Miz Kelly that I came here today?"

"Don't worry about Angel," he assured her. "I'll make her swear not to tell, and when Angel swears, that's it. She may act a little loony at times, but when she gives her word, you could pluck a silver dollar down that she won't break it."

They reached the porch steps, and Will went up to the front door leaving Emma in the yard. "You stay here till I tell Angel I'm back. If you want, go ahead and have a look around, and I'll come get you in a minute." Before he went inside, he tried to bolster Emma's confidence with a wide grin. It was so good to have her at his home and to know she trusted him enough to come. He wanted her to feel that she belonged. She gave him a little nod and a wave, and he went inside to find Angel.

She wasn't in the parlor where he'd left her, and she wasn't in the kitchen. He looked in Abby's bedroom and, not finding her there, called up the ladder to the loft. He was just about to go out back and see if she was in the vegetable garden or the apple orchard when he heard a howl that froze him where he stood. He couldn't tell if it was a shriek of pain or anger, but it was uttered in fierce desperation, and it came from the direction of the big willow tree.

Will ran through the house, bounded down the front steps, and tore across the yard toward the lean-to. He tried to scream for Emma and Angel, but his breath burned in his lungs. No sound came from his constricted vocal cords, but fear raged in his veins and pounded in his ears.

He hit the entrance to the shed with the force of a locomotive, and only by grasping the tree and the side of the lean-to was he able to stop his forward motion. His head and chest pitched forward, but his booted toes dug into the loose soil of the yard, the only thing that kept him from falling directly onto the body of Tucker Brandywine.

Will's wild stare swept the cramped, dim interior of the lean-to. He tried to piece together the fragments of the grizzly puzzle before him. Emma, trembling violently, stood over her father. Her fingers clawed at her mouth, making her words, if they were words at all, incoherent.

Angel lay in the dirt with her knees drawn up to her chest. Her lips moved, and a low, droning sound came from them that seemed to beat to an inner drum no one else could hear. Her skirt was pulled up to her waist, and she clutched frantically at the open neckline of her dress.

Tucker Brandywine was on his back pinned to the ground by a pitchfork. The handle, with its shiny new bands of metal reinforcements, stuck straight up from his abdomen. Will realized with a sickening churn of his stomach that the prongs were in so deep they were barely visible. Blood streamed down Tucker's bare skin onto the dirt, pulsing in spurts from the four holes in his midsection.

Will choked back the bile that rose to his throat. He gripped the bark of the willow tree until its sharp ridges cut into his palm. "Angel? What's wrong with Angel?"

he cried. But the horrifying clues were all around him, and he knew.

Emma lunged at him and grabbed the front of his shirt. ''I done it, Will. I kilt him. I kilt Tucker.'' Her glassy stare darted to Angel and immediately returned to Will. ''He was about to do to her what he always done to me. I had to stop him.''

Will dropped his arms and teetered on the threshold for a moment, then regained his balance and started toward Angel. Emma refused to let him go. Her fingers held on to his shirt with the force of a bear trap.

''I couldn't let him do it, Will,'' she said. ''I just picked up that pitchfork and said his name real soft, and he turns around and looks at me. He starts to laugh, Will, like he never thought I'd do it. Then he tells me to wait my turn. So I hollered, Will. I hollered so's his ear would burst with rememberin' it. And I stuck him. I stuck him clean through.''

Emma's face turned deathly pale. Her fingers slipped from his shirt, and she sank to the ground. Choking sobs racked her frail body, and she looked up at Will with pleading eyes. ''Tell me I done the right thing, Will, please tell me.''

He bent down and put his arms around her. She hid her face against his shirt and cried. ''Of course you did the right thing, Emma,'' he said, ''the only thing you could a' done.'' He looked over her head to Angel. He had to get his sister inside the house, but right now she didn't seem to know where she was or even that he was there. But Emma did know, and she needed him. ''You saved my sister, Emma. You're a hero.'' He stroked her hair. ''Everything's gonna be all right. Just let me think about what to do now.''

A spasm shook her and she lifted her face. Her eyes were suddenly alert and very frightened. ''Will, I'm gonna go to jail. They're gonna put me in jail for what I done.''

"No, no, Emma. Nobody would put you in jail for killin' that evil snake. Everybody'll thank you most likely, 'specially when they hear what he was about to do to Angel.''

Realizing that Angel was the key to Emma's innocence, Will looked over at her again. She hadn't moved, and was still mumbling words he couldn't understand.

Emma's gaze followed his. "Will, I don't think that girl even remembers what happened. And I'd bet that a month a' Sundays will come and go before she's ever able to tell it. That girl's the most scairt I ever seen anybody be.''

Emma was right. Angel was even worse than when she first came to the farm over a year ago. Her family had lived in the neighboring county in an isolated cabin a long way from any town. Her father had abandoned them, and after scraping out a miserable existence without him for some time, her mother had taken a man into the house to live with them.

Will had heard Papa James tell Miss Abby that the man was mean to Angel, not like Tucker was to Emma, but he was violent and often took his fits of rage out on Angel. She stopped going to school, and no one saw her for months. Then one day her mama and the man just up and left. No one knew where they went, and the county sheriff found Angel, or Rebecca St. John, as she was known then, weeks later, in her cabin with no food left and no one to care for her.

The sheriff wrote Papa James, and he'd gone right away to fetch her. She was skinny and pale, and she never said a word for the longest time until Papa James just gentled her into talking. And since then, Will realized with a rueful smile, she hadn't stopped jabbering about something. But when he looked at her now, he knew she was broken again, and he didn't know what it would take to bring her back this time . . . especially since there was no Papa James to help her.

He went to where she lay and got down on his knees beside her. "Angel, it's me, Will. Are you okay?"

She cried out a protest at his closeness and cowered away from him. She wouldn't look up, just kept mumbling—he could tell now . . . it was something about the devil.

"I got to take you inside, Angel," he said. "I'm gonna put you in Miss Abby's bed. You'll be all right there. You'll feel better, I promise." She was backed up against the willow tree, with nowhere to go, so he just reached out and picked her up as if she was a doll. She whimpered, but he kept talking softly to her until she calmed down a little. He couldn't tell if she knew who he was or not, because her vacant eyes gave no clue as to what was going on in her head.

"I think you're right, Emma," Will said as he left the shed with Angel. "She may not recollect what happened here, but don't worry. I'll make sure you don't go to jail."

"How're you gonna do that?"

"No one'll ever say you killed Tucker if there isn't a body to prove he's dead." Her eyes widened, showing her bewilderment, and Will managed to give her a little half smile. "Just stay here till I get back. Then I'll tell you what we're gonna do."

When Angel finally fell asleep, Will came back to the lean-to. It was well past noon, and he knew Abby would be coming home before too long. He hadn't had much time to think about the trouble he was going to be in when she learned he'd left Angel alone on the farm. But he figured punishing him wouldn't be the most important thing on her mind. She'd be worried about Angel most of all, and he'd already decided to tell her the truth about how Tucker had been there and what he'd almost done to Angel. He'd have to tell her about Emma too, and how she got Tucker with the pitchfork. Blood was everywhere around the shed. But he sure wasn't going to tell anyone that Tucker was dead.

It wasn't easy getting the pitchfork out of Tucker's body, but once he did, Will, with Emma helping him, began the difficult job of moving the body to the Little White Tail. They each took a leg and dragged Tucker across the yard, through the cornfield and the apple orchard. When they reached the riverbank, they covered him with branches and left him for later. They had to bury him, but there was no time now. They had just made it back to the orchard when the buckboard came over the rise toward the house.

"You stay here, Emma," Will said. "I'll come and get you in a while after I've explained some things." He took several steps away from her and looked back over his shoulder as a thought occurred to him. "You're not gonna run, are you, Emma? You're gonna stay, right?"

"You done all this for me, Will, I ain't about to back out on you. I'll be here waitin'."

Abby hadn't even gone in the house when Will began telling his story, and it was as if a terrible nightmare had come true for her. "Tucker Brandywine was here?" A familiar chill crept down her spine, and she shivered. "What happened, Will? Are you all right? Where's Angel?"

The rest of the story tumbled out of his mouth, including the part about him knowing Emma Brandywine for a long time and bringing her to the farm today. When he told Abby about what happened in the shed, her heart pounded with fear, nearly drowning out his words. The chill she'd felt before had become a cold stark terror. "Where is she? Where's Angel?"

"She's in your room, Miss Abby. I know she's gonna be okay."

Though she was aware that Will was talking, she had stopped listening to him. He trailed after her into the house. She ran to the bedroom and halted at the doorway. Could that frail, thin body that hardly made a wrinkle under the coverlet be her beautiful, sweet Angel? She was so pale, so small, so wounded. Abby felt her heart break as if it were a fragile piece of china. She crept across the room on feet that didn't seem to be on solid ground. When Abby sat on the edge of the mattress, Angel opened her eyes. A muffled scream came from her lips and she cringed to the other side of the bed, but Abby took her hand and stroked her fingers.

"It's okay, my angel," she crooned, though her throat burned with the effort to keep from crying. "It's Miss Abby. I'm here." Will stood on the threshold looking lost and hopeless. "Go to the village for the doctor," she told him. "Don't tell anyone what's happened here. Just tell the doctor that Angel's had a fright. Then fetch Melissa for me. Tell her I need her."

When Will had gone, Abby leaned against the headboard of Papa James's big featherbed and stretched out beside Angel. She gathered the girl into her arms, resting Angel's head on her shoulder. It seemed like hours, though it was probably only minutes that Angel lay stiff and trembling in Abby's arms. Over and over again Abby whispered, "Everything will be all right, I promise. No one will hurt you again."

Finally, Angel's body grew slack, and Abby felt her own strength dissolve with the easing of the girl's tension. When she saw tears glistening on Angel's cheeks, Abby cried too. "I'm sorry, Angel, so sorry," she sobbed.

Angel spoke the first words she'd said in hours. "Don't call me Angel anymore. I'm not an angel. I'm just Rebecca—that's all—not an angel."

Abby blinked back fresh tears. "You'll always be an angel to me. You have the sweet, pure soul of one of God's own angels, and I see His light in your eyes every day. No one can ever take that away from you. But I think Rebecca is a beautiful name. It's from the Bible, you know, and I will be proud to call you that."

"You're going to be fine young lady. Stay in bed a few days and rest," the doctor said when he finished examining Rebecca. After he put his instruments back in his bag, he motioned for Abby to precede him out of the bedroom. They went to the parlor, where they could speak candidly. "There's nothing physically wrong with her, Abigail," he said. "But she is so withdrawn ... much like she was when she first came to you. There are some marks on her neck that might indicate a struggle, but she wouldn't tell me how they got there. Has she told you what it was that frightened her?"

"She hasn't said much of anything, Doctor," Abby answered truthfully. "Do you think she'll come out of this?"

"In time I believe she will." He reached for his hat. "I'll be back to check on her in a day or two. In the meantime, if you learn anything that will help us speed her recovery, you'll let me know, won't you?"

"Of course."

Abby accompanied the doctor to the front door and watched him leave. When she came back into the parlor, she sat next to Melissa Mitchum.

"You're not going to tell him, are you?" Melissa asked.

"I can't. It would cause too much gossip and Rebecca would be hurt even more than she is now. You know how people talk about her as it is. Besides, it would be Rebecca's decision to ever tell her story, and I think it will be hard enough for her to finally discuss what happened with *me.*''

At last giving in to exhaustion, Abby leaned against the back of her mother's settee and closed her eyes. She hadn't said anything to Will, but she knew he had been sitting in the parlor waiting for her. The time had come to settle things between them. She kept her eyes closed, and when the room became quiet, she asked, ''Why did you do it, Will? How could you have left her alone?''

His voice was raspy and low, and she had to strain to hear him. ''I'm sorry, Miss Abby. If I could do things over, I would. I was only gone for an hour. I never thought . . .''

His words were broken by a great shuddering sigh, and Abby couldn't stay angry with him. His big heart was shattered by what had happened today. She knew it was. ''Where is Tucker now, Will? Do you have any idea?''

He cleared his throat, and took so long answering that Abby became wary. She opened her eyes and looked at him. ''Will?''

''I don't know where he is now,'' he said. ''This isn't easy to tell you, Miss Abby. It was Emma that found Tucker with Angel in the shed. She's the one that stopped him.''

''How? What did she do?''

He swallowed hard, and Abby saw his Adam's apple bob in his throat. ''She ran a pitchfork through him.''

Abby's stomach clenched, and she bolted upright on the sofa. ''Did she kill him?''

''No. We just let him lay there while we took Angel inside. When we came back, he was gone. The pitchfork was leanin' against the tree. Tucker just ran off, I guess.''

Abby grabbed Melissa's hand. ''I've got to tell the sheriff. Oh, Melissa, I don't want to do that. Rebecca will have to tell what happened. What should I do? Tucker could be dying . . .''

Melissa's calm cool voice broke through Abby's anxiety. "You're not going to do anything, least of all tell the sheriff. How badly do you think the skunk was hurt, Will?"

"Prob'ly not too bad, Mrs. Mitchum. Otherwise how could he have hightailed it like he did? No, I think Tucker's gonna be okay. In fact, if he's got any brains at all, he'll have left Seneca for good."

"That's very possible," Melissa agreed. "You see, Abby, it's likely that Tucker's gone. If you want my advice, be done with it. Let the old dog cower in some hole and lick his wounds. You've got to take care of your family, and do what's best for Rebecca."

Abby nodded. Her friend made sense. No one outside the family need ever know about Rebecca's ordeal today. Suddenly a chilling thought gripped her, and all the good advice in the world wasn't able to chase this new fear away. "What if he's not gone, Melissa? What if Tucker decides to come back?" She thought of the one certain magnet that was likely to draw Tucker back again . . . his daughter. "Where's Emma now, Will?" she asked.

He stood up and went out of the room. In a moment he came back to the parlor, holding the hand of a pale, thin wisp of a girl. "This is Emma, Miss Abby. I told her you might let her stay."

The girl's tiny voice sidestepped all logic and cut a path directly to the core of Abby's emotions. "I won't be no trouble, Miz Kelly. I promise I won't. I can do lots of things . . . carry my weight. I'm sorry as I can be about what happened to Angel. I'll make it up to her for what my pappy done if you'll let me stay."

There were more problems with letting Emma live at Chadwick Farm than Abby cared to think about, but the biggest one was obvious and terrifying. Tucker wanted the girl back, and he'd no doubt stop at nothing to get her. How could Abby feel secure about her family if she suspected that Tucker could be hiding behind any tree on Chadwick Farm?

She might have said no, but she couldn't even imagine the horrors the girl had endured living with Tucker, and for this reason she couldn't turn Emma away. "Of course you can stay, Emma."

Abby looked at her friend and whispered, "This changes things, Melissa. What am I going to do now?"

"I think you know what you have to do."

Abby nodded. "I've got to go get Sam. He's got to come home." Melissa agreed. "Will you and Jake stay here for a couple of days while I go to Pennsylvania?" Abby asked.

"It's done. Now go start packing."

It was well after midnight when Will crept out of the house, met Emma in the yard, and walked with her back to the Little White Tail. Will carried a shovel and Emma carried a lantern. Neither of them talked much. The ghoulish job ahead of them was too heavy on their minds.

When they reached the spot where they'd left Tucker, Will noticed that the branches had been moved. An eerie feeling pressed down on him. He picked through the underbrush while Emma held the light. All he saw was the indentation of a body in the damp soil by the river. Will raised his eyes to Emma at the same time her startled gaze met his. "He's gone, Emma," he croaked. "Tucker's gone."

Chapter Thirteen

Early the next morning Melissa came into Abby's bedroom carrying a hatbox. "Will's brought our buggy around to the front," she said. "Are you ready to go?"

Abby finished tying the bow under her bonnet and checked the belt buckle at the waist of her slim black skirt. "I guess I am. All I have to do is fold my mother's good silk blouse and put it in the valise." She ran her hand over the sleeve of the coarse muslin blouse she was wearing. "I'll change when I get to Pittsburgh. Sam says he's staying with these rich folks, and it wouldn't do to show up in this old thing."

Melissa began folding the silk blouse. "This is so pretty, Abby, and I've got just the thing to go with it." She pointed to the hatbox she'd set beside the bed, and moved it with her toe toward Abby. "Here, take it. My aunt sent it to me from Kingstown. She says it's all the latest rage on the lakes."

Abby lifted the lid and took out a stiff straw hat with

a wide band, a flat top, and a forest-green ribbon around the crown. "What is it?"

"It's called a boater, and it's worn at all the summer regattas back east. It's quite fashionable. Go ahead, take it with you."

Abby set the hat on the bed. "I'm not going to a regatta, Melissa."

Melissa held the hat out to Abby again. "But you are going to see your husband after a month and a half, aren't you? And you told me he lives in a carriage house. Folks wealthy enough to have a carriage house will appreciate seeing you in this boater." A reserved grin played around Melissa's mouth. "And though bonnets are fine for farm life, I'm told women in the cities don't wear them at all anymore."

"Then their faces must be as tough as leather," Abby countered, but she wrapped the hat in its tissue, put it in the box, and slipped the handle over her arm. "Okay, if it makes you happy, I'll take it with me. After all, I'm going to the train station in your buggy. I might as well take your hat!"

Looking over at Rebecca, she said, "Melissa, will you tell Will I'll be out in a minute?" When Melissa left the room, Abby sat on the bed next to Rebecca. "You remember where I'm going, don't you? I told you last night."

Rebecca stared at her, but there was no indication in the girl's dull eyes that she remembered at all. She picked at the threads in the coverlet while Abby talked. "I'm going for Sam, Rebecca. I'm going to bring him home so he can take care of us . . . just like Papa James always did. And you remember what our new friend Emma told us . . . the mean man that hurt you will be plenty scared of Sam. He won't ever come back as long as Sam's here."

Rebecca squinted slightly as if she were trying to understand. Abby patted her hand. "Don't you worry, darling.

Mr. and Mrs. Mitchum are here. They'll watch out for you while I'm gone." She got up and went to the door, but before she crossed the threshold, Rebecca stopped her.

"Miss Abby?"

"Yes?"

"You're coming back, aren't you? You *and* Sam?"

There was such pain in Rebecca's eyes that Abby wished she knew how to make up for all the times people had left her during her short life. But she couldn't. Some heartaches would never be erased. All she could do was try and reassure her now. "I promise you, Rebecca . . . just two days and I'll be back. Okay?"

"Okay."

Abby discovered it wasn't much easier to tell the other children good-bye. Since the little ones had lived with her, they had never seen their caretakers leave with suitcases in hand. After all, when one lived the simple life of a country minister and his daughter, opportunities for travel were indeed rare.

"You mind Mrs. Mitchum now," Abby cautioned the twins. "I shall miss you very much, and when I come home, I will expect Melissa to tell me what good boys you've been."

Susanna interrupted with a solemn pledge to keep the boys under control. "You needn't worry, Miss Abby," she said. "I will watch them carefully and not allow them to misbehave."

Abby smiled. "I know you'll help, Susanna, but remember that you still need some watching too."

"Let's go, Miss Abby, or you'll miss the train!" Will called from the buggy.

She quickly hugged each of the children, handed Lizzie to Emma, and climbed up next to Will. It was hard to believe that when the train left the depot and headed east, she'd be following Sam's trail away from Chadwick Farm.

* * *

When the locomotive reached a moderate, steady speed, the big wheels clattered away with mind-numbing monotony. Having nothing to occupy her time, Abby allowed her thoughts to wander. She contemplated the details of her journey—what she would do when she reached Pittsburgh, and how she would contact the man whose name and address were tucked into her satchel.

She hoped she wouldn't have any trouble finding Harland Carstairs. She had consulted an atlas before she left home, and knew that Fox Hill was a small village north of the city. That should make locating one of its citizens relatively easy.

Casting aside her doubts concerning Carstairs, Abby concentrated on what was most important to her—seeing Sam again. Three emotions warred for dominance within her. First there was the pressing need to locate Sam and persuade him to come home. She had to convince him that whatever amount of money he had saved, in addition to what he had sent her, had to be enough. Even if they had to settle for a slightly smaller barn, made of slightly cheaper materials, they would have to do that. She and the children needed Sam at home.

Next Abby pondered the future that she and Sam would have together, and she prayed that this future hadn't been jeopardized by their separation. Sam's letters indicated that returning to her was nearly all he thought about, but was he being completely honest?

What if he had decided that he preferred the civilized atmosphere of town to the isolated monotony of the farm? What if being around the wealthy people where he lived had made him want to be among them again? What if he had decided that he missed the academic life and wanted to return to it, finding the cultured realm of Chilton-Howe more appealing than the mundane labors of Chadwick

Farm? These possibilities eroded Abby's peace of mind and threatened the life she envisioned building with Sam.

Once again she pushed her doubts to the back of her mind. What she really wanted to think about was the imminent delight of seeing Sam again. She conjured up an image of his face as easily as if he were sitting beside her, and she was awed that he could be so quickly and thoroughly recalled to mind. Many times through the long weeks, she had visualized his dear, handsome face the way it had looked hovering above hers for the instant after their quick, passionate kiss at the depot.

She remembered his soft, touchable hair settling on his forehead in the afternoon breeze. A half smile had tilted his full lips. It was a smile that she knew was meant to inspire her trust, but instead it fired a longing she never thought she possessed. And she could still see his charcoal eyes—intent upon delivering a promise to his new wife and yet sad as if he had already begun missing her.

Thinking of Sam this way, Abby vowed that she would persuade him to come home. She leaned her head against the window of the train and caught glimpses of the stars lying still on an ebony blanket, and realized with a quick, strong shudder that she could hardly contain her desire to be with her husband again.

It was barely dawn when the train pulled into the Pittsburgh station and jolted Abby from a fitful doze. She stood up and stretched her back muscles, relieving the tension from trying to sleep in an uncomfortable position. Then she retrieved her valise from the overhead compartment, exited the train, and made her way to the depot.

She passed among a small gathering of early morning travelers and went to the street entrance of the station. Looking out the front door, she spied a cafe on the other side of the awakening thoroughfare. It was a small establishment but appeared well kept, and the cheerful lights in the windows were inviting.

She freshened up in the ladies' lounge of the train station and changed into her good blouse. She would have coffee and a light breakfast in the cafe and inquire about hiring a cab to take her to Fox Hill and Harland Carstairs.

After she'd eaten breakfast and tidied her hair, Abby felt refreshed and ready to undertake the last leg of her journey. She procured a cab from among many lined up in front of the train station at eight o'clock. Having been assured by the driver that they would be in Fox Hill by noon, she settled back in the comfortable seat and watched the activity of the bustling city outside her window.

If all went as planned, she and Sam would return to the depot this afternoon. They would take the night train back to Akron, and Abby would keep her promise to Rebecca to be at Chadwick Farm in two days' time. If all went as planned ... She wouldn't allow herself to imagine any other possibility.

Sam arrived at the Rosemont Furniture Manufacturing Plant shortly before eight o'clock, and noticed that a crowd had gathered outside the company gates for the third morning in a row. Today, however, the numbers of workers assembled had swelled to well over four dozen. He now knew most of the men by face and name, and had established a growing rapport with many of them.

Rosemont employees, or ''the boys'' as they were called, knew Sam's tenuous position in the company hierarchy, and knew too that he was out of favor with ''the brothers.'' That, and the fact that Sam worked alongside them, had made him an equal in the factory brotherhood.

As he maneuvered among the crowd, Sam clearly heard the booming voice of Mike Fogarty carrying over the heads of the workers with vitality and persuasiveness.

Every eye was on Fogarty's swarthy face, and every ear seemed tuned to his fervent message.

" 'Mornin', Kelly." Gifford McIlvaine whispered his greeting while his gaze remained intent on the speaker who stood on a wooden crate several yards in front of him. "I'll say this for the sorry sot—he's a persistent mick by anyone's standards." In his gruff Scottish accent, McIlvaine hinted at a genuine respect for the fiery-talking Irishman.

"Have you seen the Pinkertons yet this morning?" Sam asked.

"No, but you know the brothers . . . I've a hunch the hired guards have been told to go for Fogarty's throat this time and not let him off with a warnin'. I'm sorry to say this about your own kith and kin, Sam, but Frederick's a mean bastard, and he'll not let this go on for long."

Sam nodded in agreement, but was unable to dwell on the likely unpleasant result of Fogarty's bold appearance again at Rosemont. He, like the others, was soon caught up in the orator's dynamic rhetoric.

"And how many of you will go into work this morning and find your jobs have been taken over by foreigners or convicts—men willing to work for any wage at all? Talk to your brethren in the city mills. They'll tell ya it happens every day . . . that American men go home jobless to face a cryin' wife and the hungry faces of their little ones."

Fogarty suspended a quivering fist in the air, and his intense green eyes scanned the visages of every man assembled. "By God, friends, it could happen here, and you could be starin' right into the face of starvation and misery. And even if you do keep your jobs, you're hardly a sight better off, now are ya? Your wages are pitiful, and the conditions in your factory so deplorable, you're lucky if you go home at night with all your fingers."

He brought his fist down and clasped his hands together

over his chest, prayer-like. "And what about the little children—the boys barely out of grade school comin' to the factory and the sawmill every day, doin' the dirty work of the brothers, just to bring home a few miserable pennies to ease their mamas' sufferin'. Is this what you want for some poor bloke's tads—to bow and scrape for the likes of the Rosemonts?"

A resounding "no" echoed through the throng, and Fogarty adjusted his stance. He leaned forward from his waist, hands on hips, bringing his face closer to the attentive workers. "A fair deal is all Mr. Samuel Gompers is offerin' you, men. An honest deal for yourselves and your families. I'm only the voice of Mr. Gompers. The message is his, and he's tellin' you to unite with us against the oppressors. Otherwise you stand alone, and the fight will surely be lost."

Gifford McIlvaine screwed his face up with cynicism. "A fat lot of good unitin' will do, Kelly. That's where Fogarty's all wet. We've been united for twenty years and it's done us no good at all."

Fogarty began pacing within the limited confines of his crude dais, and his next words struck at the heart of Gifford's beliefs. "I know what you're thinkin'. You're a cabinetmaker, and the cabinetmakers' union is a grand and glorious institution befitting a noble occupation. And it *was,* my friends, it surely was for many years, but it's outlived its usefulness in today's world of capitalist aggressors.

"The laboring man has been trodden down by the capitalists for so many years that he can't see a way out of the depths of poverty and despair." Fogarty stopped pacing and pointed his index finger at his chest. "I'll show you the way out, my friends. Samuel Gompers will show you the way and the path is the American Federation of Labor!

"Under the leadership of Mr. Gompers, our numbers

now total in the thousands. We have secured firm contracts for our members, with wage increases, the abolishment of child labor, and improved working conditions. The AFL, my friends, is the only way to meet the needs of America's labor force, and we're doing it every day!''

Pounding his beefy fist into his palm, Fogarty drove his final point home. ''We have the power to strike. We can bring the Rosemonts and the entire country to a stand-still to get what is just and fair for the American working-man!''

A commotion on the road leading to the factory drew Sam's attention away from the mesmerizing Mike Fogarty. Nearly three dozen Pinkerton detectives had climbed out of open wagons and were advancing on the crowd. Their only weapons were stout clubs, but it was enough to part the wary throng and allow the detectives to swarm on Fogarty's makeshift stage.

Still shouting his threats and promises, Mike was pulled away from the crowd and dragged to one of the wagons. Most of the Rosemont workers backed away from the melee; however, several of the men shouted bold warnings to the Pinkertons.

''Leave him be!''

''This is America! You can't drag a man off for speaking his mind!''

One of the detectives came forward and shouted above the protests. ''Get to work! Orders from Mr. Rosemont! Any man who's late will forfeit his wages for half a day!''

Any notions of a fair deal and a secure future were quickly overshadowed by the very real threat of diminishing wages. The men grudgingly dispersed and headed for the factory gates. Sam lingered behind and approached the detective.

''I'm Sam Kelly, Frederick Rosemont's half brother.'' He inclined his head toward the still-struggling and blustering Mike Fogarty. "What are you going to do with him?"

The detective eyed Sam for a moment before apparently deciding there was no harm in telling the truth. "Just haul him a good ten miles out of the village for now." He gave Fogarty a menacing look that would have made most men cringe. Fogarty only growled back like an angry dog. "But if he ever shows his face again, the brothers have vowed to teach him a lesson he won't soon forget."

An angry fist shot into the air from the wagon as a partially bound Fogarty hollered, "You're in league with the bastard oppressors, and you'll fall just as they will. This isn't over, not by a long shot!"

"Take him away," the detective ordered, and the wagon lurched forward. Fogarty's epithets were soon lost in the wind and dust.

Sam walked through the gates, and was met by Gifford McIlvaine. "So what d'ya think, Kelly? You're closest to them—the brothers, that is. Do you suppose they're giving Fogarty an ear? What will all this mean?"

"Come on now, Giff, I've told you more than once. I'm not close at all to my brothers, and they'll tell you the same thing. I'm here to serve my three months, and then I'm hoping to make a deal with Frederick to get out with my dignity still intact. But I'll tell you what I think this means, and that's trouble."

Gifford rubbed his chin. "That man Fogarty makes some kind of sense to me, Sam."

"He makes sense to a lot of people, and Samuel Gompers has organized hundreds of local trade unions into his federation. It's the wave of the future, I suspect, for all of us—join forces for change or flounder alone."

"But the brothers, they'll never go for it, will they?"

"Not without a fight, Giff, and that's what scares me. You can't stop the voices of the Mike Fogartys of the world, and you can't change the minds of the Rosemonts.

It all boils down to who can push the hardest and carry the biggest sticks.''

"If the brothers won't listen to Fogarty, Sam, you got to talk to them. You got to make them see reason.''

Though what Gifford suggested seemed like an impossibility, Sam had become a believer in miracles. "I'll try, Giff, I'll try.''

McIlvaine put his hand on Sam's shoulder and walked with him to the factory door. "We got faith in you, Kelly. All the boys have.''

When he entered the factory, Sam tried harder than he ever had to block out the whirring of routers and sanders and sewing machines, the acrid smell of varnish and wood glue and the stench of sweat. He longed more than ever to breathe in the fresh, earthy scents of soil and plant and animal. And the clean fragrance of castile soap on just-washed skin and hair. He'd do what he could to help the boys in the time he had left, but he longed for Abby, and he wanted to go home. There were still almost six weeks to go.

Abby decided the village of Fox Hill looked like a picture in a magazine, or the cover of one of the Christmas cards she received from relatives in Connecticut. The town square was perfect in its charm and symmetry, and invited a guest to stop and rest on one of the benches bordering the plush green lawn. It was nice to realize that Sam had been living in such a pleasant little town.

The people who crisscrossed the square and entered and left the brick buildings completed the quaint tableau. Ladies in ribboned and ruffled dresses and feathered hats strolled leisurely along the sidewalks. Men in starched pin-striped shirts or three-piece vested suits carried canes and tipped their bowlers in well-mannered greetings.

Abby despaired of her own simple attire, wishing that

her blouse had the ballooning leg-o'-mutton sleeves that were all the rage, but grateful that at least the material was the finest quality. She was suddenly thankful that Melissa had talked her into bringing the flat boater, which now sat atop her head.

''Here's the address, miss,'' the cab driver said, pulling up in front of a two-story building.

Abby took a few precious coins from her reticule and gave them to the driver. She stepped down from the cab and saw the name of Harland Carstairs on the plaque leading to the stairwell. She drew a deep breath. *This is it,* she thought. One step closer to Sam.

The driver had kept his word and delivered her to Fox Hill by midday, but Abby hadn't counted on the office being closed for dinner. She muttered her disappointment when she tried the locked office door, but decided it was a good time for her to take her noon meal anyway.

After buying a boxed lunch at a cafe, she sat in the square and watched the sights around her. She took special notice of the men who walked across the grass, imagining that any of the tall, lean ones could possibly be Sam. Though she felt sure she could tell his strong, confident stride from far away, whenever she saw a man in the distance who even resembled Sam's stature, her heart beat a little faster, and her sandwich became a little more difficult to swallow.

When the clock tower sounded one o'clock, Abby sighed with relief that she had something to do again. She headed back to the lawyer's office and this time, the door was not locked.

A pleasant-looking woman looked up from her desk and smiled at Abby. ''May I help you?''

''Yes, I've come to see Mr. Carstairs. Is he in?''

''He's due back any moment. Do you have an appointment?''

''No, I'm sorry. My plans to come to Fox Hill today

were rather sudden, and I didn't have a chance to wire ahead.''

"That's unfortunate. Mr. Carstairs has several engagements today, and I'm afraid he won't have time to meet with you. Will you be in town tomorrow?''

"No, I must see him today. I don't need much of his time. I only want to ask him for some information. You see he's a friend of my husband's . . .''

The woman picked up her pen and poised her hand over a piece of paper. ''May I ask your husband's name?''

"Certainly. Samuel Kelly. I'm Abigail Kelly.''

The efficient secretary suddenly dropped her pen and stared across the desk at Abby.

"I sent several letters to my husband over the last few weeks to this address,'' Abby explained. ''Do you remember receiving them?''

"Yes, of course I remember the correspondence. Mr. Kelly does pick his mail up here, but naturally I don't know who it is from.'' The secretary came around her desk and stood in front of Abby. ''I apologize for my abruptness a minute ago, Mrs. Kelly, but I . . . *we* had no idea Sam was married.''

Before Abby could respond, the office door opened and a large, well-dressed gentleman came in. He nodded a hasty acknowledgment in Abby's direction and spoke to the woman. ''Miss Merriweather, I'll need my briefs on the Hathaway case. Bring them to my office as soon as possible.''

He brushed by the women, but stopped when Miss Merriweather suddenly announced, ''Mr. Carstairs, this young lady would like a word with you. She's Abigail Kelly, that's *Mrs. Samuel Kelly.*''

Carstairs spun around as efficiently as his considerable bulk would allow and leveled his gaze on Abby. ''Mrs. Samuel Kelly?''

"Yes, sir.''

The shock on his face mutated to amused interest as a grin caused the waxed ends of his handlebar mustache to curl even tighter. "How long have you been Mrs. Samuel Kelly, my dear?"

"Just six weeks."

The grin broadened, and he muttered, "Just *traveling here and there,* eh, Sam?" Then, as if suddenly remembering his manners, Carstairs swept his arm gallantly toward his office. "Do come in, Mrs. Kelly. I think I can spare a few moments. Some tea, if you please, Miss Merriweather."

Abby preceded him into the office and sat down. She didn't wait for him to occupy his desk chair before revealing the importance of her visit. "I need to get in touch with Sam, Mr. Carstairs, and he told me I could contact him through your address. That's why I've come. Apparently Sam neglected to tell you about me, and I'm sorry for surprising you."

She tried to keep a mounting resentment from showing in her voice. Why hadn't Sam mentioned his family to this good friend? Was he ashamed of them?

"Well, yes, you have come as a surprise, Mrs. Kelly, but Sam is nothing if not secretive, wouldn't you say?"

That was certainly true, but Abby hated admitting that she too had been kept in the dark about much of Sam's life. She shrugged off Harland's question and returned to her reason for coming. "Will you tell me where Sam is? I really haven't much time."

"Of course. I wish I could take you there myself, but it's not possible. I will arrange for your transportation, however."

"Is it far?"

"His brother's house? No, not far at all. Though it's likely Sam will be at the factory at this time of day."

A hum of confusion droned inside Abby's ears. She felt lightheaded and alarmed at the same time. What had

Carstairs said? *His brother's house?* "Where did you say
Sam is staying?" she asked.

"At his brother's, of course. I wondered why your
letters hadn't gone directly to Rosemont Manor, but then,
knowing Frederick, perhaps that was wise . . ." Harland
bit off the end of his sentence, and his eyes widened with
bewilderment. "You *do* know of Frederick and Simon,
don't you?"

Abby clasped her hands together to keep them from
trembling. "I . . . I . . . can't really say . . ."

"Oh, dear," Harland mumbled. "Well, let me procure
a cab for you, Mrs. Kelly. You may as well get started.
I have a feeling this is going to be an eye-opening afternoon for you." He darted from his office with surprising
alacrity. "Miss Merriweather!" he bellowed. "Hail a
coach!"

When Harland took her to the cab, Abby asked the
one question that had been haunting her since she met
Carstairs, and its significance had grown considerably in
the last few revealing minutes. "Mr. Carstairs, you must
tell me one thing. Are you really a longtime friend of my
husband's as he told me, or has he need of your services
as an attorney?"

The question obviously made Carstairs uncomfortable.
He cleared his throat as seconds ticked by. "I am definitely
a friend of Sam's, Mrs. Kelly," he finally said. "I'm
quite fond of him. And as for how long . . . well, friendship
cannot be measured by time, now can it?" His puffy
cheeks colored a deep crimson. "In my heart, Mrs. Kelly,
I feel like I've known Sam forever."

He hastened to grab her elbow and assist her into the
cab, then barked the directions to the driver. They were
pulling away from the curb before Abby had a chance to
challenge the attorney for not answering her question in
its entirety.

Chapter Fourteen

Once the driver turned on Sawbuck Road, the hire cab went past many fine residences, but none of them was as grand as the impressive Tudor, which looked very much like a castle. The tall iron fence, sloping lawn, and sprawling mansion caught Abby's eye before the carriage slowed in front of the formidable gates.

It can't be, she thought, refusing to consider that this estate was the place Sam had been staying—his brother's house, as Carstairs had said. "Why are we stopping here?" she asked hesitantly.

" 'Cause we're where the lawyer told me to take you, ma'am." The driver jumped down and opened the gates, which were emblazoned with a gold rose. The word *Rosemont* was inscribed in metal above it. When he drove inside the grounds, he remarked, "I've never had a call to bring a fare here before. This place is a treat for the eyes, all right."

Abby was too spellbound to respond. She had never seen such grandeur before. The house was far beyond anything she had ever imagined. It was difficult to fathom how many rooms existed behind the dozens of windows or how much luxury could be found within the brick walls.

The driver stopped at the foot of a slate stone stairway leading to a pair of lacquered walnut doors. Abby stepped down from the cab and adjusted the boater so it sat perfectly level on her head.

"Shall I wait, ma'am?" the driver asked.

"I . . . I don't know." After a close scrutiny of the massive entrance, and a tug on the lion's-head knocker, Abby was quaking. What little confidence she'd managed to gain on the drive over slipped away. "Perhaps you'd better stay a moment," she finally said.

The door was answered promptly by a distinguished-looking gentleman in a meticulous black suit. He smiled at her. "Yes, miss?"

"I'm here to see Mr. Kelly, Sam Kelly," she said. Then, to avoid any embarrassing conclusion the man might draw, she quickly added, "I'm his wife."

The smile on the man's face twinkled in his eyes. "His wife? What a surprise. Master Samuel is married . . . I had no idea."

Master Samuel? Abby feared that her answering smile must have been as tilted as her entire center of gravity at the moment. Why was this man referring to her husband as if he were an aristocrat? And if everyone she'd met so far knew Sam as well as they seemed to, then why did no one know of her role in his life? She was becoming quite distressed at being a surprise to everyone with whom she came in contact.

"Do come in, Mrs. Kelly," he said. Then he stepped outside to the waiting cab. "Shall I dismiss the coach, madam?"

Since this man was much more in control than Abby, she left the decision up to him. "If you think that's wise.

I suppose if I need to get back to the village Sam can take me.''

''Of course.'' A brisk, authoritative wave sent the cab crunching over the gravel away from the house. When he came back inside, the man dutifully returned to her side. ''Is Master Samuel expecting you, Mrs. Kelly?''

''No, I didn't have time to notify him that I was coming. I hope that's not a problem.''

''I should certainly think not, madam. Have you traveled far?''

''I left Ohio yesterday and came by train.'' As soon as she thought about what she'd said, Abby concluded that it seemed as if several days had passed, not just one. ''It feels like longer ago than that actually,'' she admitted to this man whose demeanor was kind.

He nodded sympathetically. ''Traveling can take a toll, as well I know. May I show you into the drawing room and offer some refreshments? Master Samuel should be home before too long.''

''That would be lovely, thank you, Mr. . . .''

''Just Kitridge, madam. That will do.'' He bowed slightly from the waist. ''I'm the Rosemont butler. Shall I bring you some tea?''

This day was becoming more extraordinary as the minutes ticked by, but at least Abby was at ease around the agreeable Kitridge. ''Tea will be just fine,'' she said.

When he left, Kitridge closed the pocket doors halfway, leaving Abby a glimpse of the entryway she'd just passed through. It was certainly well-appointed, but not nearly as extravagant as the formal parlor she was in now. She was admiring the ornate and no-doubt expensive trinkets that adorned the room when she heard movement in the hall.

She glanced up to see a tall, severe-looking woman peering through the doors at her. The woman's face was set in a stern mask, and without displaying any obvious reaction to Abby, she turned abruptly from the doorway and apparently ran into Kitridge returning with the tea.

"Pardon me, madam," Abby heard the butler say.

"Who is that woman?" The question was delivered in harsh, clipped tones. "If she's come for the scullery position, why in heaven's name have you shown her to the drawing room? Remove her to the kitchen at once!"

"I can't do that, madam," Kitridge responded in a gruff whisper, "because, you see, she's not a servant at all, but Sam Kelly's wife!"

"His wife?" came the shrill response. "No one told me he had a wife! Why didn't someone tell me Sam Kelly was married?"

"I assume that no one knew, Mrs. Rosemont."

A feeling of dread snaked down Abby's spine. Though the butler had been accommodating, she definitely sensed that she was not a welcome guest in the Rosemont house. *Sam Kelly,* she thought, *I have a horrible feeling that all your secrets are about to come tumbling down on top of my head as if the bricks of this mansion were shaken from their foundation!*

She gripped the arms of the chair she was sitting in to wait for what the woman would say next. One thing was clear—Mrs. Rosemont was doing an extremely poor job of concealing her opinions. But then, she probably rarely had to.

"She's nothing but a rustic, Kitridge, and certainly has no place in my home. Why, she's as much a peasant as Moira Kelly was!"

Kitridge must have been blocking the woman's entry to the drawing room, because she spoke crossly to him. "Get out of my way. I'm going to ask her to leave and settle this matter once and for all before Sam Kelly surprises us with more of his country kinsmen!"

Abby rose from her seat, propelled by a fit of temper that this haughty woman could so easily dismiss her as unworthy. *After all, I am Sam's wife,* Abby said to herself, *though it appears the dubious honor carries little respect around here!* She prepared to meet the ill-mannered matron of Rosemont Manor face-to-face.

A confrontation between the two women was forestalled, however, and the doors to the drawing room remained partially closed. Kitridge diplomatically suggested to the woman that she call her sons before acting hastily. Abby heard a disgruntled *har-umph* followed by the rustle of stiff skirts as Mrs. Rosemont traipsed down the hall. Seconds later, the butler entered alone.

Abby waited until Kitridge set his tray down and looked at her. By that time, she had calmed herself enough to speak without biting his head off. After all, the butler might very well prove to be her only ally in the house. "I'm not usually in the habit of eavesdropping," she said, "but I found it impossible not to hear the conversation in the hallway."

"That was most unfortunate, madam," Kitridge said. "I'm afraid the mistress of Rosemont Manor is in a bit of a snit due to your arrival."

"She's in a *bit of a snit,* like this is a *bit of a house,"* Abby responded.

"Yes, well, not to be a prophet of doom, but I should warn you to consider her reaction as the calm before the storm." He poured a cup of tea and handed her the cup and saucer. "I'll see that you're left alone for now, madam, and I will telephone the factory and suggest that Master Samuel find the quickest means here." With another courteous bow and a hesitant grin, Kitridge left the drawing room.

Abby did not have to wait long before a carriage arrived at the manor, followed by several sets of firm footsteps resounding through the hallway to the drawing room. A tall man with a full crop of coarse red hair slid back the door and entered the room. He was accompanied by a slightly built fair man and Mrs. Rosemont. Abby rose, clasped her hands at her waist, and waited for one of them to speak.

The red-haired man spoke first, without any regard to initial pleasantries. "I'm Frederick Rosemont," he said, as if his name were descended from kings. "And just exactly who are we supposed to believe you are?"

You pompous, arrogant . . . Any number of fitting labels ran through Abby's mind. She had no reservations about letting this man know she didn't like his attitude. Before she could explode with the tart reply that sat on the tip of her tongue, Kitridge slipped inside the doorway and stood against a wall. He stayed clearly in her line of vision and cast her a warning look.

She clamped her lips shut in deference to the one person in this house she felt she could trust. Kitridge sent her a thin smile of encouragement. *All right,* she thought. *I'll mind my manners—for now.*

"I'm Abigail Kelly, Sam's wife," she responded in a controlled voice.

Mrs. Rosemont bristled like an angry mama bird. "See, Frederick, I told you . . ."

"Just a moment, Mother," Frederick said, holding his hand up to silence her. He glared at Abby with cold, penetrating eyes. "How very interesting, *Mrs. Kelly,*" he ground out. "Considering that Sam never mentioned that he even *had* a wife."

Here we go again! Once more Abby didn't exist to this gathering of strangers, and she was beginning to wonder if she existed to her own husband! "I don't know why he didn't, Mr. Rosemont, but I assure you that he does indeed have one."

"Why have you come here?" Frederick asked.

"Isn't it obvious?" Mrs. Rosemont exclaimed without

giving Abby a chance to respond. "When are we ever going to be free of the curse of that damnable will? Whether she's Sam's wife or not, she's come as another interloper bent on carving her share of your father's fortune."

No one tried to stop the woman's ranting this time. She was clearly set on venting her anger at Abby. "Look at her, Frederick. She's just like *she* was, dressed as a country girl, plain and simple, but no doubt with just as wicked a soul. I regret the day I ever let Moira Kelly into this house! I won't let another of her kind in!"

The younger, frailer man stepped forward and put his hand on Mrs. Rosemont's arm. "Mother, please . . . you've no reason to talk this way to her . . ."

"Let go of me, Simon!" She swatted at his hand and he dropped it. "Don't think I haven't noticed your traitorous acts since this whole miserable situation began. I've seen you stealing out to the carriage house to talk to *him*. God knows what plots you've concocted behind my back. And now you're defending this . . . this fortune hunter. I've had quite enough!"

"And so have I! I've had my fill of your venom, Delilah!" Abby's surprise at seeing Sam enter the room was matched by the startled expressions on the faces of the Rosemonts. Everyone turned toward the sound of his thunderous voice as he strode across the plush carpeting.

Aside from rare minor bursts of temper, Abby had never heard Sam's voice raised in anger, and even she was struck by the intensity of his emotional outburst. "Sam . . ." she whispered.

His intense gaze connected with hers for a brief moment before he reacted with his brothers. It was not long enough for her to sort out all the emotions reflected in his eyes. There were definitely sparks of indignation, but were they aimed at her or the others in the room? Was he ashamed of her? Was he angry because she'd come?

He approached her and stood beside but slightly in front of her. She could see the tension in the bunched muscles of his shoulders and back. The veins in his temple throbbed with the clenching of his fists.

"This is my wife," he stated almost as a challenge. "She will be treated with respect. I have put up with enough of your slanderous insults to me, but I will have none of them directed at Abby, do you understand me?"

Frederick Rosemont shrugged. "Certainly, Sam. There's no reason to be so hostile. After all, if you had bothered to tell us that we even had a sister-in-law, we wouldn't have been so shocked today, now would we?"

Sam stole a quick look at Abby before answering. "My private life is none of your business, Frederick."

And obviously none of mine either, Abby concluded miserably.

He turned to her and took her hands. "Is everything all right?" he asked. "Are you all right? Why have you come? How did you know where I was?"

They seemed like ridiculous questions for a man to be asking his wife. Abby looked away from him, and saw that Frederick was watching them with amused interest. While his mother found the situation provoking, Frederick obviously found it laughable. And Abby found it humiliating.

"I think your wife is a little confused, Kelly," Frederick said. "Could it be that she doesn't know what's going on here?" He looked at Abby and a practiced smile creased his face. "You do know, don't you, Abigail, that your husband may soon be a very rich man?" He studied her face for seconds, drew the apparent conclusion, and roared with laughter. "By God, he hasn't told his own wife. She doesn't have any idea."

Sam took a threatening step toward his brother. "Frederick, that's enough!"

Frederick's smile became a smirk of triumph. "This is

very interesting, Sam. Mother is convinced your charming wife came to Rosemont Manor to dip her dainty fingers in the cash reserves, but obviously she knows nothing about them. She's a true innocent, isn't she, Sam? Just like your mother was." He raised an orange-furred finger to his lip thoughtfully. "Oh, wait, Moira wasn't really so innocent after all. Perhaps I've drawn the wrong conclusions about Abigail as well. I seem to suffer from a marked inability to judge character when it comes to the women in your life, Sam."

Later, when she thought about it, Abby didn't know how she had been able to respond so quickly, and on reflection, she wished she hadn't stopped her husband. Out of the corner of her eye, she saw Sam draw his arm back and ball his hand into a fist at the same time he lunged for Frederick. She managed to grab his elbow as Frederick jumped back a step and ducked. Sam's ineffectual blow cut the air above Frederick's head.

"Stop it, Sam!" she cried. It took all her strength to keep him from advancing on Frederick. "You won't solve anything by acting like a barbarian."

Frederick smoothed the lapels on his jacket and stared wide-eyed at his assailant. "Listen to your wife, Sam. After all, you're really a Rosemont, aren't you? On some level anyway. Not some ill-mannered oaf!"

Sam's back was heaving with the effort to get his emotions in check, and his face was crimson with fury. His eyes never left Frederick's face, but he refrained from straining against Abby's hold. "Funny thing, Frederick," he ground out, "but I thought being ill-mannered oafs was what made us Rosemonts! It's the mark of our exclusive fraternity."

A curious sound came from the third male player in the room, the fair-complected one whose momentary gallantry to Abby had brought censure from his mother. Abby looked at Simon. His mouth curled up at the corners,

and she knew the sound she'd heard had been a chuckle
. . . a stilted, constrained one for sure, but a chuckle none-
theless.

"Simon, stop that this instant!" Mrs. Rosemont shot
her younger son a scathing look that erased the grin from
his face. "There is nothing at all humorous about this
situation. I for one have had quite enough of all of it!
I'm beginning to wonder if Tobias's will is going to haunt
me for the rest of my days. My life is in a shambles my
household is in a constant uproar. I don't know what to
expect from one day to the next. And now *you* appear
on my doorstep."

The last comment had been directed at Abby. "For all
I know," Mrs. Rosemont raved, "you may have dozens
of your country cousins in a wagon outside my gates
waiting to swarm upon us at any moment." She fanned
her hand in front of her face and scanned the room.
"Where is Kitridge? I'm beginning to feel faint."

"I'm here, madam," the vigilant butler said, raising
his eyes to the ceiling. He slowly and deliberately crossed
the room to aid his mistress.

Sam and Frederick remained locked in a maddening
staring contest. Simon had retreated to a far corner of the
room, and Abby was beginning to feel like a hopeless
outsider who was never going to fit anywhere into this
ridiculous picture.

In one agonizing day, the life she believed she was
going to be living with the man she thought she had
married had been turned upside down. She was caught in
a maelstrom of uncertainty in which she was an unwitting
principal player. She was an actor who knew nothing of
her script, and she realized with a wrenching sob that
she didn't want to play her part any longer. She didn't
understand any of these people. And what was worse,
she didn't want to.

All she wanted to do was get away . . . go back to her

farm, her family. All her doubts and fears had come true. Sam wasn't who she thought he was after all and never would be. While he was with her, he had been living a lie, and she could only guess at the depth and magnitude of his deception. Maybe he wasn't capable of telling the truth ... ever, and she should never have believed anything he told her.

As if reading her thoughts, Sam turned pain-filled eyes upon her. He reached out, but she brushed his hands away. She couldn't hide the disgust she felt at that moment.

"Abby, I know what you're thinking," he said.

"Oh, no, you don't, Sam. You have no idea." She saw the hurt in his eyes, but it could not equal the pain that sliced her heart at his betrayal. He was sorry, yes, maybe he was ... sorry that at last his game of deceit had been revealed.

What he had hoped to gain by including her in his charade she couldn't imagine. She only knew that she wouldn't let him manipulate or humiliate her anymore. She'd had her fill of the Rosemonts. She'd had her fill of Sam. She viewed the open doors of the fancy Victorian drawing room as a prisoner would an open jail cell, and she ran.

"Abby, wait ... let me explain."

Don't listen to him, she told herself, but Sam's voice still managed to cut a straight path to her wounded heart. She had to get away before he wrapped more of his wicked lies around it and stopped her from getting away.

She blocked out the rest of his words and ran from Rosemont Manor, down the gray slate steps and onto the sloping lawn. She ran for the front gates, paying no heed to the hot tears that coursed down her cheeks. She was only dimly aware that Melissa's boater had flown off her head and was rolling topsy-turvy across the grass.

She paused outside the gate just long enough to recall which way she had come, and then, without looking back, she ran toward the village of Fox Hill. She wouldn't stop running until she'd found a hire coach to take her to the depot in Pittsburgh and a westbound train. But even as she devised this plan, an image of Sam's face taunted her. *Go away, Sam Kelly!* a silent scream echoed in her mind. *Go away and leave me alone!*

Chapter Fifteen

Abby hadn't run far before a pair of strong hands gripped her shoulders and jerked her to a sudden stop, nearly knocking her to the ground.

"Stop, Abby! Don't run away from me!" It was a desperate command as Sam spun her around to face him.

His face was flushed, and his breathing labored. He looked at her with eyes that glinted like molten silver. She could feel the heat from both his gaze and the hands that held her arms in a vise-like grip. It radiated from his body to all her nerve endings. She strengthened her resolve to get away. *Not this time, Sam!*

"Let go of me," she spat out, daring him to refuse the cold, hard edge to her voice.

"Not until you listen to me. I have to explain."

She tried to twist out of his grasp, but soon realized her attempts were useless, as were her efforts to keep the tremors from her words. She hated herself for showing such weakness. "Don't . . . don't touch me, Sam. I . . .

I don't want you to. I've already heard enough inside your house.''

"You don't mean that, Abby. You're hurt, I know that, but remember what we had before I left . . . think back."

A hard, coarse laugh answered him. "What we had never existed, Sam, but I never knew it. Only you did!"

"Of course it existed. It was real. You felt it and I did, too. This . . . *place* you came to today—it's what doesn't exist for us. It's not real."

"Stop lying to me! I'm not your fool any longer!" She swiped at the tears that streamed down her face.

His eyes softened and he loosened his hold on her for just an instant. "Oh, Abby . . ."

It was the opportunity she needed. She pooled her strength in her hands and shoved at his chest. He stumbled backwards, and she fled into a thick stand of trees that bordered Sawbuck Road. Pushing aside the offending branches that snagged her blouse and whipped against her face, she ran into the woods. But she was no match for Sam's swift pursuit.

Suddenly the leaves at the tops of the trees spun crazily overhead as she felt herself tumbling backwards. She landed with a thud on Sam's body, his work-hardened muscles providing little padding.

They rolled over in the brush and pine needles until he was on top. He pinned her to the ground, pressing his thighs against her hips and preventing her from raising her knees to shove him off. He captured her wrists and held them on the ground at each side of her head.

Though she was winded, she thrashed against his grip until she only succeeded in aggravating the parts of her body already smarting from the fall. Finally she lay still, her anger bursting from her lungs in sharp pants. *I hate you, Sam Kelly,* she cried out in her mind. She tried to stop the flood of tears that ran from her eyes. *I hate you all the more because hating you is the last thing I wanted to do!*

Determined he wouldn't see the hurt in her eyes, she blinked away the moisture and stared up at him. His face was set in grim, taut lines that didn't reflect the first signs of regret. His voice reverberated with strength, not contrition. She began to wonder if Sam even had a heart.

"You are going to listen to me, Abby. I will not let you throw away what we have."

"We have nothing." God, how she wanted to hurt him.

"Then why did you come here? Why did you come all this way . . . to tell me it's over?"

She wrenched her face away from the piercing eyes that held her almost as surely as his hands. "I came to see Sam Kelly. I have no idea who I've found. I have no idea who those people in that house are."

"You've found me . . . the same man who kissed you at the depot six weeks ago, the same man who has thought of nothing else but coming home to you."

She risked looking at him again. "The man who lied to me."

"The man who married you."

"Oh, yes." She laughed bitterly. "I am married to you. And because of that, I'm supposed to accept all of your lies as if they made sense? Well, nothing does make sense to me, Sam. Nothing from the very beginning makes any sense. Who are you? Why were you with Duncan Walthrop? Why did you offer to stay with me? Why, in God's name, did you propose to me?"

Time stopped as she waited for the answers to her questions. Their gazes remained bound together in a fierce struggle of wills. Finally, in the charcoal embers of his eyes, gold flecks flickered to life and burned into her. Had she angered him? Had she succeeded in shaming him? Did he at last feel her humiliation?

He sat up and his shoulders sagged, but his heated gaze

never left her face. She pushed herself up and sat on her heels. She could have run away again, but she didn't. Even if he hurt her more, she would hear what he had to say. It was the only way she could put an end to what he had done to her.

"Why did I propose to you?" he repeated. His voice was calm, but at what expense she could only guess. His temples pulsed with pent-up emotion. "Do you want the truth?"

"I'm not sure you're capable of telling it."

He took a deep breath and let it out slowly. "I proposed to you to save the children . . ."

"So you said at the time," she snapped back, disguising her pain with sarcasm.

All at once, the hard planes of Sam's face transformed into softer curves that hinted of pain, vulnerability. What was he thinking of? What was he remembering? Desolate memories seemed etched in his handsome face. At that moment Abby saw the facade of Sam Kelly, the man, slip away and leave behind a young man's anguished reality.

". . . and because it gave me a reason to confront my past and the demons of Moira Kelly's," he said. "And fulfill a promise at the same time. And because I believed your need was greater than my desire to leave the past buried."

She could no more control her traitorous emotions than she could stop the sun from shining above them. Pity began gnawing away at her anger. She tried to push it away, but if the truth were ever to come from Sam Kelly, she believed it would come now. "And have you confronted it?" she asked.

"Yes. Six weeks ago I did."

"This house? These people are your past?"

"They're a link to my father and to who I am and to what my mother wanted me to be."

"And what have you found out, Sam? Are you who your mother wanted you to be?"

His fingers wrapped around her upper arms, firmly, but not with the fierceness of before. "I found out that I proposed to you to save the children, but I married you because I love you. And it matters more to me now that I am what *you* want me to be."

His gaze moved over her face, and his hands moved on her arms. Their heat penetrated the silken fabric of her blouse. She felt it in her core. His hands moved down from her shoulders and back up again, as he pulled her closer. With a sob that released her anguish, she let herself be drawn into his sphere of warmth.

"I've missed you, Abby," he said hoarsely. "When I told you that in my letters, it wasn't just words—it was what was in my heart. All I could think of was coming home to you. Being with you and picturing us all together again has sustained me, and now you're here, and it's nothing like what I wanted it to be. I don't want to start all over with doubts and suspicions. I only wanted to provide for you. I never meant for it to be like this."

His full mouth, so close to hers, turned up slightly at the corners. "I thought it would be you who fell in love first. I thought you were so close to being there, but before I ever got off the train in Pittsburgh, I knew I was already in love with you, because it hurt so much to leave."

"Oh, Sam, I did love you, but I don't know what to believe anymore . . ."

Suddenly his hands were on her back, and she was spinning through a tumultuous eddy that led to his embrace. The last measure of space that separated them was closed when her breasts met the muscled tautness of his chest.

He stroked her back, the curve of her spine, then found her waist and moved up again. His hands never stopped moving, pulling her in, urgently, needily. His lips were on her throat, and she lay her head back giving him access.

"Sam, don't . . ." she heard herself say before her feeble objections died on her lips, her words lost in the rush of his breath on her skin.

He raised himself to his knees and bent over her, taking her lips in a crushing kiss that erased the last of her protests. She let him lower her into the pine needles and realized he was falling with her, his lips slanted over hers, molding and shaping her mouth to perfectly form with his.

She wrapped her fingers around his shoulders feeling the tense muscles flex when she touched him. Her hands moved as feverishly as his, sliding down his back and up again to hold his head over hers, inviting the kiss to deepen.

His tongue probed the crease of her mouth, and she opened to him. When he thrust inside, the emotional turmoil of six long weeks and the last agonizing hours exploded in her mind like a white, hot flash, obliterating everything but the feel of his tongue, his lips, his exquisite hands.

This was the man she wanted, the man she had dreamed of. He awakened all the passion that she had only imagined existed between a man and a woman. If he were a deceiver, then at that moment she wanted to be deceived. She could forgive him anything if only she could believe that this ecstasy would last for a lifetime.

When at last he raised his head and looked down at her, his eyes, like blue-gray ash, caressed her face. She didn't want to move. She wanted to stay wrapped in the blanketing warmth of his gaze forever.

He planted his elbow in the needles beside her, and rested his head in his palm. The impassioned grin he gave her showed just the tips of perfect white teeth set in the dark shadows of a day's-end beard. It spoke to her of his pleasure and his desire. She wondered if his heart were pounding as furiously as her own.

His voice floated above her, husky and deep. "Abigail Chadwick, minister's daughter, friend and heavenly tormentor . . . recent bride of the very lucky Samuel Kelly . . . you amaze and astound me. It is true what they say about ministers' children. Still waters do indeed run deep, and it has been my good fortune to explore the fathomless depths of your soul."

His words were like a cocoon she could have wrapped around her, but instead she pulled herself up from a heady daze and squirmed out from under him. She took a moment to steady her ragged breathing and find her equilibrium again.

She knew she looked a mess. Her hair was down around her shoulders, and the tails of her silk blouse trailed on the ground. Her face was on fire where his lips had been, and her arms and back tingled everywhere his hands had roamed. Abigail Chadwick was flushed with passion for the first time in her life!

"D-don't think your Irish charm will make me forget what we were talking about, Sam Kelly!" she warned, looking away from his gaze and the power it had to banish all common sense. She fussed with her appearance, but her hands were trembling too much to make many repairs.

"And what were we talking about?" he whispered in her ear before his mouth struck a path down her neck.

"You know very well!" She halfheartedly tried to push him away.

"I believe it was how happy I am to see you. I'll beg off work tomorrow and we'll go to Pittsburgh this afternoon and get the fanciest suite in the finest hotel. We'll start this marriage off right." He raised an eyebrow and grinned mischievously. "Not that the last few minutes weren't a pretty fair beginning to my way of thinking!"

"Tonight!" Abby scrambled to stand up. "I've got to

go back." Then realizing that Sam still knew nothing of her mission, she added, "I came all this way to get you. We must return tonight."

Worry creased the fine lines around his eyes. "What are you talking about? Why do we have to go right away?"

"It's Angel," she said, "and that horrid Tucker Brandywine. That's what I've come to tell you. Oh, Sam, we've got such troubles at the farm." As she related the events of the last few days, she watched Sam's face change from shock to anger.

"So you see," she finished, her back straight as a ramrod, and her resolve to protect her family now firmly planted in her mind, "I've got to go back. I promised Angel I'd be home tomorrow morning. She's shattered, Sam. I don't know how long it will take her to recover from what happened. I told her I'd bring you with me. But either way, I'm going."

She leveled cool eyes at him as she issued a bold challenge. "You must make up your own mind, Sam. Are you coming with me or not?"

"Damn that man!" he swore. "How could anyone do this? Of course I'm going with you."

"Will you stay?"

She didn't know yet what price he would pay for leaving Rosemont Manor, but she assumed it would cost him dearly. A moment of indecision flashed in his eyes, but soon passed. "Yes, Abby, I'll stay. Let's go."

He grabbed her hand and cut through the trees toward the road, holding the low branches away from her face. They retraced their steps along Sawbuck Road to Rosemont Manor. The mansion loomed before them, a hulking stronghold of buried secrets. But it was a long journey back to Ohio, and maybe now Abby would learn what those secrets were. Since it was not within her power to stop loving Sam, she had to learn to believe in him.

Chapter Sixteen

When they reached the end of the drive that led to the mansion, Abby assumed that Sam would go inside the house to gather his belongings. Instead he kept walking toward the back of the estate. "Where are you going?" she asked.

"To my room." He pointed to a large outbuilding behind the main residence. "I live in the carriage house. Remember, I told you that in one of my letters."

"Yes, I remember, but . . ."

"But you thought it was another lie?" A guilty grin gave her away, and Sam smiled. "Everything I wrote in my letters was the truth, even when I said I lived on the grounds belonging to some very rich people. I just didn't happen to mention that I was related to them."

"No, you didn't. I wonder what else you forgot to tell me." As they walked to the carriage house, Abby was grateful she would have the opportunity on the train to delve into Sam's past more thoroughly. But in the meantime, she was curious as to why he had lived away from the main house. "Did they ask you to sleep out here, Sam, or was it your choice?"

He chuckled ruefully. "Being Tobias Rosemont's son may have a certain rank, but that does not guarantee that it comes with its privileges."

He showed her his hands, callused on the palms and colored a light brown with mysterious stains. "Further proof," he said without bitterness. "You won't see such smudges on Frederick's lily-white hands." He held up the index finger on his right hand. "Goldenrod Oak. That's what we call it. A House of Rosemont exclusive which I personally applied to three bureaus and a sideboard today."

She pouted in exaggerated sympathy. "It looks as though Frederick has worked you harder than I ever did."

"And with far fewer rewards! Frederick can't even cook." He chucked her under her chin with an oak-stained knuckle. "Wait here. I'll run up to my room and throw everything in my suitcase. It's pitifully small quarters up there, I'm afraid. Hardly room for one, much less two."

He lowered his voice in seductive teasing. "Besides, after what happened in the woods just now, I doubt I'd be able to keep from tossing you onto my bed, and the springs squeak. We'd set the horses to whinnying and Kitridge would surely come to investigate."

Abby felt a warmth creep up her neck. Imagine her being teased about such a thing. She felt almost giddy with delicious embarrassment. "You'd best stop all this silly chatter, Sam Kelly, and get your things," she scolded with a transparent attempt at pretending offense.

After Sam disappeared inside the carriage house, she marveled at how the last few minutes had changed everything she had been feeling about him. He was the old Sam again, whoever that might be, she concluded with an optimistic smile. She was becoming more hopeful by the second that they would be able to return to Ohio and

mend the rift that distance and misunderstanding had put
between them.

While she waited for him, Abby tried to make repara-
tions to her disheveled appearance. When she heard footsteps on the gravel behind her, she spun around to face
Kitridge, who, she decided, must have a sixth sense about
what was going on everywhere in the estate.

She abruptly stopped her grooming, leaving a number
of hairpins sticking out from her mouth. Her hands ceased
their mechanical working of a thick shock of long hair
she'd planned to twist into a bun, and she let it fall. "Oh,
Kitridge, it's you," she mumbled through the pins.

"Yes, madam, and I see that you might require the use
of a looking glass. May I get one for you?"

"And some soap and a tub with a washboard and a
hot flatiron if you don't mind," she said. Realizing from
the shocked expression on the butler's face that he had
taken her seriously, she quickly amended, "I'm just teasing, Kitridge. I'm fine. I'll make do, though I admit I
must look utterly hopeless right now."

"Not at all, madam," he replied politely. "I'm gratified
to see that you and Master Samuel had a nice stroll along
our beautiful countryside. Your husband has had far too
few pleasant diversions since arriving here."

Abby thrust the last pin into her hair and smoothed
her blouse. "Yes, we had a delightful time," she said.
"Perhaps Sam can use some help in his room. If he's
looking for me, tell him I went around to the front of the
house to search for my hat."

He nodded and headed to the carriage house. Abby
walked to the front lawn feeling as light-headed as she
could ever remember in her life. *We had a delightful time,*
she had told Kitridge. So fine, in fact, that she couldn't
suppress the giggle that bubbled up from her throat and
sounded as carefree as a young girl's.

* * *

"Pardon me, Master Samuel. I thought I might be of some assistance to you."

Sam turned to see the butler standing in his doorway. "Kitridge, I'm glad you're here. Come in."

Kitridge ducked his head to avoid hitting the low door-frame, then squeezed between the narrow bed and dresser to settle on the wooden desk chair. Sam continued tossing his belongings into his case, aware that the butler watched him with wary eyes.

"You're giving up the ghost, are you, sir?" Kitridge finally asked.

Sam smiled. The term "ghost" was certainly appropriate to describe the situation, for he was, in fact, giving up his quest to settle Tobias Rosemont's will. "I have to, Kitridge. Abby's come with bad news. My family needs me. That's more important than continuing my feud with the Rosemonts."

"Quite so, sir, but does it say in the will that you must complete your obligations within a span of three *consecutive* months?"

"I'm not sure, but no, I don't think so."

"Well, of course, it's none of my business, but perhaps when things quiet down a bit, you might consider coming back. I wonder if your father's inheritance hasn't become more meaningful to you since you've been here. The House of Rosemont is a fine business, Master Samuel, despite the rather authoritarian way it has been run of late. And if I may say so, you seem to have a knack for creating exceptional pieces of furniture. Besides, there are those of us, here and at the factory, who regret your leaving . . . with the exception of the family naturally."

Sam grinned at him. "Naturally." He closed the lid on his suitcase and snapped the latches in place. "Thanks for your kind words, Kitridge, but I can't see myself returning. I did enjoy working on the furniture, and I'm probably a better craftsman than I am a farmer, but, well . . . you saw her.''

The butler smiled knowingly. ''Yes, indeed I did, sir, and I heartily agree that in this instance, farming has a most remarkable appeal.''

''Which reminds me . . . I need a favor.'' Sam placed his hand on a six-foot hutch that occupied the one free span of wall space remaining in the room. He ran his fingers down the sienna patina of its maple finish. ''It's almost done. Just needs one more coat of wax. Would you mind applying the last coat for me, Kitridge? It's a present for Abby, you know.''

Kitridge nodded. ''I would be happy to, sir.''

''And when that shipment I've been waiting for from New York arrives, you'll send it and the hutch to me in Ohio?''

''Consider it done.''

Sam took Kitridge's hand in a firm grasp. ''You've been a good friend,'' he said. Then he stunned the discomposed butler by pulling him into a bear hug, which culminated in several robust slaps on Kitridge's back.

Slinging his jacket over his shoulder and picking up his valise, Sam left his room above the carriages and climbed down the ladder to the main floor. He passed the assortment of Rosemont buggies and proceeded to the exit. On his way out, he ran straight into Simon, who was hurrying through the door at the same time.

Simon fixed his startled gaze on the case in Sam's hand and stepped back from him. ''What's going on, Sam? You're not leaving?''

''I'm going home, Simon. You Rosemonts can finally breathe a sigh of relief. I'm no longer a threat to our venerable father's fortune.''

''But you've only got a few weeks to go! You can't leave!''

Simon's outburst sent a shock wave of astonishment through Sam. True, the two half brothers had managed to forge a tenuous bond of friendship. In fact, Sam almost *liked* the younger Rosemont, but he certainly hadn't expected Simon to be so distressed at his departure.

Sam tipped his hat back on his head to get a better look at Simon's face. There was nothing there but sincere disappointment, and Sam wasn't at all sure how to deal with it. "Tell you what, Simon," he said. "You keep my share. You once told me you thought you deserved it."

"I don't feel that way anymore, Sam. I've gotten rather used to having you around. And, well, the truth is, I think you're good for the House of Rosemont. The men like and respect you. They never have felt that way about me, and they only fear Frederick."

"You have to earn their respect, Simon, and you can do it. But you'd better keep a watchful eye out. There's a wind of change blowing, and it's touched our father's precious company in ways I doubt Tobias ever thought of."

Sam put his arm around Simon's shoulder, and the two of them walked down the drive. "Consider this a warning, brother. There's a current of unrest rippling beneath the saws and sanders, and it's not going to go away, no matter how many Pinkertons Frederick hires. Freddie may find that all his rules will be broken in time, on the backs of a lot of good men."

Sam left Simon standing in the middle of the drive as he continued toward the mansion with a brisk step. Then stopping to take a quick look around the estate, he wondered where his wife had gone.

"There you are," Abby muttered to Melissa's straw boater. It fluttered by its ribbons from a low branch of an oak tree in the Rosemont front yard. "I've been looking all over for you."

She rescued the hat, found it free of damage, and began to cross the lawn the way she had come. When she reached the front entrance of the house, Frederick came out the door and descended the steps toward her.

Since she couldn't avoid him, she simply nodded and spoke curtly. "Good day to you, Mr. Rosemont." She proceeded to sidestep the position he had taken in front of her.

He grabbed her elbow. "Wait a minute, Abigail. What's your hurry? Where are you going?"

"Why should you care, Mr. Rosemont?"

He seemed unaffected by her abrupt response. "Frederick, please. After all we are family. Now that I've had time to think, I regret the unfortunate events that occurred in the drawing room this afternoon. I acted most ungraciously, I'm afraid, and treated you unfairly."

She gave him her most withering glare. "You'll get no argument from me on that admission, *Mr. Rosemont,* but you needn't worry about it. Sam and I are leaving."

"Is that so?"

She thought she saw a hint of triumph in his eyes, but quickly cast aside any concern over it. Frederick couldn't hurt her, and once Sam was back in Ohio, he couldn't touch him either. "Yes, Sam is coming home with me," she said, allowing an edge of arrogance to creep into her voice.

"For a visit, you mean?"

"Certainly not. He's going to stay."

"And throw away his chance at a substantial chunk of Rosemont money? I hardly think so."

Abby wanted nothing more than to put this arrogant man in his place. "Not everyone believes that money is the most important thing in life, Mr. Rosemont. My husband's priorities are in the right place. He came here to earn enough to rebuild our home. He has done so, and now he's leaving. He has a family to consider.''

Frederick looked down at her with an unmistakable smirk. ''Why, Abigail, my brother is absolutely god-like in your eyes, isn't he? A paragon of the Puritan work ethic.''

Abby felt her cheeks flame. Maybe she'd gone a little too far with her assessment of Sam. ''He's not a saint at all, but he is aware of his responsibilities.''

''But are you aware of what he stands to lose by leaving here today?'' He waited for her to answer, and when she didn't, his lips curled up in a self-satisfied grin that said he was privy to important information she didn't have. ''You haven't been married very long, have you, Abigail?''

''What does that have to do with anything?''

''Perhaps nothing, but I fear you don't know your husband all that well. I've been watching him carefully for the past few weeks, and I've drawn my own conclusions about young Sam's character. He may go with you now, but my guess is, he'll be back.''

That was exactly what Abby didn't want to hear. She stuffed Melissa's hat under her arm and started to walk away. ''I won't listen to your opinions, Mr. Rosemont. Sam is waiting for me.''

''It's greed, Abigail, pure and simple, and Sam suffers from it as profoundly as any man I've ever known.''

She stopped and whirled on him. ''How could you possibly know anything about him?'' she demanded. ''You didn't even allow him to live in your house! If anyone is greedy in this family, I believe it's you, *Frederick!*''

''You're quite right, Abby, and that is precisely why I can recognize the trait in someone else. Sam has worked hard while he's been here, broken his back, so to speak. He wants this, Abigail.'' Frederick glanced at the mansion beside them and shrugged with a smug superiority that infuriated Abby. "He's had a taste of this life, and he wants it, more than I've ever seen a man want anything. Oh, maybe he'll share it with you and your brood. I'm not saying he won't, but one thing I know for certain is that he wants it for himself."

She refused to believe what Frederick was telling her. "You're wrong. Sam isn't like that."

"Oh, but he is, Abigail. It's Simon who isn't like that, I must sadly admit." His attempt at a smile conveyed bitter resignation. "My mother never forgave my father for his dalliance with the lovely Moira Kelly," he said wistfully. "She couldn't let it go, and I've always believed she plotted her revenge against him.

"Just as Father took Moira to his bed, I think Mother likewise took a mongrel to hers. Simon is the result. He's not a Rosemont, surely you can see that yourself. But Sam, ah, Sam . . ." Frederick faltered as if it pained him to go on. "He is a Rosemont through and through, and he and I are very much alike."

"You're nothing alike," Abby said, but it sounded more like a plea than a conviction.

He stepped close to her and went on as if he hadn't heard her. His gaze raked her face. "For instance, I envy Sam his choice of a bride." He smiled at her obvious affront. "It's true, dear sister. I could have fancied you for myself."

She was too stunned to speak, and her discomfort only seemed to spur him on.

"You find this hard to believe? I find you very attractive, Abigail. There's an earthiness about you, a robust quality that could be coaxed into wild passion, complete abandonment." He reached up as if to touch her face, but held his hand suspended inches from her cheek. "Beneath your maiden's milk-fed rosiness, I sense a smoldering fire that needs only the right touch to be kindled."

His hand dropped and he grasped hers, turning her palm up. "Such a strong, capable hand. I can imagine what pleasures you could give . . ."

She jerked out of his grasp and slapped him so hard her hand stung. "You are a loathsome, vile . . ."

He raised both thick eyebrows mockingly and chuckled. "Probably so, but I think you could have learned to love me if you hadn't met my brother first."

"I could never even stand to be near you!" she bit out.

"It doesn't really matter, now does it, Abigail? After all, you've already chosen your Rosemont, and alas, it wasn't I."

His brown eyes darkened threateningly, and he glared at her. "Keep him in your bed then," he commanded. "Keep him home. I don't want him back here any more than you do."

His voice was low and menacing, and Abby was certain he used the tone to intimidate her. "I'll strike a bargain with you," he said. "You keep Moira Kelly's mixed-breed son in Ohio where he belongs, and I'll make it worth your while. I can make your little plot of land the envy of all your backwoods neighbors, and no one need ever know how you did it. I'll pay you for a job well done, and your success will be our little secret."

She tried to slap him again, but he held her wrist. His grasp was so strong that she winced. He shook his head regretfully. "Such a pity, Abigail. You're a hell of a woman, and Sam's a lucky man." He thrust her hand to her side. "Now go to your husband before I forget I'm a gentleman."

She ran from him as fast as she could, but not fast enough to escape the sneering laughter that followed her.

The Rosemonts' driver took Sam and Abby into Pittsburgh to catch the train. They had a light supper in the same cafe where Abby had had breakfast, and boarded the westbound Erie when the moon was already fully risen in the sky.

Having exhausted a reservoir of idle conversation, they settled comfortably in their coach seats, both nearly overcome with the fatigue that results from an easing of tension. They gradually relaxed in each other's company as the train reached a steady speed.

When they were accustomed to the easy rocking of the passenger car, Sam began talking. It was as if a dam had been holding back the floodwaters of his past. Though bits and pieces had trickled through the cracks in recent months, the heightened emotion of the last hours caused the dam to burst and the memories to come rushing out.

While Abby sat spellbound by the soft, mellow tone of his voice, Sam told her about his youth at Chilton-Howe and how he'd earned his education by doing chores around the campus. He'd started by helping his mother clean offices, and as he grew older he began fixing things, painting and plastering and hammering together whatever needed mending. Patching and gluing whatever seeped or leaked.

He next apprenticed to the campus gardener and learned to trim the tall hedges that bordered the shaded walkways of the school. He mowed and snipped and pruned whatever needed to be made more uniform. And he did all this under the critical eyes of the same boys who sat next to him in his Chilton-Howe classrooms and judged him because of his lowly position in the school's hierarchy.

And always at the end of a day, he explained to Abby, while he studied under the flickering gaslights in the small room he shared with his mother, Moira Kelly would say, "Aren't you lucky, Samuel, to have this fine opportunity? You must work hard and show respect, so the professors will know you are grateful. You must be ready when your father comes for you."

Though Moira Kelly always believed the noble Tobias Rosemont would come, Sam told Abby that *he*
never did believe it. Otherwise, he reasoned, why would
the great man have left his mother to toil long hours
in the halls of Chilton-Howe? And would a virtuous
man have let her grow sicker and more despondent and
more prone to wild imaginings as the years went by?
Tobias Rosemont was a fantasy that Sam Kelly learned
to hate as surely as he learned all his other lessons at
Chilton-Howe. That night on the westbound train, Sam
told Abby all of this.

"And you never met his family in all those years growing up?" she asked.

"Of course not. Tobias Rosemont would not have let
that happen . . . would not have invited the living reflection
of his infidelity into his home. I doubt my father ever
thought of my mother or me until he lay dying and the
sins of his life weighed heavily upon him." Sam smiled
ruefully. "As a matter of fact, I'm quite certain that I
thought more of him than he ever did of me."

"And you knew nothing of the will until you heard
about it from Mr. Carstairs?"

"That's right, and when I did hear about it, all I could
feel was resentment at Tobias Rosemont's back-door
attempt to make amends. But to my mother, it was as if
that damn will vindicated Tobias for all the pain he'd
caused her. I know she died thinking her former lover
was close to achieving sainthood for offering the status
of Rosemont to their son. She made me swear I would
claim my inheritance."

"You promised her that you would?"

"I did, but when she died, all I thought about was
getting away from Chilton-Howe. Even though I had
climbed to the dubious rank of tutor, I still felt trapped,
almost like an indentured servant. And the prospect of

succumbing to the demands of the will seemed even worse.''

He leaned his head against his seat and looked to the top of the rail car. His gaze wandered, unfocused. ''I had never been free, Abby. As a boy I never knew what it was to run with friends. The young masters at the school scarcely looked in my direction unless it was to gawk at the servant boy going about his chores. I spent my little spare time alone. I gathered twigs and sticks and built things, like those hickory cowboys I made the twins. Working with my hands brought me an inner peace. I found comfort in what I created.

''When I was older, I went into town sometimes, made a few friends of the village lads whose fathers were shop-keepers, but when I came back, I was still the servant's son, bound by duty and birth to the school and my mother. Her death was the most profound grief I'd ever known, even though it released me from my servitude.

''After her funeral, I simply walked off the campus and down the road. I didn't know where I was going, but for the first time in my life I knew what it was to be free. When Duncan Walthrop stopped beside me a few hours later and offered me a job, I took it, without thinking twice and without looking back.''

Sam's gaze shifted to Abby and washed over her like warm rain. ''That was the wisest choice I ever made.''

''So why *did* you go back, Sam? To fulfill your promise?''

''Only partly. Mostly I went back because of you.''

''Me?''

''I had a reason to care about the money. I didn't care for myself, and probably never would have. But when I took on the responsibility of the children, I knew it was time to go back. What my father left me would mean something to them.''

Frederick's words came back to Abby, and she tried

to push them away. *He wants this, Abigail, more than I've seen a man want anything.* "How do you feel now, Sam?" she asked. "Do you care about the money for yourself now?"

The lights dimmed in the passenger car, making it difficult to see his eyes. All at once, they became two dark orbs looking down at her, passionless and unreadable. "I left, didn't I?" he said. "To earn my inheritance, I would have had to stay another six weeks. Shouldn't that tell you what I think of the money?"

She knew it should have. She wanted to believe, but what if Frederick was right? *And give up a chunk of Rosemont fortune? He'll be back.* What if Frederick knew her husband better than she did? Better than he knew himself?

It had grown very late. The sky was black as coal and the steady clacking of iron wheels on steel rails was hypnotizing. It was much easier not to think anymore. Sam put his arm around Abby and pulled her close to him. She rested her head on his shoulder, closed her eyes, and fell into a fitful sleep that was haunted by the faces of Tobias Rosemont's family.

Will glanced toward the kitchen entrance when he heard the soft padding of Emma's bare feet on the wood floor. The candle she carried provided the only illumination in the otherwise dark room. He hadn't bothered to light a lantern.

She set the candle on the table and shivered, though it wasn't cold. "What time is it, Will?" she asked.

"Must be about four."

"I heard ya get up. Can I fix some breakfast before you leave to pick up Miz Kelly?"

"That'd be fine, Emma, thanks. How's Angel?"

"She's sleepin' now, though every once in a while she

makes this pitiful little sound, like a bird that's had his wing broke.''

A fresh stab of guilt jolted through him. ''She'll be all right once Abby and Sam get home, don't you think, Emma?''

''Sure I do. Don't fret. She'd be better now if she weren't such a delicate thing.'' She nodded her head slowly, and when she looked at him, it seemed there was a lifetime of wisdom in her eyes. ''Some girls learn to come back quicker from somethin' like what Tucker done than others. It's just what they gotta do to git on with things.''

She busied herself getting a skillet from a hook and a slab of butter from the crock on top of the icebox. When she reached inside to get eggs, Will noticed for the first time that the door on the old icebox didn't squeak anymore. Thanks to Sam, he thought. The man had certainly done a lot of good around the farm. Will hoped he'd be able to take care of that evil . . .

Tucker was back again, as he often was since he showed up in the shed. Tucker Brandywine seemed to be in Will's thoughts constantly, no matter what he did to try to block out the man's leering face and those bloody, awful wounds. Will shifted in his chair and shook the image from his head. He must have made a noise because Emma's voice came from the stove, and she sounded worried.

''Are you okay, Will?''

''It still doesn't make any sense, Emma. I thought for sure ol' Tucker was dead. What's he made of anyway? I can't believe he wasn't there when we went to bury him.''

''I can believe it,'' she stated with harsh certainty. ''The only feelin' Tucker ever had was hate. He's made of nothin' but meanness, and he's too mean to die. Even the devil don't want Tucker Brandywine, 'cause he throwed him back.''

Will looked at her, but all he could see was her back. Her thin shoulders churned furiously as she whipped the eggs in a bowl. Maybe she was right. Maybe that was exactly what happened.

Chapter Seventeen

The chatter at the supper table was nonstop, with all the children trying to talk at once and ask the thousand questions they had been saving up for Sam. The one who was noticeable for her silence, however, was Rebecca. Though she didn't say anything, she did look at Sam quite often, and he made certain that when she did, he met her gaze and smiled.

When she finished with the little food she managed to eat, she placed her napkin by her plate and asked softly, "May I be excused, Miss Abby? I'll come back and help clean up."

"Yes, of course, Rebecca."

She carried her dish and cup to the sink. But before she left the kitchen, she stopped next to Sam and said, "I'm glad you're back."

"Me too, Rebecca. Very glad."

Thomas waited until she'd gone before a scowl took up most of his face and he grumbled, "Ain't she ever gonna be better, Miss Abby? She's like that all the time, so quiet she might as well be sleepin'. And her eyes don't look like they're seein' much of anything. I made the best face at her this morning, and she didn't pay any mind to it.''

"Of course she'll be better, Thomas. You must be patient with her, that's all.''

Timothy didn't seem any more convinced than his twin. He placed his elbows on either side of his plate and rested his chin on his fists. His lips pulled down in a frown that tugged his freckles with it, and he spoke sternly. "Sam, you 'member when we were all at church and that ol' Tucker Brandywine came in and scared the dickens out of everybody?''

Sam delivered his answer with appropriate seriousness. "Yes, I remember that very clearly.''

"Well, don't you wish you'd a' whomped ol' Tucker good that day when you had the chance?''

Thinking about it, Sam bit back the response he truly wanted to give the boy. "It's bothered you ever since then that I didn't fight Tucker, hasn't it, Tim?'' The boy's sandy-colored curls bounced with the nod of his head. "What I really wish,'' Sam said, "is that Tucker hadn't hurt Rebecca. But I still believe what I told you that day . . . there's a time to fight and a time to give way. I didn't have a reason to fight Tucker that day.''

"But you do now,'' Timothy amended wisely.

"Yes, son, I surely do now.''

Tim's face brightened. "How would you do it, Sam? Would you hit him in the kisser or break his arms? Maybe tie him up to the big willow tree and punch his stomach till he belched out all his meanness . . .''

Sam looked at Abby. She was staring open-mouthed at the boy, but there was something in her eyes that suggested a subtle pride. "Timothy! You stop that kind of talk right now,'' she said. "In fact, you boys go on and get ready for bed. It's been a busy day for all of us.''

The twins reluctantly followed orders, while the girls cleared the table. When the dishes were washed and put away, Sam went out the back door. He'd seen Emma go out there a few minutes before, and he found her sitting on the stoop gazing out over the backyard.

She glanced at him briefly and then looked away. He sat down beside her and found his own spot in the darkness to focus on. They stayed that way, neither one looking at the other for a while.

Finally Sam said, "Sorry about what we said about Tucker in there. I know he's your father . . ."

"It don't matter none to me what you say about him," she said. "I wish you'd a' whomped him that day too."

"That does seem to be the popular opinion," Sam admitted. He continued to stare at the horizon. "Imagine this," he sighed after a moment. "I never thought I'd be sitting next to Emma Brandywine."

She snorted through her nose and kicked at a loose clod of dirt by her shoe. "It ain't exactly like meetin' the queen of England now, is it?"

"I don't know . . . for a few days you were a very important person around here. A lot of folks did nothing but search these fields and woods for you."

"Just 'cause they were scairt of Tucker, that's the only reason. Even Will said I was nothin' but a troublemaker when he first found me."

"If that's the case, then he's sure gone to a lot of trouble himself for a troublemaker." She shrugged, going along with Sam's conclusion about Will. "People here care about their children, Emma, theirs and everybody else's."

"Even Tucker's?"

"Even Tucker's. I'm not saying I blame you for hiding out like you did, but it sure caused quite a commotion. A lot of folks missed work and put in long hours looking for you. I'm one of them. You could have saved us all a lot of time by letting someone know where you were.''

She leaned over and stared up at him with fight glittering in her eyes. He knew she hadn't expected him to be so callous.

''I can't do nothin' about how you spend your time, Mr. Kelly, *sir,* but if it makes you feel better, you can send me a bill!''

He plucked the top off a dandelion that grew stubbornly from between the two wooden steps, and began mechanically pulling at the wispy seeds. ''I've been thinking along those lines actually.''

From the corner of his eye he could read the shock on her face. ''You're just gonna hafta wait for Tucker to die then, till I get my inheritance,'' she shot back.

He liked her. She might have had to take a lot of abuse from her father, but she sure as hell didn't take any from anybody else. ''I wasn't necessarily talking about money,'' he said.

She leveled a hard stare on the night shadows again. ''Why don't you spit out what's stuck in your craw, Mr. Kelly?''

''This afternoon, Timothy came out here and asked you what was written under a picture in the Sears and Roebuck Catalogue. You told him you were too busy to help him and he should go ask Susanna.''

''So?''

''You weren't busy. I saw you. You were drawing a heart in the dirt with a stick.'' He picked up a limb that was resting against the steps. ''I believe this is the very stick, now that I look at it.''

''I was thinkin' about somethin'. It was real important. Besides, kids can grow to be a real nuisance if you let 'em.''

''That's true enough, I guess, but I don't think that's why you didn't help him.'' The dandelion was almost bare, but he still kept his eyes on it. "I think you can't read, Emma."

"And I think you're actin' awful free with your high-'n'-mighty opinions, 'specially for a man who don't know nothin' about me."

"So you can read?"

"Enough. I git by."

"Good. I'm happy to be wrong." He took a piece of paper out of his pocket. "When I was in Fox Hill, there was a woman where I lived who was a wonderful cook. Even though it was July, she made me a special treat from her home in England. It's called Christmas pudding." He handed Emma the paper. "If you can tell me even three of the ingredients on this list, I'll leave you alone."

Her eyes were like blue ice, and they met his head on. She took the paper and stared at it a long time before she finally thrust it back at him. "I don't care much for pudding."

Sam put the recipe in his pocket again. "I can teach you to read, Emma. You're smart, I can tell that. Just a half hour each day, and if you study hard so that by Christmas you can read one of Timothy's primers to me, I'll consider all debts paid. And I'll personally make you a Christmas pudding that will melt in your mouth. It's not that I didn't believe you about your reading ability, Emma. It's just that I know *everybody* likes pudding."

Her eyes softened just a little, and he thought she just might have smiled. Pointing down at the dusty remains of her stick-drawn heart, he added, "Besides, a heart without a name in it seems kind of lonely to me, and I'm pretty sure I know what name you'd like to put in there."

"There you go, bein' Mister Know-It-All again." She chewed on her lower lip and thought a moment. "You ain't gonna let up on this, are ya?"

"Not likely, sweetheart."

"Okay, I'll give it a try, but only 'cause I don't cotton to you pesterin' me all my daylight hours."

Sam stuck his hand out. "You are most gracious, Miss Brandywine."

She shook the proffered hand. "Oh, what the blazes? What else have I got to do anyway?"

Abby had been acting differently all day. If she were an actress, Sam would have thought she had stage fright. If she were an explorer, he'd have thought she was certain the next step was quicksand. But she wasn't either of those things. She was a bride, and he was pretty sure he knew what was wrong.

And he also knew it was difficult to enjoy privacy in a house the size of theirs populated with so many people. He decided that if he were successful building the barn, he would next add a couple of bedrooms to the house— out back behind the kitchen. But in the meantime, he'd have to contend with thin walls and a bride with the jitters who'd wrapped herself in an icy exterior.

At least everyone was settled in for the night . . . the boys in the loft and the girls in the parlor. Sam knocked on the door to James and Daisy Chadwick's old bedroom.

"Come in," Abby said. He could barely hear her.

He entered the room and closed the door. She was in bed with the covers tucked securely under her chin. He moved about the room quietly and efficiently in the soft lantern light trying to act as casual as he could. "It was sure nice of the Mitchums to stay here while you were gone."

"Yes, it was."

"And the kids . . . it was great to see them again."

"They were happy to see you too."

He pulled his shirt from the waistband of his pants and began unbuttoning it, aware that she watched him. When he shrugged out of it, he said, "I sleep in my drawers, Abby. Is that all right?"

"Fine."

He undid the buttons on his trousers and began to slip them down his thighs. He glanced at Abby, and his heart swelled with compassion at the sight of those huge, frightened eyes. What the heck did she think was going to happen anyway?

Leaving the pants hugging his hips, he went to the end of the bed and wrapped his hands around the spooled footboard. She bent her knees, pulling her feet up from the end of the mattress and away from his hands. She looked around the room at everything but him.

"Are you uncomfortable, Abby?" he asked.

"Of course not," she answered too quickly, for when her gaze came to rest on his naked chest, her cheeks flushed and she clenched her fingers around the blanket at her shoulders.

At the same time, Sam's own hands flexed more tightly on the footboard. Did she have to look so almighty beautiful, even in her distress? Her hair was loose and ran over the pillow like liquid flame. Her cheeks were a delicate rose that highlighted her finely sculpted facial bones and brought out the dewy emerald of her eyes. How he wished that blush were one of expectancy, but he knew it was not. She was clearly embarrassed, uncertain, and afraid.

Sam took a deep breath to steady his rapidly increasing heartbeat. His body was paying no heed to the messages being sent by his logical brain. Every nerve ending was responding to her, and if he took his pants off now, she would surely know it. It took all his willpower to sacrifice his desire to her trepidation. "I told you, Abby, that I was a patient man, that I would wait for you, until you're ready, and I meant it."

She closed her eyes and fell back against her pillow.

Relief, like fine gauze, veiled her features. "Sam, I'm sorry . . . I'm very tired, and the children . . ."

"I know. It's all right." With a great deal of effort, he presented her with a tight little smile. "It's okay if I sleep in here, though, on the floor? Under the circumstances I think I'd lose face if I climbed the ladder to the loft and found my old spot between the twins."

"Of course." She scrambled out of bed and got him a quilt from the cupboard. When she bent to spread it on the floor, the lantern light outlined the tempting curves beneath her nightdress. He saw the rounded fullness of her breasts peaked above the flat plane of her stomach.

She handed him a pillow. "Will you be comfortable?" she asked.

"Fine. I'll be fine." He almost choked on the words.

"Well, then, good night, Sam."

"Good night, Abby."

He lay down and listened to her get back into bed. He heard the little puff of her breath as she blew out the light, then the shuffling of bedclothes. She was wrapping herself in that tight cocoon of blankets again. Didn't she realize how ridiculous it was to bundle up in the middle of the summer?

He threw off his own light cover and turned on his side, facing the wall. He wouldn't think about the way she had been just the day before in the woods off Sawbuck Road . . . responsive, eager, alive with passion.

Think about something else, Sam, he told himself. *How much lumber do I need for the barn? How many nails? Hinges? Shingles . . . soft green eyes and rosy-tipped . . .*

She hadn't lied, Abby told herself. She really was exhausted. And what if one of the children needed her? What if Rebecca called out in her sleep as she had the first night after Tucker's attack? And how much noise did making love make? She'd heard once that the first time a woman did it, it hurt so much that she cried out loud. Will and Emma . . . they were old enough to know.

And what if she got pregnant? Abby pushed to the back of her mind the little thrill that raced through her at the thought of having Sam's baby. Don't think about babies, she scolded herself. All they needed now was another mouth to feed. And what if Sam went back to Fox Hill after all?

She turned to her other side. Why couldn't she get comfortable? Why did Frederick's voice continually haunt her? *He wants this, Abigail. He'll be back . . . a chunk of Rosemont money . . . as much as I've ever seen a man want anything . . . you don't know your husband.*

But it had been her husband who stood at the foot of the bed. The hair on his chest coiled so softly and ran down . . . down into the V his trousers made. And his hair, so thick she could imagine the feel of it around her fingers. It fell low on his forehead so she couldn't tell where his eyebrows began. And his eyes, like the last golden flecks of smoldering ash . . . so warm her skin felt hot where he looked.

She tossed onto her back. It was definitely too warm under these blankets. A sheen of perspiration dotted her upper lip. But if she got up to open the window, he'd know what she'd been thinking. What if he did? She lay her open palm on the side of the bed where Sam would be sleeping if she had let him. She imagined the impression his body would make, the way the mattress would bend to the center, ever so gently, pulling her into him.

Turning slowly to her side, she pictured the way his face would be in repose, his long dark lashes against his cheekbones. Her fingers crept from under the covers and reached for his face, finding only still, warm air. *He'll be back . . . you don't know your husband . . .*

She pleaded for sleep to come. She listened to his

breathing and believed he was asleep. Then his voice drifted up to her, low and hoarse, barely a whisper. "Don't make me wait too long, please, Abby."

She hugged her pillow to her chest trying to quench an unfamiliar ache in her breasts. How could an ache hint of such sweet pleasure?

Chapter Eighteen

When Abigail Chadwick's new husband left her at the altar and ran off to Pittsburgh for Lord knows what reason, it was certainly fodder for the gossips of Seneca Village. But when she left home to go to the city to drag him back ... why, that was almost the biggest news anyone had ever heard. Tongues would still have been wagging about the newlyweds had Andrew Purcell of the mercantile not gotten a telephone the next day. The Kellys' escapades had to be back-shelved in favor of modern technology.

It was because of the telephone, a device which Sam had become accustomed to using at Chilton-Howe and Rosemont Manor, that he went to Purcell's two days after he arrived home. The odd-looking oak box with its center speaker horn and twisted cords leading to small metal earpieces was mounted on the wall behind the counter. The case had been polished to a golden sheen and the brass fittings glistened.

"I heard you were back, Sam," Andrew Purcell said

when Sam came into his store. "Fact is, my wife tells me Abigail boarded a train and went to the city to fetch you herself. That's mighty unusual behavior for Abigail, leaving the young ones behind."

Determined to keep the story of Angel's incident with Tucker from being ground into the gossip mill, Sam responded evasively. "Abby has always wanted to see Pittsburgh, Mr. Purcell. I thought it was time she did. She enjoyed herself and can't wait until we go again."

Andrew seemed disappointed by Sam's logical explanation of Abby's sudden journey, and he quickly moved on to more important matters . . . his pride and joy on the store wall. "You'll notice the big city has nothing on us, though, Sam." He shooed away a small gathering of customers who clustered around the telephone. "Did you come to see her?" he asked proudly.

"I've come to *use* her," Sam said. "Can I call the lumber yard in Akron and have them send the wood for my barn?"

Andrew swept his arm toward the phone, giving Sam permission to enter its hallowed sphere. "You're gonna rebuild the reverend's barn, are you?"

"Just as soon as the lumber arrives, Mr. Purcell, and thanks to your telephone, it will be sooner than later."

When he finished his call, Sam picked up the supplies Abby had told him to get and carried them to the counter for Mr. Purcell to ring up. As the shopkeeper methodically packaged the items in paper sacks, he kept glancing at Sam with a look that could only be interpreted as guilt. He refrained from sliding the bags across the counter, and Sam finally asked, "Is something bothering you, Mr. Purcell?"

"Yes, Sam, there is."

"What's that?"

"I feel bad that I didn't go out to your place the whole time you were gone. I should have checked on Abigail and those kids to make sure they were okay out there. I want you to know, it's not that I don't like Abigail, 'cause I do. Always have, even though she can be a bit standoffish at times.''

Like the last three nights! Sam readily agreed. ''It's all right, Mr. Purcell . . .''

''No, it isn't, and I'm ashamed of myself for listening to gossip. Some of the wives were talking up a storm about Abigail while you were living there, before marrying her. It never mattered to me, of course, but you know how women are . . . always poking and prodding around till they get the juicy fruit to chew on. As for me, I just think a lot of you for making Abigail an honest woman.'' He leaned close to Sam. ''It couldn't have been easy, what with her picky nature and all.''

Sam stifled a chuckle. ''I can assure you, Mr. Purcell, I had nothing to do with making Abby an honest woman. She did that long before I ever met her. But I did have to meet a set of rigid standards to qualify for the job of husband.''

Andrew nodded sympathetically. ''I can well imagine. You're a good sort, Kelly. You've taken on that whole Chadwick brood, and I remember what you did organizing the search to find that lost girl. I think you're all right, and I want you to know that.''

The first fingers of acceptance reached out to Sam when Andrew Purcell offered his hand. ''Thank you, Andrew,'' Sam said, using the merchant's first name. He picked up his packages, but before he left, he added, ''What you just said made me think of something. Have you heard anything recently about the missing girl's father, Tucker Brandywine? I looked for him over at his place, but there was no sign of him.''

''I haven't seen him in several days, but I can't say as I've been looking for him either. Brandywine's the sort this town can do without.''

"Thanks just the same, Andrew. And by the way, it's a fine-looking telephone. Works good too." Andrew Purcell was beaming when Sam left the store.

The lumber arrived the very next morning on a flatbed wagon pulled by a pair of mules. The driver, Sam, and Will unloaded every one of the fir-pine posts, beams, and siding planks next to where James Chadwick's barn had stood. The dirt floor was still hard-packed and level, which would make the job of erecting a new structure simpler than it might have been.

Soon after the lumber was delivered, another wagon, this one a closed delivery type, arrived at the farm. It was brightly painted on the side panels with the name *Purcell's Mercantile* and was driven by Andrew Purcell himself.

The wagon slowed in front of the house, and Abby came out and stood with Sam. The expression he saw on her face matched his own bewilderment. As Andrew nodded to both of them and halted the wagon, Arne Swenson dropped the back gate and jumped out. He was followed by Ernest Sholski and his two strong boys.

"Good morning, gentlemen," Sam said. "What brings you out here?"

"You got a barn to build," Arne observed. "Ve are here to help you build it." He handed a large wicker basket to Abby. "Martha says you von't be able to feed us all, so she sends her chicken and biscuits."

Ernest Sholski then thrust three boxes at her, muttering a few succinct words of explanation. "Harriet sent some pies."

Laden with the packages, Abby managed a stuttering "thank you," before leveling wide eyes at Sam. He shrugged his own astonishment back at her. After the men traipsed off toward the lumber, she whispered, "Do you think the pies are poisoned?"

Sam couldn't hold back a choking laugh. "No, but I think something's definitely gotten into the well water around here."

Just two weeks later at daybreak, Abby stood outside the back of her house admiring the new barn. Sam had applied the cheerful apple-red stain to the siding the day before, and it contrasted nicely with the coffee-colored roof shingles.

She could hardly believe that the project had been completed so quickly. While she and the girls had tended the crops and prepared the first harvest of vegetables for market, Sam and Will had worked each day until dusk erecting the barn. They were often helped by one or more of the men from the village, whose appearances continued to amaze Abby. She was beginning to see her neighbors in a more favorable light.

The only one who had not been able to help much was Emma. Whenever someone from the village was in the yard, Emma stayed in the house. It was likely that Tucker was still looking for her, and everyone in the family understood that they must not reveal her whereabouts. Just because no one had heard any news of Tucker in many days didn't mean that he wasn't out there. The Kellys had learned that lesson before.

There was also a threat that Emma might be taken away and put in another home. Abby knew that such an occurrence would be heartbreaking for Will, who watched over Emma with a protective nature that Abby had never seen in the young man before. Emma's presence had changed Will in other ways too. His resentment of Sam and misguided feelings for Abby had disappeared, and Abby credited his new maturity to his deep feelings for Emma.

Sighing with contentment, but realizing she still had

several chores to finish before the sun completely cleared the eastern horizon, Abby went back in the house. This was the first day of school, and soon Will would take Rebecca and the younger children over the rise and down the village path. It would be a long time before Abby felt safe letting them walk alone.

At midmorning Abby heard the rumbling of wagon wheels in the yard once more. Sam had gone to the Little White Tail to check the dam. Will and Emma were working in a distant field beyond the apple orchard, so Abby went alone to investigate the visitors. It was the first time she'd ever seen a Wells Fargo wagon at Chadwick Farm. A Wells Fargo delivery usually meant the cargo had traveled some distance.

She greeted the driver and peeked around the panels at the sides of the wagon to get a glimpse of the crates inside. One of them stood out from the others because of its size. It was at least six feet tall, bound by blankets and ropes and a framework of lumber. It was hard not to speculate about what this package contained.

"I'm lookin' for someone named Kelly," the driver said from the wagon bench.

"I'm Mrs. Kelly."

"Okay, you'll do then." He jumped down from his perch, and unlocked and opened the back gate of the wagon. Then he called for his helper to come around and give him a hand.

Abby's interest escalated as the driver pushed boxes to the side to get to the one destined for Chadwick Farm. And her jaw literally dropped when he leapt onto the wagon bed and began scooting the large mystery crate to the gate. "You catch 'er down there, Floyd," he said to the helper.

"What is it?" Abby asked, as much out of curiosity as to prevent the delivery men from dropping off a package that was misdelivered and would have to be picked up again. She certainly hadn't ordered anything this big from the Sears and Roebuck Catalogue.

The driver grunted while lowering the crate to the ground. "I have no idea, ma'am." He followed the large package with a smaller one that had packing straw protruding from its slats. "I need you to sign for these things."

She had just taken a clipboard and pencil from him when she spied a label on the side of the crate. The words *Rosemont* and *Sawbuck* seemed to jump out from the paper. She went closer to convince herself that her eyes were not deceiving her, and her worst fears were confirmed. The package had indeed come from the Rosemont Manor on Sawbuck Road. Her stomach clenched, and she thrust the clipboard at the driver, hitting him in his waistline. "Put it back on the wagon," she said.

The sweating driver narrowed disbelieving eyes on her. "What did you say?"

"I said, put it back. I don't want it."

"Beggin' your pardon, ma'am, but just a minute ago you didn't even know what it was."

"I still don't, but it doesn't matter. Take it away."

The man's face screwed into an impatient grimace. "Are you crazy?"

"Absolutely not." She felt her temper rise. It was enough to have to put up with the sneering image of Frederick Rosemont without being the recipient of the delivery man's rude behavior.

The driver widened his stance, folded his arms across his chest, and stared down at her. "I ain't puttin' this thing back in the wagon. Now you be a good girl and sign that delivery slip."

"I'll do no such thing! You brought that monstrosity here, and you can very well send it back where it came from."

The beefy arms unfolded and a stubby, thick finger wagged at Abby. "Now see here, missy . . ."

"What's wrong?"

Abby hadn't heard Sam come around the house, and she jumped at the sound of his voice. She watched him walk up to the red-faced driver, seemingly not the least bit curious at the sight of the wagon or the giant crate. "What's wrong?" she echoed incredulously. "Don't you see that . . . that thing?"

"I see it. Sign the man's paper and let's have a look inside."

"I *know* what's inside," Abby stated emphatically, "and I don't want it."

Finally Sam's face registered the confusion that the situation demanded. He looked from Abby to the package, to the driver, who was gaping at Sam with a blend of irritation and sympathy in his eyes. "Well, then, Abby, what is it?" Sam challenged.

"I can't say exactly, but it's a bribe."

Now she had his full attention. "A bribe? From who?"

"From Frederick."

His eyebrows shot up, and he shook his head slowly. "Abby, why would Frederick bribe you?"

"Look, folks," the driver cut in. "This is about as interestin' as water drippin' off a tree limb, but I've got deliveries to make. I'm late already, so if I'm gonna load this monster back on the wagon, I'd just as soon get started. And if I'm not, then would one of you kindly sign this."

Abby bestowed upon Sam her most impressive glare, the one designed to ward off any rebellion, but he took the clipboard anyway and scrawled his name across the bottom of the sheet. She refused to speak to him while the driver refastened the wagon gate and pulled out of the yard. But as soon as the wagon crossed the rise, Abby whirled on Sam like a dervish. "Sam Kelly, how could you? Now you've played right into his hands. I didn't want to have to tell you this, but Frederick and I had words . . ."

"Wait a minute, Abby. I'd like to hear all about what Frederick said to you, but first, listen to what I have to say. This time it's just possible that you might be wrong."

Her toe was tapping in the dirt, and she hadn't even realized she'd started it going. "All right, Sam, I'm listening."

"I'm guessing that what's in that crate stands on bracket-front feet, has two recessed panel doors on the bottom and a drawer above them with a soft felt lining. On top of all that is a pair of brass-hinged cupboard doors made of the finest convex glass in western Pennsylvania. And if I'm wrong, I will personally carry this thing on my back to the village and ship it back to Frederick for being the bribe that it obviously is."

"Well . . ." The single word came out in a rush of breath that died in the still morning air. Mortification left Abby momentarily speechless. "How . . . how do you know that?" she finally asked, disliking the taste of crow.

"It'll all become clear to you, I promise," he said. "In due time . . . after I get a crowbar."

He came back from the barn with the tool and loosened the tightly nailed corners of the packing wood. When the skeletal remains of the protective lumber lay splintered on the ground, it was an easy task to remove the rest of the packaging materials. Soon a finely crafted maple hutch stood in the middle of a puddle of blanket wraps. It looked exactly like the description Sam had just given Abby.

"It's beautiful," she readily admitted, though something inside forced her to remain stubbornly aloof and slightly wary of its grandeur. "But why is it here, and how did you know about it?"

Sam's demeanor took up where the driver's had left off, and his face revealed the tense lines of impatience.

"Why do you think? Because I made it." He almost shouted at her. "It's for you."

"For me?"

"Of course. What did you tell me happened to the last hutch you had?"

She desperately sought to recall the exact conversation she'd had with Sam months ago.

Too agitated to wait for her answer, he blurted out, "You said it was destroyed in the storm, and you used the pieces to build a bed for Lizzie."

"That's true, we did," she confirmed. "I told you that?"

"Yes, you did, though it seems to have lost its significance right now."

The relevance of the hutch was suddenly absolutely clear. "Oh, Sam . . ." she whispered. She clasped her hands under her chin and stared longingly at the beautiful piece of furniture. She truly couldn't recall all of the details of Sam's first visit to the farm—she'd still been reeling from the tragedy wrought by the storm—but she did remember telling him about the hutch. And she certainly remembered how kind and sympathetic he had been that day. "The hutch," she said, "it's the finest thing I've ever owned or ever seen for that matter."

The irritation ebbed from his face when she walked up to the hutch and touched the door. The sun's rays had penetrated the bubbled glass, and she felt its warmth in her fingertips. She ran her palm down the rich russet patina of the cabinet's side. Never in her life had she felt wood so smooth and satiny, even considering the factory-made pieces her mother had brought from Connecticut. And it was certainly unlike the make-do chairs and table she had grown accustomed to in her kitchen. "Thank you, Sam. I hardly know what to say . . ."

"That's a first," he quipped with an easy grin that spread the warmth in her fingers deep inside the rest of her. "The hutch is basically utilitarian." He pointed to the smaller crate. "This is your wedding present."

Abby slowly opened the box. Soon, pieces of wood lay scattered around her, and she dug through the straw packaging. She brought the first piece out of the crate. The shimmering glaze over the muted-flow blue-and-white pattern on the dinner plate caught the sunlight. Abby immediately recognized the pagoda in the center and the birds in flight on the rim. "Blue Willow!" she cried. "Just like my mother's set."

"I was hoping it would be," Sam said. "I remembered you told me that she had gotten a set for her wedding, but it was destroyed. I ordered a service for twelve. Considering this family, I calculated we would need that much . . . eventually anyway."

Abby removed several pieces of the china and set them around her in a semicircle on the ground. She wanted to tell Sam how much his gift meant to her, but the words couldn't find a pathway from her heart to her mouth. They were blocked by emotions that covered old scars she hadn't even realized she'd ignored for so long.

The magnitude of his gesture was almost more than she could bear. All her life she'd been the one who'd done for other people. And now someone had done something so wonderful for her. And not just any someone . . . the man she loved.

She should have basked in his unselfish act of kindness, found joy and comfort in knowing he cared. She wished she could stand up and throw her arms around him to show her gratitude and her love. But Abby felt the heavy hands of guilt pressing down upon her so that she couldn't move, could not even raise her head.

She was aware that he had gotten down on his knees beside her. He waited several moments before asking, "Abby, is something wrong? Did I make you unhappy by giving you the china?"

She set a cup in its saucer with an unsteady hand, then threaded her fingers tightly and put her clenched hands in her lap. She squeezed her palms together to keep her body from shaking, but it was no use. Her trembling shoulders gave her away, as did the tears that ran unchecked down her cheeks.

Sam's voice was strained and anxious beside her. "I'm sorry. I should have known that the memories were still too painful."

She slowly raised her face to look at him, and hated herself for the anguish and guilt she saw etched in his features. She had put them there, though all the pain and remorse should have been hers. She swallowed hard and swiped at the tears. "Why did you do this for me?"

He drew back from her, concern and confusion knitting his brows. "What are you talking about, Abby? You're my wife."

"I've done nothing but treat you with mistrust and doubt. In my mind I've accused you of things I had no reason to believe you'd do. I convinced myself that you cared nothing for me, and that one day you would go away. I have been unforgiving and narrow. And now that you've done something so wonderful, I can't even allow myself to accept that perhaps you did it because you do care. It scares me, Sam, that I don't seem to be able to trust anyone. I don't deserve your gifts and your kindness. I don't even know how to thank you for them."

He reached out for her, but she stumbled to her feet, and ran into the house. She fled to the bedroom which she shared with her husband as mutual accommodations— nothing more. She lay across the bed, clutching her pillow, and wept because she was not the woman she wished she could be to this man she so desperately wanted. *What is wrong with me? Why can't I give as freely as he does? Why can't I just love him?*

Minutes later, Lizzie scratched at her door. "Miss Abby, I'm hungry."

Pulling herself up from the bed, Abby stood erect. She thrust her chin out and drew a deep breath. Opening the door, she gathered Lizzie in her arms and said, "I know, sweetie. It's time for Miss Abby to fix things, isn't it?"

"Like sam'iches?"

"Kind of, yes. We'll start with sandwiches anyway." She took Lizzie's hand and went to the kitchen. The beautiful Blue Willow dishes had been unpacked and were sitting on the table, but Sam was not there.

"Do you know where Sam is, Lizzie?" she asked.

"Yes'm. He went out to the barn."

Then that's where I shall go to mend my fences.

Chapter Nineteen

Abby and Lizzie took sandwiches to the field where Will and Emma were working. When she saw the two of them sit under a shady tree to eat, Abby knew they'd be content there for quite some time. After Lizzie had her lunch, Abby tucked her into her bed for a nap. "You stay now, sweetie," she said. "Don't get up until you've had a good rest."

The child nodded drowsily, and Abby sighed with relief. Then she went into the kitchen and got her picnic basket from the pantry. She filled it with ham and biscuits and a pint of cold lemonade and covered the food with a checkered cloth. Without stopping to question her plan for the hundredth time, she went to the barn.

The big double doors were open. Sam was at the far end of the building beyond the buckboard and stalls that housed the mules and dairy cow. The animals were out grazing, so the only nonhuman creature that Abby saw in the barn was the fat gray cat Arne Swenson had brought Lizzie during one of his visits. It yawned and stretched lazily on a bale of hay. No mice had taken up residence yet.

Sam was working hay into the stalls with a pitchfork. The back barn door was open and sunlight streamed in, illuminating swirling motes of straw and turning them into flecks of gold. They glittered in Sam's dark hair and in the fine, lighter hair on his arms. The sweet scent of fresh-cut hay mingled with the tangy pine of new wood. Abby breathed in the pleasant fragrance, and her confidence in what she was doing was bolstered. A new barn, a new life. They went together and symbolized what she wanted for her and Sam.

He noticed her when she came around the buckboard and set down the basket. Leaning the pitchfork against a stall door and settling his long frame next to it, he watched her without speaking.

"I've brought you some lunch," she said.

He acknowledged with a disinterested nod.

"I thought I'd eat out here with you, if that's all right."

His gray eyes were unreadable. Did he want her to stay or not? Shrugging with continued indifference, he mumbled, "Suit yourself."

She took out the cloth and spread it on the ground, determined not to let his curt response sway her from her goal. She sat down and smoothed her skirt around her ankles, then removed the food from the basket. "I love the dishes and the hutch," she finally said when he made no move to join her.

"Oh? It was a little hard to tell."

"I know, but I do love them. My reaction had nothing to do with my appreciation of your gifts. You shouldn't feel responsible."

"Who should then? Frederick?" His tone was both sarcastic and skeptical.

She hadn't expected him to be so cold and distant, but really couldn't blame him. She wished he would walk away from that darned stall door and sit with her, but he appeared as immovable as a block of granite. "I guess I should explain about Frederick," she ventured.

"Maybe you should."

She held out a biscuit topped with ham and mustard, and he had to come a few steps closer to take it. *Okay,* she thought, *it's a beginning.* "When you were packing in your room to come back with me, I met Frederick in the yard. We had a conversation I've been trying to forget."

Sam slowly lowered himself to the ground, but stayed coolly remote from her. He nibbled mechanically at the biscuit. "Go on. What did he say to you?"

"That he didn't want you to come back to Fox Hill . . . ever, but he believed you would. He said you wanted the Rosemont life, that you were greedy for it. He swore you would come back for the money, for your share."

A vein worked in Sam's temple. "And you believed him?"

"I didn't want to, but he seemed so sure. He said he'd been watching you, that he knew what you were like. That you were like him actually." She fixed an unwavering stare on his face. "You'll remember that on that day I wasn't so sure I knew you at all, and I'd just discovered you had a brother who probably knew you much better than I did."

There was the faintest flash of guilt in his eyes. "What about the bribe you mentioned? What was that all about?"

Keep him in your bed, sister, and I'll make it worth your while. "He told me to keep you . . . here, and he would compensate me. I'm not sure what he meant, but when I saw the Wells Fargo wagon and the large package from Rosemont Manor, I thought he was rewarding me for doing my job. I was so angry, Sam."

His eyes glittered darkly, and she prayed his fury was

not directed at her. "Why didn't you tell me about this conversation when it happened?"

"Because I knew you would have been furious with Frederick, and I'd already seen once that day how you react to his taunts. And you would have only reassured me as you've done in the past. Frankly, I'm not sure I was ready to believe you that day."

"And now? Do you believe me now?"

"Now I have proof. You haven't gone back. You're still here."

"So where do we go from here, Abby? How long will you continue to test me?"

"Test you? What do you mean?"

"Isn't it obvious? You've held yourself away from me to see if I would leave you. Are you convinced now that I'm going to stay?"

She'd never thought of it that way, and she was forced to admit that his accusation was true. She wished with all her heart that she could honestly tell him she had no more doubts, that Frederick's threats meant nothing to her anymore.

"I guess it has been a test, Sam," she finally said, "but it's over. I've lived so long with my fears and suspicions that it's almost as though I've wrapped them around me. They've become a fortress protecting me from hurt and preventing me from showing what I truly feel."

The hard lines of his face softened, indicating that his icy attitude was thawing, that he was beginning to understand. "And what do you truly feel, Abby?"

"Shame. Today, you showed me more kindness than I deserve. That's why I reacted as I did. I couldn't face your kindness because I couldn't return it. I had to let go of the doubt first."

"And you have?" His voice was husky and low, riding the waves of the space that separated them, a space that suddenly was charged with expectancy.

A shiver ribboned down her backbone, a reaction to his difficult question and the sound of his voice, seductive somehow, and exciting. "I want to, Sam. I'm trying. You must believe me. Trust does not come easily to me. But I do believe you want to do what's right for this family . . . for me."

"Then you don't believe Frederick?"

She wished she could give him a simple answer, but she couldn't. "I don't want to think about any of the Rosemonts ever again. I want to believe in you . . . only you."

He glanced away, and she was afraid she'd said the wrong thing. She desperately wanted to be honest with him, but how could she tell him she had no more doubts when it wasn't so? *Dear God,* she prayed, *don't let him stay angry at me forever.*

When he looked at her again, his eyes were bold and sure, but no longer angry or challenging. He met her gaze head on, with a confidence that suggested how he would face their lives together. "Then I will just have to see to it that you do believe in me," he said. "I'll keep trying."

Her spirits soared, and his pledge emboldened her to say what was in her heart. "I love you, Sam." The words, when they finally came, flowed from her as easily as if she had believed them all her life.

"And I love you. It's what I want to do for the rest of my life."

He spoke to her with his body as well as his words. He leaned toward her, placing his palms on the ground on each side of her knees. His face was only inches from hers; his eyes were a window to his hope and an emotion so powerful she drew a shuddering breath in anticipation of what he would say next.

"I want to whisper it in your hair with my arms around you in the dark of night."

She felt light-headed, as if she had finally reached a

precipice that she had been climbing her whole life but whose summit had always eluded her. She was already beginning to feel the glorious flight into its mysterious depths. All she needed to do was let herself go, quit hanging on to a lifeline of insecurities and doubts. "What about the light of day, Sam?" she heard herself ask. "Will you whisper it to me now?"

His smoky eyes said what words could not. He reached out his hand, she took it, and he pulled her up with him. Gathering the cloth they had been sitting on, he led her into an empty stall. The floor was covered by the new-mown hay he had just spread upon the floor. It smelled of clover and earth, fertile and rich. He lay the cloth at their feet, closed the stall door, and slipped the bar lock into place. When he faced her, he said the first words he had spoken in moments. "Are you sure, Abby?"

She nodded, her gaze never leaving his face. "Yes, I'm sure."

Her breath caught in her throat when he reached for the high collar of her blouse. His knuckles, roughened by labor, brushed against her throat as he slipped the first button free, then the second. With the backs of his fingers he caressed the line of her jaw while his gaze moved over her face, lingering on her eyes, her lips.

The coarse muslin of her blouse might have been the finest satin, for when Sam had finished loosing the buttons, the fabric slipped easily from her shoulders. He tugged the blouse from the waistband of her skirt and pushed the sleeves down her arms. It fell somewhere in the straw.

When he bent his head to her shoulders, Abby's pulse raced. A mysterious quivering began in the pit of her stomach that felt strangely like a slow-burning fuse, sizzling and snaking to where his mouth journeyed over her skin, leaving a tingling, damp trail from her collarbone to her neck.

He pulled the pins from her chignon, and her long hair

fell down her back. It was her hair, yet somehow lighter, softer than she remembered, like a silken blanket whispering over her bare shoulders. His fingers trailed through it to find her nape, then moved outward. The fuse he had lighted inside her crackled and twisted a fiery path to where his hands captured her face. His thumbs rested on her temples holding her immobile to his penetrating gaze.

She gave in to the pleasures he lavished upon her heightened senses until her eyelids grew heavy and her vision blurred. She closed her eyes just before his mouth settled on hers, soft and tantalizing. She savored the delicious blackness that blocked out everything but the feel of his lips, pressing and shaping hers.

Her hands were on his elbows, but they moved up the slightly damp skin of his upper arms and over the soft bunching of his rolled shirtsleeves to his cotton-clad shoulders. She settled one hand on the hair that covered his collar. Her fingers flexed against the tense muscles of his neck, and his mouth pressed more urgently on her lips.

When he moved his tongue insistently along the crease of her mouth, she did what he demanded and opened to allow him inside. Hesitant at first, she soon responded to the expectations of his searching tongue, circling and mating with him. The fuse reached higher and burned brighter.

His hand dropped to her chest, moving slowly above her breast, his finger working its way under the ruffled fringe of her chemise. He brushed the swell of one breast teasingly, moving closer to the crest. He kissed the corner of her mouth, the soft skin under her earlobe, her temples, bringing her more pleasurable sensations than she had ever dared to imagine, yet it was somehow not enough. *Merciful heaven, I never knew.*

She was hardly aware that he had unbuttoned the waistband of her skirt, or that the garment had fallen to the checkered cloth beneath them. She submitted willingly when he raised the chemise over her head. Out of the corner of her eye she watched it flutter to the ground. The whole process seemed to take only a fleeting second before he resumed his fervent exploration of her lips.

His palm cupped her breast from underneath, and a jolt of pure rapture coursed through her. When his thumb moved tantalizingly over the peaked top, deep within her, a burning need was fueled by his touch and crept upward to his hand, expanding and growing with a mysterious hunger for fulfillment.

''Take my shirt off,'' he whispered hoarsely, and her hands obeyed, trembling yet eager to comply. Seeking the hard plane of his chest, she rubbed her palms over the matting of damp, coiled hair. He took one of her hands and moved it down, below the waistband of his trousers, and pressed it against the mound between his legs. Her fingers cupped the swelling and it grew larger, rounder.

He moaned and lowered his head to her chest. His lips closed on one breast, and he pulled the budding nipple into his mouth and played over it with the tip of his tongue. The longing inside her swirled to where his lips became the center of her universe. She arched back, surrendering her breasts, her chest, her neck. His lips explored; his tongue left warm, wet trails on heated skin.

By degrees she slipped the bonds that held her to this earth to soar with him. So this was what it was like . . . gentle yet wild, sweetly coaxing yet feverishly demanding. The crackling fuse grew shorter, the sparks brighter. She wanted it to last forever, yet she yearned for the explosion that was somehow sure to come.

He stepped back and his gaze roamed over her. Only her flimsy pantalets hid the rest of her body from his eyes, and those were soon abandoned when he slipped them down her thighs. A breeze wafting over the stall door cooled her fevered skin, bringing with it an unwelcome awareness of her worldly surroundings, and she became conscious for the first time of her nakedness.

She suddenly felt awkward and unsure, and crossed her arms over her chest, barring the sight of her still tingling breasts. She stared at the checkered cloth under her feet as an inbred modesty grew more intense even as she attempted to reject it. *Believe in him,* she repeated over and over again, while the first inklings of unbidden shame washed over her.

"Abby, Abby, look at me." She raised her eyes tentatively, and he smiled, a tender, knowing gesture that brought a choking sob from her throat.

"You're beautiful, Abby," he said. "You're as nearly perfect as anything God ever created. Don't hide from me. I love you with all my heart. Trust me and believe that I always will."

He took her hands and coaxed her arms to her sides, then gently, tenderly, lowered her to the covered bed of straw. His calloused palm, a strangely pleasurable combination of silk and sandpaper, traced the lines of her body, beginning at her neck, curving over the swell of her breasts, and flattening at her stomach. His hand stopped at the point where all the mystery was centered. His fingers bent around her own secret swelling and pressed against her.

She sucked in an urgent breath while he brought back the glorious fluttering, warm and wonderful inside her. A wetness appeared on her inner thighs. *Sweet Jesus, what is happening?*

When he lifted his hands from her body, Abby moaned her displeasure. She yearned for his touch to continue, to fan the fire he ignited, to fulfill the promise his hands had pledged. She focused on his swift actions as he removed the last of his clothing and came back to her. Positioning himself above her, he cupped her face in his hands and pressed his lips to hers in a mind-shattering kiss of such urgency and need that Abby trembled under its onslaught.

His voice, honey smooth, came in heated pants in her ear. "Let it go, Abby. Let go of the doubt." His hands slid over her taut nipples, down her rib cage, and rounded her hips to settle underneath her. He lifted her slightly. "Go with me, Abby, my love. Let me take you."

At that glorious moment she could do nothing less than believe every fervent word he uttered. He was her Sam, the man she wanted him to be, and he was showing her how to be the woman she had only imagined she could be.

He claimed her lips again, thrusting his tongue inside at the same time he entered between her legs. Slowly he penetrated until he couldn't go any farther. "Abby," he breathed against her hair, "you know that the first time . . ."

Her voice came out as ragged as his. "Yes, I know. It's all right, Sam."

There was a brief hot flash of pain. She gritted her teeth and dug her fingers into his back. Then he began a slow rhythm that increased with each thrust until she matched his movements, climbing higher and higher to the precipice again as the fuse crackled and burned inside. The anticipation rumbled through her until it burst in a dazzling culmination of heat and light. Clutching him to her, she felt him shudder, and she knew that he had felt it too.

She cuddled against him, her spine against the curve of his stomach. She refused to open her eyes the whole way, and blurry splotches of red and white checks danced in her foggy vision. *A horse's stall on a tablecloth!* The image brought a chuckle to her lips.

"What's so funny," Sam murmured against her hair.

"This setting somehow seems just right for a farm girl," she said, "but I'm not so sure it's fitting for a Rosemont."

He laughed and stirred beside her, moving his fingers over her skin. She realized he was picking pieces of straw off her shoulder and arm, and she sighed contentedly at his gentle ministrations.

"It suits a *Kelly* just fine, though," he said, "but I won't turn down an invitation to that big bed you've been hogging for nearly three weeks now."

"Hmmmm ... just in time for you to keep my feet warm in the autumn chill." He started to respond, but she heard other voices besides his, and they were coming closer. "It's Will and Emma!" she cried, disentangling herself from Sam's arms.

"Well, at least Will's timing is better this time," Sam remarked more casually than Abby would have thought possible.

"What's he going to think?" she demanded in a panicky squeal.

"Will's a farmer too, isn't he? I bet he'll *know!*"

Abby jumped up to her knees and flung a pile of clothes at Sam. "Hurry up, put these on."

He quirked an eyebrow at her and grinned. "I don't think they're my size."

She stopped her own frantic search through the straw to stare at him. Wrinkling her nose at his humor, she grabbed the pantalets he was dangling from his hand.

When they were discovered, Abby and Sam were fully clothed. Will came into the barn with an armload of various sizes of hickory limbs. "Oh, here you are," he said, nodding at Abby. "Emma took the lunch things inside. Didn't you hear us call?"

Packing the picnic basket gave Abby an excuse to avoid

direct contact with Will's eyes. "No, I didn't hear you," she said. "We must have been talking too loudly, right, Sam?"

When she looked over at Sam for verbal support, he only shrugged a noncommittal answer. He was clearly enjoying her discomfort. She widened her eyes and prodded him with a forthright stare. "Oh, yes," he finally said. "We were practically yelling in here."

Will continued through the barn, seemingly unconcerned with their activities, and Abby followed him. She turned her attention to the wood in his arms. "What's all that for?" she asked, grateful for a change in topic.

"It's for Sam." Will caught Sam's eye and grinned. "It's a pretty good batch, don'cha think?"

"It's wonderful." Sam joined them and took a two-inch-thick limb from the top of the bundle. He turned it over several times, as though measuring it for a particular purpose. "Put the rest over there with the others."

Abby followed his line of vision, for the first time seeing the accumulation of branches and twigs in the corner of the barn. She went over for a closer look. There were several pieces of long gray-black limbs she recognized as coming from the paper birches that grew by the Little White Tail.

Next to them stood an assortment of twigs whose bark curled outward in shaggy patterns. "Shagbark hickory," she said.

"Right," Sam confirmed. "And you know what these are, of course."

He pointed to a pile of green pliant branches standing in a bunch. Identical ones had been bound into coils and were soaking in water in a galvanized tub. The coils were weighted down with heavy stones. "Willow branches," she said. "From our tree?"

"Yep, but don't worry. The tree's fine. In fact it's long been in need of a good pruning."

"What are you planning to do with all this?"

"It's just a little idea I had . . . something to keep me busy when winter comes. I hadn't intended to show you until I'd finished one whole piece, but since you're here now . . ."

Sam bounded up the ladder to the hayloft. In seconds he walked to the edge carrying a wooden contraption that Abby couldn't identify. "Here, Will, take it."

Will grabbed hold of part of the "thing" and brought it down to earth. By the time Sam came down from the loft, Abby had pretty well decided that his creation resembled a chair.

"It's a chair," he said, as though her face still registered some doubt on that point.

"I knew that . . . I did," she said, walking around Sam's handiwork and noting the curved back and arms. A hickory-slat seat was mounted on thick birch legs. Abby took hold of one arm and gave it a good shake. Yes, it was a chair, all right, and was as sturdy as everything else Sam had built on Chadwick Farm.

Sam folded his arms and peered proudly down at the oddly shaped masterpiece. "Oh, it'll hold you all right," he said. "That chair will hold anyone from our Lizzie to Duncan Walthrop, I guarantee it."

Picturing the bulk of the portly drummer settling onto the deceivingly frail spindles of the chair brought a smile to Abby's lips. But she suddenly had an overwhelming desire to test the chair's mettle herself. She turned around and lowered herself onto the seat.

"Remember, it's not quite done yet," Sam said. "There are still a few rough pieces of bark that have to be snipped off and sanded. And as for the wood-boring beetles . . ."

"What?" Abby jumped up as if the chair had caught fire. Will snickered in the background.

"I was just going to tell you," Sam explained. "I've

treated each piece with turpentine. They're clean and likely to remain so.''

''Oh.'' She sat back down and wiggled her bottom to find the best spot on the surprisingly comfortable seat. In fact, the entire chair felt pretty darn good. The back twigs were bent to accommodate the curve of her spine, and the soft pliable willow branches at the top flexed slightly with her head, creating an almost pillow-like effect. The thick bark-stripped post that formed the front of the seat was smooth under her knees, allowing the material of her skirt to slide easily along its waxed surface. She looked up at Sam. ''It's nice,'' she said, embarrassed that her voice still expressed an element of shock.

He grinned. ''You didn't think it would be, did you?''

''Well, no, actually . . .'' A totally ludicrous notion popped into her head and she asked, ''Are you going to sell these to Frederick?''

Sam laughed out loud. ''It's a Rosemont exclusive if I ever saw one!'' He got down on a knee beside her, and she watched the excitement dance in his eyes. ''I did talk to Andrew Purcell, though, and he's agreed to put them in the store when I get a bunch finished this spring. I don't expect any to sell before then anyway, since they're outdoor pieces, but by April I ought to have several chairs done and maybe some tables. Who knows?''

''Who knows indeed?'' she said. His enthusiasm was infectious. ''And all this from the simple beginnings of hickory cowboys,'' she mused.

He took her hand and pulled her up from the chair. ''Here, look at this.'' He turned the chair over and pointed to a design that had been burned into the bottom of a seat support. She recognized the simple shape of her farmhouse, with its two-story living quarters and add-on kitchen.

''Frederick has his rose,'' Sam declared, ''and we have

our farmhouse. You're seeing the very first piece of hand-crafted furniture from Chadwick Farm, Abby.''

She saw the hope in his eyes and looked at the strong, capable hands that just moments before had taken her to a plateau of delight and completion. *It's going to be all right, Abigail,* she told herself. *You must have faith that the steadfast core of Chadwick Farm, the strength of family, and the promise of a future will bind this man to you and make him forget Fox Hill.*

He'll be back. He wants this more than I've ever seen a man want anything. It was time for Frederick's voice to stop taunting her. *No more!* she shouted in her mind. *Frederick Rosemont and Tucker Brandywine, leave us alone!* Abby gripped Sam's arm and leaned against him.

"What's wrong, Abby?" he asked. "You're shivering."

"Nothing." She dismissed his concern with a shrug of her shoulders. "It's a wonderful chair, Sam. Truly it is."

Chapter Twenty

Chadwick Farm—Spring, 1893

Christmas had been one of the happiest times of Abby's life. All the children received store-bought gifts that she and Sam, in a moment of frivolous generosity, had selected from catalogues with each child's unique personality in mind.

And since holidays were a time for remembering, that was what the children of Chadwick Farm did. They talked about their memories of James Chadwick and how much they missed him. Rebecca sat by the decorated fir tree with Lizzie in her lap and listened to what everyone else said. Often a quiet smile appeared on her face, and Abby knew she was recalling one of her own fond memories of the man she had so cherished.

For Christmas dinner, when Abby served the turkey Sam purchased from Ernest Sholski, she used her Blue Willow china for the second time. And for dessert, the whole family enjoyed Sam's Christmas pudding. But it was Emma who was the envy of everyone as she was given two helpings in a Blue Willow bowl set ceremoniously on top of Timothy's primer, the book she had mastered by Thanksgiving.

Once the holidays were over, the rest of the winter dragged on as only a damp, frigid Ohio winter can ... colorless and bleak. Most mornings when they went to the barn, Sam and Will, with collars turned up around their ears, plodded through fresh snowfalls and high winds. In gray, dreary dawns, they fed the mules and milked the cow, stopping often to blow on their chilled fingers.

The industrious cat, who had been an almost constant companion to Sam before the snow came, abandoned the barn for the winter. The few mice who stubbornly refused to find warmer climes burrowed so deep into the hay that the cat gave up his efforts to find them and spent his days curled in a furry ball by the parlor fireplace.

When snow covered her house for weeks, Abby realized that the passionate abandonment that she shared with her husband that late summer day in the barn was a luxury she was not often to enjoy. That winter her house was much too small, her family too large, and the winter too cold. While she longed to feel her husband's arms around her and the same fervent kisses he had given her in the barn, she most often had to be satisfied with a hug, or a whispered word of endearment.

Even when a welcome but unexpected calm did settle over the crowded farmhouse at night, it was often too cold to enjoy it. Once the fires and kerosene heaters had been extinguished and warm bricks secured under the bedcovers, it was unthinkable to throw off one's flannels and expose bare skin to the wintry chill.

While everyone at Chadwick Farm waited impatiently for spring, their supplies and money dwindled. Each day there were fewer Mason jars on the cellar shelves, and scantier portions of pork in the smokehouse. This year there were two more mouths to feed than last, and while Sam's generous salary at the House of Rosemont had seen them through some hard times, it was nearly gone. Abby faced each day with the same question that had always plagued her at the end of winter ... would the ground ever thaw so she could plant the crops that would feed her family and sell at the marketplace?

Finally, in April, the snow melted and the Little White Tail swelled its banks with cold nourishing water from the hillsides and spring rains. Each day when the last of the nighttime frost disappeared under a warm sun, Abby, Sam, Will, and Emma broke through the hard ground to the rich warm soil below and planted the seeds that would sustain them for another year.

When her father had been the village religious leader, Abby had felt justified in asking the community for help, but she could no longer do that. She and Sam had willingly taken on the responsibility for the children. And Sam would never accept charity. He was determined to support his family, and Abby did not question her husband's resolve to succeed. Sam's pride had been won on the fields of manicured lawns and in the dusty classrooms of Chilton-Howe, and she would never strip him of the dignity that he'd earned in boyhood battles for recognition and equality.

"Everything will be all right," he told her often, and she found comfort knowing their loft was full of sturdy Chadwick Farm chairs and tables. Sam believed that with those fine, handcrafted pieces lay their future, and Abby encouraged him, because if they failed, the consequences were too awful to think about. And, of course, one of those consequences for Abby was still the image of Fox Hill and the inheritance that was Sam's for the taking.

He never said he wanted to go back, but Abby feared the possibility always existed for him. He loved her, she believed he did, but perhaps Rosemont money would become too tempting when weighed against the challenges of Chadwick Farm. Would the tug of his Ohio family be enough to hold him from that other prosperous family, when the burdens became too heavy for one man to carry? And if Sam went back, Abby couldn't imagine herself going with him. As much as she loved him, she doubted she could ever leave her home or subject her children to the scorn of Delilah and her sons.

She didn't bring these doubts up to Sam, hoping that if his wealthy family remained in the background of his thoughts, he would be less likely to go back to them. She prayed his enterprise in the hayloft would bring him contentment and the financial stability they needed.

Once selected pieces of Sam's handiwork were on display in Andrew Purcell's store, trips to the establishment took on a new significance. Abby always met the buckboard when Sam returned to the farm. She asked if any of the pieces had sold, but so far, Sam's answer had been, "Not yet."

"I'm sure they will," she kept repeating despite her misgivings, but as the month of April came to an end, she began to wonder if they ever would.

Then one bright May afternoon a smart open carriage pulled by two perfectly matched Appaloosas come over the rise toward the house. The driver was ensconced on a padded seat above his passengers. He wore a well-tailored suit that reminded Abby of royal livery she'd once seen in a book.

On one of the plush passenger benches, a man in a dark three-piece vested suit sat with the confident posture of prosperity. A spotless derby topped his trim gray hair, and his hands were folded over an ebony cane that was propped upright between his legs.

Next to him was an attractive lady every bit as elegantly attired. She sat primly beside her companion, the breeze lifting the ruffled trim of her high-necked blouse. In a gloved hand, she held a cream-colored parasol that shaded a small hat trimmed with a black ostrich feather.

The carriage had two large passenger seats, and what was most remarkable to Abby was that the spare seat was filled with various pieces of Sam's rustic furniture! And that wasn't all. More of it had been strapped to the back of the carriage with ropes and blankets, the whole effect being one of a gypsy traveling band . . . an amusing contrast with the dignified appearance of the travelers.

Lizzie squealed and pointed a chubby finger. "Look, Miss Abby! What is it?"

Abby picked the child up and balanced her on her hip. "I'm not really sure, Lizzie, but we'll find out, I guess."

When Abby walked up to the carriage, the driver looked down and inquired, "Is this the home of Samuel Kelly?"

"Yes, it is," Abby answered, looking around for Sam. She was relieved to see that he had noticed the mysterious arrival and was coming toward them from the apple orchard.

"This is it, Mr. Rockefeller," the driver said, turning to his passengers and peering at them through the legs and arms of a small mountain of furniture.

Rockefeller? Abby had heard of a man by that name who'd started an oil company in Cleveland, but surely this wasn't the same man. She knew *that* Mr. Rockefeller was enormously wealthy. Why would *he* be in Seneca Village?

The man climbed down from the carriage and came toward her. "Are you Mrs. Kelly?"

"Yes, sir."

He tipped his hat to her. "John D. Rockefeller, madam. I've come to see your husband. I understand he is the artisan responsible for the pieces in our carriage."

It is *him . . . John D. Rockefeller!* "H-how do you do?" she stammered. She reached for Sam, but her hand only fluttered in the air since he was still several feet away. "Sam, this is Mr. Rockefeller. He's come to see you."

"Mr. *John* Rockefeller?" he asked, taking the man's extended hand.

"The same. That's my wife in the carriage."

Sam and Abby looked at the woman, and she acknowledged them with a polite nod while her husband continued. "We've just come from that quaint little store in the village where we stumbled upon your creations, Mr. Kelly. As you can see, we rather fancied them. So much that I persuaded the owner to direct us to your factory."

Factory? Abby saw the same amused expression on Sam's face that she suspected was on hers. "That's it over there," Sam said, pointing to the barn.

Mr. Rockefeller stated the obvious. "It's a barn."

"Yes, it is."

"You made all these pieces there?"

"I did."

"Have you any more?"

"Would you care to follow me, Mr. Rockefeller?" At the man's assent, Sam led his guest to the barn.

Abby had a hard time picturing the well-dressed man climbing the ladder to the hayloft to inspect the other pieces of Sam's furniture, but she guessed that was exactly what he was going to do. Meanwhile she turned her attention to his wife. "Would you like some tea, Mrs. Rockefeller?" she asked.

"How kind of you, Mrs. Kelly. Indeed I would." She allowed the driver to assist her out of the carriage, then preceded Abby into the cool kitchen of the farmhouse. Sitting on one of Sam's straight-backed rustic chairs that now surrounded the large table, Mrs. Rockefeller exclaimed, "Ah, these chairs are a marvel." She rubbed her shoulders against the bent-willow back. "I can't wait until we get them to our summer home in the Adirondacks."

Abby had no idea what was going on in Sam's *factory*, but she was awestruck at the picture of Mrs. John Davison Rockefeller sipping tea from one of her own Blue Willow cups. And Lizzie O'Donnell was sitting in the woman's lap sharing her cookie!

Thirty minutes later, Mr. John D. Rockefeller poked his distinguished gray head over the Dutch door of Abby's kitchen and motioned to his wife. "Come along, dear, or we'll miss the train."

As they walked to the fancy carriage, Mr. Rockefeller kept up a lively conversation with Sam. "So you can do special orders?" he asked.

"As long as it's furniture suitable for the outdoors, Mr. Rockefeller, I can make it."

"And you can ship the pieces in the barn to Saratoga Springs as soon as I notify you?"

"Sure can."

Mrs. Rockefeller gave her husband a subtle poke in his ribs. "Why, John, you must have had the very same thought I did. Once we get the furniture we bought today on our porch, it will be quite the rage. Everyone will want to know where we got it."

"That's exactly what I think will happen, and I want Sam here to be ready. You could be a very busy young man soon, Kelly."

"Nothing would make me happier, sir."

Mr. Rockefeller assisted his wife into the carriage and climbed in beside her. "Let's be off, Raymond," he said to his driver, and then touched the brim of his bowler at Sam and Abby. "Nice doing business with you folks," he said. "You'll be hearing from me."

Sam and Abby watched the loaded conveyance sway on its rockers and finally settle into an equilibrium suited to its cumbersome cargo. As soon as the Rockefellers

disappeared over the rise, Sam turned Abby toward him.
He wrapped his arms around her waist, lifted her off the
ground, and spun her around twice before setting her
down again. Lizzie clapped her hands and hollered, ''Me
too,'' and Sam obliged her.

''You know what life is all about, Abby?'' he mused
when he'd deposited Lizzie on the ground and she'd run
off after her cat. ''It's fate—that's it, plain and simple—
and sometimes fate has golden opportunities in store. We
must be alert enough to recognize them and prepared to
grab on with both hands. Like when Duncan Walthrop
picked me up on the road in Cooper's Glen. And like
today when John D. Rockefeller happened into Seneca
Village.''

A bright glow of wonder dawned in Sam's eyes, and
it tickled Abby to see how the events of the past hour
had turned him into a philosopher.

He clasped her hands in his, looked heavenward for an
instant as if thanking whatever force had sent fortune his
way, and returned his gaze to her face. ''They could have
taken the train in Cleveland, that's what he told me, Abby.
But his wife likes to shop in little out-of-the-way places,
so they'd made a trip of it driving from Cleveland to
Akron in their own carriage.

''And they wandered into Andrew Purcell's Mercantile
today. Can you believe it? If they hadn't decided to catch
a train in Akron, this never would have happened. It's
fate, Abby, my love, a miracle really, and this time, the
miracle is ours.''

Once again, she recalled her father's words on the day
he'd presented her with the Sears and Roebuck Catalogue.
Most often what we're searching for is the little miracles,
Abigail, the ones that just sort of sidestep into our lives
without a lot of fanfare.

Sam raised her hands to his lips and kissed her fingers.
She smoothed a lock of his hair off his forehead and

looked into his eyes. "I think this situation deserves a little better than that, Sam Kelly, from a man who believes in miracles."

He lowered his eyelids in teasing seduction, and the grin he gave her hinted of a bold sexuality that was all hungry male tempered with a boyish innocence that made Abby's heart race.

"Right you are, Abigail Kelly," he said. He wrapped his arms around her and lifted her again, this time to meet his eager mouth.

Sam and Abby didn't see Mr. Rockefeller again, but the man's predictions proved absolutely correct. During May and June Sam received over a dozen orders from the Rockefellers' wealthy Adirondack neighbors. And the best thing about the orders was that they were always prepaid. Apparently John D. had convinced his summer acquaintances that the artisan who crafted the unusual pieces was a man who could be trusted. To prove himself worthy of that trust, Sam worked long hours to make the furniture and ship it when promised.

His efforts paid off at the end of June when a letter bearing the Standard Oil Company's Cleveland address arrived for him at Purcell's. As soon as he returned home, Sam immediately went into the house to find Abby. He then tore open the envelope and read its contents.

Abby waited impatiently as Sam's facial expression changed from interest to shock and finally to joyous exhilaration. "What is it, Sam?" she prompted, thinking she might very well jump out of her skin if he didn't tell her soon. "Is it from *him?* What does it say?"

Sam was bursting with spectacular news. "It's from John D., all right. Maybe you'd better sit down, Abby."

She reluctantly did as he suggested. "Okay, I'm sitting. Now tell me what's going on or pay the consequences!"

Sam grasped the arms of her chair. Abby had never seen a light quite like the one that shone from his eyes. "How'd you like to go to Chicago?" he said.

"Chicago?"

"To the Columbian Exposition. Mr. Rockefeller says an exhibitor has to take an emergency leave from the American Design Building, and he wants to sponsor Chadwick Farm for the two weeks the vacant spot will be available. Look here, Abby, read what he says."

Sam pointed to a line in the middle of the letter. *"It's about time this overindustrialized nation of ours got a kick in its collective backside from good old American hands-on ingenuity."*

Abby grabbed his wrist. "The Exposition! Oh, Sam, this could be a chance for you to gain real recognition. I've read that thousands of people attend every day. But what will it cost?"

"Nothing for the two of us. He said to be sure and include my *lovely wife* ... the man has excellent taste, don't you think? As soon as I let him know if we're interested, he'll reserve the space in the exhibition hall and a hotel room nearby for the last two weeks in July."

Try as she might, Abby couldn't make the skeptical side of her nature surrender completely to the spontaneous joy of the moment. Somehow their benefactor's offer just seemed too good to be true. "Why would Mr. Rockefeller do this, Sam? What's in it for him?"

Sam smiled. "I knew you'd ask that, the suspicious but beautiful realist that you are. I didn't show you the second page of the letter. Ol' John D.'s a businessman first, last, and always. He's a major contributor to the Exposition, which is how he's able to pull these strings, but he wants me to agree to split the profits from all orders received as a result of his efforts to get us in."

Abby thought about the terms. "That certainly seems fair."

"That's what I thought."

"But what about the children? Mr. Rockefeller's only paying for two tickets. We can't leave them alone. Tucker could still be out there somewhere . . ."

"Already thought of that," Sam said. "Abby, in the mountains of New York State there are at least a dozen summer home porches that are crammed full of Chadwick Farm furniture. I think the *corporation* can afford to purchase seven additional train tickets for the employees who've helped make this possible."

She nodded her head. That was reasonable, all right.

Sam must have seen the lessening of doubt in her face, because he was beaming with anticipated victory when he grasped her shoulders. "So what do you say, Ab? Are we going to Chicago?"

The city on the shore of Lake Michigan might have been Paris, France, glittering on the Seine for all the glamor and adventure it conjured up in Abby's mind. Oh, yes, she wanted to see Chicago! "There's just one thing, though . . ."

"What is it?" he asked impatiently. "Whatever it is I'll fix it!"

"We'll have to have two large hotel rooms . . . one for the boys and one for the girls. Can the hotel accommodate all of us in just two rooms?"

He grinned and a hint of wickedness lit his eyes. "Already thought of that too. We'll get three rooms . . . two large enough for all of them, and a slightly smaller, blessedly quieter, wonderfully *private* one for us. Last summer I promised you a honeymoon, and it's time I made good on that promise."

Chapter Twenty-one

Nearly half the population of Seneca Village came out to watch when the Kelly family passed through to catch the train to the World's Columbian Exposition. It wasn't so much that their neighbors wanted to wish them farewell, although many of them did. It wasn't even that it was an opportunity to see that Brandywine girl who had become a recent topic of conversation. No, the townspeople had known of Emma's existence for quite some time, and they were content to leave her exactly where she was—at Chadwick Farm.

After all, Emma Brandywine was a skinny teenaged girl, and therefore possessed few desirable skills and talents in a farming community such as Seneca Township. And she was the seed of that awful Tucker Brandywine, a fact that didn't endear her to Seneca citizens who firmly believed that an apple doesn't fall far from the tree. All in all, Emma was not considered adoptable.

No, the reason the people came out to see the Kellys off on their momentous journey was because John D.

Rockefeller himself sent a personal conveyance to pick the family up and transport Sam's furniture to the depot. No one wanted to miss seeing a wagon that had come all the way from Cleveland and belonged to such a notable individual.

Curious eyes were not disappointed. The large freight wagon that passed through Seneca Village that day was painted a bright red with the words ''Standard Oil Company'' scripted in glossy black paint across its sides. Sam and Abigail Kelly rode in the elevated front seat with the driver, and the children rode on benches behind them. Samples of Sam's rustic furniture were loaded in the deep open well of the wagon, and wonder of wonders—the whole lot of it was truly going to Chicago.

The westbound train left Akron at dinnertime, and it was all Abby and Sam could do to keep the twins in their seats in the plush dining car. Thomas and Timothy finally settled down when they were each given a window seat. But it meant that they kept their minds on the passing scenery more than their supper.

Susanna, at eleven, was nothing like the rambunctious boys. She sat primly in her chair beside Thomas. She grimaced in disgust at a blob of ketchup that fell from the boy's fork to land on his clean white shirt, and she hastily stuffed his napkin in his collar to prevent another mishap. He responded with a theatrical display of choking sounds, which caused Susanna to roll her eyes with impatience. ''For heaven's sake, Miss Abby,'' she remarked with the air of a world-weary traveler, ''you'd think these boys had never been away from home.''

Thomas squinted up at her in confusion. ''Well, geez, we haven't! Ouch!'' He snapped upright in his seat and reached down to rub his shin as Susanna innocently lifted her own fork to her mouth.

Timothy continued staring out the window, a half-eaten biscuit poised midway to his mouth. ''I don't see the reason of somethin', Sam," he mused. "If them trees are flyin' by so fast out there, how come these plates ain't slidin' off the table?"

"I'll take that one for you, Sam," Will said. He looked across the table at Emma to make sure he had her attention before answering. "It's because the plates are glued down and the trees aren't. You better not touch the bottom of your dish, or you'll be stuck to the table too, and you'll have to ride in this dining car all the way to Chicago."

Emma giggled, as Timothy jerked his hands away from his plate. Sam scowled at Will before placating the frightened boy. "Don't you worry, son," he said. "It's the train that's moving. The trees are staying put just like all of us, these dishes, and everything else inside. Your plate will move if you pick it up, so you can finish your meal without fear of getting stuck."

Sam pointed his fork at Will and gave him a halfhearted frown of rebuke. "And you, Mr. Professor, I have a hunch you'll get your reward for that answer tonight."

The Kellys occupied four sleeping berths. Rebecca shared with Lizzie, Emma with Susanna, and Will slept between Thomas and Timothy. Sam poked his head in on the three young men before climbing into his berth with Abby. "Comfortable in there, Mr. Buckman, sir?"

Wedged between two limp bodies, Will had to remove a chubby hand from his face before he could answer. "They're already floppin' around like a couple of bluegills outta water. Now all I need is for the pair of 'em to grunt like billy goats!"

"It's the least you deserve," Sam said. "And good practice. My guess is, someday you and Emma will have kids of your own. And I'd lay a twenty-dollar gold piece down right now that you'll be a fine daddy when the time comes."

Will cast him a surprised look, but it was soon replaced with a grin of satisfaction. When he closed the privacy curtain, Sam noticed that Will was tucking the covers around his two charges.

Just after eight o'clock the next morning, the conductor announced that the train was pulling into the Chicago station. Sam put Will in charge of the luggage since he himself would have to arrange for the hasty unloading of the Chadwick Farm furniture. When the pieces were transferred to a wagon, Sam gave the driver instructions to deliver the cargo to the American Design Building at the Exposition. Then the family hired a cab to take them to the Piedmont Hotel located on State Street, just a few blocks from the fair.

During the hectic maneuvers, Emma had hastily ducked into the depot, where she grabbed numerous brochures highlighting the exhibitions and activities of the Exposition. She read silently from pamphlets as the cab progressed to State Street, and then she related what she'd learned to the family. "It says all the buildings are like the ones built by an . . . an . . ." She turned to Sam and pointed to a word.

"That's 'ancient,' Emma."

". . . ancient Greeks and Romans. That means they look real old, right, Sam?"

"Yep, that's right."

". . . with columns and arches and something called atriums filled with flowers." She looked at Abby. "Don't . . . *doesn't* that sound just beautiful?"

"It most definitely does."

"And they built lagoons right in the middle of it all with statues and fountains. And look at this!" She held up a photo for everyone to see. "Runnin' right smack down the center is somethin' called Midway Playsance."

Sam looked at the caption under the picture to see what she was talking about. "That's Midway *Plaisance,*" he said. "It's French, and it stands for pleasure. And it looks to me like that's where all the fun is."

"They got a thing called a Ferris wheel there. It climbs way up into the sky and holds hundreds of people at one time. I can't wait to see it." All the children agreed with Emma, and begged for an immediate trip to the midway.

"Tell you what," Sam said. "Let's drop the bags off at the hotel and tell the doorman to send them up to our rooms. Will and I can meet the freight wagon and set up our display, and the rest of you can go on ahead to the fair. Later when we join up, you can show us around. How does that sound?"

Sam's suggestion met with instant approval, and for the rest of the journey to the hotel, everyone concentrated on the sights and sounds of Chicago. None of the children had ever seen a skyscraper before, and they were awestruck by buildings that soared ten stories above the street.

When the hire coach entered the bustling center of town located inside a web of streetcar tracks, its pace slowed considerably due to increased traffic. The driver threaded his way through numerous carriages and wagons to stop under a brilliant red marquee which identified a multi-storied gray stone building as the Piedmont Hotel.

The children clambered out of the coach anxious to be on their way to the fair. The only one who seemed daunted by the crush of vehicle and pedestrian traffic was Rebecca. After the coach was dismissed and the suitcases were inside the hotel, she quietly whispered to Sam that she wanted to go with him and Will rather than face the crowds on the midway.

"Then that's exactly what you shall do," he told her, and the three of them set off for the American Design Building soon after the rest of the family had left for the fair.

* * *

The first floor of the American Design Building was a collection of furniture of such distinctive and opulent styles that Sam began to wonder if perhaps John D. Rockefeller's confidence in him wasn't a bit misplaced. There certainly was a need for the furniture Sam created, and no doubt a locality where it fit in perfectly, but somehow the Columbian Exposition did not seem to be that place.

The ceramic-tiled floor of the exhibition hall was not the appropriate platform for his creations. Likewise, the swirled plaster walls painted with scenes from Greek mythology were hardly a fitting backdrop.

Nevertheless, Sam set up his exhibit amid the displays of polished Victorian mahogany, solid carved Eastlake walnut, and intricate Oriental wicker and bamboo. He knew he was the object of curious stares and whispered comments from other exhibitors, but he told himself that the opinions that really mattered were those of the general public. Glancing every few minutes at his pocket watch, he waited nervously for the doors to the hall to be opened to visitors.

"Sam! Sam Kelly, is that you?"

The familiar voice captured Sam's attention. He peered over the heads of fellow exhibitors to see a thin, fair man edging his way through the crowd. The man's pale face was lit with joyous recognition, and his hand was outstretched long before he was close enough for Sam to grasp it.

"Simon!" Sam clasped his brother's hand and patted his shoulder, his surprise at seeing the younger Rosemont catching him off guard. He should have anticipated that the House of Rosemont would have an exhibit at the fair, but in all the hectic activity of the past weeks, the thought hadn't really occurred to him.

Sam realized with more than a little astonishment that he was truly glad to see Simon. He considered his brother's flawless fair visage a friendly face among the crowd. He knew too that he would not have experienced the same reaction had his unexpected visitor been Frederick. And if Simon was here, could Frederick be far behind?

"It's good to see you, Sam!" Simon exclaimed. "As a matter of fact, it's unbelievable. What are you doing here?"

Obviously Simon was so caught up in the reunion that he hadn't noticed the rustic furniture display. Sam smiled a little thinly and swept his hand around his small area. "I'm an exhibitor actually."

"Go on!" Simon hooted with surprise and delight. He scanned the sample pieces and shook his head in wonder. "What is all this? I've never seen the like."

Simon's reaction was not at all critical. He was, in fact, genuinely and forthrightly curious, and Sam found himself relating the origin and details of his unique designs with pride. Simon listened attentively, a good audience for Sam's enthusiastic oration.

"Who knows, brother? These pieces just might be the hit of the show," Simon encouraged. He rubbed his chin thoughtfully. "Imagine . . . outdoor furniture that actually melds with the environment. A novel idea to be sure. I can see where these designs might catch the eye of stylists and grace the verandas of lake cottages and . . ."

He suddenly stopped talking, and stood absolutely still as if stunned by an electric current. Sam thought for a moment that Simon might even have stopped breathing, until he noticed that his brother's unblinking gaze was fixed, not on the furniture any longer, but rather on the silent young woman who sat on one of the chairs. Rebecca's eyes were cast down to her lap as if she was acutely aware of Simon's ill-concealed interest and wasn't at all sure how to react to it.

Without taking his eyes off Rebecca, Simon sidestepped closer to Sam. "My God, man, she's an angel," he whispered behind a cupped hand.

The truth of Simon's appraisal struck Sam as ironic, and he smiled. "Yes, as a matter of fact, she is."

"Who is she?"

"She lives with Abby and me. Remember I told you about the children we care for?"

"She's not a child, though, is she, Sam?"

Simon sounded so desperate that Sam chuckled. "No, she's seventeen."

"Would ... would you consider introducing me to her?"

"Come on." The two men walked toward Rebecca, and seeing her through Simon's eyes, Sam noticed for the first time the changes that had occurred in the girl's appearance since he'd come to the farm sixteen months ago. She had seemed just an innocent child then, and now, though the blush of pure innocence had been taken from her by Tucker Brandywine, the tender fragility was still there. But it was tempered by more mature qualities, and Sam could understand Simon's attraction to her.

Rebecca had become a young woman while Sam had been too busy to notice the subtle metamorphosis. Her long hair, which had always streamed down her back with girlish freedom, was now captured in a cluster at her crown, a blue ribbon that matched her blouse entwined in its mass. Her lips and cheekbones were colored a delicate pink. Was it because she blushed under Simon's appreciative stare, or had she started using facial tints? Sam felt suddenly awkward and embarrassed that he didn't know for sure.

She sat in the chair with the appearance of self-possessed dignity that one might have taken for haughtiness if her sweet disposition and simplicity were not still reflected in the deep blue of her eyes. In truth, there was not an iota of pretension about Rebecca. The gentle, pretty girl that she had been had become an artlessly beautiful woman.

"Rebecca," Sam said, and she looked from him to Simon. "I'd like you to meet my half brother, Simon Rosemont. Simon, this is Rebecca St. John."

She raised her hand slowly from her lap and offered it to Simon. "How do you do, Mr. Rosemont?"

He bowed slightly over her hand. "Very well, Miss St. John. It is indeed a pleasure to meet you."

Sam thought it wise to keep the details of his relationship to Simon simple. Of all the children, it was only Will who knew of the animosity that existed between Sam and his father's family. "Simon is from Pittsburgh, Rebecca. I stayed with him when I worked there last summer."

"I see."

"Is this your first visit to Chicago, Miss St. John?" Simon asked.

"Yes, it is."

"And are you enjoying the Exposition?"

"Well, I haven't seen too much of it yet, but the buildings and especially the gardens are very beautiful. I've always liked flowers."

Sam passed an astonished glance between the two. Simon was obviously smitten to his core. But Rebecca . . . she'd just uttered two full sentences, more than she'd said at one time in months, to a virtual stranger. Sam was amazed.

"Have you walked the midway or passed along the lagoons, Miss St. John?" Simon asked.

"No, not yet. We only just arrived this morning."

"Well, then, if Sam doesn't object, perhaps you'll allow me to escort you this evening. The weather promises to be mild."

At that moment Will returned from exploring the exhi-

bition hall, and made his presence known with an unexpected outburst. "You stay away from her! She won't
go anywhere with you."

Sam glared at him, Simon stiffened, and Rebecca shrank
back into her chair. "Will, what's wrong with you?"
Sam asked. "I know this man. He's my brother, Simon."

"If that's supposed to make me feel better, it doesn't.
I know how your family treated you in Pittsburgh. And
besides, I don't care who he is, Rebecca's not goin' off
with some fella she doesn't know." Will tried to position
himself between Rebecca and Simon, but Sam prevented
him from doing so.

"In the first place," Sam began calmly, "I hold no
animosity toward Simon, and secondly, no one has said
Rebecca is going off with him, not even Rebecca herself.
But more importantly, it's not your decision to make."
Sam wondered if Will would ever forgive himself for
what had happened to Rebecca. If he didn't, he was surely
going to smother her. "Now, I know Simon, and I trust
him. Let's see what Rebecca wants to do."

"But does he know she's . . . different?" Will whispered hoarsely.

"Maybe it's time we stopped treating her so differently,
and let her make her own decisions. We can't shelter her
from the world forever. Will you stay out of this?"

Will grunted his reluctant assent, and Sam returned to
Simon and Rebecca. "Simon, will you excuse us for a
moment? I'd like to speak to Rebecca alone."

"Certainly." Simon stepped to the side, as far away
from Will as he could go.

Sam bent down and took Rebecca's hands. "Sweetheart, Simon has asked you to go for a walk with him
this evening. I believe him to be a nice man, a gentleman.
Would you like to go?"

"I think maybe I would. I like him, Sam, but I want
you to go too, and Miss Abby, and Will and Emma . . ."

He patted her hand. "I think that's a wonderful idea. May I ask him to join us for dinner?" Rebecca's smile was his answer.

Sam put his arm around Simon's shoulders and led him a few feet away. He explained the plan, and Simon readily agreed. "She's rather shy," Sam said, "and if I may put it bluntly without offending, not at all like the Rosemonts."

Simon laughed. "Why do you think I was drawn to her, Sam? Don't I know what it's like to be different from the Rosemonts? And two days from now when Frederick gets back from Pittsburgh with Mother, I will certainly be reminded!"

Sam didn't know how Abby would react to hearing the House of Rosemont had an exhibit at the fair. He could only imagine how she'd feel seeing Frederick and Delilah again. And he was most concerned about what she'd say when he told her he'd invited Simon to have dinner with them. But one thing Sam did know for sure was that he was looking forward to seeing Abby after the long day, and the last thing he wanted to do was upset her.

He took Will and Rebecca to their hotel rooms. Emma, who was in charge of the youngest children, whispered at the door when she saw them. "The little 'uns are sleepin' so don't you all make any noise." She flashed Will a challenging little grin and added, " 'Sides, Will Buckman, I want you to save all your screamin' for that Ferris wheel. Wait till you see the size of that thing! You'll swear you're flyin'."

Sam chuckled as Will's face turned stark white. "Where's Miss Abby, Emma?"

"She's in the next room, and you be just as quiet when you go in there 'cause she's restin'. I promised her we'd leave her be till seven-thirty, when we go to supper."

Sam held his finger to his lips. "Don't worry about

me. I'll be quiet as a mouse.'' Then he exaggerated by tiptoeing away until Emma had closed the door.

The door to his room was unlocked. It was cool and dark inside. The draperies were drawn, so that just remnants of the afternoon sun filtered around the thick damask material. It was enough light for Sam to appreciate that the room was elegantly appointed.

Ivy-decorated wallpaper climbed to a ceiling border of acanthus leaves. The bedspread and linens matched its forest-green color, as did the upholstery of the two wing chairs flanking the marble fireplace. A brass fire screen closed off the hearth for the summer. A triple-door wardrobe stood along one wall and a lowboy bureau against another. Sam recognized his and Abby's personal items on top of the bureau.

The room was well-furnished and functional in all respects, but one thing was definitely missing . . . Abby. The bed linens were unwrinkled, refuting Emma's story that Abby was resting. He was about to return to the children's room to question Emma further when the faint scent of lavender assailed his nostrils.

He turned toward the origin of the pleasant aroma and spied the door to the lavatory, which was open a few inches. A soft gold glow spilled onto the floral patterned carpet and drew Sam as if it were a beacon.

He looked inside, but with the limited viewing perspective afforded by the small opening, he couldn't see directly into the room. What he did see was a full-length mirror tilted on its mahogany frame. Gaslights on either side of the mirror burned with flickering low flames inside frosted tulip shades and cast the room in soft illumination.

A large oval porcelain tub was visible in the mirror, and drew Sam's gaze. As he watched, a long shapely leg slowly raised from one end of the bath. Frothy white bubbles dripped down the calf. Sam followed the path of the bubbles to where a thigh disappeared into the tub. He then looked at the opposite end of the bath, where Abby's head rested against the curved edge, her face in repose.

Most of her hair had been artlessly piled on top of her head, but red-gold strands of it trailed down her throat and into the foam sparkling at her shoulders. While Sam stood spellbound, Abby lifted her hand from a mound of froth and pressed a thick sponge to her knee. When she squeezed, bubbles cascaded into the tub, leaving only bare, cream-colored skin to tempt him.

His wife had spectacular legs! He'd never before viewed them as he was at this moment. The one exposed to his appreciative stare was magnificent. The light reflected off her calf and it seemed as though her flesh were made of wet satin . . . sleek, gleaming, immensely touchable.

A tightness pooled in Sam's loins while he considered what he should do. The proper thing, the thing he assumed his Midwestern wife would expect, would be to announce his presence, and immediately forsake the secret pleasure he was experiencing by watching the purely natural, yet intensely arousing, scene of her bath. But he did not believe he could summon the words that would break the artistic splendor of the vision in the mirror. There was something deeply stirring about being the lone spectator of a live tableau, and Sam kept silent.

All of his senses were heightened and focused. He breathed in the sweet lavender. His eyes feasted. This exquisite woman was his wife, yet different from who she'd always been, recognizable as the woman he loved, yet unforgettable as the one he desired.

"Why are you standing out there, Sam Kelly?" Her voice trembled low and soft, like the base notes of a violin.

Ah, caught in the act. Sam's eyes widened to see the smile form on her lips. "I-I'm sorry," he stammered. "I have something to tell you. I was going to come in."

"Then why haven't you?"

He opened the door wide enough to slip inside. She watched him with warm, welcoming eyes. "I didn't want to intrude," he said. The hell he didn't. *Intrude* was a ridiculous understatement of what he wanted to do. It was all he could do to keep his hands at his sides, to keep from reaching out and gliding his fingers along her slippery wet skin to find the warm, glorious parts of her hidden beneath the foam.

"This bath is luxurious, Sam," she said. "Lying here is probably the second most pleasurable thing I've ever done."

"The second?"

"I'm sure you can imagine the first." She looked at him from under thick, dark lashes with a coy flirtation that was not at all like her, but was decidedly exciting. The ridge in Sam's pants grew harder, straining against the closure.

"Do you see how large the tub is?" she asked. "Why do you suppose that's so?"

He grinned down at her. "Perhaps it's to accommodate husbands who have promised their wives honeymoons."

"That's exactly what I think." He began unbuttoning his shirt. "If you'll come a little closer," she said, "I'll do that for you."

He stepped to the side of the tub and waited. She wrapped her fingers around the porcelain rim and stood up, reaching almost to his height since the bath was elevated on brass claw feet. Trickles of frothy water cascaded down her chest, parting at her rosy upturned breasts. The bubbles looked like violet crystals in the soft light.

She unbuttoned the rest of his shirt. With damp hands she pushed the material off his shoulders and let the shirt fall to the floor. She rippled her fingers up his back, finally entwining them in the hair at his nape and pulling him closer.

Strands of her hair, heavy with water and gleaming a rich, dark burgundy, clung to her breasts. With the backs of his hands he brushed the tresses over her shoulders, exposing her breasts to his touch. The nipples hardened instantly against his palms. He kneaded each puckering tip between his thumb and forefinger until she moaned her response.

It was more than he could bear. ''Oh, Abby,'' he groaned, hardly recognizing the urgency in his own voice. He crushed his mouth over hers and jerked her hard against him. Her hands tightened on his nape, and her breasts flattened against his chest, soaking his mat of soft, springy hair. Her breasts felt warm from her bathwater, yet the skin surrounding them was cool from exposure to the air. Her touch refreshed him from his walk in the afternoon sun, at the same time inflaming his senses with a burning need only she could quench.

While he worked his mouth over hers, opening it to the thrusts of his plundering tongue, his fingers fumbled with the tousled mass of waves at her crown. He pulled two pins from her hair, releasing it in a thick tumble down her back. He raked trembling fingers through it, finding her back and stroking her spine. He was hardly aware of her hands working feverishly to unbuckle his belt and unbutton his trousers.

Somehow he managed to kick off his boots and socks and step out of his trousers. With all barriers removed, he grasped her buttocks and lifted her slightly, pressing her dampened triangle of hair against his enlarged flesh.

A throaty giggle erupted at his ear, and Abby slipped down. He held her tightly, protectively, but she clasped her fingers around his shoulders and pulled him with her into the tub. He was just able to step over the side and release her in time to spread his hands on the bottom of the bath to support his weight.

Water sloshed over the side as Sam straddled her. "Good God, Abby, I could have crushed you," he said.

"I dare you to try," she challenged with desire and amusement dancing in her green eyes. She reached between his legs and guided him to her. His mouth covered hers and his arms wrapped round her, lifting her to meet his entrance, and he was lost in the wondrous wet warmth of his wife.

An hour later, evening shadows washed the room in a charcoal haze. Towels lay on the carpet beside the tousled bed. Abby rested her head in the crook of Sam's shoulder while he ran a lazy finger up and down her arm. They had made love again, this time slowly, languorously, luxuriously. "So what was it you were going to tell me?" Abby cooed in a soft, sated voice.

"What do you mean?"

"When you came back to the hotel. You said you had something to tell me. What was it?"

"Oh, that's right, I did." Reality suddenly intruded on their idyllic setting, and Sam knew he had to face it. He still had to tell Abby about Simon and the Rosemonts. "You're not going to believe this," he began.

"Believe what? That Simon is here, and he's interested in Rebecca?"

He sat up and leaned over her. "How did you know about that?"

"When a dozen yellow roses arrived for Rebecca St. John this afternoon, I couldn't resist looking at the card."

"The poor boy's really gone overboard," Sam remarked wryly. "I invited him to have dinner with us. I hope you're not angry."

"Since it's Simon and not Frederick, no. But that *I* didn't get any roses, maybe a little angry."

"My darling wife," he said, grinning at her, "let me

show you today's orders, and tomorrow we'll buy you an entire hothouse of flowers!''

"Sam! You never said anything. You mean we did well today?''

He winked at her and kissed her forehead. "I can't imagine how it slipped my mind to tell you, but yes, my love, we did.''

Chapter Twenty-two

Sam positioned a pair of twig chairs around a bent hickory table, then stepped back to appraise the setting for its aesthetic value. His efforts failed, however, because his gaze was drawn instead to the tempting derriere of his wife. Abby was bent over a low table arranging a vase of flowers, and her meadow-green satin skirt swayed gently as she moved. The black velvet ruffle at the hem brushed against the backs of her slim ankles until she straightened, allowing the ruffle to sweep the floor once more.

"You look quite elegant," he said. "I like the clothes you bought at the dress shop."

She turned to him, and the carved malachite brooch at her throat caught the early morning sun coming through long arched windows along the wall. She ran a finger down the onyx buttons of her blouse and puffed out the stylish leg-o'-mutton sleeves. "I don't look like a country peasant then?"

He smiled. "No, not a bit, and I know what you're

thinking. Frederick and Delilah arrive today. I wish you wouldn't worry about what they think of you. It couldn't be any less flattering than their opinions of me, and I couldn't care less.''

''That's easy to say, but . . .'' She glanced down the row of exhibitors to where Rebecca was helping Simon set up for the day. ''Look at them, Sam. If you ever needed a definition of love at first sight, you'd only have to look at Simon and Rebecca to understand. Rebecca's timidness and melancholy have all but disappeared the last two days, and Simon . . . well, he's positively moony. Yet when I look at them, all I can see is a modern version of Romeo and Juliet.''

Sam slipped his hand under the green velvet net that held the chignon at Abby's nape, and gave the tense muscles a gentle squeeze. ''I don't think it's that tragic, love. After all, we don't know for certain how Frederick and Delilah will react to seeing us here. And how can anyone not like Rebecca?''

''I fear the Rosemonts will find it quite easy to, and Sam, we must be ready to step in and protect her.''

''I'm ready in case that happens, and oddly enough, so, I think, is Simon.''

As if on cue, a commotion at the end of the aisle drew their attention once more. Sam stared at the Rosemont exhibit and reached for Abby's hand. ''Chin up, Ab,'' he said. ''The Royal Family has arrived.''

Frederick's bright carrot-hued hair would have been recognizable anywhere, as was Delilah's full, flouncing dark skirt and severe ash-streaked coif. They had arrived with as much pomp and circumstance as would have heralded true royalty, and Sam found the sight of them almost comical.

Mirroring his thoughts, Abby said, ''I'm surprised they aren't attended by an entourage of liveried servants.''

"I know what you mean. At least we won't have to wait long to see how this Shakespearean play concludes."

The House of Rosemont booth was instantly surrounded by other exhibitors who appeared to be currying favor from the grande dame and her son. Abby folded her arms across her chest and tapped her foot on the ceramic floor. "The queen and prince regent are holding court," she remarked. "I suppose that's a tribute to House of Rosemont furniture. It obviously has a noteworthy reputation."

"Indeed it does," Sam said. "I worked there long enough to know that. Old Tobias may have been an even bigger bastard than his illegitimate son, but he knew how to build some fine furniture."

The throng circling Frederick and Delilah suddenly parted. The group's attention had shifted to the Chadwick Farm exhibit. Sam could almost feel the heat of Frederick's glare, and though at least fifty yards separated them, he could see Delilah stiffen, and the features of her pale face turn to stone. She pushed her son from behind, and Frederick was propelled down the aisle.

Sam gave Abby a last-minute encouraging grin and clasped his hands behind his back. "Don't let him get to you, darling," he muttered out of the corner of his mouth. "But be prepared. I think it's about to get downright frosty in this building."

Frederick blustered to a stop in front of Sam and bestowed only a cursory glance over the exhibit before he vented his anger. "How dare you? You've made me a laughingstock with this . . . this *campfire* rubbish. How do you think it feels to have all the chaps hooting at me because they've discovered you're a Rosemont . . . " Frederick's head and shoulders shook with the repugnance of the thought, and Sam gripped his hands even tighter to keep from connecting his itching fist with Frederick's face.

". . . and you represent our good name with such trash as this!"

"Actually, *Freddie,*" Sam began, "I'm representing myself. Do you see the sign?" He gestured toward a burnt wood placard which read *Chadwick Farm Furniture.* "I've spent most of my life *dis*associating myself with the Rosemonts, and I'm not about to change now. So how do you suppose your *chaps* even knew I was a Rosemont? I assure you it's not something I brag about."

Frederick's face turned crimson with anger. "I suppose that sniveling puppy dog of a brother told them. He actually acts as if your accomplishments are a matter of personal pride for him. As if the little turncoat had any pride. He's even gone so far as to take up with one of your backwoods brood. I'm going to have a devil of a time wresting him away from her greedy claws."

That was definitely *not* the thing to say, Freddie, Sam thought. He saw Abby take a few threatening steps toward them, and acted quickly. He put one arm around Frederick's shoulder and maneuvered him to the side of the exhibit away from her and the mainstream of pedestrian traffic. With his free hand he motioned for Abby to stay back.

"Sorry to disagree, Freddie," Sam ground out in a low voice, "but you could take a lesson or two from your brother on the definition of pride." He applied pressure to Frederick's shoulder, and prevented him from breaking free of his grip. "And a lesson in manners wouldn't hurt you either."

"Get your hands off of me, you caveman!"

Sam tightened his fingers on Frederick's collarbone, and felt gratified when his brother winced. "So sorry, Freddie, if I'm hurting you, but we need to have a little understanding about Rebecca."

Sam held Frederick tight against his side so he couldn't get away. At the same time, he found the painful pressure point in Frederick's shoulder that he was searching for. Frederick cried out in a muffled groan and seemed to shrink several inches in height.

"Now get this straight, Freddie." Sam's voice was a growl in his brother's ear. "Simon likes Rebecca, and she likes him. You may not understand how that can be possible, but I think it's nice. I think they're good for each other, and I'm willing to overlook the fact that Simon comes from a family of crude, ill-mannered, overbearing, *stupid* people. But the thing that I won't overlook is any mistreatment of Rebecca from you or Delilah, and I mean even the *slightest little thing* like a sigh, or a glance, or an ill-chosen condescending word from either one of you."

Sam leaned even closer so he could look into Frederick's glazed eyes. "If Rebecca so much as hints that you have been anything less than a gentleman, I will beat that highbrow Rosemont stuffing right out of you, Freddie. It's something I've dreamed of doing for a long time. Do you think you can relay this information to your mother, or should I come down there and tell her myself? Because if she says anything to Rebecca, I'll give you a lathering for that too."

The capillaries of Frederick's face seemed about to explode, and his lips twisted into an agonized grimace. "All right, let me go, for God's sake."

Sam released his grip and flicked his hand across Frederick's jacket lapel as if brushing away a speck of lint. "Good," he said, feigning amiability. "We understand each other."

Hatred blazed from Frederick's eyes. "I'll ruin you, Kelly. I promise you that. You'll have to cart your load of firewood back to Ohio with your tail between your legs."

"We'll see about that, brother. But that's between you

and me. It's just business. But you remember what I said about Rebecca.''

Frederick shrugged his shoulders and straightened his jacket. Then he glared at Abby. She smiled sweetly at him and asked, ''What do you think of our display, Frederick? Do you like it?''

Frederick opened his mouth to speak, but Sam answered for him. ''As a matter of fact, my brother was just telling me how much he admired my work, isn't that right, Frederick?''

It was almost possible to see steam issuing from the pink-tipped ears under Frederick's bushy red hair, but the irate man was prevented from saying anything by a crowd of people advancing on the exhibit.

''Looks like we're open for business, Freddie,'' Sam said. ''Good luck today.''

Frederick clamped his lips together, whirled around on his heels, and ran right into a distinguished gentleman approaching Sam's booth. Clearly flustered, Frederick sputtered a hasty greeting. ''Mr. Delacorte, sir, wh-what a pleasure to s-see you.''

The man acknowledged Frederick with a nod. ''Hello, Rosemont, how have you been?'' Without waiting for an answer, Mr. Delacorte entered the sphere of Sam's exhibit. ''I see you're admiring this young man's craft . . . quite amazing, isn't it? I've ordered several pieces for my lake house in Akron.'' The man smiled with satisfaction. ''Imagine, coming all the way to Chicago to discover Kelly's unique talent, and he lives but a few miles away from me. Can't get over it.''

Sam figured Frederick was seething, but to his credit, he managed to keep his temper. ''Stop by the House of Rosemont exhibit, Mr. Delacorte,'' Frederick said. ''We've got some exciting new pieces this year.''

''I'm sure you have, but I've got quite enough of that type of thing. Got my eye out for the truly rare finds, you know . . . like Kelly's work.'' Mr. Delacorte dismissed Frederick with a wave of his hand and went to Sam. ''I've decided on that rocking chair after all . . .''

The last Sam saw of Frederick was his red head bobbing agitatedly down the aisle.

Chapter Twenty-three

Two weeks after they left Seneca Township, the Kellys headed back home with fond memories of the Exposition and Chicago. The children had eaten their fill of frankfurters, roasted peanuts, and a delightful new snack called Cracker Jack, a molasses-coated smorgasbord of treats. They played games of chance for a penny a piece on the midway, and rode the Ferris wheel and the carousel until their stomachs threatened a revolution.

Abby bought each of them bathing outfits. At first, the twins laughed at the tight-fitting sleeveless tops and knee-length drawers, but they eagerly ventured into Lake Michigan. The girls, however, found it difficult to cast modesty aside. Even though the beach dresses flounced at their hips with a full six yards of material, they still revealed more feminine curves than would ever have seemed proper in Ohio. So Susanna and Rebecca contented themselves with soaking their ankles at the water's edge, while Emma, not to be vanquished by gender, plunged into the waves with the boys.

Satchels and suitcases were stuffed full of souvenirs on the return trip—a toy for each child, new clothes, and several packs of the latest craze, a sweet, chewy, spearmint-flavored substance invented by a man named Wrigley. Sam's special mementos, the dozens of orders he'd taken for Chadwick Farm furniture, were bound in a leather notebook that he kept in his valise.

Tucked protectively in Rebecca's handbag was her most prized possession from the fair, a photograph of her and Simon in bathing outfits in front of a shooting gallery along the boardwalk of Lake Michigan.

When he'd first seen the photograph, it was all Sam could do to keep from chuckling out loud. Abby had had to silence him with a stern look and a whispered warning. "I know what you're thinking, but don't you dare laugh at his legs," she'd said.

Sam had discreetly covered the skinny appendages with his hand and responded with sputtering laughter. "In that case, I'd best not look at them at all." Then he'd whispered back at her, "Besides, how would you know what I'm thinking if you didn't think the same thing?" He'd almost sent them both into fits of laughter.

When they arrived back at Chadwick Farm, Sam and Abby were relieved to see that the crops hadn't suffered from neglect or scavengers. The scarecrow Will had set in the field before they left had kept marauding birds away, and Lizzie's cat had done a good job scaring ground invaders. Of course they owed a debt of gratitude to Jake Mitchum for his daily visits to tend to their small family of livestock.

Everyone picked up with their chores and prepared for school to start, but it was impossible for life to completely return to normal ... especially for Abby. In the short time she'd known Sam, he had triumphed over despair with hope, and destruction with renewal. Now she'd seen him conquer the family's financial struggles with a grow-

ing security . . . and he'd done it without having to fall
back on Rosemont money.

It was an entirely alien feeling for Abby . . . this comfort
that came from knowing the next penny wouldn't have
to be eked out of a meager livelihood, that life would
be easier. Even the crops seemed to flourish, as if they
instinctively knew they didn't have to any longer.

How different Abby's little piece of the world became
when the burdens were lifted. How green the grass, how
sunny the marigolds in front of the porch, how much
friendlier her neighbors. And of course, how wonderful
her husband. She beamed inwardly with pride at his
accomplishments. And since the farmhouse no longer
seemed as small as it had, she began to think of adding
another child to the family . . . hers and Sam's . . . and
he wholeheartedly agreed with her.

Sam divided his time between tending the crops and
building his furniture in the barn. He hired Ernest
Sholski's two oldest boys to help him.

Herbert and Laurence had never been too fond of their
father's lackadaisical enterprise of raising and slaughter-
ing livestock, and since Seneca Village offered few pros-
pects for young men of limited skills and pampered
backgrounds, Ernest was happy to see them hire on with
Sam. He no longer had to devise ways of keeping the
boys busy, and could pursue the activities of the landed
gentry, which was always what he wanted to do anyway.
And the boys turned out to be attentive and enthusiastic
learners.

The only dark spot in Abby's life was Rebecca. Abby
didn't know what the future held for her and Simon, and
she had several reservations about Rebecca becoming
involved with the Rosemonts. But she had to admit that
the girl had flourished during her courtship. And she
seemed lost without Simon now that they were home.
She didn't revert to the silent, desperate world that had

kept her isolated before the trip, but she was certainly not happy ... at least not unless she was talking about Simon.

The younger Rosemont brother had been the tonic Rebecca needed. He had lavished affection on her, and she had soaked up his attentions the way a dry riverbed soaked up a spring rain. There seemed to be no end to the patience and understanding Simon had displayed toward Rebecca, and the more he'd shown her, miraculously, the less she'd needed. For that reason, no matter what Abby thought of the rest of the Rosemonts, she was definitely grateful to kind, amiable Simon.

Summer crept lazily into fall with a golden-leafed understatement that soon gave way to a resplendent riot of bright russets and reds. Abby enjoyed the cool autumn air on her face and the crackle of dry leaves under the buckboard wheels as she came down the village road from the gristmill. Rebecca was beside her, her feet propped on a sack of newly milled provender ground from the last of Chadwick Farm summer corn. She was reading the latest letter from Simon for perhaps the tenth time since they'd picked it up in the village.

"He wishes he could come see me, Miss Abby," she read. "He says his heart is fairly breaking with missing me." She let the letter fall to her lap and stared wistfully into the trees. "I feel the same ... I do. I long to see him again."

Apparently time and distance had not cooled the ardor of the young lovers, and though Abby worried about Rebecca's future, she recognized the depth of the girl's feelings. This was a matter to be taken seriously. She smiled and patted the hands that clutched Simon's letter. "I know, dearest. Why doesn't he come? Surely he knows we would welcome him."

"Oh, he does, yes. But he says things are not going well at the factory where he works. I don't know what's wrong. Simon is so considerate; he doesn't trouble me with his problems. He wants to come desperately, and he says he will as soon as he can. But sometimes I think I can't wait!"

"Then I'm sure he will come. You must be patient, Rebecca, and have faith that everything will work out in the end."

A strange feeling suddenly came over Abby, prompting a subtle smile to curl her lips. She remembered when she had heard those words before . . . a year and a half ago when she was riding in the buckboard with her father and he had gently admonished her with the exact same advice. She raised her eyes and gave a shrug of capitulation to the heavens. "I think faith is something we've all learned a lot about lately," she said to Rebecca.

Abby guided the mules over the rise, and the farmhouse came into view, the newly constructed framework of the two-room addition just visible beyond the back wall. Unexpectedly, a smart coach stood by the front porch, its single horse tied to a railing. "Now who could that be?" she asked.

Rebecca grabbed her shoulder and stood up. Her face brightened with recognition. "It's Simon!" she shouted. "Oh, he's come, Miss Abby, he's come!"

The pale face and thin frame of the mysterious visitor were undeniably Simon's, and Abby chuckled to herself. "My, but you work fast, Papa."

Sam and Simon rose from porch chairs, and Simon came down the steps at a run. He had his arms outstretched before Abby had even brought the buckboard to a complete halt. Rebecca jumped down from the bench and into his embrace.

Sam climbed up beside Abby and took the reins. She gave him a questioning look, and he lifted a corner of his mouth in a lazy grin. "Who says life isn't full of surprises?" he quipped.

"Not me," Abby said.

Sam slapped the reins on the mules' backs and headed toward the barn. "We might as well give them some time alone together. Not that I think they even remember we're here."

Abby looked over her shoulder and saw that Rebecca was lost in Simon's adoration. Their hands were clasped and her face was turned up to his, intent on every word he said.

After supper that night Abby learned the reason for Simon's unannounced visit. She sat beside Sam on the front steps and looked out toward the apple orchard where Simon and Rebecca had gone for a walk. Their silhouettes, dark against the light gray shadows of night, were visible in the moonlight. Simon drew Rebecca close, and she raised her face to accept his kiss.

"We're losing her, Sam," Abby said, unable to keep the sadness from her voice. "I know he loves her, but can he protect her from . . . *them.*" She sensed Sam stiffen beside her, and looked into his face. "That is why he's come, isn't it? To ask her to marry him?"

Sam focused on the horizon and began to shred a wide blade of grass he'd been holding. "Oh, I'm sure he wants to marry her, Ab," he said, "though that's not the only reason he's here."

A familiar but unwelcome tingling of dread, which she had been quite certain she would never feel again, worked its way up Abby's spine to the wispy hairs on her neck. "Then why?" she asked.

He didn't look at her. "You're not going to like this."

She placed her hand over both of his, stopping him from shredding the grass into thread-thin fibers. "You're starting to scare me, Sam. Say what you have to say."

''He came to tell me what's been going on at the factory and to ask for my help.''

His announcement had the effect of a fist slammed into her abdomen, and Abby's response was pushed out on a weak flow of air. ''Wh-what did you say? What kind of help?''

Finally Sam looked at her. ''Things are really bad over there, Ab. It started before I left. The American Federation of Labor sent a union organizer to the factory, and his speeches had the boys pretty stirred up by the time you came and got me. Frederick hired some Pinkertons to rough him up and run him off . . .''

''That sounds like that pompous ox, trying to rewrite the Constitution to exclude freedom of speech! From what you wrote in your letters, it seems to me the House of Rosemont could *use* some reorganization.''

''Yeah, well, that's what I thought too, and I warned Simon before I left that the boys were buying into the union idea. I thought maybe Frederick would eventually listen to reason.''

''Are we talking about the same Frederick Rosemont I know?'' Abby asked. ''The one with all the compassion of a rattlesnake?''

Sam smiled. ''I guess it was sort of like pinning my hopes on the moon. Anyway, the situation only got worse, and last week erupted into a full-blown battle.''

''Was anyone hurt?''

Sam nodded and drew a deep breath. ''Two of the boys were killed by Pinkerton strikebreakers, and a dozen or more were injured. Simon said the ground looked like a massacre had occurred there.''

Abby put her arm through Sam's and leaned close to him. ''I'm so sorry, Sam. Did you know the men who were killed?''

''Yeah, one of them real well. His name was Gifford McIlvaine, and he was a good man, Ab . . . a real good man." Sam pinched the bridge of his nose and squeezed his eyes tightly shut. When he opened them and looked at her, moisture glistened on his lower lids. "The factory's been shut down since it happened."

This last revelation made Abby think that perhaps there was some compassion after all in the rock-hard soul of Frederick Rosemont. "At least he had the decency to let the men mourn," she said. "He showed good sense by closing down for a while and letting things cool off."

"He didn't shut it down, Abby. Simon did. The day after the fight Frederick was shot in his carriage. Two bullets hit him, one in his skull and the other in his back. He's been in a coma since."

A knot that had been forming in Abby's stomach twisted tighter. "My God, Sam. How horrible! What's Simon going to do? How does he think you can help?"

"He wants me to come back and take over operation of the factory. For some reason he thinks the men will listen to me, and I'll be able to restore some sort of order."

"What?" Abby had suspected that Sam's story was leading up to this conclusion, but it didn't make hearing it any easier. "Can't Simon restore order himself? After all, he's been a Rosemont a lot longer than you have."

"I've *never* been a Rosemont, Ab, you know that. And despite what Frederick may have told you that day, I never will be. But I have worked side by side with those men, and I care about them, and as much as I despise the memory of my father, I care about the House of Rosemont."

She knew that what she was about to say would sound spiteful and selfish, but she couldn't help it. The thing she had most feared was about to happen. The Rosemonts were pulling Sam away from her. "But Sam," she said, "it's not our battle to fight!"

"It's Simon's battle, Abby, and he's my brother. And it could be Rebecca's future."

She tried one last argument. "What about Delilah? Surely she doesn't want you back."

"That's the amazing part of this. According to Simon, she does. I think when Delilah weighs her dislike of me against the downfall of the business and the erosion of her financial security, she's willing to bury the hatchet. Rosemont Manor is an armed camp right now, and Delilah's afraid to leave the grounds. She actually supported Simon's idea to come here today."

Abby believed she'd dealt with her animosity toward the Rosemonts and gotten over it, that she'd finally abandoned the fear that Sam would one day return to Fox Hill as Frederick predicted. It had helped that Frederick and Delilah didn't want him there, but now that barrier had been removed. And here she was, unwillingly struggling with the same old doubts again.

What would happen now that Sam was *welcomed* into his father's family? He would be living in the manor and assuming a position of authority in the factory. This was a much different situation than had existed for him when he was there before. Then he had been an underling, a subordinate. Now he was suddenly an equal, with equal power and status . . . and a fortune waiting for him to take.

How could he feel the same about her and the life he'd carved for himself at Chadwick Farm? How would he continue to be satisfied with his handcrafted creations built in the simple barn he'd constructed himself? To believe he would seemed ludicrous. And yet, if he wanted to go, how could she hold him back? Abby was facing the biggest gamble of her life, and she hadn't the slightest idea how to play her hand.

"You're so quiet, Abby," Sam finally said. "What are you thinking?"

Her head snapped up at his question and she stared at him. He looked the same . . . handsome, strong, dependable. He was the same Sam on the outside. Yet there was an eagerness in his eyes, a zest for facing a new challenge, and while that unquenchable fire of ambition should have made her proud, instead it only frightened her. ''You've already made up your mind, haven't you?'' she said. ''You're going back there.''

Was she wrong, or did he suddenly look sad, as if he knew that he would betray her, that his future might very well lie under the far-reaching thumb of Tobias Rosemont. He slowly nodded his head. ''I'll see if I can get one of the men to stay out here with you while I'm gone. I know we haven't seen Tucker for a long time, but I'm still not convinced he's gone for good.''

Simon and Rebecca came toward them from the apple orchard. Abby didn't want to face them anymore than she wanted to face Sam's decision. She got up from the porch steps and walked to the front door of the house. Before she went in, she turned back to Sam and said, ''It's no secret I never liked Frederick, Sam, but I wouldn't have wished this horrible fate on him. I used to fear the man he was, but of course I don't anymore. I'm not afraid of Tucker either. They're just men. I wish I weren't afraid of anything at all, but that would be an impossibly perfect world, wouldn't it?''

She felt his lingering gaze on her back after she'd gone inside.

Simon left the next morning, but Sam didn't go with him. In spite of Abby's statement that she was no longer afraid of Tucker, Sam was still very much concerned about him, and he was determined not to leave his family until one of the men from town agreed to stay at the farm at night. Besides, he had several loose ends to tie up before he left. Even though he believed he would only be gone a short time, he wanted Will and the Sholski boys to keep working on the Chadwick Farm furniture orders from the Exposition.

Abby had been quiet and remote since their talk on the porch the night before. The tension that hung between them was so thick Sam could practically see it . . . touch it. Whenever he spoke to her, she responded with a succinct answer that left little doubt of her feelings about his return to Fox Hill.

He had tried to reason with her after breakfast that morning, explaining that if everything went well, he expected to be home within a week.

"I'm sure you'll try, Sam." She had sighed and resumed her chores in the kitchen without so much as a glance over her shoulder at him.

When he found her in the vegetable garden that afternoon and offered to help her, she dismissed him with a wave of her hand. "I can manage."

That was the last straw. "I'm sure you can manage to pluck a few tomatoes from the vines, Abby," he said. "But I don't think you can manage a few simple words with me that aren't delivered with poisonous darts!"

She looked up at him with green fire in her eyes. "Oh? You want a pleasant conversation with me, Sam? Well, you're a little late. We should have had it *before* you made your decision without asking my opinion."

He threw his hands up in frustration. "Look, Abby, this is ridiculous. It's not as though I volunteered for this job of peacemaker. Simon came to *me*, remember. He asked *me*. I didn't ask to be connected to the House of Rosemont . . . for that matter I didn't ask to be connected to Tobias Rosemont in the first place!"

She tore a tomato from its vine so forcefully that juice squirted from a slit in the fruit and ran down her arm. "Well, you certainly did a good job of avoiding your dear father's family for twenty-six years!"

She was being unreasonable. Didn't she know that he

hated to leave her? Was he ever going to be free of the obligation to constantly prove himself to her? Hadn't he paid enough for his deceit at the start of their relationship?

Sam paced in a tight circle and raked his hand through his hair. He was just about to ask all these questions when Emma and Will came around the house and stopped at the edge of the garden. They looked at Abby and him and then at each other. The tension was as thick as autumn fog on Chadwick Farm, all right. Sam could even see it in the faces of Will and Emma.

He clamped his mouth shut and took a deep breath. Abby's fiery gaze had never left his face. She was just waiting for him to say something that would fuel her anger. Well, he wasn't going to do it. "I told you, Abby," he said with barely constrained calm, "I only expect to be gone a week. If things aren't better by then, I'll come home anyway to check on you and the children."

"And then go back again?" It was definitely a dare.

"Maybe. Maybe not. I don't know. Right now I've got work to do."

He stuffed his hands in his pockets and strode toward the barn. Will and Emma watched him go until they heard Abby muttering something. They looked at her just as she threw a pair of pruning shears into the dirt.

"Is somethin' wrong, Miss Abby?" Will asked.

She didn't look at him, but stood up and watched Sam go into the barn. "No, Will," she said, tapping her foot in the dirt. "Why would you think that?" She tugged at the sleeve of her blouse as if she were as mad at it as she was the shears. She started toward the back door with a determined stride. "I've just got a little tomato juice on my shirt, that's all."

"Miss Abby?" She stopped. "Emma and I were gonna take a walk. Is that all right?"

"Do as you please. That's what everyone else does."

Chapter Twenty-four

"What do ya suppose got into Miz Kelly, Will?" Emma asked as they crossed the rise that led away from the farm.

"I don't know, but she looked awful mad about something."

"No more'n he did. I never saw those two speak an ugly word to each other before. Sounded to me like Sam was fixin' to go off somewhere . . . maybe back to Pennsylvania. Do ya think that's why Simon came . . . to get Sam?"

Will thought about what she said. It made sense. He'd believed the smitten Simon had only come to see Rebecca, but now he wasn't so sure. And Will knew enough about Abby's dislike of the Rosemonts to understand that if Sam went back there, she'd be plenty mad . . . about as mad as she was now. "I think you're right, Emma," he said. "Simon was here for more than just to spark Rebecca, that's for sure."

Emma grabbed Will's arm and held tight. "If Sam goes off, what about Tucker? What if he shows up?"

"Aw, don't worry about him. He's long gone, and besides, I can handle him now. I've grown a lot since he hurt Rebecca, and Tucker doesn't scare me."

Emma didn't look entirely convinced, and Will worried that the thought of Tucker and the quarrelsome atmosphere at the farm would spoil their afternoon together. He didn't want that to happen. It had been a long time since he and Emma had been alone, and they hadn't been able to sneak back to the cave in weeks. "You're not gonna get all down in the mouth now, are you, Emma?" he asked. "We're gonna have a nice time this afternoon. All the problems between Sam and Abby will have worked themselves out by the time we get back, you'll see."

She slipped her hand into his and shrugged her shoulders. "You're right, Will. Sam and Abby'll patch things up, and you and me . . . we'll have a fine time."

His lighthearted mood restored, Will pulled Emma toward the footpath to the Little White Tail. They had just about crossed over the border of thick ferns and oak trees that hid the path from the road when Will heard his name called.

"Will! Where're you goin'?"

"What do those two want?" Will muttered angrily. He waited for the twins to catch up to them and then spoke sharply. "You go on home now!" He gave both twins a push toward the farm.

"We want to go with you," Timothy said. "We got no homework, isn't that right, Tom?" The quieter brother nodded. "You goin' down to that place where you found Emma?"

Will answered vaguely. "Maybe. But it doesn't matter anyway, 'cause you're not comin' with us. Miss Abby will be watchin' for you, so you'd best get on home."

"We'll just walk a little ways with you then . . ."

"I said, go!"

Will shot a no-nonsense glare at Timothy and he gave

in. "Awright, we'll go, but I hope your ol' cave is grown over with poison ivy and your skin gets red and scabby and falls off!"

Will snorted. "If I find any poison ivy, I'll be sure and bring you a bouquet. Now scat on outta here." He tugged on Emma's hand and she followed him into the woods.

When they'd gone, Thomas looked at his brother and asked, "Why do ya think they're goin' to that cave, Tim?"

"Boy, are you dumb," Tim answered. "They're gonna go smooch and carry on." Tim pranced around in a circle pretending he was courting his brother. "Oh, Emma," he drawled in a high voice. "I love you. You're the prettiest thing I ever saw. Let me smooch on you." He smacked the air around Tom's head with wet-sounding kisses.

"Cut it out!" Tom protested, swatting at the offending lips.

Timothy stood up straight, and smiled. "I've got a great idea. Let's follow them. It'd serve that ol' king of the cave right to have us spy on him and his sweetheart."

The boys took off down the footpath in pursuit of Will and Emma. They had only gone a short distance when Tim suddenly jerked on Tom's arm and pulled him down into a thicket of wild mulberry bushes.

Tom rubbed his arm. "Ouch! What'd you do that for?"

"Listen up. Someone's comin'."

The boys crouched in the bushes and waited as the sound of footsteps on the path grew louder. Finally a large shape lumbered from the trees, pushing away overhanging tree limbs and branches.

Tom nearly gasped his alarm, but Timothy clamped his hand over his brother's mouth. His own voice quivering with fear, he whispered, "It's him, ain't it, Tom?" He felt his twin's head bob shakily against his grip, and knew Tom was as scared as he was.

Tucker Brandywine passed within feet of the boys'

hiding place. The year's absence hadn't changed him much. He was still wearing the same old clothes, and they were even dirtier than before. His hair stuck out from the same tattered hat and hung in limp greasy strands over his shoulders. The only real difference Tim could see was a slight bend in the old devil's back, giving him a humpbacked posture. But all in all, Tucker Brandywine was as big as ever and looked every bit as mean.

When Tucker was several yards down the path, Tim slowly dropped his hand from his brother's mouth and croaked out, "Ol' Tucker's back, Tom, and it sure ain't for any good reason."

"We got to tell Sam," Tom sputtered. "He's got to stop Tucker before he gets to Will and Emma."

The twins ran like the wind out of the woods toward the farm. Tim never once looked back, but all the way home, he could just about feel the old snake's hands wrapping around his collar and stopping him cold.

From the entrance to the barn Sam saw the boys approach. At least he thought it was them. It was hard to pick the twins out from the clouds of dust they were kicking up. He crossed the yard to meet them, figuring if there were a problem, he'd best deal with it. Abby wasn't in any mood to handle more catastrophes.

Timothy ground to a stop and panted. "Sam, Sam, you gotta come now! It's him! We saw him!"

"Who? Who'd you see?"

"Tucker. Ol' Tucker's back!"

Just hearing Brandywine's name caused adrenaline to pump through Sam's veins bringing a long-suppressed anger to the surface. "Are you sure?" he asked.

Both dusty heads bobbed up and down. Fear was etched in both freckled faces, and Sam knew that no one else but Tucker would likely have put it there. "Where'd you see him?"

"Over yonder by the footpath to the river," Tim answered. "He was followin' Will and Emma."

"You boys caught your breath yet?" They nodded. "Good. Show me where you saw him. We've got to hurry."

They ran over the rise and back to the exact spot where Tucker had passed by the twins. Tom pointed down the path. "He just kept goin' that way, Sam, the same way Will and Emma went."

Sam started into the trees and called back to the boys. "You did a good job. Now I want you to go back to the house."

"We're comin' with you!" Tim announced.

"Oh, no, you're not. You go inside the house and stay there. No arguments and no sneaking back."

"Sam?"

He turned around at Tim's voice. "What?"

"Now is it time to fight Tucker?" the boy asked.

"Yes, son, now it's time." He listened to the boys' retreating footsteps, and squinted into the thick trees that obscured the path before him. He remembered that Will had once told him that the path was dense and difficult to pass and ended at a waterfall. Sam prayed he'd find Will and Emma before he ran out of trail. And before Tucker found them first.

Emma stretched the top of the canvas drawstring sack she'd carried from the house and took out a book. She looked up at Will with an impish grin as if she knew what his reaction would be. He didn't disappoint her. "You're not gonna read one of those love poems again, are you, Emma?"

"Maybe I am," she said smartly. "And they're called *sonnets.*"

"Sometimes I'm sorry Sam told me to get you that

book for your birthday. Now all you do is sit and sigh over it.''

"Don't be sorry, Will. This is the best present I ever got.''

"But we're here, Emma! In Lucy's Kitchen, and we haven't been back in a coon's age. Surely you can think of somethin' you'd like to do as much as read what some dead English fella wrote hundreds of years ago.''

She grinned at him and patted the dirt beside her. "I know why you were so all-fired anxious to get down here, Will Buckman, and you can just sit down and hold your horses. I'm gonna let you kiss me, but first I want you to be all romantic-like. This Mr. Shakespeare . . . he knew all about that kind of thing, and it won't hurt you to listen.''

He plopped down beside her and stared at the crumbling rock igloo that had once served as an oven for Emma's drop-biscuits. They'd sure come a long way since he'd first found her in the cave. Once he'd decided that she wasn't going to bash his head in, he'd started right in liking her. And even if she did get all gushy over a dead Englishman, he liked her even more now. "All right, Emma," he pretended to grouse, "get it over with and read your old sonnet.''

She crossed her legs Indian-style and spread the book open on her lap. Then she cleared her throat and straightened her shoulders. Her face took on a prim, serious look, as if she were an actress on a stage and this was her most important role. "Shall I compare thee to a summer's day?" she read. "Thou art more lovely and more temperate . . .''

Her voice was soft and sweet, like church music, and if he didn't understand everything she read, or if she didn't exactly get all the words right, it didn't matter to Will. It was enough to just sit and listen to her. Most times, if she wasn't mad about something, Emma had a nice, gentle voice that was just right for a girl . . . just right for her.

"Rough winds do shake the darling buds of May . . ."

"Well, ain't this just about the homiest sight I ever laid eyes on? I'm surprised the honeybees ain't swarmin' around the two a' you to get some a' that sugar."

The voice was an icy blast, stinging Will's nerve endings like daggers of sleet in a blizzard. He didn't have to look up to know it was Tucker. Emma had turned to stone beside him, and her face was as gray and hard as the rock walls of the cavern.

"Tucker . . ." Her voice came out in a raspy whisper when she said his name. No other sound followed it.

"So you remember who I am, do ya gal?" He stood at the entrance to the cave, his giant form outlined by filtered sunlight. Then he stepped inside, moving slowly like a preying animal, crouched, ready to spring. "Ain't you gonna inquire as to my well-bein', seein' as you're the one who run me through with a pitchfork."

Will watched Emma's face. Her eyes had grown so big and round they seemed to leave no room for her little nose and mouth. He had to tell himself to breathe, and when he did, it hurt. He put his hand on her arm. She swallowed hard and glanced at him before looking back at Tucker. "How've you been, Pappy?"

Tucker came closer until just the rock oven separated them. He put his large hands on his waist and stared down at Emma. "Oh, I been fine, gal. Them holes in my gut barely slowed me down. I just crawled like a skunk back to West Virginy to the Blue Bottom and found me a shack to dig into till I healed. Though it might interest you to know that I almost died!"

The last three words were flung at Emma as if Tucker had delivered them with a slingshot, and she cringed backwards, nearly falling into the dirt. Will caught and steadied her. "I'm sorry, Pappy, about what I done to you, but you was about to . . ."

She stopped talking when he leaned over so his grimy face was very near hers. Tucker's few stained teeth were framed by a snarl. Though his voice seemed calm, Will sensed there was a terrible anger boiling inside him, making everything he said a threat.

"I done nothin' all them months but think about you, gal. A father and his daughter ought never to be torn apart, don't you agree, Emma? Ain't you glad I come lookin' for you as soon as I was able?"

"There was no need, Pappy," she said weakly. "I'm doin' good, you can see that. You don't need to worry over me."

"That's right, Mr. Brandywine," Will cut in. "Emma's stayin' with us at Chadwick's, and she's welcome for as long as she wants to stay. You can go on your way without fussin' about how she'll get by."

"Now ain't that a comfortin' thought," Tucker said, his lips contorting into something oddly resembling a smile. "Too bad I don't give a gnat's wing whether she gets by or not. Any more than she cared whether I lived or died when she run me through."

Will stood up and wiped his palms on his pants legs. "Mr. Brandywine, you got to leave Emma alone. I care for her, and Emma and me . . . we're gonna get married someday. I haven't asked her yet, but she knows how I feel, and she's stayin' right here with me . . . with us."

Tucker closed one eye and leveled a flinty glare at Will with the other. "You think I can't see what's been goin' on here, you ruttin' little pig? You been feastin' plenty on Brandywine Stew, ain't you, boy? She tastes purty good, don't she? Ain't much of her, but she'll do instead a' starvin'. Well, the feedbag's empty, 'cause she's comin' back to the Blue Bottom with me." He crooked his finger in Emma's face and made a clucking sound with his tongue. "Come on, Emma, gal. You and me got some miles to put between us and these parts."

She stood up beside Will. "I'm not goin', Pappy."

"Now looky here. You're still my daughter, though you don't hardly act like it. But the law says you do what I say."

"I don't know any such law, Pappy. I only know what I say, and I say I'm stayin' here."

"You're uppity as a peahen, ain't ya, Emma? Well I'm here to tell ya that all the books and fancy dresses don't change what you are, gal. You're still a lazy ol' cur bitch from the Blue Bottom, not much good for nothin' but one thing. You're lucky I'll still take ya back after what you done. But I got a generous heart, and you're comin' with me."

He grabbed for her. Will flew over the rock oven, connecting his head with Tucker's chest. The big man stumbled back, but quickly regained his footing. Will charged a second time, but Tucker sidestepped out of his path. The wind whistling past Will's ears mingled with Tucker's mocking laughter.

"You surprise me, boy," Tucker chortled. "I'd figured you a mite smarter than to risk life and limb for this pitiful prize. But come on. Let's have at it." He wiggled his fingers in Will's face.

Will's anger drummed in his ears. He clenched his fists into tight balls and lunged for Tucker a third time. His adversary moved out of the way at the last second and stuck a booted foot in Will's path, sending him sprawling to the ground.

Tucker howled. "Look at your hero, Emma. I'm more scairt of that ornery Miz Kelly than I am this banty rooster."

Will never hated anybody as much as he hated Tucker. He wanted him dead, and he wanted to be the one to kill him. He spied a large rock from the oven just a few feet from his hand and reached for it. While Tucker continued his taunting laughter, Will sat up on his haunches, ready to attack.

Ignoring Will, Tucker turned his attention to Emma, and despite her wails of protest, he began dragging her to the cave entrance. That was just the diversion Will needed. He uncoiled his tense body and sprang like a wildcat, landing on Tucker's back. Tucker whirled around in frustration, trying to rid himself of the pesky baggage. Will pounded the rock into the side of Tucker's head.

"Damn you, boy!" Tucker grabbed Will by the waist and wrenched him around until Will landed on his feet in front of him. There was fire in Tucker's eyes now. Will just had time to recognize its menacing glint before Tucker's fist slammed into Will's jaw.

Shooting stars lit the ceiling of the cave. Will landed against a rock wall, and was immediately hauled upright by a thick fist clutching the front of his shirt. Tucker landed a gut-wrenching blow to Will's abdomen. All the wind in Will's lungs spewed out in a painful whoosh. He doubled over as another well-placed punch connected with his cheek.

His head snapped back against the cave wall, and Will watched his world turn black. The last thing he remembered before he lost consciousness was Emma's pitiful sobs.

"You've kilt him, Tucker. I hate you!" she cried.

Poor Emma. Will wished he could tell her he wasn't dead.

The footpath was overgrown with thick vegetation, but Sam pressed on, mindless of low-hanging limbs that whipped against his face and arms, and gnarled tree roots that threatened to trip him. His vision was blurred from perspiration running down his forehead and into his eyes, so he scarcely noticed surrounding landmarks. And fear beat in his brain so loud that he didn't hear the thundering water rushing over the rocks until he was upon the waterfall. Any fleeting appreciation for the fall's powerful splendor was soon replaced with the growing terror that the footpath ended here and he hadn't found Will and Emma . . . or Tucker.

He stood on the bluff, looking down at the pool of water into which the waterfall emptied, and contemplated his next move. He was just about to go back the way he had come when sounds coming from below drew his attention to an area near the pool. Tucker was dragging a screaming Emma from an opening in what looked to be a granite wall. But where was Will? What had Tucker done to him?

The path down the side of the waterfall looked treacherous, but Sam knew he had to risk a hasty descent to confront Tucker before he hurt Emma. The sound of the water deafened his quickly executed scramble down the rocks. He landed at the base of the falls before Emma and Tucker reached it for the upward climb. He spun around to face his adversary just as Tucker and Emma saw him.

"Sam, oh, Sam," Emma cried through tears of hysteria. She tried to break away from Tucker, but he held her tightly. "He's kilt Will . . . oh, God, Sam, Will's dead!"

"You shut your mouth, you stupid gal!" Tucker threatened. "That simple boy ain't dead."

"Where is he? Where's Will?" Sam demanded, scanning the woods around them.

Tucker pointed to the cave. "He's in there. You can go in and take care of yours once I git mine outta this hole. The boy'll be a mite dazed is all, but it ain't likely to matter much considerin' he's a damn fool to begin with."

Emma continued struggling with Tucker trying to free

her arm from his grasp. In desperation she leaned over and bit his hand. "Ouch!" Tucker hollered, and jerked her to the ground.

"Let her go, Brandywine," Sam said, wanting to help Emma, but edging toward the cave to see for himself that Will was okay.

"This ain't no concern of yours, Kelly. You just git outta my way. I ain't got no quarrel with you."

"You're wrong, Tucker. Emma *is* my concern. She's not going with you. You're unfit to be a parent, and if I have to, I'll go to the circuit judge and tell him so. You're not leaving here with Emma."

"You can't take a young 'un from her pappy. The law's on my side!"

"What about all the laws you've ignored, including the ones you broke on our property last summer."

Tucker's eyes dawned with remembrance and his lips curled up in a sneer. "If you're talkin' about what happened with that half-wit gal, no one'd believe her anyhow. Besides, what took place that day was more hurtful to me than to her. I was the one that got poked and drug through the mud to the river."

The thought of Tucker's hands on Rebecca ignited the old anger that had been simmering in Sam for months. "If I'd been there that day, Brandywine, I'd have dragged you to the White Tail myself and seen that you were food for the mud fish."

Tucker cocked his head to the side and glared at Sam with narrow, dark eyes. "You ain't entertainin' the thought that you could whomp me, now are ya, Mr. Kelly?"

Sam was close enough to see into the cave. Will was there, all right. The boy rolled his head from side to side and moaned. He was alive. "I'm damned anxious to try," Sam swore. "Right here, right now."

A low chuckle that bristled the hairs on Sam's neck

came from Tucker's throat. "I ain't had me a good fight since I left the Blue Bottom," he said. "There's a sorry-arse miner 'bout twice your size who's still lickin' his wounds from my thrashin'."

Sam rolled up his sleeves. He nodded toward Emma, who was still clawing at Tucker's hand and sobbing. "Now that we've established what we're going to do, you let her go and let's get at it."

Tucker thrust Emma aside, and she scampered away to the cave entrance. Then Tucker held up his hand and taunted Sam with a coaxing wave. "My fist is itchin' bad," he jeered.

Sam took a deep breath. He was no fighter, and he knew it, but there was no closing the door on this challenge now. He just prayed that no matter what happened, Emma would have the good sense to get out of the gorge . . . and hopefully Will would come to and follow her. Sam had to make this fight last as long as he could so the young ones would escape. He held his fists in front of his face and danced around on the balls of his feet. If he couldn't lick Tucker with strength, maybe he could dazzle him with confusion.

Tucker backed away a few steps, and Sam actually experienced a burst of confidence that his bravado was working to frighten his opponent . . . until Tucker's mocking laughter rent the air. "You're mindful of a rooster prancin' on hot coals, Kelly, though I 'spect a rooster's a mite faster on his feet."

Tucker picked up a thick limb near the water's edge, and Sam's heart raced frantically. The scornful smile faded from Tucker's face, and was replaced with a menacing determination that was accentuated by the expectant flexing of Tucker's fist on the club. He brandished the weapon in tight little circles and advanced on Sam.

Sam fixed his gaze on the dangerous club, blocking out everything else in the gorge until a loud shriek broke his concentration. Emma crashed into her father with all her might, hitting Tucker at his waistline. The blow surprised him, but barely caused a misstep.

"Get back, Emma!" Sam cried, but the warning came too late. Tucker swung the limb at her, hitting her in the side of the head with a resounding crack. She moaned once and fell in a heap at his feet. An open gash at her temple dripped blood into the dirt.

From that moment, Sam was no longer capable of rational thought. He was a machine bent on destruction, not as powerful as his adversary, but infinitely more determined. He rushed at Tucker and the big man fell backwards, but not before he grabbed Sam's neck and brought him down with him.

The combatants rolled in the damp soil landing blow after blow on each other's bodies. Sam never felt the pain from the wounds Tucker inflicted. His attention was focused on causing the most damage he could to the massive, heaving body tumbling with him. He swung his fists and jabbed his elbows and knees into any body parts he came in contact with, heedless of the fact that Tucker was doing the same to him.

Shaking his head to clear his mind of the dazing effects of Tucker's blows, Sam retaliated with all the strength he could muster. But he finally realized he was losing the battle. All at once he felt as though he were suspended above the struggle, and he saw himself slipping away from consciousness.

His hands split the air uselessly, no longer finding a target, even though Tucker's fists landed mercilessly on Sam's own body. The world started spinning, and Tucker's face undulated into a leering caricature of triumph.

Mercifully the blows stopped, but that was just before Sam began sliding along a wet slippery path. He was being hauled from behind, and his collar was constricted around his throat so tightly it was impossible to breathe.

His eyes were nearly swollen shut, but through blurry slits, he could make out the tips of his boots swaying at the ends of numb legs.

Sam heard Tucker's labored breathing above him, followed by a low, grunting sound like laughter. Then water splashed around Sam's head, and a cold dampness seeped through his clothes. It revived Sam enough for him to realize that he was being pulled into the pool.

Tucker's large hand clamped down on Sam's forehead. *I'm going to die,* he thought, *and there's nothing I can do about it.* The idea was almost pleasurable. The water sloshed around his body, refreshing and cool. He floated as if on a cloud for a few seconds until his face was brutally thrust under the water to the muddy bed of the lake.

Water rushed into his ears and his eyes opened wide. Through Tucker's thick fingers, Sam saw water swirling and bubbles gushing in sparkling cyclones to the surface. He smiled at the memory. Bubbles . . . beautiful, white, frothy bubbles on a long, shapely leg. Abby laughing and pulling him into the tub. Her body, soft and sleek, her lips warm and wet. *I'm going to die!*

The awareness hit him with a force greater than any of Tucker's blows. *Hell, no, I'm not!* In that instant, Sam began to fight. He clawed and scratched and battled his way back. When his head broke the surface, he gasped for air and targeted his opponent with gritty tenacity. Tucker Brandywine was just a man, and like any man, he could be broken. Sam plowed through the water with sure, bold steps, outmaneuvering Tucker and closing the distance Tucker tried to keep between them.

Though he managed to back out of the pool, Tucker repeatedly stumbled and righted himself. Unintelligible muttering came from his cracked lips. Recognizing the weakness in his adversary, Sam advanced. He'd never felt so strong. He was in control, and it felt so damn good!

With the last of his waning strength Tucker headed for the rocks by the waterfall. "Oh, no, you don't!" Sam challenged. "You're not getting away just to come back and plague this family again!"

Sam pursued Tucker up the gorge, grabbing at his boots as they slipped time and again out of his grasp. When they were almost at the top, Sam lunged for him once more, but his hand missed its aim. Tucker looked down, and a snarl of victory slanted across his face. "You ain't gonna get ol' Tucker this time," he mocked. "And you ain't never . . ."

Those were the last words he spoke. Tucker's boot slid on the rocks. His fingers clawed unsuccessfully at the slick granite. His big body arched backwards and he fell. Forty feet down the ravine he tumbled, as if in agonizing slowness. Sam had only climbed halfway back down the rocks when he saw the lifeless eyes of Tucker Brandywine staring up at him.

He checked Brandywine's pulse and confirmed that the man who'd seemed indestructible was indeed dead. Sam supposed he ought to feel some remorse, maybe even Christian compassion for the wasted life snuffed out at his feet. But he didn't. All he felt was relief, so powerful and all-consuming that his head bowed and his shoulders sagged from the weight of it.

He looked around for Emma, but she was nowhere in sight. She couldn't have gotten past him and Tucker on the climb out of the gorge, so she had to be in the cave. He entered and found her kneeling next to Will. She was holding his hand and bringing him back to consciousness.

Will rubbed his head and blinked his eyes open. "Emma, oh, geez, Emma, are you okay?" He touched the spot where the blood congealed at her temple.

"I'm okay, Will. How 'bout you?"

He sat up straight. "Where's Tucker?"

"Dead," she said without emotion. "Fell down the gorge tryin' to run from Sam."

"Sam?"

"I guess that's my cue," Sam said, coming toward them. He looked down at Emma. "I'm sorry about Tucker. No matter what he did, he was still your father."

"I won't have much trouble forgettin' about him," she said. "You been a lot more father to me than Tucker ever was."

Will got to his feet slowly. "Sam, what are you doin' here? How'd you know?"

"Seems you had a couple of seven-year-old spies following you, and they saw Tucker. They ran back to the farm like they'd seen the devil himself." The irony of Sam's statement brought a wry smile from Will and Emma. "Can you walk?" Sam asked them. "We've got to report this to the sheriff."

It was a slow, cumbersome climb out of the gorge for all who left Lucy Cameron's Kitchen that day. Wincing with aches and cuts and bruises, each one offered help when he could, and no one refused it when it was offered.

Once on the summit, Sam, Will, and Emma faced the long walk down the footpath. But at least they had the satisfaction of looking to a future without Tucker in it. The ordeal was over, and they were headed home.

Abby ran through the dense foliage. Her lungs felt like they would burst but she couldn't slow down. The twins' words still echoed in her mind. *Tucker's back. He's after Will and Emma, and Sam's gone after him.* Before tearing toward the river, she'd shouted instructions to everyone around her at Chadwick Farm. She'd made Laurence Sholski promise to stay with the children, and she'd sent

Herbert to Purcell's Mercantile to call the sheriff and bring help.

Please let them be all right, she prayed as she ran. She'd seen the waterfall a couple of times when she was younger, and the sight of the upended canoe reminded her that she was nearly there. She rounded a bend in the path and stopped. Like wounded Crusaders, her family appeared through a break in the trees.

Will and Emma saw her first and ran toward her. She embraced them each and heard a brief, breathless version of their story, which included the harrowing demise of Tucker Brandywine. Her heart ached when she saw their bruises, but she knew they'd be all right. They left her, and she remained staring down the footpath at her husband. Abby had never been so happy to see a person in her life.

Sam's injuries were evident from many yards away. She felt his pain, imagined his fear, and exalted in his bravery in standing up to Tucker. He could have been killed saving Emma and ridding this demon from their lives.

Tears of guilt and gratitude sprang to Abby's eyes, rippling Sam's battered face and torn clothing. She blinked the tears away. She wanted to see Sam as clearly on the outside as she now perceived his soul. She drew a deep, ragged breath. Her heart swelled with love and compassion for this man she once believed she couldn't trust. What an idiot she'd been.

He leaned against a tree and smiled crookedly. "I guess I look even worse right now than when you saw me terrorizing that poor mare hitched to Duncan's wagon. That day I worried that you might not even want to shake my hand. I wouldn't blame you if you cut a wide swath around me altogether today."

"Or cut a path straight to you, you big wonderful fool," she said. The tears fell then, hot and salty down her cheeks and into her mouth. He pushed himself away from the tree and opened his arms to her. She ran into them and pressed her lips on his. It was an awkward kiss, because she was half crying and half laughing, but it was a kiss she knew she'd always remember.

He held her tight until his knees gave way, and clinging to each other, they sank into the sweet sumac. They both tried to talk at once.

"I'm sorry, Sam, about everything. You go to Fox Hill and help Simon. I don't know why I acted the way I did . . ."

"You saved me down there, Ab. I saw you in my mind's eye, and it made me fight back . . ."

"I'll never doubt you again, Sam. I trust you. I always will. I love you . . ."

"It's for Simon and Rebecca, Ab. That's the only reason I'm going. My future's always been here, maybe from the first moment I saw you. I love you, Abby . . ."

She placed trembling hands on either side of his face and saw beyond the cuts and sweat and grime of the gorge to the selfless, loving man that was inside. Voices sounded indistinctly through the trees, and she knew the men from the village were coming. It didn't matter one bit to Abby if they found her passionately kissing her husband on the old Iroquois trail to Lucy Cameron's Kitchen.

Epilogue

The day couldn't have been more perfect. Too excited to sleep, Abby had been up to see the sun peek through the last gray shadows of night with golden splendor. April had certainly done itself proud on Chadwick Farm. Its gentle, soaking rains had produced the most brilliant profusion of May flowers Abby could ever remember, and now they absolutely sparkled in the noon sun.

"Mama, I have one more ribbon. Where can I put it?"

Abby adjusted the circlet of flowers on Lizzie's nest of soft strawberry curls. She would make a beautiful flower girl. In the three years since the child had been with them, she'd occupied a place in Abby's heart as rooted in love as if she'd been born to her.

"Let's see," Abby said, making a show of studying the gaily festooned porch rails already dripping with satin garlands and ribbons. She chose the only bare spot she could find. "I think it will look best right here."

With capable little hands, Lizzie tied the white ribbon on a spindle of the farmhouse porch. Picturing how Rebecca would look when she stepped out of the house into the pink-and-white fairyland the women of Chadwick Farm had created for her special day, Abby smiled. Of course, Rebecca would have been a breathtaking bride if she'd been surrounded by burlap and butcher paper. She was simply beautiful, inside and out.

"Miss Abby, are you out here?"

"Around here, Emma." She waited as Will and Emma came from the back of the house. James Kelly, at eleven months of age, was a bouncing, squirming bundle of energy on Emma's hip. He spread his arms wide when he saw his mother.

"What a handsome lad you are, James Kilbourne Kelly," Abby said, taking him from Emma and planting a noisy kiss on his chubby neck.

Emma passed an appraising glance at the decorations and sighed. "Just look at all this, Will. Isn't it the prettiest sight you've ever laid eyes on?"

"It's okay, I guess," he said, kicking at a clod of dirt. "All I can think of is how this shirt collar scratches my neck."

"You stop your complainin', Will Buckman," Emma scolded. "Why, when we get married, you're going to have to dress up even finer than that."

Will faked a frown at Abby. "Tell me one more time, Miss Abby, how bein' married is worth all the aggravation a man has to go through."

"You'll have to ask Sam about that," she said, shifting her gaze to her husband, who worked near the apple orchard.

"Hey, Ab," he called out, "have I got this thing straight yet?"

Carrying James, she walked over to the arched trellis Sam had made for the ceremony from bleached hickory and then draped with white rambler roses. With the apple trees in the background, budding with small pink blossoms, the trellis looked enchanted. She raised up on her toes to give Sam a kiss. "It's a work of art by a master craftsman," she said, and meant it.

He rubbed a finger along his jaw. "I dunno. James, what do you think? Should I raise this side just a little?"

James gurgled and stuck out his tongue.

"Just what I thought, son. Better to leave well enough alone."

"You'd better quit fussing with it anyway, Sam, and set up the tables. The ladies will be here with the food in Mr. Purcell's wagon any minute."

But it wasn't the mercantile's wagon that first crested the rise to the farmhouse. It was a much fancier open carriage, and it had traveled all the way from the inn in Cuyahoga Falls. The defining features of the two occupants identified them to Abby. The groom wore a shining black top hat, and the woman beside him sat under a cream-colored parasol with delicate fringe bouncing with the sway of the buggy.

Sam put his hand on Abby's shoulder. "So what do you think, Ab? You still get the same old feeling when you have to face Delilah?"

Abby waved at the carriage, and Delilah's gloved hand came up to fan a simple, dignified response. "She's coming around, Sam. One of these days she'll be almost human."

Sam greeted his half brother with hearty congratulations, a loud clap on his back, and some good-natured teasing. Simon beamed.

"Samuel, Abigail," Delilah said when she'd set her polished goat leather shoes on Chadwick soil. "Your home looks quite charming." She almost smiled.

"Thank you, Mrs. Rosemont," Abby said. "Why don't you come up on the porch and have some lemonade. Or would you like to go inside and help Rebecca get ready?"

Delilah hesitated, then looked at her son.

He nodded. "I think she'd like that, Mother."

With a tilt of her head, Delilah announced her decision. "I think if it's all the same to you, Abigail, I'll go inside."

To her credit, she didn't even flinch when she had to step out of the way of two stampeding freckle-faced nine-year-old boys being chased by a scolding raven-haired girl waving two neckties as if they were weapons.

"Boys! Susanna!" Abby called before they could turn around and launch a second attack on Delilah.

"Let them go, Abby," Simon said. "Mother will adjust. In fact, she almost enjoyed telling Frederick we were coming to Ohio for the wedding. He's not the most good-hearted invalid you'll ever meet, and I think Mother draws a sort of perverse pleasure from goading him now and again. And she's actually looking forward to having a daughter-in-law living close by the old mausoleum."

Sam's voice assumed the husky timbre of seriousness when he asked, "How are things going at the factory now, Simon?"

"Good. Since we've let the AFL men hold meetings once a month, production has gone up fifteen percent. I still don't know which way the wind blows on this union issue, but I think either way, we can live with it."

Abby gently tugged on Sam's arm. "You'll have to talk business later," she said. After giving Simon a conspiratorial wink that said she realized business would be the last thing on his mind, she pointed to the rise. "There's the wagon with Harriet and Martha and all the food."

"Right." Sam hurried toward the lumber and sawhorses that needed to be set up for tables. "Will, get on over here! We've got work to do!"

An hour later, the sweet strains of a violin and guitar announced that the first wedding ever to take place on Chadwick Farm was about to begin. Under Sam's hickory arch, the minister who'd come to Seneca Village eighteen months before smiled at Simon.

Standing in front of friends and neighbors seated in rows of chairs, Will ran a finger around the inside of his collar. Next to him, Thomas and Timothy craned their necks to get the first view of their sister when she came out of the house. Emma, Susanna, and even Lizzie stared straight ahead in rapt attention, probably with dreams of their own special days in their heads.

Her heart bursting with love for all of them, Abby, with James on her lap, finally turned toward the house to see her husband and Rebecca step onto the porch. To those who knew her, and especially to those who loved her, the bride, an ethereal vision of organdy and lace, was as perfect of soul as she was of body. She smiled at Abby across the lawn, and then turned her gaze to her groom, whose adoration shone clearly in his eyes.

Sending her thoughts on the spring breeze to the two people just stepping off the porch, Abby felt her eyes mist with tears. *You are my dearest angel,* she said to Rebecca, *and Sam Kelly, you are my love.* Turning her gaze to the heavens, she added, *And Papa, you were right. These are life's miracles, and I've been blessed with so many. Just like you said, it all came out right in the end.*

ABOUT THE AUTHOR

A native of the Midwest, Cynthia Thomason now lives in Davie, Florida, with her husband, teenaged son, black Persian cat, and Jack Russell terrier. When she's not writing romances, she is an auctioneer and estate furniture buyer for the auction company she and her husband own. Cynthia would love to hear from you at this address: PO Box 550068, Fort Lauderdale, FL 33355. Or visit her Web site at www.tlt.com/authors/cthomason.htm. You may E-mail her at cynthoma@aol.com.